# CLOCKWORK PLANET

...ubaki Himana

Illustration: **Sino**

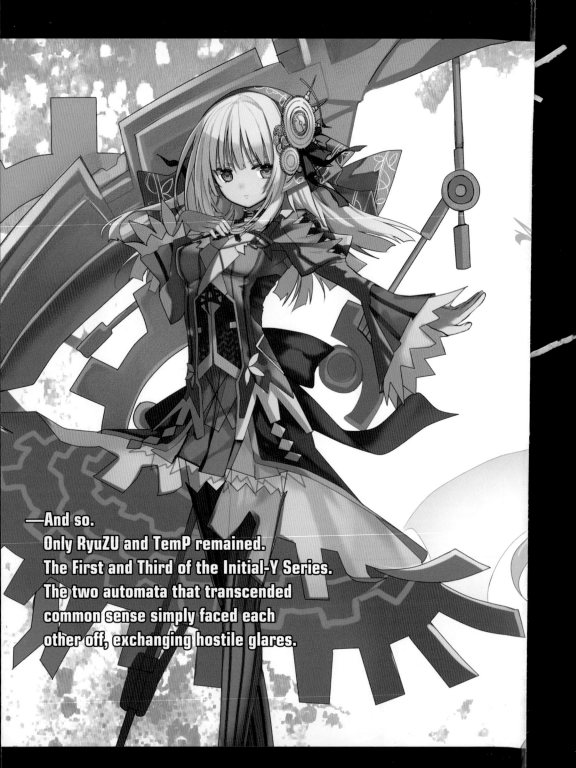

—And so.
Only RyuZU and TemP remained.
The First and Third of the Initial-Y Series.
The two automata that transcended
common sense simply faced each
other off, exchanging hostile glares.

TemP sneered scoffingly, then said,

## "Definition Proclamation—"

It felt to her almost as if the world had been submerged under a sea of tar. As her awareness expanded widely, deeply, and sharply and her perception was honed, Marie made her move.

She kicked up the coil spear by her feet, swimming through the viscous spacetime she was in.

She could see everything.

She saw everything in the hallway, the dumb faces of the clowns pointing guns at her, the parts that made up their facial mechanisms, the manufacturers of those parts, the model numbers, even their respective release dates. Everything.

The only things she couldn't see were what were behind the stupid faces of the soldiers—their brains. Well, if they really had any in there, anyway.

# contents

♡ TemP ♡

# CLOCKWORK PLANET

CLOCKWORK PLANET, VOLUME 4

©2015 Yuu Kamiya, Tsubaki Himana
Cover illustration by Sino

First published in Japan in 2015 by Kodansha Ltd., Tokyo.
Publication rights for this English edition arranged through
Kodansha Ltd., Tokyo.

Follow Seven Seas Entertainment online at
sevenseasentertainment.com.
Experience J-Novel Club books online at j-novel.club.

TRANSLATION: fofi
J-NOVEL EDITOR: Andrew Hale
COVER DESIGN: Nicky Lim
INTERIOR LAYOUT & DESIGN: Clay Gardner
COPY EDITOR: Stephanie Cohen
PROOFREADER: Dayna Abel
LIGHT NOVEL EDITOR: Nibedita Sen
EDITOR-IN-CHIEF: Adam Arnold
PUBLISHER: Jason DeAngelis

ISBN: 978-1-64275-002-7
Printed in Canada
First Printing: April 2019
10 9 8 7 6 5 4 3 2 1

# CLOCKWORK PLANET

## IV

Presented by
**YUU KAMIYA** *and*
**TSUBAKI HIMANA**

*Illustrated by*
**SINO**

## ● Prologue / 14 : 00 / Traditore

IN THE BEGINNING, there was nothing; the universe burst suddenly into existence.

The various myths we have concerning the creation of the world all share this feature.

Like how God created the world in just seven days. Or that the world was the result of our mother deity and father deity's lovemaking. Or, in some stories, that a giant or a dragon had been killed and that everything in the world had been born from its corpse.

However, though there are plenty of stories regarding how the world began, there are none about *why* it began.

All of the stories simply say that the universe suddenly materialized for one reason or another, each with preposterous concepts that make one's head spin—like eternity, infinity, and chaos.

Even science defines its explanation, the Big Bang, thusly: our universe was suddenly born from a nothingness where time and space couldn't be differentiated, and immediately expanded explosively upon its birth.

Whether the story was about gods, love, monsters, or physical singularities and enormous amounts of energy, there was no explanation as to why the things that created the world were there in the first place. Had they had simply popped up by chance, out of nothing? Or is there some special reason why they were there?

There isn't.

Well, there might actually be one, but at the very least, no human can get an answer to that question, as there's no convenient existence which can answer it.

Is there any point to asking such a question in the first place?

Take, for example, the one who created this Clockwork Planet, the latest demiurge who recreated the world with gears.

In other words, if "Y" were asked, "Why did you create this world?", how would he have answered? For the sake of humanity? To save our planet, which was on the verge of death?

Could a creature who would return such a sensible response create such an absurd contraption in the first place?

Surprisingly, he might have tilted his head perplexedly and said, "Hmm, I've never even thought about that."

You don't have to be a god to create worlds.

Simply write a poem. Draw a picture. Spin a tale. Making music or sculptures would do just fine, as well. You don't need to force yourself to create a new world in reality; simply fantasizing inside your mind is enough.

Inside of our minds, we can create universes that belong only to us. There is no particular reason or meaning behind us doing so. Nor do we need any.

People who do such things for work, such as novelists, manga artists, or composers, might answer that they do what they do because they want to express something, or to entertain others.

However, to the end, that too is mere sophistry. They're just pretending.

"I made this because I wanted to." That is the one and only reason. I assure you with confidence that all other reasons are purely afterthoughts.

In the beginning, there had been nothing; the universe had suddenly burst into existence.

There isn't any particular reason why things turned out that way.

Of course, mediocre as we humans are, we're free to imagine there to be some higher intent, some lofty aim behind the miracle that is the creation of our world, but...when all is said and done, that attempt to find meaning is also meaningless.

And, just as meaninglessly, the genius known as "Y" remade the world with gears.

A thousand years afterwards...

· · ● ● ● · ·

Vainney Halter didn't believe in fate.

He had been this way ever since he first stepped onto the battlefield long ago—no, even before then, and continuing to this day.

He had made it through countless battles and brought about

countless deaths. It was, without a doubt, an overwhelming reality to bear.

That kind of first-hand experience gave him an unwavering conviction that a chain of coincidences was just that and nothing more. He thoroughly rejected and eliminated sentimentality towards things that happened in his life.

To him, there was no meaning to this world, no value to life, no significance to truth. Fate was something which sometimes simply vanished; depending on the situation, it could even be burned through more easily than paper scraps, just as currency that has lost people's confidence instantly loses its value in turn.

Once fate is stripped of the belief in greater meaning, it instantly devolves into mere circumstances.

Which is precisely why belief itself often ends in not a bang, but a whimper.

*If I have one talent as a soldier, it'd have to be that I understand this cold truth,* Halter thought.

· · ● ● ● · ·

Along Chang Klan Road in the eastern part of Shangri-La Grid was a type of marketplace called a night bazaar.

The street stalls which haphazardly lined the street used to display items like traditional handicrafts, and were a popular attraction among tourists.

However, the merchandise that lined the stands now was stuff like dangerous light and heavy weaponry, suspicious-looking narcotics, child pornography, and snuff films. Items that would get one sentenced to a hundred years of imprisonment in any developed country were being sold as casually as candy.

As Halter casually glanced through the merchandise of one such stall, he found an enormous transforming pistol on its rack. He took a closer look at it.

Soon after, a plump shop assistant leaned forward from across the counter to greet him. "Ah, ye like this one? Ye've got a good eye, Mister."

The assistant looked so eager that Halter wouldn't have been surprised if he started rubbing his hands with glee. Chuckling to himself, Halter replied, "It looks powerful. Is it handmade?"

The assistant began his sales pitch. "Oh yeah, it's a one-of-a-kind item made by a master craftsman in this city. Its engraved name is Monarca. It's a trans-system pistol that's capable of both sniping and strafing. The maximum firepower this thing's capable of is twenty rapid-fire shots of 15 mm armor-piercing bullets, y'know? I hear there was a fool who fractured his arm when firing some test shots from this thing, but that wouldn't be a problem for ye, Mister."

The assistant wasn't flattering him. Halter was a full-body cyborg.

Though he wasn't sporting one of the latest models, his body was still a standard fifth-gen model that many militaries around the world used. Judging from his physique—which far exceeded that of a typical man—one could tell that his body wasn't a model with lesser strength built for reconnaissance. It was one built for assault, for users who sought to wield weapons with firepower greater than what a body of flesh could handle.

The transforming pistol spanned forty centimeters in length and weighed seventeen kilograms. It was a heavyweight that pushed the definition of the word "portable". Still, the assistant deemed that Halter could easily handle the gun, and rightly so.

Tracing his finger along the barrel of the gun that had been polished as sleek as a mirror, Halter nodded. "I see. Looks interesting. I'll take it."

"Yessir, thank ye very much. Ye can try test firing it at one of Arsenal's outlets. Just mention that ye bought it from us, and they'll give you an hour at their shooting range for free."

"Thanks, mate."

After paying for the gun, Halter put on the included holster and stuck the pistol into it.

The item looked more like a light cannon than a pistol, but when worn around the waist of a giant like Halter, even a gun like that looked scarily small.

Straightening up his ruffled suit, Halter went on his way, slipping past the many bustling stalls.

After continuing for a while, he found himself in an area where, rather than weaponry, the primary items being sold were parts for military machinery and automata with illegal modifications.

Here, he found a group that stuck out like a sore thumb with their ruckus. Upon confirming the state of affairs, Halter approached them with a nonchalant expression.

"Naoto! What do you mean, you don't know the parts she

needs? You were so full of it when you boasted that you knew AnchoR's structure in its entirety! Shall I take that as a declaration of defeat?!"

The one yelling in the shrill voice of lingering prepubescence was a blonde-haired girl. She was sporting a casual look, with a thin white shirt over a camisole with black and white stripes and a denim skort to complete the outfit. The awfully-worn tool belt around her waist stood out quite a bit in that context.

"How many times do I have to tell you, Marie?! I know the parts she needs; I just don't know their names!"

Shouting back angrily at the girl was a black-haired boy named Naoto. He, on the other hand, was wearing a cheap T-shirt with a logo of some sort and light blue overalls. On his head was a pair of fluorescent green noise-canceling headphones, restraining his tousled hair.

Neither of them looked too out of the ordinary for a boy and girl in their teens, but they stood out like sore thumbs in the midst of all these stalls selling questionable wares.

"I'll know it's a part she needs when I see one, so what's the problem?!" Naoto yelled.

The blonde-haired girl—Marie—snorted and scoffed, "Oh, is that right? So you plan to find the parts she needs by going through every single place that sells parts around here, do you, Mr. Naoto the Great? Might you be aware of how many parts she needs in total?"

"I told you, we only need 68,323,405 parts to do the basic repairs!"

"Even if you find a part every second, it would still take roughly 790 days for you to find them all, you know? Do you want to live in this nasty city that smells like the sewers so badly? Are you an idiot?"

Marie glared sharply at Naoto with her emerald eyes, to which Naoto responded in kind with his light gray gaze.

The two of them looked like they would glare at each other all day long if they were left like this, so Halter called out in a deliberately cheery voice, "Yo, did I make you guys wait?"

Without taking her eyes off Naoto, Marie replied, "No, not really. Did you find what you wanted?"

"Yeah, I found a pretty good item. How about you guys? ... What, are you two quarreling?"

"No; I would say the current discussion is not on a high enough level to be called a quarrel."

The one who replied dispassionately was the silver-haired automaton girl standing by Naoto's side, RyuZU.

She had an exceptionally beautiful face, and the bewitching curves of her arms and legs were apparent even underneath her black formal dress. Even in a different place, she would draw the eyes of all around her.

"Mistress Marie was simply venting her jealousy towards Master Naoto for knowing what parts AnchoR needs, something that she was unable to do despite racking her shoddy brains. Though I can understand that, it would be nice if you would at least have the modesty to try to hide your jealousy, as you are making quite the ruckus."

In response to RyuZU's long-winded venom, Marie turned towards her and yelled, "Me, jealous? Could you not spout off baseless claims? Thanks! Now, in the first place," Marie pointed at Naoto, "if this. Guy. Right. Here. Simply did the things he said he could with his big mouth, there'd be nothing for me to yell about—"

"Umm... Motherrrr..."

The one who interrupted Marie in her rant, tugging on her sleeve, was the automaton with the appearance of a little girl, AnchoR.

With her lustrous black hair and cherubic expression, her cuteness put even top-class love automata to shame. However, though her head was in good condition, the rest of her body was terribly damaged. Even though the traditional Thai dress she was wearing covered her entire body, the areas where she had received a patchwork level of repair were painfully apparent.

AnchoR begged as she clung onto Marie unsteadily, "Let's stop fighting, okay?"

Marie immediately broke into a grin as she hugged AnchoR tight. In a complete reversal from her angry shouting, she said in a sweet, doting voice like someone soothing a kitten, "What are you saying, AnchoR? Mother isn't fighting ♪."

"...Are you mad, though?"

"No, no. I'm not mad at allll! In fact, I'm in a great mood," Marie said as she held AnchoR in her arms, rubbing her cheeks against hers.

Judging by how she was acting, it was clear that she had already forgotten about her own attitude from just a few seconds ago.

"Now then, we can't be dilly-dallying. We've gotta get you some new parts already. We're leaving now."

"Well, fine, I guess... Your one-eighty is so extreme it's even refreshing in a way, I have to say," Naoto grumbled with an un-amused gaze as they began to move.

Halter thought, *I wonder how many people would hold their heads in disbelief if they heard this conversation.*

This was the current state of Second Ypsilon—the armed ter-rorist organization behind all the happenings in the "Uprising of 2/8," like the Akihabara Terror Incident, Akihabara's Magnetization Crisis, and the Battle By Sakuradamon Gate—all incidents that shook the very core of Japan.

That was the official account, anyway.

Of course, the truth differed. Second Ypsilon had prevented a world crisis by smashing through all the conspiracies, and then had willingly chosen to wear the hat of dishonor of the conspira-cies that they had crushed. Far from terrorists, one could even call them Messiahs.

That much was surely common knowledge among those who knew even a little about the reality behind the scenes in the world. However...

"Come to think of it, I wonder where old man Vermouth went off to. It's been two days and he hasn't come back yet."

"Who cares? He's probably just getting cosy in an indecent establishment somewhere, anyway."

"In that body of his? What kind of pervert do you take him to be?"

"Isn't it already well-established that the hoodlum's a pervert?"

Just then, RyuZU interjected in a subdued voice, "I deeply apologize for interrupting you while you are displaying exceptional interest in Vermouth's sexual life, Master Naoto, but there is a little something I would like to report to you."

AnchoR, who was being carried in Marie's arms, also warned with a stern expression, "Father, Mother, there's someone dangerous around here..."

Naoto immediately strained his ears, then muttered, "I see. Indeed, there's someone aiming at us..."

"What's this about? Halter, we've already made a deal with the local syndicate, haven't we?"

"With the syndicate, yes. But you know, there are swarms of drooling idiots who detest orders and marches and fancy themselves lone wolves in this city. Did you think all of them would politely follow the rules?" Halter replied while pulling out the pistol he had just bought.

*We're regarded as the most dangerous group in the world right now, after all. The hefty bounty to capture us dead or alive is more than enticing enough by itself, not to mention there are surely as many crime syndicates set on seizing Second Ypsilon's talents for themselves as the number of stars in the sky.*

Halter went through the various reasons in his head, but didn't bother to explain, simply sighing instead. *That's the real problem,* he thought.

*It hardly mattered* that those in the know knew they weren't actually terrorists. These two automata had *war capabilities* that transcended common sense, and this boy and girl had easily seized control over the central mechanisms of a nation.

Before those overwhelming facts, neither the truth, nor whether they were good or evil, mattered one bit.

If only the two of them were gods. If everything they did had been convenient "miracles," distasteful "magic," and undefiable "fate," no one would object. No one would be able to complain.

However, in reality, they were mere humans like anyone else. But despite being private persons who weren't under the control of any state, they did have absurd abilities.

Regardless of what they themselves thought of their abilities, the fact is, they possessed overwhelming power—power on the level of gods.

However...

Vainney Halter didn't believe in God. At the very least, he would never believe in a sole, absolute, and almighty one.

The reason being was that he knew the cold truth: it didn't matter how powerful one might be—there isn't a single thing in this world that's absolute.

Since the chain of events in Tokyo, various police forces, militaries, and crime syndicates had readied their armaments and closed in on them, but every single one of them had made a fundamental mistake.

Simply having the idea of challenging nonsense like the Imaginary Gear or the Perpetual Gear with simple violence was already a mistake in and of itself. One shouldn't seek to fight against enemies whom one cannot defeat—one should seek to remove them from the picture, instead.

Vainney Halter was not a Meister.

He didn't have any superpowers he could seize the world with, like the boy and girl walking ahead of him. He didn't have the technical skills of the specialists who worked for the Meister Guild, either. Even bearing in mind his handicap as a cyborg, he was nonetheless still only a Geselle as far as clocksmithing goes—which had been hard enough already for an average Joe like him, without much talent to achieve.

But he was fine with that. After all, even a single part falling into dysfunction would be enough to make any clock, no matter what kind of godly technique was used to make it, cease to function.

No clocksmith, no matter how talented they were, could change that fact. That's why all he had to do was this.

Halter grabbed Naoto by the scruff of his neck and shoved his pistol against his temple in a most casual manner.

The air froze. RyuZU slowly turned towards Halter. "What do you think you are doing, you piece of junk?"

"That's how it is, miss. To put it in a clichéd bad-guy-from-a-lousy-movie line: if you don't want this guy to die, then shut up and do as I tell you."

"Old man?" Naoto muttered in amazement.

"Halter, what are you—"

Marie was so astounded that she couldn't even finish her sentence.

Dragging Naoto along, Halter slowly put some distance between himself and the others. As he did so, he thought to himself, *I'm still alive. That's already a victory in and of itself.*

Normally, should RyuZU have taken a cyborg like him to be an enemy, she would have already minced him to pieces so quickly that he wouldn't even be able to realize what had happened.

Even if, considering their relative positions, it would be impossible for her to slice the bullet along with the gun in half during the few milliseconds it would take for the bullet to pierce through Naoto's cranium after he pulled the trigger...RyuZU had a trump card, Dual Time. If she used Mute Scream, the situation would be turned on its head in an instant.

However, RyuZU didn't do so. She couldn't.

After all, she knew that even if she did, it would be futile.

"I appreciate your quick understanding." With a smile on his face, Halter continued, "If you had misunderstood that I was the only one with a gun pointed at Naoto's head, then if nothing else, both Naoto and I would be dead, so..."

"..."

"And just in case, I'll have you know that I've got more than just snipers in position. I know both your capabilities and Naoto's, so it wasn't very hard to set up a situation where they would be fully suppressed."

Indeed, it hadn't been difficult.

For RyuZU to enter Mute Scream, she would need several seconds to prepare. Even in the unlikely case that she somehow had a way to shorten that prep time, she would have no follow-up attack afterward.

Once she entered Mute Scream, it would end with her exhausting her spring.

If she were to enter into Mute Scream without knowing the total number of snipers targeting Naoto, their threat level, and their positions, Naoto would be left defenseless should she fail to take down just a single enemy. There was no way RyuZU would accept that kind of risk.

"...So?" RyuZU said in a dispassionate voice. "What do you plan to do now?"

"Get the hell out of here, of course. Your black scythes are scary."

"That is just fine with me. Please, run off now to wherever you want. Even if you hide inside a shithole—I apologize, that was vulgar of me—a *toilet*, I will still find you and drag you out. Even if I have to mince this entire city into pieces..."

"Great, I'd very much like to see you try...though it'd probably lead to *a fight between sisters.*"

"Does that mean—?!"

Naoto squirmed inside Halter's arms. However, Halter responded by calmly twisting the muzzle of his pistol roughly against Naoto's temple.

"Sorry, Naoto, but I'm not gonna let you ask any questions or give any hints. If you say just one more word, I'll pull the trigger. If you say something unnecessary, it might end up ruining my entire plan."

"...Ngh."

Naoto almost said something, but the cold feel of the weapon pressed against his temple shut him up.

Meanwhile, Marie shouted in a trembling voice, "What's going on?! Halter, what kind of joke is this?"

Bewilderment. Anger. Seeing these two emotions overtake and ooze out of the girl who was glaring at him, Halter replied with a bitter smile, "Sorry, Marie. This is also *one of my jobs*, you see."

"Your job, you say...?"

"There's a personage who's putting up a high price for this guy's head and ears. You don't need me to explain the value of the talent to even seize control over a core tower, do you?"

"Why...did you betray us?!"

"Betray?" Halter parroted with a blank face for a second before snickering in amusement. "Sorry, princess. I don't remember ever signing a contract with you, nor do I remember ever receiving pay from you. Me helping you out up until now was done out of pure kindness on my part. Proper adults can't let personal feelings interfere with their work, understand?"

"Halter!!" Marie shouted vehemently, her mouth trembling. Her voice oozed absolute hatred. In any case, the boy and the machines who shook the world had been overcome with just this simple maneuver.

In the midst of an atmosphere which was like standing in front of a bomb that was seconds away from exploding, Halter smiled confidently as he thought about his "job" this time around, as well as its significance.

This all began two days ago...

# Chapter One / 09 : 15 / Attore

"**T**HIS IS THE WORST," Marie muttered sullenly as she stepped off the gangway of the cylinder train.

Even with her necktie loosened, the sultry air was still terribly unpleasant. The sensation of her blonde hair sticking to her face from all the sweat felt equally intolerable, and the suffocating stench of raw garbage made her want to vomit.

Marie looked around the platform through her sunglasses. The floor was sticky from unidentifiable filth. The walls were covered with obscene graffiti and flyers. The illumination from the ceiling lights was dim, and the station sign dangled unsteadily from above, its text blotted out.

Despite looking like an abandoned station that no one was maintaining, the platform was jam-packed with people who had just disembarked from the cylinder train that arrived just a short while ago.

"The absolute worst," Marie repeated as she tore off her

sunglasses. What the shaded black lenses had kept hidden was the now-exposed insuperable scowl she had on her face.

"So a city that looks like trash apparently smells like trash, huh? But of course. This is the worst, the absolute worst! It's making me feel queasy, goddamnit. How about we just burn it all to the ground?"

"Oy oy, that's the first thing you have to say, missy? This place is the world's hottest tourist destination, you know. Can't you say somethin' a li'l more cheerful than that?" someone said from behind to try to pacify her.

Marie turned around and stared right at Vermouth, who had a cynical smile on his face.

He had the look of a glamorous blonde beauty, but his voice was frivolous and deep, like a man's. He was a bizarre existence whose face, voice, and gender expression didn't match one another at all.

Marie said, sounding fed up, "Tourist spot? A trash dump's more like it. Or a cockroach den."

"Sure, you could say that. But aren't you forgetting that, from the world's perspective, we're also a bunch of creepy-crawlies? And extremely big ones at that," Vermouth said, curling his lips. He then took a nice, deep breath and slowly exhaled it out, savoring the taste of his cigarette.

"Ahh, this stagnant air that smells like it came from the sewer... how nostalgic. Just breathing it in calms me down..."

"Before that."

The one who interjected was Naoto Miura. It appeared that

the roar of the cylinder train had hurt his ears quite a bit, for he had a pained look on his face. "Would someone mind telling me where this is already, please?"

"Well, for starters, it's a place where you can get changed into something that *doesn't make me want to puke,*" Marie said coldly, giving him the stink-eye.

Naoto was wearing a colorful traditional garment normally *worn by women,* made of many layers of cloth which hid the contours of his body. With his short stature and voice that hadn't fully dropped, he looked just like a real girl wearing it.

Of course, it wasn't that crossdressing was a hobby of his.

"Are you serious? I'm a wanted terrorist whose face is known—and not just that!!" Naoto unrolled the piece of paper he'd been holding in one hand and shoved it in Marie's face. "You're the one who told me to disguise myself so we wouldn't be identified, since we made a huge ruckus at the naval base right upon landing!!"

The piece of paper Naoto had unfolded was from a tabloid written in English. On the page was a photo of the Thai destroyer docking at the harbor and a flashy headline sprawled in large font.

*"Hijacking a Destroyer and Destorying a Thai Naval Base, 2nd•Y Strikes Again!!"*

It was a news article on the global terrorist group still at large that had one-sidedly wrecked a Thai naval base and repelled the local military and police with nothing but brute force, thrusting the Thai people into the depths of fear: Second Ypsilon.

Marie slapped the news article down, growling, "I told you

to *disguise* yourself. I didn't say anything about becoming a drag queen!"

"Master Naoto, there is no need to concern yourself with the outbursts of the lower class."

The one who interjected with a cool, calm voice was the automaton RyuZU. She had stepped forward to defend Naoto.

"It is only natural that you should feel inferior when comparing your own looks to Master Naoto's, who scores far higher on the attractiveness scale than you do, even crossing gender lines. To try to cover that sense of inferiority up with anger is the last right of those who are the very embodiment of mediocrity and foolishness. I beg of you, Master Naoto, please, do not take that very last right of hers away from her—"

"You're the one who made him wear this! That was directed at you as well, you piece of junk!"

"Hey, princess."

The one who interjected this time was the cyborg Halter. The giant man made the door look small as he bent down to get off the train, after which he sighed and said, "That's enough, yeah? Or do you plan to put on a comedy act right here on the platform?"

"Tell that to this piece of junk first! She's the one who makes a giant mess out of every little thing! Shall I tell you how many times I've been cursed at in these last two weeks?!"

"My, are you bragging that you can count above ten? Well then, far be it from me to take that accomplishment away from you..."

"Sixteen times!! All! Because! You keep making a scene!" Marie shouted, glaring at RyuZU.

It was two weeks ago now that they had hijacked a destroyer that had tried to arrest them as they were sailing in the Indian Ocean, and then used it to dock at Phuket Naval Base.

The plan had been to take a land route and stay on the down low while on the move, but they had ended up being chased around everywhere by police, military, and even the media, sadly enough.

Every time a gun—or rather, anything even remotely suspicious—was pointed at Naoto, RyuZU would respond automatically, as befitting an automaton, by cutting it down regardless of whether there was any actual malice or murderous intent behind it.

And so, *this* was the result. Every time they attracted even the slightest attention, there would be a disturbance.

And that's how their pursuers would find them.

Therefore, they had to continuously change their destinations to lose their pursuers, taking them on an aimless journey.

They had gone from Chumphon to Bangkok, then Pattaya. At one point, they had even briefly gone into Cambodia before re-entering Thailand through Ubon Ratchathani. They then headed north to Khon Kaen, then Nong Khai.

They made their rounds through nearly all the major cities of the country and slipped their way into Laos before finally arriving at this station without a nameplate. During that time, they got into trouble a total of sixteen times.

If they could have just stayed on the down-low, coming here shouldn't have taken them more than just three days with free use of the local transportation systems, yet it ended up taking them nearly five times as long.

As for why things turned out that way...

"It's all because you punks draw way too much attention!!"

"But you know, princess, I'm afraid I have to say that trying to move undercover with these members was a tad hopeful to begin with, don't you think?" Halter said in a conciliatory tone.

Marie fell silent. Even with her blood boiling, she had to admit that Halter had a point. Halter and Vermouth weren't a problem whatsoever. Marie and Naoto in drag could also pass as teen foreigners here on holiday.

But the problem was RyuZU. Her beautiful, well-proportioned face and radiant silver hair were simply too bewitching to be concealed. On top of that...

"Hey, Father? Where are we?"

"Oh, hey AnchoR. Sorry~ Daddy doesn't know either because that shitty old hag—shoot, I said a bad word in front of AnchoR—that blonde walking landmine won't answer me."

The one whom Naoto had replied to in a fawning voice was the automaton AnchoR, who had the appearance of a young girl.

Her black pupils wavering in unease, her plump, soft-looking cheeks, her pink lips—all of these adorable features, plus her waddling about due to the fact that she still needed further repairs, stirred a fierce protective instinct in the hearts of those who saw her.

*As Halter said, it was probably impossible to begin with to try to move around undercover with this group, but—*

"You! Don't try to brainwash AnchoR with your lies!"

"Mother, where, are we?" AnchoR asked, tilting her head.

Marie instantly beamed at her, despite having the sulkiest of faces just a moment ago, and said, "We're in Chiang Mai Grid, AnchoR."

"You're not wrong, missy, but no one else calls it that these days, you know?" Vermouth teased with a smirk.

Marie frowned in protest. "The official international name for this city is still Chiang Mai."

"But even Thailand, the state to which it originally belonged, no longer uses that name in its official documents. Its nickname is pretty much its official name at this point, isn't it?"

Naoto asked, looking perplexed, "What nickname?"

"People call this place 'Paradise,'" Vermouth replied.

Naoto furrowed his brows as he looked around him and skeptically asked, "A city with a beat-up station like this?"

"There's nothing that isn't sold here and nothing that you can't buy here. Arms, weapons, automata, everything from illegal clockwork parts to drugs—even humans and their human rights if that's what suits your fancy. For criminals, terror syndicates, armed groups, extremists and the like, it's absolute paradise. And so, this place became known as..." Vermouth grinned, then said, "...the crime capital of the world: Shangri-La Grid."

· · ● · ·

Chiang Mai—a city that had once been the next biggest city in Thailand, after its capital.

It used to be a landlocked city a thousand years ago, but after the planet was remade with clockwork, the city boundaries were adjusted to fit the grids. It had obtained access to a harbor that was connected to the open ocean, and had since developed as a port city.

However, when Thailand, Malaysia, Myanmar, Vietnam, and Bangladesh had signed the treaty to set their new borders, the city of Chiang Mai had declared independence from Thailand in opposition to the treaty.

On the surface, the city had declared independence because it wanted to liberalize its international trade, and complying with the treaty would have meant establishing tariffs. However, the truth behind the city's opposition was quite simply that multiple crime syndicates and armed groups had wanted to create an enormous black market for themselves.

As a result, Chiang Mai turned into a capital of vice which permitted all activities that would typically be illegal anywhere else. And so...

"No one knows who first coined it, but people began calling the city Shangri-La Grid. The name comes from a fictional utopia in one of Hilton's later works, *Lost Horizon*. A place where you can get anything there is in the world; a paradise for villains. Quite ironic, eh?"

Marie shrugged her shoulders cynically as they exited the nameless station and passed through Tha Phae Gate, an ancient castle gate made of brick, heading towards their hotel.

The central marketplace of Shangri-La Grid was enclosed by this castle gate which, by tradition, must never be closed. Said marketplace was currently under sweltering heat and filled with clatter.

In the midst of the all-engulfing tropical heat, a large number of people were walking every which way. There were men and women of all ethnicities, as well as—quite noticeably—cyborgs and automata, which would be rare sights in normal cities.

Garishly colored parasols and sunshades, flyers, and link wires used for transmissions could be seen everywhere.

The enormous throng of people made the visibility exceptionally poor, yet the pulled rickshaws, auto rickshaws, and pickup trucks adapted into minibuses were somehow nimbly weaving through the mess. There was virtually no distinction between the road and the sidewalk, so it would hardly be surprising if an accident were to happen. However, no one was bothered by this.

"So basically, there's no such thing as the law here. That would be far too civilized for this place—a lawless city where anything goes, including but not limited to human trafficking, drug dealing, the illicit manufacturing and smuggling of arms, and automata with prohibited mechanisms."

"Oy oy, aren't you forgetting the best part, miss? Maybe you just don't want to say it, in which case, I'll say it for you," Vermouth cut in. "To add to what she said, the docs here'll do anything from illegal organ transplants to body modifications. As long as one pays up, even a wrinkly old grandpa can turn into Cinderella over a single night. For example, that booth over there's sellin' all sorts of fresh human organs for transplants."

"...You're kidding, right?" Naoto asked with a pale face.

Marie sighed. "Think of all the illegal activities, all the inhumane deeds you possibly can in your mind—all of it, bar none, is being sold as souvenirs here."

"Hahah! There're only two things you can't buy here," Vermouth said with a wink. "A conscience and character. Unfortunately, those two things are very hard to come by here, though everything else is easily accessible. They might sell for a high price here if we import some, y'know?"

"That's a great idea—if you ignore the fact that there's no demand for them, that is."

"Sorry if I'm asking the obvious, but...is this really acceptable? What do the police, militaries, and IGMO even exist for, then?"

Marie answered with a scowl, "Of course it's not acceptable. IGMO and the UN security council have already taken all possible sanctions against the city, aside from military intervention. Just so you know, the situation here is always discussed in every international summit as a threat to world stability."

"It's ironic to hear you say that, considering that nowadays, y'all are the ones at the top of that list."

Ignoring Vermouth's snide comment, Marie continued, "Even so, no one will lift a finger against this city—or rather, they can't."

"Why?"

Marie raised her index finger as she answered lethargically, as if she didn't want to admit something. "The first is that both the core tower and the clock towers here are actually governed more strictly than the five signatory countries of the border treaty."

"What? I thought this city was a lawless place."

"It's true that this place is lawless and doesn't have any form of government. Instead, there are countless mafia gangs and armed groups continuously fighting for turf here. At present, the three top syndicates here are managing and maintaining the core tower and the twelve clock towers."

"Why do criminal syndicates have that kind of technical capability?"

"Because the fact that you can do anything you want in this city, unrestrained by any laws, draws tons of technicians and researchers from all over the world."

In the first place, the supreme duty of any nation in this Clockwork Planet was the maintenance of city mechanisms. If the core towers weren't properly taken care of, it would lead to a world crisis. To that end, things like a sound government or human rights were simply secondary. That was the true stance of international society.

Because of that, even if a national government was formally recognized by other countries, should that government be deemed incapable of managing its grids, its only choice would be to accept technical support from a group like an IGMO affiliate or Meister Guild, either willingly or by force.

"It isn't just human resources that this place is rich in. This city is overflowing with so much money from secret slush funds and its black market that the IGMO trade sanctions don't even put a dent in the economy. Plus, its borders with the surrounding countries are as full of holes as a colander, so enforcement of the sanctions is basically impossible."

"That ain't all of it, y'know? 'Just imagine what'll happen if you thoughtlessly use force and aggravate the hoodlums who reside there. Heaven knows just how much damage that would cause to the core tower and the surrounding countries.' ...That's the argument from industries and small nations who use this city as their base for money laundering when they pressure IGMO not to take armed action."

"So, does that mean...?"

"Savvy? You can get your hands on anything here. In other words, for any given product, there are producers, sellers, and buyers here," Vermouth said with a wink, his lips curled.

Naoto inadvertently stared up at the sky, then buried his face in his hands and sighed deeply, "Politics really is over my head..."

"Well, to each his own, but personally I don't dislike this city, y'know? The clever fool who asks himself, 'I wonder why killing people isn't acceptable,' will find a straightforward answer here. Heh heh," Vermouth snickered sardonically. "There ain't any police or any lawyers in this city. They won't give you something so easygoing as a trial here. There ain't a single thing that's forbidden in this city. That's why the rule is simple—*if you go too far out of line, you'll be killed*. Troublesome crap like due process is omitted in favor of lead in your head. It might seem paradoxical, but precisely because this place is lawless, the public order is strictly preserved. Screw lawyers and their pretentious sophistry. There's nothing easier to understand than a country that permits even murder. That's why I like this place."

"In short, a hangout for degenerate savages," Marie summarized sharply, then went on. "Degeneracy! Evil! Moral compromise! Misinformation! Deceit! This city's like all the shit I hate stuffed inside a pot and boiled down into concentrate. Ugh, God, the stench here is so bad I feel like it's going to permanently stick to my clothes. I know purging is never the answer, but shouldn't we make an exception for this city? I'm serious. Hasn't it been enough? Let's forget excuses like proper grid management and purge this filth to the bottom of the Earth, yeah?"

"Princess, I know you're joking, but purging a city based on personal feelings is plenty evil as well, y'know?" Halter muttered in exasperation.

Vermouth nodded with a smug face, "Yep, that's right. This place simply supplies what people demand. Well, I suppose it'd be just like an extremist terrorist to try to eliminate something because she doesn't understand it or she doesn't like it."

"Shut the hell up. There's a limit to everything!" Marie scowled, clicking her tongue.

Vermouth suddenly stopped smiling. "Say, little princess. I have some serious words of advice for you. I'll give you some change, so find yourself a male prostitute for a night. Once you cry from the ecstasy of climaxing while high on drugs, you'll understand deep down in your womb that we noble humans are really just beasts like any other animal."

"If you take that unfunny joke a single line further, I'll dismantle you down to your screws and sell you off as spare parts," Marie said, her body emanating a chilling aura.

However, Vermouth persisted with a straight face, sighing,

"You don't get it, do you? If I was just joking, I'd ask if you wanted to get it done with me. Sure do wish you could figure out by yourself whether I'm serious or not."

"If it's a joke then it's in poor taste, and if it's not, then it's absolutely abominable."

"I've thought this for quite some time now, but you're too damn prudish. Typically, dirty jokes bother men more than women, y'know? Yet, the way you overreact to them negatively shows that..."

"That what?"

"It's backlash from your frustration, yeah? If you'd like, I could show you the place my past colleague Strega favored. Rest assured, they guarantee that with one of their pros, even a virgin with sexual arousal disorder will turn into a nympho in one night or your money back."

"I'll say this one last time, Vermouth," Marie said slowly, enunciating each syllable before finishing with a sweet smile. "Shut up or I'll kill you."

Sensing true murderous intent from her words—that probably wasn't the only reason, but in any case—Vermouth raised both hands up as if to say, "All right, all right, I give up."

Marie snorted as she took her eyes off of Vermouth. She then turned towards RyuZU and asked, "I guess this kind of talk doesn't bother you?"

"What? Are we talking about humans? The same animals that even insects would object to being grouped together with? Whether a human puts on or takes off their clothes does not change anything on the inside. It is my firm belief that humans who are aware that they are beasts and act along those lines are far more respectable than imbeciles who pretend to be civilized, unaware of their own stupidity. As such, I don't really have any opinion on your exchange on human sexuality just now, nor does it bother me in any way—so long as Master Naoto doesn't harbor any carnal desires for animals such as yourself, anyway."

"Huh? Me? Feel any desire for that lump of protein and noise?"

"Rest assured, kid, this city's got people like you covered, too. Got any interest in the super erotic techniques that the state-of-the-art Dutch Wives in this city can do that would never be even remotely possible for real humans?"

"Wha?" Naoto stiffened. He clearly imagined something for a moment before catching himself and shaking his head, flustered. "N-n-no, that's a bit... I mean, I-I-I'm underage to begin with..."

"Don't you worry, there ain't such a thing as underage here. Ain't no problem if you want to walk yourself to a brothel with the same legs that came out from your mom's crotch."

"But, well, I mean..."

"Master Naoto?" RyuZU said in a chilling voice.

"Eek!" Naoto gulped with a start. "I-I'm not considering it at all, you know?! Not at all! Not even a little! I'm not interested in playing with dangerous thrills like that in the slightest! I wasn't thinking 'Well, maybe I would like to try it seeing how much you recommend it' at all!"

"Is that so? I am sure it is," RyuZU said as she wrapped her arms tightly around Naoto from behind, like a snake constricting its prey. She then caressed Naoto's face with her smooth, pale hands. "Incidentally, Master Naoto, allow me to give you a strong word of advice. Being young and healthy is one of your few merits, but allowing yourself to be easily swept up by the impulses of youth would be equivalent to voluntarily lowering yourself from your position as one of the few intelligent life forms on this planet. Should you plead that your urges are simply too difficult to suppress with self-restraint, then I propose I help by surgically pulverizing the source of your urges. How does that sound to you?"

As she spoke, she stretched one hand in front of Naoto so he could see it and violently tightened it into a fist before opening it back up, as if to demonstrate how she would crush *a certain something*.

"Eek! That won't be necessary, I think!"

"Is that so? That would be for the best, I'm sure." After repeating herself to make her point, RyuZU slowly released Naoto. She then shot Vermouth a sharp gaze. "And you, Mr. Junkbot. If you keep luring Master Naoto with odious temptations, I shall deem your existence as undesirable and take the liberty of disposing of you myself, so mark that in your head going forward."

Vermouth raised both hands flippantly as he apologized. "I get it, I get it. I was wrong; forgive me."

"B-by the way...should we do something about that?" Naoto asked, hoping to change the topic.

"By 'that,' do you mean the guys who've been monitoring us for some time now?" Marie asked as she quickly surveyed their surroundings.

*One, two, three...* The pedestrian who passed them by earlier, the auto-rickshaw driver driving on the other side of the street, and the worker selling juice at a nearby stall. By paying just a tiny bit of attention, she was able to quickly find people who were paying an awful lot of attention to them.

And this was just from Marie's eyes; she hadn't taken any professional training. If the pros who were used to this kind of work were to look around, who knows just how many people in this area they would discover secretly monitoring them.

RyuZU's expression turned cold. "If they are a nuisance, shall I clean things up?"

"Leave them be."

The one who stayed her was Halter. Though he himself was surely aware of the piercing gazes of surveillance coming at them from all directions, one wouldn't be able to tell that from the relaxed manner in which he walked.

"The group that tried to sink Tokyo has entered their own turf. It's only natural the local syndicates would send an observer or two to monitor us. It isn't anything to get all up in arms about."

Naoto tilted his head, a blank expression on his face. "In that case, shouldn't we disguise ourselves after all?"

"Nah, we're fine. The syndicates here aren't stupid, either. They surely have no intention of giving the military or the police of the neighboring countries an excuse to meddle in Shangri-La's affairs."

Vermouth nodded in agreement. "Yep, that's right. As long as we remain respectful guests, simply feigning ignorance to the neighboring countries about us being here will work, and there isn't anyone stupid enough to disrespect that pretense and stick their meddling hands into this city to arrest us, either."

Halter sighed. "But if we cause any needless disturbances... well, let's just say that being sold as hostages to the neighboring countries would be the best conclusion we could hope for."

Marie asked, perplexed, "There are groups that can actually beat us here?"

Those who were well informed already knew—Ypsilon members included two Initial-Y series automata and two clocksmiths who were skilled enough to seize control over an entire grid—so Marie was wondering if there really was anyone who would actually pick a fight against their lineup.

However, Halter and Vermouth exchanged a glance before shrugging at her. "Oy oy, missy, you still have much to learn about the world, don't you?"

"I don't want to say this, princess, but aren't you getting a bit full of yourself lately?"

Repudiated in stereo sound, Marie became quite blatantly offended.

"What, are the syndicates here that dangerous?"

Vermouth didn't answer her. Instead, he turned towards RyuZU and asked, "Question, miss doll. How many of the Initial-Y series can you win against?"

"If the question is *which* of the other Initial-Y series I can win against, then the answer would be all of them," RyuZU answered readily. "If I make the first move and activate Mute Scream, no one can counter that. That's true for any of my sisters—even the strongest in raw combat among all of us, AnchoR."

"Oh, I see. Then let's say you either can't, or fail to make the first move. If you end up having to straight up fight against any of them in a contest of strength, how many would you lose to?"

"Though as a whole, none of my younger sisters surpass my capabilities," RyuZU replied, "the answer is all of them, as I am the most humble one of the Initial-Y series in terms of strength."

The problem was the nature of Mute Scream. Once RyuZU entered Dual Time, not even AnchoR, the strongest Initial-Y, could deal with her.

If RyuZU rent AnchoR in half in Dual Time before AnchoR could activate Bloody Murder, AnchoR would be helpless even if she were in perfect condition.

However, if it were a straight-up one-on-one fight, then it was just as she said—she was the weakest Initial-Y.

Vermouth nodded, then turned back towards Marie with a flippant smirk. "Hear that? Should the worst happen and we get attacked by an Initial-Y that's brainwashed like the little pipsqueak was, would you still be able to keep up your complacent attitude?"

"Are you saying Omega's hands could reach as far as this city?"

"Is there any reason to think that isn't possible?"

"It's a simpler problem than that," Halter said sharply. "If there's someone out there who truly wants to eliminate us, then things like combat or technical prowess don't mean a damn thing. *There are any number of ways someone could use to eliminate us.*"

Halter's speech was even, neither overbearing nor threatening. His attitude was simply that of a teacher who was gently warning a rebellious student, which gave his words greater weight.

Feeling that the mood had become a bit solemn, Naoto sighed. "For now, is this place really safe? From what I've been hearing from you guys, it seems pretty dangerous."

"Don't worry," Halter said as he shifted the luggage on his back. "So long as we remain nice guests, the local groups won't do anything to us. Of course, there'll be a million eyes on us at all times, and a rash underling here and there might try to make a move against us. In any case, the local groups here aren't so anal as to make a fuss over a few cannon fodder-tier dimwits being disposed of."

"In the first place, they're in the same business as us," Vermouth said. "There are swarms of real terrorists gathered here. No one will mind a few more joining the party at this point. Besides..." He paused, his feet coming to a stop. "There are strange things here, like hotel rooms that come with full-scale workshops, y'know?"

• • ● • •

Pandora's Inn could reasonably be called a luxury hotel. At the very least, it was a building that looked somewhat out of place in the messy streets of Shangri-La.

That said, one shouldn't even bother comparing it to a five-star hotel in a developed country. But in the context of this city of villains, it certainly passed the mark of luxury.

Naoto and his friends entered the hotel. There was a café on the first floor that shared the front counter with the hotel's reception. They walked up to the shared counter.

Halter said to the receptionist, "I'd like to book one regular room and one that comes with a workshop, if possible, as neighboring rooms located near the emergency staircase."

Upon which the young receptionist of indiscernable Asian heritage showed them to their rooms. Just as Halter had requested, the rooms were located near the emergency staircase and came with a workshop. The room's interior was spacious and well-designed. Marie and Halter went to check out the workshop.

"How's it look, princess? Are we good?"

"It's sufficient."

Though the workshop's machine tools and facilities were slightly dated, all of them had once been the best models on the market. If one wanted access to a better workshop than this, then the only choice would be to use a lab at a university or a research facility.

Halter nodded in response, then gave a generous tip to the receptionist and drove him out of the room.

After the receptionist left with a beaming face, Marie immediately got down to business. "So Halter, mind explaining what this is all about?"

"What do you mean?" Halter asked calmly.

Marie furrowed her brows sharply. "You need me to say it?"

"Don't even have the slightest clue what you're referring to."

"Oh, is that so? Then I'll kindly inform you, so listen carefully."

She paused for a breath. "Why! Am I! Sharing a room with Naoto—ngh!!"

Marie's bellow shook the air as it rippled through the room.

RyuZU shot Halter a grim look as well. "Though it pains me deeply to agree with Mistress Marie on something, I would also very much like to hear an explanation for this. No matter how I try to interpret it in my mind, I can only think that this is an elaborate suicide plan of yours."

Being stared down coldly by both the blonde girl and the silver-haired automaton, Halter sighed. "Right, well..."

As Halter thought about what to say, he opened the window of the room. Humid air blew in from outside. As he looked out at the filthy streets of Shangri-La Grid, Halter continued, "First of all, you wanted to share a room with AnchoR, right, princess?"

Marie nodded. "Yes, that's right. Of course. I'm the one who's gonna fix her, after all."

"And Naoto stated that he wouldn't budge on sharing a room with RyuZU and AnchoR."

Naoto and RyuZU nodded.

"Obviously."

"But of course."

Halter nodded back. "Right. And AnchoR has to stay within a certain distance of Naoto—in addition, she expressed her wish to 'share a room with Mom and Dad.'"

AnchoR nodded deeply several times.

"Finally, there's only one room in this hotel with a workshop on each floor that one can book for a longer period of time if necessary. So, taking all that into consideration, was there any other way?"

"There sure was. Isn't it obvious? You could have just ignored Naoto's nonsense and given AnchoR and me a room to share."

"Yes, I do believe there was. You only had to reject Mistress Marie's indiscreet demands and grant Master Naoto's wishes."

"And if I were to say no to one of you?"

"I'd beat you to death, of course."

"I would dismantle you then, naturally."

"...Right. By the way, I imagine that this is news to both of you, but I don't want to die yet," Halter said. He then turned around and gestured with his chin at Vermouth, who was smirking in a corner of the room while enjoying the unfolding drama. "Also, though I'm not happy about it, I'm sharing the room next door with this greenhorn. If you're envious, you're welcome to join us."

"Oy oy, are you implying something? Geez... You're not as uptight as you seem, after all. Well, it's true that right now I'm in a body that can answer your wishes, but—" Vermouth jested.

"Greenhorn, if you don't want to be slaughtered, then shut the hell up," Halter growled in a low voice.

Meanwhile, Marie pouted with displeasure. "But, hey... doesn't this room only have one bed?!"

That was, in fact, true. Their room was only meant for two people. Although the interior was spacious, most of that space was taken up by the workshop—and, *for some reason*, a king-sized bed. Therefore, the living space was quite constricted.

However, Halter simply shrugged. "Even if you tell me that,

there's nothing I can do. There isn't any other room available, so you'll just have to deal with it."

"What are you suggesting I do?"

"It's not like you're a little kid. Decide where you're going to sleep by talking it out with your roommates, like any civilized person would," Halter replied as he left the room with Vermouth.

Having been left behind, Marie stared at the door resentfully for a while, but eventually dropped her shoulders with a sigh. "... Well, guess it can't be helped."

*It's not like the number of beds will increase if I keep complaining like a brat.*

In the first place, Marie was exhausted, both mentally and physically. Even though she had both Halter's and RyuZU's protection, she never managed to get a good night's sleep while she was on the run.

Whatever the case, she was now in a proper bedroom. With her dusty baggage finally off her shoulders and a soft bed in sight, she wanted nothing more than to fall down and sleep like a log.

"Argh...! I'll be using the shower first. I feel strangely tired today, so I'm gonna sleep right after I finish my bedtime routine."

Naoto blinked, looking confused. "Eh, you're gonna sleep now? In the morning? I mean, I'm tired, too, but..."

"Whatever we decide to do, it's easier to act at night." Marie raised her index finger towards Naoto and continued, "Shall I guess what you're thinking? You're thinking that, despite everything we've said, it's a rather peaceful city, aren't you?"

"Well... it doesn't look that different from the places we've been to up till now."

The sticky, hot air, the dust everywhere, the lurid and congested streets...indeed, if one only considered those qualities, then it might not be so different from the many other Southeast Asian cities they'd passed through.

Just then, a gunshot rang out. It was loud enough that one could hear it clearly from where they were, even without Naoto's superhearing.

"Oy, what was that just now?" Naoto rushed to the window to take a look outside.

Marie replied, "Just some fireworks."

"Yeah, right! That was clearly a gunshot just now, you know?!"

"Gunshots are a dime a dozen in this city. Don't bother yourself with them. If you hear *bombs exploding*, then let us know."

"How are you able to be so calm about this, Marie?"

Marie let out a sigh. "Let me tell you something, Naoto." Her emerald eyes wandered upwards, as if she were seeing a scene that was far away in the past.

"Though there are exceptions from time to time, like Japan, for the most part there are only two kinds of places the Meister Guild is dispatched to," she told him. "Those that are so poor that they can't even properly maintain their own grids, and warzones without a functional government. Try doing an emergency repair job over two or three consecutive all-nighters. You won't care about a gunshot or two after that. Though admittedly, there aren't many places I've been to that were as rotten as this city."

She tossed her backpack away, then took off her summer coat and hung it on a hanger. She then pulled her necktie off and was just about to undo the buttons on her shirt when she stopped. "By the way, if you look my way right now, I'll murder you."

"Are you dumb? What demand is there for a scene of you changing? You don't have to tell me; I wouldn't look anyway. To begin with, I already have RyuZU."

"Rest assured." RyuZU nodded with a chilling expression. "On the off chance that Master Naoto tries to turn his head around, I shall kindly and swiftly return his neck to its resting position."

"Eh?" Naoto said, taken aback.

Marie tilted her head, also looking perplexed. "That's pretty unusual of you, RyuZU. What's gotten into you?"

"Nothing. It is simply that I cannot allow Master Naoto's precious eyes to be dirtied from seeing the seedy disappointment that is Mistress Marie's naked body."

The vein below Marie's temple popped out. "Oh, is that so?"

Meanwhile, Naoto sprung up excitedly. "Hell yeah, RyuZU's jealous! Did you see that, AnchoR? The expression on my wife's face when she's worried about me cheating on her, even though that would never happen!!"

"So, Big Sis, you make those kinds of faces too..." AnchoR muttered quietly.

Seeing the disappointment in AnchoR's eyes, RyuZU furrowed her brow. "Master Naoto, could I ask you to keep your delusions within reason? I did not say that to Mistress Marie out of any such base emotion. It is natural that, as an assistant to my master, I should act to prevent any danger from happening to you."

"Yeah, uh-huh, right. I know. I believe you."

"Hmm...I wonder what this is? It seems that errors of unknown cause are building up in my behavioral algorithm. If I had to put it into words, I would say that I feel 'extremely irritated' right now."

As Naoto jumped about in joy with a smirk on his face, RyuZU's mood worsened even faster.

*Go ahead and keep that circus act up your whole lives, you idiots, Marie muttered internally. As she took off her shorts and undid the clasp of her skort, she said, "AnchoR? Their idiocy will infect you if you watch them, you know. Come over here and take a shower with Mom. I'll wash you."*

"Ah, coming..."

All of a sudden, Naoto forcefully turned around and yelled, "Stop right there, Marie! I won't allow you to strip AnchoR-chan without my permission!"

In that instant, he saw AnchoR with her arms up, in the middle of taking off her top...and Marie in her underwear, her fair, soft maiden's skin fully exposed.

"Eeeeeeeeeek! Stop looking, you punk!"

"Master Naoto."

"Ah—! No wait, RyuZU, I was just—gwah!"

RyuZU sandwiched Naoto's cheeks with her hands and forcefully twisted his head back to face forward.

That was when Marie, whose face was totally flushed, landed a powerful back spin kick on the back of Naoto's head.

· · • ● • · ·

When Naoto regained consciousness, Marie and AnchoR had already finished taking their shower.

As he tried to enter the bathroom while rubbing his head and neck, which were throbbing in pain, RyuZU followed him casually, as if it were only natural.

Then she said, "Please sit over there and take off your clothes."

Naoto didn't defy her. He sat by the edge of the bathtub and took off his feminine top—which he had been wearing to disguise himself—just as he had been told, exposing his upper body.

His body was covered in bandages. Protective sheets were wrapped tightly around the entirety of his upper right arm and back, and were kept in place firmly with medical tape and bandages.

RyuZU carefully removed them, one by one, upon which severe burn wounds became visible.

There were large patches of melted skin and burnt flesh. His entire back was purple. It must have been as painful as it looked, for he recoiled as RyuZU unwrapped his dressings. These wounds were from when he'd carried RyuZU in Akihabara. The nanomachines he had been injected with prevented his wounds from festering and continued to heal him, but...

RyuZU remained silent as she gently felt one of his wounds with her finger. A healing membrane was stretched over the wounds, but the flesh underneath was still a mess. Disturbing the membrane even just a little bit should cause unbearable pain and itching, yet Naoto didn't make a single noise.

His wounds wouldn't be able to heal completely without a transplant of either real or artificial skin, and his body wouldn't be able to return to its original state.

His flesh had been pressed tightly against an object that was hot enough to melt construction materials. He was lucky he didn't just die. That it didn't disable him was close to a miracle.

Naoto addressed RyuZU solemnly, "Don't let it bother you."

"That is not possible."

"It's not your fault. It's something I did by my own accord. So—"

"That is not it," RyuZU said as she offhandedly grabbed Naoto's head and thrust his face into the sink.

"Bwahh?!"

Ignoring Naoto's cry of alarm, she turned the stopper of the pullout shower. She then added some shampoo and vigorously scrubbed Naoto's hair and scalp.

"Wha, RyuZU—"

"To put it bluntly, you stink."

"Hahh?!"

"Your burns may be one thing, but having a master who smells like a sewer reflects poorly on my dignity as well, so..."

"No way...I smell that bad right now?!" Shocked, Naoto stopped resisting as he was left speechless.

Thankfully, RyuZU had soaked a towel with hot water, with

which she now wiped his entire body thoroughly, but also meticulously so as not to irritate his wounds. She then applied ointment on top of his burns and redressed his wounds with new protective sheets, then set them in place with bandages and medical tape.

"Are you done? Has my stink gone away?" Naoto asked, concealing the pain he felt.

RyuZU nodded. "Yes. Though the usual body odor that is stuck to Master Naoto is still there, the sewer-like stench has gone away. With this, you should be nominally presentable again."

"I see. In that case, it's your turn now, RyuZU. Take off your clothes."

"...Oh?" RyuZU tilted her head in confusion for a bit before nodding. "How embarrassing. Of course, how did I not realize? Considering that, even under normal circumstances, you are already oozing with lust, you must have a lot pent up within you right now. Plus, we are alone here, so there is no need to worry about AnchoR catching us, either—this is what you are implying, yes?"

"Wrong," Naoto replied crisply as he turned RyuZU around so that her back was facing him. He briskly stripped off her clothes, which were made of gear fibers, and picked out a flat jar from his bathing products bag.

On the lid, the words "Repair Kit (Cream Type)" were printed in English. It was an artificial skin restorer.

The artificial skin used for high-class automata was made from shape-memory polymers that auto-regenerated from trauma up to a certain point. However, if the damage exceeded that point, the built-in nanogears would run out and would need to be replenished.

"Man, I'm really glad I can finally mend your artificial skin, RyuZU. I would've never imagined that a hotel room could come with a workshop, much less one as upscale as this. Old Man Halter doesn't disappoint, does he?" Naoto said as he opened the lid of the repair kit while humming happily.

He scooped out some of the milky-white restorative cream and applied it broadly onto RyuZU's skin.

*Ever since I awoke to my abilities in Kyoto, I've had to push RyuZU too hard too many times to get through the messes I've found myself in, he thought to himself. Though Marie and I repaired her each time, if I look closely at her skin under a bright light like this, the tiny little chafes in her artificial skin become quite apparent. I really want to be able to give her some proper care soon.*

*This had been on Naoto's mind for some time now.*

His fingers traced a circle as he spread the cream on RyuZU's back gently, attentively. He didn't use much force. After he spread the cream out sufficiently, he began to rub it in with the palms of his hands.

As the milky-white cream permeated her skin and became indiscernible, her skin became smooth and springy again. Forget merely being on par with human skin—her restored artificial skin was far more pleasing to both the touch and the eye.

"Master Naoto, I demand an explanation for this act of utmost disrespect," RyuZU said suddenly, sounding sullen..

"Huh? What'd you say?" Naoto uttered with a blank expression.

Offended, RyuZU objected, "It is simply splendid that you appear to be having a grand old time, Master Naoto, but for my part, to have my clothes stripped away, yet not get any sort of response is a bit—no, it is in fact *considerably* baffling. I cannot imagine that it is due to some imperfection in my beautiful form, either. The only explanation I can think of, Heaven forbid, is that you have a bodily dysfunction of the male kind."

Naoto's eyes popped out as he yelled, "That's not it, you know!!"

"I must say, a good number of things make more sense now... like how, even though you are always jabbering on about how I am your wife, you have never targeted me with your beastly passions. They say that one can get one's hands on anything in this city, yes? Perhaps you should seek treatment to restore your male functions in addition to your burns—"

"Wait, don't jump to conclusions, Ms. RyuZU! Would you please notice just how hard I'm trying to restrain myself...nggh!!"

• • ● • •

*Would you shut the fuck up already?* Marie muttered threateningly inside her head as she clicked her tongue loudly.

Even from where she was in the workshop, the commotion in the bathroom was loud and clear. Marie didn't need Naoto's superhearing to understand the gist of what was going on: a wife who, unsatisfied with how her husband wasn't doing anything despite stripping her naked, was expressing her discontent to a husband who, mindful of their child—AnchoR—was trying to calm her down.

Love talk and lovers' spats had never interested Marie. Frankly, they never bothered her before because she cared so little about such things. Despite that, the current situation was enough to make her irate. *Yeah, go ahead, keep clowning around like that your whole lives, she thought. Just keep it away from me.*

Concerned about the angry click of the tongue she heard, AnchoR raised her gaze anxiously. "Mother?"

"Ahh! Don't mind me. Everything's fine, so just stay still and don't move, okay?"

Marie formed a smile on her face in a hurry as she returned her attention to the work ahead. Before her, AnchoR was naked, lying on her back on a workbench. What Marie was doing for AnchoR was the same thing that Naoto was doing for RyuZU— mending AnchoR's artificial skin.

What was different, though, was that unlike RyuZU, who needed only some restorative cream to be applied, AnchoR needed something closer to full-on grafting and replastering.

An automaton's artificial skin served two purposes: both as a case and coating for its internal mechanisms.

As far as its function as coating goes, there wasn't much need for it. If Naoto heard someone say such a thing, he would probably fly into a rage in protest, but in the end, the coating function of artificial skin was just a question of aesthetics. One could go so far as to say that if that were its only function, artificial skin wouldn't be a necessary component for automata.

The issue was its function as a case. Though it might be obvious, the joints for the moveable parts of the complex mechanisms that automata and cyborgs were equipped with—like legs and arms, necks and waists—were inevitably vulnerable.

If a maker tried to cover them up, they would have no choice but to add more plating on top of the artificial skin. As a result, it would greatly limit their range of motion, in which case the automaton would be unable to move naturally like humans do.

However, if the joints were fully exposed, there would be enough space for foreign particles like dust and dirt to penetrate the mechanisms, which could ultimately lead to a malfunction in clockwork that used fine parts on the scale of nanometers. Because of that, a highly durable and elastic material—basically, artificial skin—was needed to protect those joints.

Marie understood that, and so she had no intention of objecting to Naoto's wish to repair RyuZU and AnchoR's artificial skin as fast as possible, even if his motivation for it was questionable.

Since AnchoR was already barely moving right now due to the patchwork state she was in, Marie wanted to prevent any further functional impediments.

However, looking down at AnchoR, Marie let out a small sigh.

When it came to materials for artificial skin that could endure the full extent of AnchoR's and RyuZU's capabilities, the candidates were considerably limited.

Materials of that grade weren't something one could casually pick up from a hardware store. Their prices matched their rarity, and handling them required technical expertise...yet such materials were in fact available in this rental workshop.

The logical conclusion was that there was demand for such materials—which, in turn, suggested that the main users of these rental workshops were illegal high-output artificial bodies and automata, and the back-alley clocksmiths who dealt with them.

It wasn't just the materials for their artificial skin that were uncommon. Any spare parts that could endure the full capabilities of an Initial-Y automaton were all rare and difficult to obtain.

All the more so for ones that fit AnchoR, who was a child-sized model. It was difficult to scale down automata and cyborg bodies even without any special goals, because even the adult-sized ones were already "scaled down" to human size. It was incredibly technically difficult to use clockwork to replicate the complex system of mechanisms that was the human body to begin with, so the more compact someone wanted to make one, the harder it was to make.

As such, the child models of automata and cyborg bodies typically sacrificed output and functionalities relative to their size. There would normally be absolutely no need to make one that was the size of a child if what one wanted was power.

Yet, to deliberately and forcibly make one both as small and as powerful as AnchoR...

"The only explanation I can think of is that 'Y' was either trying to disguise AnchoR's capabilities, or that he was simply a hardcore pervert. Either way, only a criminal would think of doing such a thing."

"Mother...?"

"Oh, it's nothing. I was just talking to myself."

• • • ● • • •

Just as Naoto had finished with RyuZU and Marie with AnchoR, and sleep was on everyone's minds, another quarrel sprang up.

Marie stood in the dead center of the room, while Naoto was sitting on a sofa several meters away and facing her. She pointed to the gigantic, solitary bed and said, "'Once boys and girls reach the age of seven they should no longer eat together.' I do believe that's how the saying goes, yes? And we're not talking about just eating, but *sleeping* here."

She was dead serious.

However, Naoto replied to her contention with as cold a gaze as he could muster. "Look here, I've got no idea what exactly you're wary of. I mean, I guess technically I get what you're implying, but why does my presence worry you in the first place?"

*Okay, so as a budding girl, you're uncomfortable with the idea of sharing a bed with a boy of the same age, Naoto thought. I get that. Of course you would. Makes sense, I agree.*

*But in the first place, I'm not even the slightest bit interested in real human girls. Not only that, I've publicly proclaimed myself as*

*RyuZU's husband many times now, and proudly so at that. I'm a married man, so to speak.*

*Not to mention—though frankly, I can't see it happening even if the universe somehow turns upside-down—if I were to make a move on you, isn't it obvious that none other than RyuZU would immediately halt me with overwhelming violence that is both absurd and unstoppable?*

*Actually, considering that you've got enough CQC skills to easily KO a well-trained soldier, if anyone's in danger, isn't it me, not you?!*

RyuZU narrowed her eyes threateningly. "...Mistress Marie? I understand that the desire to conceive with outstanding genes is the instinct of all females, so it is only natural that you would be conscious of Master Naoto, the finest male specimen there is on this planet... However, could I please ask you to discern your place? Because if not, I would be forced to settle this dispute at its core. That is to say—a dead man needs no bed."

"Look here, now... I can swear in the name of God and my late mother that I've never looked at this punk as a man for a single second up to now, and never will. Even if hell froze over, such a thing would never happen."

"Then what's the problem?" Naoto asked with a shrug. "It's not like I'd be interested in a clump of flesh that isn't even loaded with a single mechanism myself."

Marie replied with a serious look on her face, "You see, Naoto, the issue here is rather that I genuinely find you, from the bottom of my heart, repulsive. That's all it is. You understand where I'm coming from, right?"

"Hey now... Do you think I don't have feelings or something?"

"Just desserts for someone who calls a girl a 'clump of flesh,' don't you think?"

The two of them glared at each other briefly, then sighed at the same time. Naoto slapped his hand on his forehead. "Well, whatever. I reluctantly agreed to share a room with you since it was AnchoR's request, but now that I think about it, you'd have to be a total freakazoid to do something like sleep together with a clump of flesh."

RyuZU nodded with a refreshing smile. "I am glad the problem appears to have been resolved. Now then, Master Naoto, please, make yourself comfortable on the bed. A clump of flesh surely needs no bed. Any old hanger should be more than sufficient for its storage."

"On the other hand, automata do need beds, huh...? Yeah, you don't have to say it. I can see it written on your face," said Marie.

"...Waahh, AnchoR is sleepy..."

"Oh AnchoR, you're welcome on the bed, you know? Come now, over here with Papa ♪."

However, Marie would have none of that, taking AnchoR by the hand, leaving the sleepy-faced automaton looking lost as to what to do.

Meanwhile, RyuZU sat down on the edge of the sofa, then called attention to her thighs by slapping them. "On second thought, Master Naoto, all things in life are a matter of perspective. A bed that a clump of raw flesh has touched can no longer be used unless it is first decontaminated and disinfected. As such, though it would not be as comfortable as the bed, how does making do with my lap pillow sound?"

"'Making do with'?! Feels more like getting a bump from a standard room to a suite, if anything!" Naoto scrambled right onto the sofa without a moment's hesitation, then rested his head on RyuZU's lap.

"But what about you, RyuZU?"

"Automata do not require sleep nor feel any fatigue, so I would say this is not a problem at all." RyuZU paused, putting a hand on her cheek. "...Normally, AnchoR would not need to sleep—or more accurately, recalibrate—either, were it not for the misalignments of the nerves in the limbs she is currently using, which heavily taxes her artificial intelligence to manipulate."

"Nnuuhh..." Torn between Naoto and Marie, AnchoR looked back and forth between the two of them as she rubbed her eyes, then asked, "Mom, Dad...can't we all sleep together?"

Even as she was clearly flustered by the upturned gaze of AnchoR's round, adorable eyes, Marie still shook her head. "E-even if you're the one asking, AnchoR, that is the one thing that Mom can't do; sorry."

"Sorry, sweetie. It's unfortunate, but humans have troublesome conventions that arise from our nature as organisms."

"...In that case, I'll sleep here...okay?" AnchoR laid out a blanket on the floor between the bed and the sofa, then flopped right onto it. It appeared she had adopted the compromise measure of remaining between her parents despite not sleeping with either of them.

Both Naoto and Marie were unwilling to sleep on the floor, but AnchoR refused to move. Before long, AnchoR was sleeping peacefully, and so the lights were dimmed gradually until they were off.

"..."

However, even as she lay on the bed that she had fought for, Marie found that she somehow just couldn't fall asleep.

It wasn't that the commotion outside on the streets particularly bothered her. She was in a safe place, and the bedding was of excellent quality as well. The cushions were soft, the sheets were clean... There was nothing to complain about. Above all, her body was thoroughly worn out. Her head even felt slightly numb, and she could feel herself losing focus.

But...there was still so much space. The bed was simply too wide.

Sure, Marie was on the small side, but there was still plenty of room left even when she stretched her arms and legs out to their maximum reach.

To be precise, the size of the bed was called "extreme ultra king size," as much of a joke as it sounds. Of course, like most people, Marie had never heard of such a thing before.

*Why does the bed have to be this big in the first place? This is supposed to be a room for two, right? No matter how you look at it, there's easily enough space for three, even four people to lie down simultaneously...*

Getting the hunch that she would reach an unpleasant conclusion should she keep thinking about it, Marie decided to stop.

That said, compared to how uncomfortable it felt trying to sleep in the corner of a freight train while holding her knees together as she was jolted constantly by the movement of the train, there shouldn't really be any problems in having too much space now, but...she just couldn't relax.

The vast amount of unoccupied space that remained even when she stretched out her body made her feel anxious. It felt almost as if, in this whole wide universe, Marie were all by herself. That's the kind of loneliness this bed made her feel.

Rolling over to her side on top of the sheets, Marie poked her head out from the edge of the bed and took a look. She saw AnchoR on the floor and Naoto and RyuZU on the sofa. AnchoR's location was indeed right about in the middle of where Naoto and Marie were, but...

"..."

Marie saw AnchoR clasping Naoto's hand, which hung down from the side of the narrow sofa.

*...What's up with this? Isn't there something weird going on here? Yes, AnchoR's sleeping in the space between the two of us, but isn't she closer to Naoto than she is to me? ...Wait, aren't I the only one sleeping alone in this arrangement? Am I the only one being left out?*

Crouching on the bed with only her face sticking out, Marie said, "Hey...RyuZU, you there?"

RyuZU was still sitting on the sofa with Naoto's head in her lap, which she was affectionately stroking with a smile. "What is the matter? Is it something important enough to disturb my

71

lofty duty of watching over Master Naoto's sleeping face from when I wish him good night to good morning?" RyuZU replied, a gentle smile still on her face. However, that smile was directed at Naoto, not Marie—she hadn't even turned her gaze one millimeter towards Marie.

If anything, it sounded like what she was really implying between the lines was, in plain speech: *"You're a nuisance. Just shut up and die."*

That lovey-dovey behavior only made Marie feel all the lonelier. "Umm...I'm sorry. I was in the wrong... So you see, uh, I'm fine with taking up just a small part of the bed... Really, just a tiny little snippet is enough for me, so could we all sleep together with AnchoR between me and Naoto? Dammit, Naoto, you're such a cheater!!" Marie yelled out, even tearing up a bit.

Just then, AnchoR, who should have been sound asleep, instantly sprang up and transplanted herself entirely onto the bed, blanket and all.

Then, after settling down around the center of the bed, she said fawningly, "Umm, Big Sis, Father...let's all sleep together?"

And so, with no one objecting to that last call to sleep together, Marie finally managed to fall asleep.

· · ● · ·

When night came, Naoto and Marie woke up naturally.

After getting changed, they went down to the first floor with RyuZU and AnchoR, upon which they found that the hotel

restaurant had become like a tavern, almost unrecognizable from how it was during lunch hours.

Under the dim lighting, the scent of tobacco smoke and pungent spices filled the room, along with the boisterous calls of the waiters. It had fully lost the sliver of respectability it had during the lunch hours as boorish, fierce-looking men and prostitutes wearing gaudy makeup had filled the seats and were talking up a loud hubbub.

In the midst of that were Halter and Vermouth, sitting at a large table near the stairs.

"Yo, did you guys get some sleep?" Halter asked as he held up his beer mug for a sip.

Naoto answered absentmindedly, "Well, to some degree, I guess... Say, isn't the atmosphere of this place completely different from how it was at noon?"

Marie answered as they both sat down, "Didn't I tell you? That when night comes, the true nature of this city will manifest itself. This is the true face of this place."

"If you'd like, you can sit at one of those seats over there and a sexy lady will pour you a drink," Vermouth said with a smirk on his face.

He jerked his chin at the table near the entrance where a bunch of prostitutes were sitting, and added, "So how it works is, you stuff some money down their cleavage. If they're satisfied with the amount, then you can go right on up to a room with her and receive some lovin'—this place's a paradise, right?"

"More like hell," Marie spat, looking deeply unamused.

Seeing that the rest of the two cyborgs' party had arrived, a hulk of a waiter came and asked, "May I take your orders?"

"A khanom chin and a sai ua for me. I don't need a drink. How about you, Naoto?"

On the other hand, Naoto, seeing not a single dish that he recognized on the menu, was at a loss. "I don't really know what any of these dishes are... Could you order something that probably isn't too spicy for me?"

"Ratna. It's basically the Thai version of Japanese gravy noodles."

"Okay, I'll have that, then."

Having finished taking their orders, the waiter left for the kitchen.

As she followed the waiter with her eyes just because, Marie asked, "So, does it look like you'll be able to get us the information we need?"

"Yep, don't worry. Though I expect you've got the money to spare to treat us to a round of drinks to loosen our friend's lips, right, bitch?" a strange voice chimed in.

As she turned back around, Marie suddenly noticed that there was another man sitting beside Halter, a stranger. It was a middle-aged man wearing a polo and jeans. His appearance was plain and inconspicuous.

*He's someone who you wouldn't remember for long, Marie thought. Though he's sitting right in front of me, I still can't tell how old he is or read his expression. I get the feeling that if this man got up and left right now, I'd forget his face in less than five minutes.*

*More than likely, he's deliberately being as inconspicuous as possible... An informant, huh.*

Marie nodded. "I do. However, I don't have even a penny to waste on treating *you*, Vermouth."

"Oy," Vermouth moaned pitifully, "give me a break, man. I'm an ex-underling who's currently out of work, you know? Not only that, my previous company is so amoral that they don't even have unemployment insurance. At least have the mercy to treat me to some drinks...as well as a new body, you damn elite."

"Please. I'm sure you've got one or two hidden assets somewhere anyway—no? Well, if you're so incompetent that you can't even manage your own finances, then wouldn't you be better off dead?"

"Allow me to deliver the breaking news to you, bitch! I'm already dead!"

"Then let me return the favor. Are you aware that the damn elite you're referring to is also dead already? What a coincidence, huh? Your shamelessness is sickening." Marie delivered a scathing retort with a sweet smile. She then looked towards Naoto and asked, "By the way, not that I'm expecting anything, but how much money do you have access to right now?"

A disheartened look appeared on Naoto's face. "Isn't it obvious that I'm broke? If only I could access my Japanese bank account, though, there should be a lot of money in there that RyuZU somehow mysteriously made for me."

"Well, it's to be expected that your assets were frozen—"

RyuZU cut in, "No, please rest assured, Master Naoto. Before we departed from Kyoto, I transferred your full balance to the Bank of Geneva in Switzerland."

"Gwah?!"

RyuZU's swift and casual reply caused Marie to have a coughing fit.

Naoto's eyes widened, his face blank from surprise. "Wha...? Uh, whose name is that bank account under?"

"Yours, of course, Master Naoto. What about it?"

"Uh, wouldn't it have been frozen already, then?"

"Rest assured, Master Naoto. The Bank of Geneva claims permanent neutrality and absolute secrecy for its clients. 'Even terrorists are customers as long as they have an account with us,' is its motto, which..."

"W-wait a sec, what? The money it takes simply to keep an account open with the Bank of Geneva is enough to build a palace, you know? Just how much money did you deposit in there?!" Marie demanded, looking flustered.

RyuZU replied with a sour face, "Are you suggesting that you have the right to know the balance of Master Naoto's bank account, Mistress Marie? Could it be that, Heaven forbid, you have taken AnchoR's figment of imagination seriously and now fancy yourself to be Master Naoto's wife? Please tell me this is not the case."

"Absolutely not!" Marie yelled, then sighed, seemingly worn out, and shook her head. "...Meh, fine. At least tell me how many digits there are, then."

Instead of immediately answering, RyuZU looked towards Naoto for approval.

Naoto himself seemed a bit shaken up, but he nodded. "Umm...a part of me is telling me that I probably don't want to know, but well, I guess I really should."

"Understood," RyuZU said as she raised both her hands palm up. She wasn't surrendering, but rather, expressing the number of digits in the bank account with her fingers.

*So a billion at the very least.* While feeling a dizzy spell come on, Marie followed up by asking, "What currency is it in?"

"What? The key currency of our time, of course."

"...So, how much is it in yen?" Naoto muttered dumbfoundedly.

Marie answered with a deep sigh, "At the current rate... Let's see, it should be roughly a hundred twenty billion yen."

Halter whistled, laughing. "Wow, Naoto. You could buy two hundred cutting-edge heavily-armored automata with that kind of money, y'know?"

"No no, Boss, you could buy double that number at what it's going for in this city, y'know? Holy balls, I sure wish we were friends, Naoto. I really could use a sugar daddy right now, y'know?" Vermouth whined, putting on a repulsively coquettish air.

"By the way, RyuZU, could I ask you where that moneys came from?" Marie asked, messing up her grammar a bit, presumably due to her shock.

However, RyuZU replied with a composed face, "What is there to say, really? Capitalism is but a game called 'ride the bubble.' Before we left Kyoto, I had foreseen the mayhem that would occur in Tokyo, so I used all of Master Naoto's assets and maxed out his credit limit to buy stocks for short selling. Is it really so surprising, then, that Master Naoto's worth would grow to this amount?"

*...I see.* Marie almost nodded in understanding before she stopped herself and groaned, "No no, for a terrorist to make a killing by manipulating the markets with her terrorist actions... It's totally a one-man insider show that you put on there."

"I fail to understand what you are saying. The one who caused Japan's stock market to crash was not I. As such, I do not think that my actions constitute insider trading. Would you object to that?"

*That's not the problem here.* Marie buried her face in her hands and groaned for a bit before pulling herself back together, upon which she said, "...W-well, all right. Though it isn't even a tenth of that amount, there's my hidden account as well. So I guess we won't have to worry about funding our activities for the time being."

Naoto retorted with his eyes half-closed, "So you're doing the same thing yourself."

"What are you talking about? Hidden accounts and off-the-book transactions are the obligations of a large enterprise."

"Apologize to all honest taxpayers in the world right now. Got it?"

"It's not like I made money off it; I simply sold off the stocks I owned before they would lose value. Of course, I secured the necessary funds for our next moves. I'm sure Halter has a hidden account or two, too."

Being called out, Halter responded while curling his lips impishly, "Oy oy, I only put enough in there for my beer money, y'know?"

"Oh, reaaally now?" Marie snorted. "You must drink some pricey beer... So, how 'bout you?"

"Oy oy, what are you expecting from an ex-underling spy? Unlike you damn elites, I'm one of the working poor, y'know?"

"Halter?"

Halter fiddled with his smartphone for a bit, then laughed. "Seems like the pay at the Audemars is quite good, huh, Mr. Ex-Underling Spy?"

Seeing his hidden account displayed on the screen of Halter's phone, Vermouth yelled in a fluster, "Wha, hey Boss! That's what's called an infringement of privacy, y'know!"

"Oh? Lemme see... Huh. Looks like you've got quite a bit stashed away, eh? Ain't that a blessing. You could easily buy yourself a new body with this much," Marie teased maliciously.

Vermouth responded, "Now look here, I was a pitiful low-level worker who could have been discarded at any time, y'know? What's wrong with me saving up with some side jobs for some extra security? Can't you just overlook the hidden stash that someone like me saved up by pinching pennies along the way? Gosh, you really take me for a scoundrel, don't you..."

"How could I possibly trust you? You're perfectly situated to earn a hefty bounty by simply informing international authorities of our location right now."

"Wow, what a bitch you are. Even though I helped you guys out so much, this is how I'm treated? Oy Boss, seems to me this twat doesn't understand the concept of honor."

"Ooh, then tell me, was this money earned through your

respectable primary occupation, or something you made from a side job, punk?" Marie asked as she pointed with a finger at a section of the screen.

"Geh," Vermouth groaned quietly.

"Looks like your side income has increased quite a bit these past two weeks, huh? You've received a total of eight deposits from Suvarnabhumi Logistics. If I recall correctly, isn't that company a front for the Thai military?"

"Huh? Don't tell me—" Naoto started to say.

"...Yes, how very interesting." Marie smiled sweetly at Vermouth. "While we were being chased around, you received eight deposits from the Thai military. *What side work* were you doing for them? Pray tell. I'm terribly curious." In contrast to her smile, her gaze had the chill of absolute zero.

On the other hand, Vermouth's countenance was the very picture of a petty scoundrel who just had his crimes exposed. He sighed deeply. "Let me off the hook, would you? We would have been found sooner or later, anyway. Given that, isn't the smart choice to take as much as we can get by informing them ourselves from the beginning? It makes their moves more predictable as well. C'mon, I dutifully helped you guys in driving them back, didn't I? This is the epitome of a win-win relationship!"

Marie said, throwing her chest out, "What? How is it win-win when you're taking all the money for yourself? How about you show some sincerity by at least giving me my share of the pie?"

Vermouth clicked his tongue sharply and said, "Tch...fine, I get it. You sure are greedy for a rich kid. How do you want to split it?"

"Nine to one, I'd say."

"What? You're okay with just that? Guess you're not that greedy after all."

"Right, nine for me and one for you. How fair and considerate of me, right?"

"Are you the devil incarnate?!" Vermouth shouted as he glared fiercely at Marie.

"Hey Father, what are they talking about?" AnchoR looked puzzled, seemingly unable to follow the conversation.

Naoto shook his head deeply to console her. "In short, there are a lot of people in the world who don't make an honest living. You're a good kid, AnchoR, so you mustn't mimic them, okay?"

"Forget an honest living, you don't even work at all. Could you not act like you're above us when you're just a kept man leeching off his wife like a parasite?!"

"The most work a normal sixteen-year-old kid can do is a part-time job! And who's the one who made it so that I can't even do that?!"

"Huh? Don't you start whining to me now this late in the game!"

An uproar ensued. As vicious abuse was flung back and forth, Halter sighed, "...Sorry about all the noise." As he apologized, he took out a stack of bills from the inside pocket of his suit and presented it to the man sitting next to him.

However, after the man took the money, he then split the stack of bills roughly in half. He tied one half back with the strip of paper it came with and returned the rest to Halter. "This is enough for me."

"Really? That can't be enough, though..." Halter furrowed his brows dubiously.

Upon shifting through the half stack he was given back, Halter found the vast majority of the information he had asked for in a note. While Halter did pay him more than market price for his services, him taking only half flipped it right back the other way, dropping the payment way below market price.

Seeing Halter's suspicious look, the man simply said, "I couldn't believe it myself until I saw them with my own eyes, but this group of brats really is the infamous Second Ypsilon, huh?"

Suddenly, the tavern fell dead silent.

Whether they were the drunkards who had been clamoring, the prostitutes who had been soliciting, or the waiters who had been welcoming customers boisterously, everyone in the tavern had all fallen completely silent.

Everyone had shut right up and was now looking intently at Halter's table.

*Guess I was too optimistic,* Halter groaned internally as he reached discreetly for the pistol at his waist. *It isn't that I complacently thought that this city was safe or anything. I simply didn't expect someone to make a move on us with this timing. Guess I misjudged the level of danger in this city...*

Halter could tell from the corner of his eye that Marie and the rest had realized the situation a second later as their whole bodies stiffened up, along with their faces.

*What should we do? It'd be a piece of cake to escape from this hotel, but then what? If the enemy's reach is faster and longer than expected, then even the backup hiding place I prepared might not be absolutely safe...*

The informant quietly stood up in the midst of the tense air. He wasn't holding a weapon. After surveying all the faces at the table, he extended his hand. "I'll give you a bargain on the information fee. In exchange, won't you shake my hand?"

"..."

*What?*

"If possible, I'd also like to ask for a commemorative photo together. All right?" the man added with an embarrassed smile on his face.

• • ● • ·

In the end, Marie was badgered into a signature on top of a fervent handshake and photograph together.

After the grinning informant had left, their table unsurprisingly remained the center of attention just the same. As she pierced her sai ua with her fork, Marie muttered, "By the way..."

"Yeah?"

"I get the feeling that I shouldn't even ask, but who was that just now?"

"You should obey your instincts, princess. You're better off not knowing. Knowing you, you might have left him at death's door then and there."

"Somehow...mmm...I can't help but feel like I've seen him

before somewhere..." Marie tilted her head as she stuffed the food into her mouth. She got that feeling when that middle-aged man, who practically seemed like a shadow with how unmemorable he was, threw away his best interests—professionally speaking—and showed a human side to himself.

Marie knew she had seen him before somewhere, but she just couldn't remember where. It gave her an uncomfortable feeling, like having something stuck between one's teeth.

"Want me to take a guess?" Vermouth interjected with a smirk. "The ringleader behind President Parham's death who is said to have died six years ago, right?"

Marie's expression immediately turned grim. She glared at Vermouth. "Hold it there. The entire region of Central America was driven into an economic depression due to that incident, you know? Do you even realize how many people were driven to suicide because of that?"

"Princess," Halter said calmly, "there are tons of people alive who are considered dead officially, just as is the case for someone sitting right here at this table."

"That's—"

"No one here has called you out for being the daughter of the Five Great Corporations, have they? The underworld has its own unspoken rules. Don't stick your nose too deeply into others' business, a'ight?" Vermouth said.

Marie replied with a surly face, "So what, that terrorist is not only related to me but also felt a sense of kinship with me? How absolutely humiliating."

"That's what you wished for, isn't it? Then you can only act out the part you've given yourself in the most vicious terrorist group in the world. Ain't that right?"

Marie almost retorted reflexively to Vermouth's snide remarks, but she ended up keeping her mouth shut. *He's absolutely right. We've become terrorists.*

*In order to force through our own will, we've kicked justice to the curb. If there is something different in what we did versus what that man did, then it'd be our motives. Had he done it for money? For a doctrine? For an ideal? ...Or for fun?*

Indeed, Vermouth was absolutely right. In the end, they did it for their own sakes. As she was right now, Marie had no right to judge others on that one point if nothing else.

"I know that much myself. So I'll bear with it...as much as it irks me."

"Relax. It's true that you guys are infamous and the center of attention right now, but it's not like we're the only terrorists in town. If you'd like, I could gather those in the same line of business who have clout everywhere in the world and hold a mixer."

"No thanks," Marie said as she stabbed the next piece of sai ua deeply with her fork.

"All right, well, I think I'll explain a little bit about this town's circumstances now. Lend me your ears as you eat," Halter began, changing the subject. "As you know, this city is teeming with countless crime syndicates and extremists and has no such thing as a government. Nonetheless, this city's questionable denizens have their own system of hierarchy and way of keeping the peace. Three principal organizations have evolved into the leaders."

"Evolved?" Marie asked with a question mark written on her face.

Halter nodded. "The organizations with those names today are entirely different from the original organizations. Of course, the original organizations were led by some other dudes from elsewhere, but after countless violent struggles, breakups, and merges, any traces of the original organizations are all but gone now."

"The names of the three organizations are simple and plain," added Vermouth, "as there isn't anyone who would name their organization something pretentious here. Nor is there any language not spoken here, as the wealthy are the best customers and they come from all over the world. And so, the three organizations are known universally in all languages as Market, Restaurant, and Arsenal."

Halter gave a rough explanation: "Market is the financier that holds the keys to commerce and information here; Restaurant is the pimp that manages drug dealing and sex trafficking; Arsenal's the militant with weapons of all scales and advanced clockwork technology under their control—straightforward, right?"

Naoto tilted his head. "Leaving Market aside, wouldn't it be confusing when someone wants to refer to a normal arsenal or restaurant?"

"No. There isn't any arsenal here that isn't under the management of Arsenal, nor is there any restaurant that isn't affiliated with Restaurant." Vermouth smiled bitterly. "So? Well, I think this goes without saying, but it's not like these three organizations are buddy-buddy with one another. That's obvious, right? All organizations do business, and if you want to sell things here you need bouncers, and bouncers need weapons to do their jobs. Of course, they eat, fuck, and get high as well."

"In short, their domains overlap," Halter said. "That's why they see each other as eyesores, but even so, they keep things smooth on the surface. That's the weird thing about this city... but anyways, for now just keep Arsenal in mind; you can forget the other two."

Naoto tilted his head. "...Why?"

"Because by tomorrow, they might become different organizations altogether. It'd be a waste of time to try to keep track of them all," Halter replied.

Vermouth expanded on his answer, "Boss mentioned this earlier too, but the three organizations didn't start how they are now. They're groups that consist of gangsters easily in the triple digits who receive assistance and meddling in internal affairs from overseas, and are even related to terrorist groups. Those who stand at the top of these groups at any given time are simply those who won the last round of infighting, where anything goes. If the head misses even one step or gives others any excuse at all, then it'll be a different head leading the group five minutes later. Aside from Arsenal, that is."

"Only Arsenal hasn't had any shuffling at the top since its inception six years ago. That's quite a feat, you know?" Halter said solemnly. "The boss' name is Kiu Tai Yu. He's the *de facto* ruler of this city. He single-handedly oversees the entire business of selling weapons, ordnance, artificial bodies, and automata and their parts. Not only that, he makes sure all the Meisters in town only work for him, and he has control of the core tower with their help."

"While we're at it, he was the key figure in heading off any excuse IGMO could use to intervene in this city, not only by showing a big stick, but also by speaking softly behind the scenes. Quite the son of a bitch, right? That he's survived for six years at the top is proof of his ability and achievements. The guy who lasted the longest after him only lasted eight months, so he's first by a long shot."

*Even if I took what Vermouth's saying with a grain of salt, that's an accomplishment you'd need an extreme level of resourcefulness to achieve. Marie gulped unwittingly and asked, "...Who is he?"*

"I don't know. I don't know anyone who's interested in knowing, either." Halter shrugged. "Well, strictly speaking, there probably are those who're curious, but those who dig into someone's past don't live very long in this city. Are you so curious that you would risk your life to know whether Arsenal's boss really once worked as a pizza delivery guy or not?"

"...I guess you're right."

"All in all, you just have to know that he's a closer. I'd imagine that, as long as we don't bother him, he isn't someone who'd make a pointless pass at us," Halter said as he produced a notepad from his inside breast pocket.

He wrote something, then tore off the note and handed it to Marie. "Regarding what you asked of me earlier, you'll find the guy in question if you go to that address. You should pay him a visit after you finish eating."

"Huh...? You aren't coming with us?"

"I've got a special type of 'immigration inspection' that I need to take care of. Don't worry. You'll be safer not coming with me, as long as you don't do anything stupid. RyuZU'll be with you as well, after all."

"Roger. And what about you?" Marie asked as she shot a sharp gaze at Vermouth, who had tried to casually step away from his seat.

Vermouth broke into a smirk and said, "What, you want me to come with you, bitch? I get that you'll feel lonely without me, but—"

"So the bastard who was just proven to have sold us out is now shamelessly trying to skedaddle off elsewhere? Hmmmmm. I'm telling you to tell me where you're going, you shitbag."

"Oy oy, calling a bald man bald is just a description, not an insult, y'know, so what's the point in calling me a shitbag? Or are you asking me for verification?" Vermouth responded flippantly.

Halter rebuked sharply, "Greenhorn, do you think I'd let you go cruising around this city on your own? You're coming with me."

"Hah hah! Sorry Boss, I'm the type who likes to visit the red light district by myself."

"I didn't ask what you'd prefer," Halter said coldly.

That instant, Vermouth's expression changed. Correction: it didn't really change. He was still smirking flippantly as always. However, the meaning behind that smirk had decisively changed.

"Hey Boss, I respect your skills as a mercenary from the bottom of my heart. I'd even dare to say that I'm a big fan of yours, but..."

Vermouth paused and snapped his fingers. Immediately afterwards...

"We all have our strengths and weaknesses."

Those words sounded from every direction. All the customers in the restaurant had spoken the same words at exactly the same time.

"...Agh?!"

For just one moment, Marie, Naoto, RyuZU, AnchoR of course, and even Halter had a small lapse in their awareness. Astonishment, wariness, and recognition over what had just happened hit them all at once.

By the time they regained themselves, Vermouth was gone, not leaving that small lapse to waste. He had disappeared without leaving behind any trace of himself, in terms of both sight and sound.

"That guy!" Marie stood up, her eyes flaring, but it was already too late.

The other customers in the restaurant had returned to their original clatter as if nothing had happened. The sight of that felt all too surreal to Marie, leaving her frozen on her feet...because this meant Vermouth had hired everyone who was in the restaurant right now to help him escape.

*When did he have the time to set this up? Considering he's been under Halter's constant watch since we arrived at this hotel, it'd have to have been before we entered the city!*

"That bastard," Halter growled, baring his teeth. "So, you think you can hold your own against me if you make me play hide-and-seek with you, huh? You've got some nerve, greenhorn, I'll give you that."

•  •  ●  •  ●  •

Nighttime in Shangri-La Grid was even more of a bustling confusion than it was at noon. Garish street stalls and signs illuminated by neon gears lined the streets.

Marie walked along the street while holding AnchoR's hand. They were enshrouded by the heat, which didn't let up even after sunset, and some weird stench that seemed like it could be from food but was just as likely to be otherwise.

Naoto and RyuZU were walking right behind them. Perhaps some on the streets recognized their faces, or perhaps their group simply stood out in this crowd, but now and then there'd be people who would stop upon seeing them and give them a suspicious gaze. Still, it didn't seem like anyone was going to make a move on them—for now, at least.

"That doesn't mean that we can let our guard down, though," Marie sighed to herself.

*There are three reasons why we we're here in Shangri-La Grid:*

*The first is to find replacement parts for AnchoR. As things are right now, we can't fully repair her. In the first place, considering AnchoR's insane capabilities, there's no way we could easily get our hands on parts that could withstand her full output.*

*Even if we assume her parts to be about the same structure as RyuZU's, we'd still need premium materials that only the manufacturing plant of an international research institute could synthesize.*

*However, though we've done what we can to fix her up along the journey, we can forget about her being combat-ready. She might even be less capable than a real child right now.*

*Both her autogyro and shock absorbers are totaled, and her frame is still bent way out of shape. That said, at least her spring—a critical component for automata—is still in good shape.*

*A good analogy for her current state would be like if a high output engine of a fighter plane were fitted onto a tricycle for kids.*

*As is, she can barely even walk. If we don't fix her up now so she can move properly at the bare minimum, her body might break down before we get to France.*

*Secondly, the only way we can make it past the many great countries in the way—like the Commonwealth of China, India, and the Arab Union—and into Europe is through the unique smuggling route that runs through this city of criminals.*

*Sure, we might have RyuZU with us, but even so, trying to cross the Eurasian continent while taking on multiple full-fledged military battalions one after the other simply isn't realistic.*

They weren't looking to fight in the first place at the moment. It might go without saying that Marie and Naoto wouldn't last through many large fights, but even Halter wouldn't hold up as he was, having lost his original artificial body. Engaging in fights right now would simply lead them to suffer injuries needlessly.

Thirdly...

"So, where exactly are we headed right now? You still haven't told us," Naoto asked, seeming to have lost his patience.

Marie replied, "We're going to order a new mainframe for AnchoR."

The mainframe for an automata was analogous to the spine and pelvis for humans. It enclosed the main cylinder, which was more important than the spring for automata, as well as sheathed the nerve wires which were finer than spider silk into bundles and connected them to other critical components. It'd be fair to say that it was the pillar of support for automata and cyborgs.

During the fight in Tokyo, AnchoR's mainframe had been broken—correction: bent.

"Unlikely as it is, even if there is a broken part in AnchoR that we could use a common spare part for, there's no world in which a mass-produced mainframe could replace her original one."

AnchoR's design was simply too unique. Though it might be obvious that her compatibility with typical replacement parts would be limited as a designer model of automata, calling her compatibility limited would hardly do it justice. Only an insane mainframe could hope to support the parts that bore the brunt of her ultra-high power output while maintaining her reaction time in a form factor that would fit inside her.

So insane, in fact, that it'd probably be easier to design a scaled-down version of a heavyweight race car to that of a palm-sized toy car while keeping its full capabilities.

Naoto thought for a bit, then asked, "Is there no way we could make it ourselves?"

"That'd be difficult." Marie shrugged. "First, the mainframe itself isn't a moving part. That means we can't rely on your ears to inspect it, but... Well, even if you could, do you think you can explain its structure to me in proper engineering terms?"

"Well, I mean...not if it's a one-of-a-kind custom part, but..."

"Are you thinking you'd be able to tell when there's a problem if we tried connecting some mainframes? But if we connect mainframes that end up being incompatible to AnchoR's body over and over again, that'll eventually take a toll on the rest of her body, you know, even as resilient as her parts are."

Unlike the arms and legs, the mainframe wasn't a part that could be casually replaced just because. It went without saying that it was left untouched during regular maintenance, but it usually wasn't taken out even in an overhaul, which might be done every few years. Normally, if an automaton's mainframe broke, the entire automaton was disposed.

However, Naoto frowned. "Okay, so it's something that even you and I can't make, right? Then just *whom* are you planning to order it from?"

"Yeah. It isn't something that a proper clocksmith could make. But..."

*If there were a clocksmith who might be able to make it happen...*

"Giovanni Artigiano," Marie declared, "He's an overclocker who is said to exceed the technical capabilities of even the Five Great Corporations when it comes to mainframe design."

"...An *overclocker*?"

Marie replied, "An overclocker is someone who mixes and

matches automata parts of different formats and connects them together adroitly."

Naoto tilted his head and asked, "Is that really as hard as you're suggesting?"

"Of course. Normally, it would be unthinkable to try to replace the parts of an automaton that isn't conformed to a standard model type. It'd be like trying to give a man the ability to fly by transplanting the wings of a bird onto his back. That's how absurd it would normally be."

The output power levels of the parts might not match. Or the material strengths. Or the capabilities. To begin with, they might come from completely different manufacturers.

"Putting incompatible parts together and making them function normally is just as hard and intricate as it sounds," Marie asserted.

That was precisely why any clocksmith who had undergone proper training would never deliberately do such a thing. After all, it'd be quicker to design a new replacement part from the ground up than to figure out how to interface two incompatible parts.

However, in this city, there was unending demand for just that service. Illegal weapons, knock-off goods that naturally weren't labeled with the name of their manufacturers, and modded articles made of parts that were intended for different models...getting such things to work required the skills of an absolute top-notch overclocker.

"I could copy what they do to some extent, but my work wouldn't even begin to compare to the work of a top tier overclocker. Those guys can even somehow coax out capabilities that exceed a part's original design. Their skills are godly, to put it mildly," Marie continued as Naoto's eyes widened. "As for whom we're going to visit right now, people call him 'Maestro Finite'. They say that no matter how incompatible the parts are that you take to him, he'll design the optimal mainframe for them and build something with capabilities exceeding those of the original parts...and that he has absolutely no interest in anything else whatsoever. An eccentric, no doubt."

"Such an amazing clocksmith is in this city?"

Marie nodded. "I'm not too sure what kind of person he is, though, myself. But I hear he brushed aside countless scouters, including those from the Five Great Corporations, to open up an independent workshop here in Shangri-La Grid."

"Wow!"

"Well, I'm sure his skills have been embellished to some extent."

Naoto's face turned blank. "What? So it could be all lies? Man, I was just thinking how cool he must be, too."

"I mean, after all, how can you create a mishmash of parts from designer items that exceeds the capabilities of those items? Theoretically, it should be impossible." Marie laughed bitterly. "Well, that said, even taking the stories told about him with a grain of salt, he's definitely got skills. That he can fit parts together no matter how incompatible they are may be deceptive advertising, but there's no doubt he's one of the world's foremost mainframe designers. He'd surely be able to make something much better than any old replacement mainframe on the shelves, or what we could make ourselves."

Having departed from the central marketplace, they now passed the Chang Phuak Gate in the north of the city.

Upon leaving the chain of street stalls that ran along the canal and water fountain, the feel of the surroundings changed greatly. The flashy flyers and garish lights, as well as the crowd of people moving about, were all suddenly nowhere to be seen. To the west was the entertainment district managed by Restaurant, but it was far enough away from where they were that the noise from the district wasn't very audible.

Instead, they now found themselves in a downtown residential area, where the houses were made with blocks and panels from scrap materials. One could tell from the ambience that they were the quarters of the permanent residents of the city, rather than visitors who were only here on business trips.

The public order in this area was particularly bad; not that it was good anywhere in the city. However, Marie stepped right into it without hesitation. While holding tightly onto AnchoR's hand, she opened up a map of the area with her other hand as they walked through the dimly lit streets. After some time, they came across a decrepit two-story building.

It was the independent workshop of the clocksmith in question; it stood sandwiched between gray apartments that had a lifeless feel to them.

"Such a great clocksmith works here?"

"That should be the case. Well, seems like he isn't a very conventional guy, to say the least." *I can see where Naoto's coming from, Marie thought.* The building was simply too dilapidated.

To begin with, despite being a workshop, it didn't even have a sign. It appeared that the pavement leading up to the door had been swept clean, but the walls had myriad little cracks in them and looked like they might collapse altogether any second. The surrounding buildings were quite run-down and unkempt themselves, but the building before them was on a whole other level.

It wouldn't be surprising if it turned out that this building actually went all the way back a thousand years ago, before the modern era. If anything, that would be more believable than otherwise. However, this was unmistakably the address written on the note that Halter had jotted down.

Marie knocked on the door cautiously and nervously, afraid that she might cause the whole building to collapse if she were to use too much force.

They waited for a while. Just when Marie was considering whether she should knock again, the door opened.

"Si— May I ask who's visiting?" The voice was clearly the synthesized voice of a robot.

Then, a maid automaton with a face like that of a bisque doll showed itself. It wore a classic-looking apron that hinted at an owner with retro tastes. Compared to the mainstream automata these days that looked very close to real humans, it was clearly an old model of automaton, much less RyuZU or AnchoR.

Looking right back at the blue eyes that one could tell from a glance were made of glass marbles, Marie introduced herself. "I'm Marie, and this girl is AnchoR."

"...Ah, I'm Naoto."

"My name is RyuZU."

"Si— Thank you very much. Allow me to introduce myself. My name is Nono Figlia, the automaton in charge of welcoming guests at this workshop," the maid automaton—Nono—said as she bowed elegantly.

As Marie's eyes widened from seeing how incredibly smooth its movements were, she asked, "To confirm, is this Giovanni Artigiano's workshop?"

"Si— Would it be correct to assume that you've come here to order something from Master?"

"Yes, there's a job that I must ask of him. Could I ask you to let me speak to him directly?"

"Si— Understood. In that case, please come this way."

Upon stepping into the workshop at Nono's invitation, Marie gaped as she looked around. The interior of the workshop was drastically different from its shabby exterior. Every nook and cranny inside seemed to be well taken care of.

They were immediately hit by the smell of kerosene. The indoor space was fairly wide, but most of it was buried in various work instruments that were clearly well-used. The shelves resting against one side of the room were stuffed with countless parts, materials, and a great number of books and documents.

Though at first glance it looked like no care was taken to keep things tidy and everything had just been thrown around carelessly, in actuality there wasn't a single speck of dust.

The walls were most likely soundproofed, as the noise from outside was completely inaudible. Instead, the overlapping sound of countless gears turning could be heard from everywhere inside. Yet it was quiet enough that one could still make out the sound of a needle falling onto the floor.

In the far back of this mysterious space was the single light source in this workshop, buried in darkness. There, an old man sat hunched over in his work chair.

*It's almost like he's a magician from the land of fairy tales, Marie thought. The image of an aloof sage surfaced in Marie's mind, one who continuously polished his wisdom in a secluded hovel away from the rest of the world, and would offer deep advice to youngsters who sought it before undertaking difficult trials.*

*The rumors may be true, after all. At the very least, I can't help but feel from seeing this workshop, and now the man himself, that he's a clocksmith who's reached an incredible height.*

Marie gently called out to the man from behind as he continued working silently, "Pardon my intrusion, but are you Signore Artigiano?"

There was no reply.

"Excuse me for interrupting you at night, but there's a job I must ask of you. It's probably something only you can do. Could you please hear me out?"

The old man started from surprise, then turned around and slowly raised his head. He gazed upon his guests with his peaceful, amber eyes for a bit, then cupped an ear with his hand, looking rather confused. "...What'dya say?"

• • ● • •

*...This might be hopeless.*

Despite falling into despair for an instant from the old man's response, Marie tried again in a louder voice. "Umm, Signore—"

"Honey, didn't you eat earlier already? Are you spacing out again?"

"Who's your honey?! You're the one who's spacing out!" Marie shouted reflexively in anger.

Grabbing Marie by the shoulder, Naoto said, "Oy Marie, you're dealing with a grandpa here, so be a little more forgiving."

"Y-yeah...you're right. I lost myself for a moment there." Marie said, then took a deep, slow breath to calm herself down.

The old man tilted his head and said, "...Marie? Oooh, are you the beautiful Queen Antoinette?!"

"Huh? What the heck are you even saying? In the first place, Marie Antoinette is someone who lived over twelve hundred years ago."

"Ahh, yes indeed, and she had huge knockers, too... Oooh, pardon me! You can't be her after all."

Marie immediately covered up her chest with her arms and shouted yet again despite herself, "Where do you think you're looking?!"

The old man gazed up at the ceiling and let out a deep sigh, "Yeah, Adelina. I too miss the sound of that canzone. Let's visit Amalfi again and drink some limoncello while basking in the sea breeze, shall we?"

"Adelina *who*?!" Marie cried out in exasperation.

Nono replied, "Si— Mistress Adelina is the Maestro's granddaughter."

"Listen to me! I'm neither your wife nor your granddaughter nor Marie Antoinette! I'm telling you that I'm a customer!" Marie screamed.

From behind her, RyuZU whispered quietly, "Mistress Marie, aside from the fact that he correctly identified your bosom as being as barren as the national treasury of revolutionary-era France, it seems clear that this senior does not have his wits about him. Yet you were saying you want to commission an extremely important part for AnchoR from him? To put it bluntly, have you lost it?"

"I'm deep in regret right now over that...!" Marie whispered back painfully, as if she were coughing up blood.

"Well, now...so that's what an Initial-Y looks like, huh?" The old man snickered as he continued, "I'm guessing that you came to ask me for a replacement mainframe for the little one with you?"

"Wha—?" Marie stared with wide eyes, flabbergasted.

"There's nothing to be surprised about, really. I may be a recluse, sure, but even I at least read the news." The old man— Giovanni—laughed like a kid who had succeeded in his prank. "I believe your group's name was Second Ypsilon, yes? For your group, which possesses two Initial-Y automata, to visit a workshop on the outskirts of town like mine with the mainframe of one of the Initial-Y's bent... Anyone could put two and two together in this case, not just me."

*Yeah, he's probably right. Or rather, he would be, if a small detail were left out...the fact that he knew AnchoR's mainframe is bent.*

AnchoR's mainframe was an internal component. There should be no way of knowing its status unless one opened her up and checked inside. Nevertheless, Giovanni was able to assert that the mainframe was neither broken nor had damaged connections, but rather that it was bent. Just as he said, anyone could know all the other premises that led to his conclusion.

Marie shivered as she became convinced. *This old man's skills are the real deal.*

That aside... "Uh, what was that about just now, then? I thought you had gone senile."

"No? I guess I may not look it, but I actually pay a lot of attention to my health. I get a checkup once every week, and I've never had the doctor bring up cognitive problems with me. Isn't that right, Nono?"

"Si— The Maestro has a few health issues that come with old age, but no observable signs of cognitive impairment, memory deficit, or disorientation."

"Then what was that just now?!"

"Well, see, usually the ones who visit are all grim-looking gangsters, so I thought I'd mess with you a bit for fun. That's all."

*This shitty geezer.*

Marie felt the veins by her temples pop out, but ultimately managed to stifle her anger. "W-well fine, I guess. If you have your wits together, then that'll save me time explaining. To repeat what I said at the beginning, there's a job I want to request of you."

His reply was immediate. "Indeed, saving time can only be good for us both. I decline. May I ask you to leave now?"

His answer had been so abrupt and unexpected that Marie was left standing still for a while, dumbfounded. She then blinked a couple of times and said, "Er, may I ask why?"

"I'm all booked for the time being, unfortunately. There's no room in my schedule for your request," Giovanni said with a shrug. "If you're willing to wait, then I don't mind accepting, but can you wait five years?"

"Of course not!" Marie yelled. She nearly lost herself to anger, but held out in the end. She took a deep breath to calm herself down, then continued. "I'm aware that my sudden request might be an inconvenience to you, but five years is way too long to wait! I'll pay the appropriate price in light of that, so could you please be just a little more flexible?"

However, the old man laughed bitterly and said, "My, my. You really don't mind asking the impossible of others, do you, missy?"

"..."

"You said that you get your request would inconvenience me, but you actually don't get it at all. Just what do you think this place is? Most of my customers are gangsters who would devour anyone who crosses them down to the bone. If I'm even a second late turning in my work at the agreed-upon time, forget paying a penalty fee. I might have my entire workshop demolished, you know?"

"That's—"

The old man shot a cold gaze at Marie, who was stumped. "And to begin with, don't you think trying to force others to follow your will by throwing stacks of money at them is a little crass?

Did they not teach you this thing called social etiquette at the Academy?"

Marie couldn't refute any of what he had said. Placing her hand on her chest, she proposed, "Th-then, could you let me help you as an assistant? I'll prove I can shorten the amount of time it'll take you to fulfill your current orders, so would you consider fulfilling mine in the time that I'll open up for you?"

The moment she finished speaking, the old man not only gave Marie a cold look, but was clearly sneering as he said, "Sorry, but a little amateur wouldn't be able to help me with the work I do."

"A-amateur?!" Shocked, Marie had trouble even getting her words out.

For a moment, she couldn't even understand what she had just been told. Never had there been any clocksmith who had shown her such disrespect. Upon regaining her senses, Marie began indignantly, "W-with all due respect, I'm actually—"

"I'm well aware. You're the prized daughter of the Breguets, yes?"

"Huh...? You know who I am?!"

"I might have heard a rumor or two about you." The old man laughed bitterly.

"Y-you called me an amateur knowing who I am, and knowing that I'm a Meister?"

"Yes, and?"

Marie's hands were curled into fists and trembling as she stood frozen to the spot.

*The old man called me an amateur.*

*Knowing full well that I'm the younger daughter of the Breguets, that I'm a Meister, and that I've served as the head of a division in Meister Guild—he still called me an amateur.*

*I've never let my accomplishments get to my head. Never. But...*

"Whether you're a Meister or the prized daughter of the Breguets makes no difference to me. You're still an amateur in my eyes. What, so you got out of your diapers earlier than most do. Is it really something to be so proud of?" The old man sneered as he rested his head in his hand.

"If you consider yourself a professional, if you pride yourself on being a true clocksmith who's pushed the boundaries of her field, then I think there's something you should do before you come crying to a half-retired dotard like myself, wouldn't you agree?"

*Snap.*

Marie heard the sound of something tearing inside her. It might have been her temple vein, or it might have been her last thread of patience. Or perhaps she had hallucinated the sound altogether.

Whatever the case, Marie was at her limits. With all of her patience depleted, she yelled, "Well then, sorry to have bothered you! Please, by all means, keep living healthily and peacefully in solitude inside this shitty city until you kick the bucket! Farewell!" Marie turned around and glared at Naoto. "We're leaving, Naoto! Staying here any longer would just be a waste of time. Let's think of another way."

Making a complete mainframe would be impossible for them, considering both the equipment and time restraints they had.

However, it'd probably be possible for them to repeatedly tune AnchoR with her mainframe's distortion in mind so she wouldn't break down, though it wasn't an ideal solution.

*At the very least, that'd be more productive than trying to coax this disagreeable old man into helping us.*

However, Naoto shook his head at Marie, who was already at the door, and said, "Take AnchoR and go back to the hotel first, Marie."

Marie's eyes widened.

*That surprised me...both the fact that he entrusted AnchoR to me, and that he thinks there's reason enough for him to stay here that he would go so far as to do that.*

"Sorry, but I've got a little more I want to discuss with this grandpa."

Naoto's dead-serious face as he said this also surprised Marie.

*You'll just be wasting your time,* Marie almost said aloud, but stopped herself.

She didn't believe that she truly understood Naoto Miura. But at this point, she already knew from the bottom of her heart that doubting his intuition and judgment was meaningless.

*If Naoto's telling me this with such a serious face, he must be seeing something I don't... That should be what it means.*

She clicked her tongue. That she couldn't see what he was seeing irritated her above all else. "Is that so? Fine, then by all means, take your time with this senile old man! I'll probably have AnchoR all fixed up already by the time you get back, so prepare to cry like a baby!"

· · ● · ·

With violent footsteps, Marie exited the workshop with AnchoR in hand.

After seeing them leave, the old man returned his gaze to Naoto and shrugged with a sigh. "Goodness me, what a feisty missy you've got with you." Despite his sharp tone, there was a faint smile on his face.

RyuZU asked, looking puzzled, "Master Naoto, I do not mean to agree with Mistress Marie, but it seems to me that staying here any longer would just be a waste of time. What are you planning to do? I mean, I cannot think that you have so much unconditional love for humanity in you that you have awakened to the joy of caring for the elderly, but it is the only explanation I can come up with."

"I stayed because I want to see how this grandpa does his work."

"Sorry, kid. If you're just lookin' to kill time, please leave. As you can see from this hovel of mine, I'm struggling to make ends meet as is, so I don't have the luxury of teaching a third-rate apprentice who hasn't even been weaned off his diapers yet."

"Dear me," RyuZU said in a piercingly cold tone, "is that my auditory mechanism malfunctioning or do you have a linguistic disorder? Actually, I suspect it is simply that you have gone senile after all. For a plebeian like yourself to speak so rudely to someone upon whom you should not even be allowed to look—"

"RyuZU, stop," Naoto interjected as he reached his hand out and covered RyuZU's mouth.

Meanwhile, the old man continued flatly, "What's wrong with calling a third-rate what he is? It's merely the truth—so you disagree, but it seems to me like the one in question is rather aware of it himself?"

"I am sorry to bother you, Master Naoto, but could you please explain?" RyuZU asked. "What valid reason could this senior have to look down on you? To be more specific, what reason could there be for me not to knock his skull a bit right now and return his lost brain to its proper place?"

"I mean, there's nothing to explain, really. As the grandpa said, I'm just a third-rate apprentice." Naoto smiled bitterly. "But still, grandpa, you're kinda twisted."

"...Oh?"

"Despite everything you've said, you never said that you couldn't do it, while understanding perfectly well that AnchoR is an Initial-Y as well."

Indeed, he had never said such a thing.

Even in AnchoR's current condition, she should still be a unit far more advanced than what modern clocksmithing could replicate; yet this old man showed no signs whatsoever of being daunted or hesitant when he had been asked to make a new mainframe for her.

Forget being astounded by her intricacy, the face the old man made when he had said that AnchoR's mainframe was bent was such that there was no way anyone could miss it. It was clear as day what he'd been thinking: *So this is one of "Y"'s masterpieces, huh? What a disappointment.*

Unconvinced, RyuZU said, "Is it not possible that he is simply a presumptuous old man with Alzheimer's?"

"A senile old man wouldn't be able to create this," Naoto said as he looked at Nono. "At first glance, she looks to be an outdated automaton. But anyone who would judge his skill as a clocksmith by that is nothing but a fool. If you take a good look, it becomes apparent she's been flawlessly maintained and that the technology used inside her is something else."

"As I said earlier, I don't have time to waste. I can't be dealing with fools who can't even tell the difference between what quality is and isn't."

Nodding at those words, Naoto continued, "Marie realized that much as well. That's why she deemed that you're a clocksmith and tried to commission AnchoR's mainframe from you. But it seems that she didn't notice the interior of your automaton."

Naoto smiled bitterly. He then looked at Nono—who looked like nothing but an outdated automaton through and through—then checked her out from top to bottom with an intense gaze and gulped. "An outdated model? Unthinkable. This one's a work of art worth more than any number of run-of-the-mill automata put together... I mean, really. How do you even make mechanisms like these?"

RyuZU asked uncertainly, "Master Naoto, unlike you, I am no expert, but is this unit really so outstanding?"

"Yeah." Naoto nodded. "The parts it uses are merely consumer ones that have been slightly tuned. The raw materials used to make its parts are also a level below what were used for yours or AnchoR's. Yet she's an amazing piece of work." He paused for a breath. "As far as basic maneuverability goes, what this unit is capable of...is no less than what you are capable of, RyuZU."

RyuZU was left speechless.

"Kaka."

The old man sneered.

Just like that, the atmosphere in the room seemed to dramatically change. The old workshop they were in began to feel like a murky cave of demons, and the man before them began to feel less like just another old clocksmith, and more like an unbelievable monster that had reached an inhuman level of mastery.

The old man said happily with a smirk, "Oh? So you're the rumored second coming of 'Y', huh? Rumors can't be trusted, or so I figured, but it does seem like you're not a complete blockhead, at least."

It seemed like the old man's transformation made even RyuZU eat her hat, as she remained speechless.

On the other hand, Naoto curled his lips, muttering, "So, you're finally showing your true self."

The old man ignored that comment and instead reached for the mug on his work desk. After drinking a mouthful of the mug's contents with ease, he continued, "I'll admit that you're a first-rate dilettante. However, it looks to me like you mistakenly believe yourself to be a first-rate critic as well. Or is that just my imagination?"

"Even a mere dilettante can see how magnificent this composition is."

"I see. It seems like you aren't conceited about your abilities," the old man said as he relaxed his eyes and nodded, upon which the atmosphere in the room relaxed just a little.

Immediately after, RyuZU shot a sharp stare at the automaton standing right next to her and said, "Nono Figlia."

"Si— What is it?"

"Excuse me, but I'd like to confirm something."

The moment RyuZU said that, black shadows flashed forth for an instant.

Her skirt fluttered elegantly as her pair of black scythes rushed out from underneath towards Nono in a lethal attack that would dismantle just about any target instantaneously, even a heavily armored military automaton.

However, Nono Figlia was able to deal with her attack without breaking a sweat.

She pulled out a brutal-looking knife seemingly out of nowhere, but it had actually been from the inside of the hem of her maid uniform. She casually parried the pair of black scythes assaulting her from left and right. At the same time, she crouched down and closed in on the beautiful, silver-haired automaton faster than the eye could follow.

The shrill ring of metal clashing sounded as sparks flew from the blades chafing past each other. They assaulted each other with slashes, thrusts, and blows from both the front and from blind spots, exceeding the speed of bullets.

Both of them stood their ground as their blades locked against each other over and over again in this contest of close quarters combat. They naturally transitioned their attacks into parries and vice versa.

"RyuZU!" Naoto yelled out chidingly upon processing the situation.

On the other hand, the old man sounded pleased as he said, "You can stop now."

"Si—" Nono obeyed the order and withdrew her knife, abruptly ending her flurry of combat movements.

As she returned to standby, Naoto checked to see if she had been damaged in the fight, and sighed a breath of relief upon seeing that she hadn't.

Then, he scolded, "RyuZU, that was way out of line! You need to apologize."

RyuZU obediently bowed as she put away her black scythes. "Please forgive my transgressions. Indeed, I see that some of this unit's basic capabilities rival mine, so it might take me *a little longer than usual* to dismantle her if I had to."

Despite the lack of sincerity in RyuZU's apology, Naoto joined her and bowed anyway. "Allow me to say it as well. I'm sorry for what happened just now."

However, the old man shook his head with a faint smile. "It's nothing to worry about. It was a rather entertaining little show, actually. I would have been perfectly fine with letting it continue, you know? I'd very much like to find out how long one of my prototypes can keep up with one of the fabled Initial-Y's."

*Huh...?*

"Prototype...? Uh, what?"

"Yep, she's one of my prototypes," the old man repeated. "She's something I made while fiddling around after I took a break from work to refresh my senses. Nono Figlia: Ninth Daughter. My naming system is simple, right?"

"Agh...! Are you serious?"

This time, Naoto stared at Giovanni with true awe and fear as shivers ran down his spine.

"Now then," the old man said as he stared right back at Naoto. "What is your name, boy?"

"Naoto. My name is Naoto Miura, Maestro."

"I'm Giovanni Artigiano. The deadline is close, so I don't have time to explain this or that to you, but if you just want to watch me at work then do as you please."

Naoto straightened his back and said in a tone of utmost respect, "Thank you very much. I'll do just that."

· • ● • ·

Upon walking through Suan Dok Gate—the west gate of the town castle in ancient times—Halter found himself no longer inside the central marketplace area, but on Restaurant's turf.

On the surface, it looked just as what one would expect from the pleasure capital of the world: a bustling entertainment district, where one could drown oneself in alcohol, drugs, and women. Lurid neon lights were everywhere and the streets were crowded with drunkards. The establishments lining both sides of the bou-levard Halter was on were all either pubs, brothels, or both.

*I'm glad I didn't bring Marie along, Halter thought as he chuckled. I can just see her squealing in disgust at every establishment we pass. Well, that or shouting angrily at them. It would have been a huge headache.*

As he continued walking, Halter rolled up the sleeves of his jacket, loosened his necktie, and opened up his vest. Just by doing that, the bald-headed giant blended right in with the resident population.

Halter turned onto a dimly lit side alley. The alley was so nar-row that if one weren't paying attention, one wouldn't even no-tice it was there in the first place.

The moment he turned onto the side alley, the atmosphere instantly changed.

Even though he could still clearly hear the lively guffaws of the drunkards and the shrill voices of the women, they now seemed distant somehow.

Practically none of the regular patrons of this district walking on the main street noticed this side alley. Even if they did, how-ever, they probably wouldn't even bat an eye.

Halter continued to walk through the alley in silence...past people in cages.

Humans were just casually out on display in front of a shop which, unlike those along the main street, had neither a sign nor any flyers posted. Inside the steel cages were people of all ages bound in chains, staring into nothingness with dead eyes.

However, Halter knew that they still *had it good*, for now.

At the very least, they still *looked* like humans. Even if it was only temporarily as "raw materials" that would eventually be "processed" down the line.

To those who lived in the light, the stores along the main street were plenty deplorable already, but this filthy, festering alley full of depravity and wickedness really took the cake. Human trafficking, body modifications, transplant surgeries... It was a place where the nastiest of all the nasty businesses managed by Restaurant operated.

Despite his aversion and repugnance to such things, Halter made sure it didn't show on his face as he continued to walk deeper into the alley.

Shortly after, he stopped in front of a store with a thick, dirty door that was falling apart. Halter placed his right hand on the gun he wore at the side of his waist as he pushed the door open with his left hand, upon which he was welcomed by poor lighting and the sound of muffled clamor—the atmosphere of a pub.

The interior was surprisingly spacious, though it was hard to see things because of the darkness and because the walls were stained pitch-black with soot. Despite these conditions, there was a good number of customers inside.

There were patrons of all races, ages, and genders; there were those who were there by themselves and in groups. However, unlike the pubs along the main road, there weren't any drunkards racking up a commotion here. That said, it wasn't exactly an authentic bar where one would go to quietly enjoy some fine wine, either.

If there was one thing that could be said about this pub, though, it would be that the community here appeared to be tight-knit, and any new faces would be judged by regular patrons. It had that kind of unique atmosphere.

The moment Halter stepped inside, piercing gazes immediately shot his way. However, Halter paid them no mind and walked through the pub as casually as a regular patron and sat down at the bar counter.

The middle-aged bar owner with the deep scar of a past gash on his face asked brusquely, "What'll you have?"

"Do you serve Macallan's here? One that's been aged for at least eighty-eight years would be perfect."

"We don't serve such pretentious drinks here."

Halter laughed bitterly. "Is that so? There should be at least one bottle lying around somewhere in the *wine cellar,* shouldn't there?"

Paying zero effort to make his morose demeanor more amicable, the bar owner looked back down at the glass he was polishing with a cloth. He then jerked his chin towards the door at the side of the room. "The cellar's over there. Go find it yourself."

"Thanks. Well then, excuse me."

Halter promptly stood up and headed towards the worn-out door at the end of the counter. Upon opening the door, he found a long, poorly lit spiral staircase beyond it.

He walked down all the way to the bottom, upon which he found himself in front of yet another door. Beyond that was yet another pub which was such a mess that it made the pub on the first floor look like a classy bar.

Well, it wasn't actually a pub.

Upon entering the room, Halter was immediately greeted by the sweet aroma of some kind of pink smoke.

It wasn't tobacco smoke; it was the smoke of opium—a terrifying, vicious narcotic that, should one inhale it directly, would make one unable to live without it. At the same time, the smell of alcohol and the body odor of grime-covered men and women mercilessly assaulted Halter's olfactory senses.

There weren't any tables or chairs inside the room. Instead, filthy sofas and mattresses filled up most of the space. There had clearly been some depraved partying going on here. Beer bottles, glass cups, syringes, bits of food, and torn clothes were all over the floor.

In the midst of all that were half-naked men and women covered by cushions and lying on the sofas and mattresses. They looked almost dead. In fact, some of them could easily pass as true corpses.

There were those who were partying as of right now as well, spanking each other and cackling hysterically as they crawled around on top of crumpled sheets and bodies.

A woman who looked barely conscious raised her body halfway up and poured alcohol over her head, upon which the men who had been lying with their faces down nearby rose up like ghosts and swarmed around her.

Unfortunately for them, they wouldn't die from this, thanks to advanced medical care and cyborgization technology. Or rather, they weren't *allowed* to die, since the ones who profited from their addiction would always help them out with a smile.

They couldn't have their precious customers dying on them, after all.

Therefore, to finance their medical fees and continued drug abuse, these addicts would end up selling away their body parts one by one. The "merchandise" on display in front of the store was how the people in this room would ultimately end up, with their minds breaking down before their actual bodies died.

One might say, perhaps, that everyone here was both a consumer and a product—a slave. Or perhaps it was even simpler than that. They were just...commodities.

*Thank goodness I didn't take Marie with me, Halter thought. If that pure-hearted, squeamish girl saw this room, she'd either report what she saw to IGMO without thinking of the consequences, or just purge this place with fire on impulse.*

*If it were that greenhorn, though, I'll bet he'd feel right at home here.*

In the back of this room of ultimate degeneracy was a parlor-like area demarked by a beautifully decorated folding screen, where a man with the air of a king reclined against a posh leather sofa.

It was a young black man who had an afro as puffy as a balloon. He looked up at Halter through his gilded sunglasses, with one hand around the scantily clad woman by his side.

The man said in an excited, high voice, "Heya, welcome! Are you Mr. Oberon?"

"Yeah. I take it you're the agent?" Halter asked.

The man rubbed the breast of the woman next to him with his left hand as he laughed in good spirits. "The name's Lodge.

Well now, have a seat. Let's get along, shall we? I know we might not look too fancy, but we've actually got a pretty good selection of both women and drugs here. Are busty blondes much your type? Or how about a brunette?"

"I'll pass on the women and drugs. But yes, I guess I'll take some fine wine, if you've got some," Halter replied.

Upon which the man—Lodge—looked a little displeased. He pouted, "Well, that's quite a shame, y'know. I wanted to give you the best welcome possible, so I prepared some first-class stuff ahead of time. Are you really sure you're good with just plain old wine?"

"I said *fine wine*, not plain old wine," Halter pointed out.

Lodge tilted his head in confusion. "You're a full-body cyborg, aren'tcha? Is mere alcohol really enough to satisfy you?"

"What's the point in living if you can't get drunk?"

As a matter of fact, full-body cyborgs that could enjoy eating and drinking were rare. That was because it would not only obviously require a taste sensor, but also special work done on the brain pod to recreate the experience.

Not only that, but to reproduce the physiological effect of getting drunk, the artificial body would have to be equipped with yet even more superfluous mechanisms. Consequently, full-body cyborgs typically ingested "drugs," which were really liquid suspensions of nanogears, as an indulgence rather than alcohol, but...

"To begin with, my brain pod isn't equipped to be affected by those kinds of drugs inside this body. Instead, I insisted they give me the ability to taste alcohol. And," he added, "My current client is rather strict, you see. A real-life Mrs. Grundy, if you would. If I were to return with the scent of a woman's perfume on me, she'd give me hell, all right?"

"Oh? Guess it can't be helped, then. Okay, let's treat you to some fine wine. Oy," Lodge said as he let go of the woman. She stood up, taking the opportunity to flaunt her half-naked body.

"Okaaay," she replied with a syrupy voice.

Her skin had been tanned golden brown, and she was wearing tremendously daring underwear. Her features were clearly defined and well-proportioned, and her waist-length hair was a brilliant silver, while her eyes were like glistening amethysts.

Her voluminous chest and butt looked awfully cramped by her underwear, while her waist was magnificently slender. She had the exceptional proportions of a model; a true beauty who would incite lust in any man.

*But, Halter thought, Whether it be her skin, her hair, or her eyes, I'm sure that none of them are what she was born with. Just like the underwear she's wearing, I'm quite sure that her beauty has been designed for the sole purpose of enticing men.*

The woman shook her hips as she disappeared into the backroom briefly before returning with a silver bar cart. Inside the cart were ice and a cocktail set, along with stuff like wine bottles, glass cups, and bar spoons.

She parked the cart right next to Halter, bowed deeply and said, "May I take your orderrr?"

"...Well, this is a surprise. You're gonna make my drink for me, miss?"

"I *am* the bartender here, you knowww, even if only in name."

The woman laughed frivolously, breaking into a smile. "But the customers who come here would rather have drugs and sex than delicious wine, sooo... I neeever get to do my thinnng. Yours is the first order in a long time, so I'm gonna go all out, 'kayyy?"

"Hah, Shirley, you say that, but you prefer having your insides stirred up over alcohol as well, dontcha?" Lodge jeered obscenely.

The woman—Shirley—puffed up her cheeks. "That's not true. I like them both about the saaame."

"Sure you do."

"Urghh, shush now. Sooo, what should I maaake?"

"Good question..." Halter said as he reclined against the sofa. He then looked up into space, stumped. He was feeling the urge to drink, all right, but for whatever reason he couldn't think of any drink in particular that he wanted.

"As long as it's good I'm fine with anything, but...hmm, I guess I'll have whatever you recommend."

"What *I* recommend?"

"Yeah. So what'll you make for me?" Halter asked.

Shirley placed her fingers on both her temples and rubbed them. "Hmm." She thought aloud with her head facing down, then suddenly looked up and asked, "Mister, is Oberon your real naaame?"

"Certainly not." Halter laughed bitterly. "Someone just arbitrarily decided to call me that and it stuck. It's like a nickname for me."

"I should have knooown. Hee hee hee," Shirley laughed.

"There's actually a cocktail that's associated with that name, you knowww? How does that sound?"

"Yeah, sounds good." Halter nodded.

Shirley began to mix the cocktail while humming happily. First she poured vodka into a shaker to use as the base, then she added several different wines and juices and a splash of rose liqueur. Lastly, she added some egg whites, then proceeded to shake the glass vigorously.

She was shaking the drink while practically naked, so naturally her voluptuous breasts jiggled about in front of Halter with only the bar cart between them.

After some time, she poured the cocktail into a glass and held it out to Halter. "Here you gooo. It's called the 'Fairy Lady.'"

"Looks like this cocktail's an awfully cute one, huh," Halter groaned as he rubbed his bald head. What filled the glass was a vivid cocktail with pink and orange shades that looked sickly sweet, like a cocktail women would enjoy.

"I'm sure you'll like iiit. It's actually one I try to get more men to try, you knooow?"

"Oh? Even someone who looks the way I do?"

"Do you know whom 'Fairy Lady' refers tooo?"

"Titania, right? The Queen of Fairies and Oberon's wife, as written in the play."

"Right, she's your wife," Shirley said, then licked her lips as a suggestive smile appeared on her face. "She's feisty, haughty, and doesn't listen to what Oberon says at alll. But she's verrry passionate. If you're Oberon, then you've gotta discipline her."

"By drinking this?"

"Subdue herrr," Shirley purred while wriggling her body in an excessively tempting manner.

Amused by her shenanigans, Halter chuckled. "I get it, I get it. I'll drink it with gratitude."

*What am I doing, shrinking away from a cocktail? In the first place, I'm the one who asked for her recommendation.*

Halter took a sip of the cocktail, upon which his eyes widened.

*It's sweet...but it burns. The acidity gives it a refreshing taste, but if it weren't for the egg whites, I think I might have just ended up spitting fire and fainting. And it seems like there's some kind of peppery spice as well to accentuate the flavor.*

Far from a cocktail that would suit women's tastes, it was so strong that even men might end up smashed after having just one glass of it.

"Wow...this thing's something else."

"I know, riiight? Titania may be the pretty wife of King Oberon, but she's also a queen who's powerful and proud, no less so than her man by any means."

"I see...so that's why it's so strong."

Though it looked sweet and tasted smooth, a weak man would definitely be blown away by it. With his pride as a man at stake, Halter calmly finished the whole glass, upon which Shirley clapped merrily like a sprite who had succeeded in her mischief.

"Shall I make another one for youuu?"

"Yeah, I guess I'll have another. Man, I really didn't think I could ever drink a cocktail like this."

"Hee hee hee, it's an original recipe of mine, you knooow?" Shirley laughed as she began to make a second glass.

Lodge, who had been keeping quiet for a while, razzed her. "Really, Shirley? You read stuff like Shakespeare?"

"Is something wrong with thaaat? Having a library of stuff to chat about with customers is part of a bartender's job, you knooow?"

"I thought the only things you'd read, if you read at all, would be porn magazines. Aren't you the surprising intellectual."

"I read porn magazines too, you know," Shirley said, puffing up her cheeks in dissatisfaction. That seemed a bit misguided, somehow. She then asked Halter, "Misterrr, have you read *A Midsummer Night's Dream* befooore?"

"Hmm...no?" Halter replied, tilting his head. "I just realized that I've never actually read it before, now that you ask. I do know the gist of the story, though."

"What a shame. It's a great read, you knooow," Shirley said as she held out another glass of Fairy Lady to Halter. "King Oberon has a quarrel with Queen Titania, then the fairy Puck smears an aphrodisiac all over Queen Titania and a bunch of humans, and in the end, all the characters have a giant orgy together through which the royal couple make up."

"...Was *that* how it ended?" Halter questioned dubiously.

"Yessireeee," Shirley affirmed in a sing-song tone, then continued, "'Now then, fairies, I want every last one of you to pump your hips like dogs in heat going at it in the bushes. As for what to sing, just follow me. We're gonna pump pump pump to the rhythm of the song.'"

"Wait a second now, oy."

"And that's when Titania badgers Oberon for it, saying, 'Show them how it's done, honey.'"

"...I think you're thinking of a parody porn flick, not the actual story," Halter said with a dubious look in his eyes.

Shirley chortled at Halter's response, then poured what was left over in the shaker into a different glass and drank it herself in a single gulp. "Ngh, ahhhhhhh!"

It appeared that she was unable to withstand the full brunt of her own cocktail, as her body began to spasm. All the while, she laughed. "That's the kind of king Oberon is, you knooow? He's haughty, inconsiderate, stirring up all kinds of hilarious trouble and chaos for those around him! Buuut..." She paused for a breath, then continued her delirious raving, "In the end, he brings everyone together in happiness. That's the kind of king he iiis."

As her voice trailed off, Shirley's eyes drooped down. It was clear from her heavily flushed face that she was on the verge of becoming blackout drunk already.

"I get it, I get it." Halter laughed bitterly as he took another sip. As he enjoyed the burning sensation in his throat, he shrugged. "Though I must say, I've been thinking for a while now that the name Oberon doesn't really suit me."

"That's not trueee," Shirley pouted. "I'm really happy nowww, because you ordered a drink from meee, Misterrr. Super happyyy... Hee hee, ehehehee..."

Hearing Shirley's words becoming more and more muddled, Lodge barked threateningly, "Oy, Shirley! The hell do you think you're doin', getting drunk on your own when we've got an important guest to take care of!"

"Ywes!" Shirley replied as her body cowered reflexively upon being yelled at. She said with a muddled voice, "Oof, sworry. Bwuuuttt, I feel so happyyy... I feel happy?"

She tried to stand up, but failed. As her consciousness faded away, she looked up at Halter with her glistening amethyst eyes and said, "I'm happy... Huh, I'm happyyy? Want me to turn on your happiness switch?"

The light of reason could no longer be found in either her eyes or her words at this point. It appeared that her heart and half her consciousness had already drifted off to the world of dreams.

"Thanks, miss. Your cocktail was delicious," Halter said gently. "I'm very satisfied. You're a good girl, so you deserve a good rest now."

· · • ● • · ·

"God, I always tell her not to drink during work, too, 'cause she can't hold her liquor worth a damn... Sorry 'bout that."

"Don't worry about it. More importantly, shall we get down to business?" Halter said as he helped Shirley onto the armchair next to his before turning to face Lodge. He picked his glass back up for a sip, then said in a dispassionate tone, "First...should I begin by thanking you guys for all your help in arranging our stay in this city? As a matter of formality."

"Oh, c'mon, don't stare at me like that," Lodge said as he raised both hands into the air in a needlessly dramatic fashion. "It's true we charged you guys double the market price, but sheltering big fish like yourselves ain't easy, y'know? I actually think we gave you quite a good deal, all things considered."

"...Well, that's probably true." Halter nodded, agreeing rather readily. It didn't seem like he cared to take this issue any further. Considering that they were wanted all over the world with an enormous bounty on their heads, they were lucky there was any organization at all that was willing to take on the job of arranging for their safe travel and accommodations.

"So, what's the deal? Still got somethin' else you want us to help you with?"

"Yeah, could you take care of this for us?"

Setting his glass on the table, Halter took out a piece of paper from the inside pocket of his suit.

Upon looking it over, Lodge's face immediately puckered up. "Hmm...the two sixth-gen military cyborg bodies should be doable, but you also want stuff like a Galvorn plate and the complete catalog of all main cylinders made of frosted glass from Leng? Those are quite hard to find..."

Most of what was written on the memo was the list of automaton parts that Marie had asked for. Parts that weren't all that special could easily be found in the markets here, but it would be extremely difficult to obtain parts made from rare materials and the latest technologies without a middleman like Lodge.

Halter glared at Lodge through his sunglasses and said, "Finding things that are hard to find is precisely your job, isn't it?

If they were things that could be easily found at a hardware store, then I wouldn't be here in the first place."

"Yes, you're quite right." Lodge sighed deeply, then flicked his finger at a particular item on the note. "But these are things that are hard to find, even for us. Especially this S200 Ether Nerve Wire here. To begin with, they aren't even sold individually."

"Yes, but I believe that a heavily armored automaton made in Spain called El Primero uses them. Get one of those and salvage the wires from it, if you would."

"That's gonna add to the fee, y'know?" Lodge said. He then gave Halter a quote for a sum shocking enough to make an average person's eyeballs pop out.

They would have to cough up nearly half of the funds in their secret bank accounts. Even taking the rarity of the items being requested into account, it was clear that Lodge was jacking up the price because he could tell that they needed these things badly... yet Halter still nodded.

As difficult to find as the items on this list were, they were all parts that were absolutely necessary to repair AnchoR, for which there could be no substitute.

They were all things rare enough that they could never be found in any honest city, so if there was an opportunity to obtain them simply by paying the right price, then that was all one could possibly ask for. Halter may have readily accepted Lodge's price, but at the same time...

"Very well. I won't bother negotiating on the price. In return, you better make sure to have everything ready by the due date.

Should there turn out to be some shoddy knockoff mixed in with what you give us..."

He made sure to drill into Lodge's head that failure was unacceptable.

Sensing the ounce of murderous intent that Halter deliberately mixed into his voice, Lodge ducked his head in fear. "Oh, of course. Reputation is key in my line of work, y'know."

"I hope that's true."

"Yes...so, is there anything besides the stuff on this note, or is this it?"

"This is it. A client of ours is going to look for the remaining odds and ends that we need in the markets here. There's no need for me to tell you what those odds and ends are, is there?"

Strictly speaking, they couldn't order all the necessary parts from Lodge, as Naoto couldn't explain them to Marie clearly enough for her to identify what they were.

"Of course not. That'd fall under Market's jurisdiction, and I wouldn't try to get in the way of a client to begin with," Lodge said. He then let out a sigh of relief as he dialed a number on the wired phone.

After finishing the call, he pushed up his gilded glasses and nodded, saying, "Thanks for the business. I explained things to the subcontractor just now. Your order should be delivered to the hotel you guys are staying at by tomorrow."

"What about the payment?"

"A different subcontractor will go to collect it. In cash, please."

That was how this city worked. The one who takes the order,

the one who fulfills it, the one who delivers it, and the one who collects the payment all belong to different organizations, so that no one person knew all the details of the transaction. Service providers and their clients avoided direct dealings with each other in this city.

*"I simply listed some things that someone else wanted. I simply gathered some goods. I simply picked up some stuff that someone had forgotten about. I simply accepted the payment for someone else."*

*"I coincidentally lost my note, coincidentally found this receipt, coincidentally found these packages delivered to me, and coincidentally lost my money somewhere."*

*"It was mere coincidence that something resembling a transaction took place."*

The transactions in this city were built upon that facade.

Of course, in the end, it was nothing *but* a facade.

Seeing that business had been taken care of, Halter emptied the rest of his glass. "I'll be going, then. Thanks for the drinks," he said as he stood up from his seat.

Just then...

"Oh, could you wait a sec, actually?"

Being stopped unexpectedly, Halter furrowed his brows in perplexment and said, "What?"

While rubbing his hands together Lodge asked, "You just placed such an expensive order. Your wallet must surely be feeling a little lonely right now, no?"

"Even if it is, what does that have to do with you?"

"Well, I thought you might be interested in a good-paying gig, you see."

"Oy."

"To tell you the truth, my boss has something he'd like your group to take care of for him."

That moment, the air froze. Something fundamental inside Halter changed gears with a clank. He casually pulled out his gun from the holster at his waist and shoved the muzzle right into Lodge's afro.

"Wait, d—"

"You're not an agent, are you?" Halter said in a low-pitched tone.

"Wh-wha...?" Lodge said, his eyes wide open in fear.

"At the very least, you're definitely not the one I was originally in contact with. Was the only thing you stole from him our business? Or did you kill him and take his place altogether?"

"W-wait a sec, you've got it wrong, I swear!"

"I see, so you were bought off, huh? Well, it doesn't matter." Halter clicked his tongue vehemently as a chilling sense of impending danger crawled up his back.

*You goddamn idiot, Vainney Halter. There's no excuse for this pathetic display. And you were telling Marie not to get carried away, too.*

He wanted to bash the living hell out of himself for letting his guard down somewhere along the way without even noticing, and in this kind of city at that.

*Transactions in this city are no big deal. They're just money and goods exchanging hands. But a commission for a job is most definitely bad news!*

*The biggest problem of all is that merely killing this guy wouldn't be enough to resolve the situation. The situation is already dire.*

*What do I do?*

*What should I do?*

Halter's heart burned with anxiety. Unable to immediately figure out how he should respond to the situation, he simply froze, speechless.

Immediately after, a gunshot rang out from upstairs.

$$\bullet \; \bullet \; \bullet \; \bullet \; \bullet$$

The gunshot was followed immediately by the agonizing scream of someone who had suddenly been placed before death's door.

Astounded, Lodge yelled out, "Wh-what's goin' on?!"

"The cleanup crew's here, dumbass. Damn it," Halter cursed, clicking his tongue and clenching his teeth. *Their response is way too fast! Or is it more that we were way too slow?*

The next moment, the sound of another shot rang out, and the one and only door to the room was blown entirely away.

"Hyaah! H-huh?!" Shirley shrieked as she got up in a fluster, having been rudely awakened from her drunken slumber.

At the same time, cyborgs donned in black mobile suits burst into the room through the now-doorless entrance, one after the other. With well-trained control, they immediately began to barrage the floor without warning with the heavy machine guns they had ready.

In those few seconds, the scenery in the room took on a whole new look.

Feathers from the sofas and the mattresses that had been punctured full of holes danced in the air like snow. Below that, the men and women who had been entangled with each other like living corpses turned into real ones, sinking into a literal bloodbath as their bodies were torn apart by the machine guns.

"A-a-ah..." Shirley stammered as she choked on air and peed herself. She had evaded the fusillade probably because she was right next to Halter and Lodge.

With perfect coordination, the cyborgs in mobile suits pointed their machine guns at Halter's group.

"Eek! Uh...s-save me..."

"Miss, if you don't want to die, then sit tight and pray," Halter warned quietly.

*Clonk.*

A footstep sounded. Someone was coming down from upstairs.

"Ah, how sad... how truly sad..."

The person who turned up was a terribly gaudy-looking and lanky Asian man. His hair was dyed crimson and cut short. He wore a double-breasted suit made of the dazzling cloth that was traditional here. His age was difficult to ascertain, however. Technically he could pass as middle-aged, but his spunky eyes looked like those of a young troublemaker.

At a glance, he appeared to be a gangster. Despite his wimpy appearance, he had the scent of someone far more dangerous than all the cyborgs around him.

"K-K... Kiu Tai Yu...! " Lodge muttered in a trembling voice with his teeth clattering.

The man—Kiu—pinched his nose with a silken handkerchief as he walked towards them with repose. "Ahh, how sad... It's a real shame, Lodge..."

"P-please wait a second, Mr. Kiu!" Panicked, Lodge staggered a few steps towards Kiu despite all of the guns pointed at him by the cyborg soldiers, not to mention Halter. It was as if Kiu was the only thing he could see. He stumbled and fell down before him.

"I beg you, listen to what I have to say! It's a misunderstanding. It's all a horrible misunderstanding, I tell you!" Lodge yelled out desperately in a pained voice.

"Ahh, how terrible. Say, don't you think it's terrible...?" Kiu replied with a gentle smile. "We agreed that none of us would get involved with them during their stay in this city. Am I remembering wrong? Tell me, Lodge, am I?"

"W-well, no, that's—"

"Breaking a promise is terrible, isn't it? Truly terrible. I'm genuinely saddened by this turn of events. So, you sought to destroy the balance of power between us by employing them, did you now?"

Out of nowhere, Kiu fired.

He had drawn a pistol in a flash and shot out both of Lodge's knees.

"G-GAHHHHHHHaaaaHHH!" After letting out a scream that was overlaid with Shirley's shriek, Lodge fainted in agony on the spot.

"Say, Lodge... There's only one rule in this city. One that's as simple as it gets. Can you remember what it is? Shall I say it for you? Yes?" Kiu said calmly as he gently placed his foot on Lodge's head.

"Ready? All right then. Make sure you don't forget this time, got it?" He paused for a breath; immediately after, his gently smiling face instantly turned into one twisted by rage as he shouted while stomping rhythmically to his own words: "Keep! Your! Promises! Or you'll! Be fed! To the dogs! Can't even remember one sentence, you empty-headed birdbrain?! Ah?!"

He cursed vehemently, chewing Lodge out as he lifted and stamped his foot over and over and over again, caught in a frenzy like a child throwing a fit. "Hey! Are! You! Listening?! Give! Me! An answer! You shitty trash bag! Imagine! How I feel! To be manipulated! By worthless monkeys! Like yourselves! Who can't do anything but shit on the floor! Won't you?! Huh?! HuhhhhHHHH?!"

He stomped on Lodge without any mercy or compassion. The sound of bones breaking rang out several times throughout the stomping. Crushed between the hard floor and the sole of Kiu's shoe, Lodge was already completely silent at this point; however, his body would still spasm a bit every time he was stomped on.

"Th-this can't be real! Please, save me!" Shirley cried out, unable to stifle her terror any longer. "Look, Mr. Lodge is already—"

"Quit the chit-chat!" Kiu shouted as he turned and fired immediately.

Blood splashed into the air as a 4.5 mm bullet pierced right through Shirley's head, and just like that, Shirley collapsed on the spot like a puppet with its threads cut. She died instantly.

"Why bother bringing up the obvious? Do you think I'm so stupid that I wouldn't know that?! That I'm dumber than this sack of shit?! Aw shucks...my shoes have gotten dirty... Geez..." Kiu said as he took his handkerchief, then turned towards the cyborg soldier standing right next to him. "Oy."

"Yes, sir?"

"Bring this shitbag's— Hmm, what was his name again? Well, whatever. Take everyone related to him, from his family to his friends, to my estate and offer them a most sincere welcome. Make sure not to kill any of them, got it? I'll be personally slaughtering them later. Now, then."

In a complete turnabout, Kiu showed Halter a refreshing smile and gave a slight bow.

"Sorry for the ruckus. Oy, clean up the trash over there. It stinks like hell in here."

"Yes sir, we'll get right on it!"

The cyborg soldiers laid out the body bags they had brought and began to stuff all the corpses in the room into them.

Kiu put his gun away, then walked around the armchairs and table to sit down on what had been Lodge's sofa in a relaxed manner, facing Halter. He smiled and said, "God, it's always rumbling in this city. Sorry about that. Well then, allow me to reintroduce myself. I'm the one who runs Arsenal, Kiu Tai Yu. Welcome to Shangri-La Grid. We're happy to have you."

Halter sighed. He had intently watched Kiu's rampage in full from the sidelines, silently and with stone-cold eyes. As he sat back down on the armchair, he said, "May I ask two questions?"

"Of course! Please, ask away!"

"Well then, for one, should I take it that pointing a gun at a customer's head is Arsenal's way of welcoming its guests?"

"What?!" Kiu uttered in shock with widened eyes before narrowing his eyes sullenly. He promptly drew his handgun and fired.

The cyborg soldier who had been pointing his machine gun at Halter from behind fell silently to the ground.

It looked like a scene from a comedy. Someone had died just like that for a totally trivial reason.

Kiu set his pistol on the table, then said in a pained voice, "That was completely out of line. I apologize from the bottom of my heart. I ordered them to mind their manners, but it appears a monkey who doesn't understand language somehow slipped into our ranks. There are all too many beasts pretending to be human in this city, you see. Please, forgive us."

Halter nodded. "That's fine. So, my second question is: Was it really necessary to massacre all of the customers here?"

"Customers?" Kiu parroted with a blank face as he tilted his head exaggeratedly to one side. "Were there customers here? That's strange. I thought I only saw worthless sacks of shit in here. Just to be sure, you're not counting those sacks of shit as *customers*, right?"

"Okay, I see. Let me rephrase my question. Why did you kill this woman?"

"Woman?" Kiu parroted yet again before looking down at the corpse sprawled on the floor. He then asked, "Hm? Was this female swine important? Oh, were you in the middle of foreplay with her? And now you're stuck with a boner? Well, that's a problem. Shall I bring over a cum dumpster with similar looks?"

"She was a fine bartender who could make cocktails that fit my taste."

"Oh, my...I've done something terrible, haven't I?"

"In addition, that cocktail was apparently an original of hers, and she hadn't told me the recipe yet, either. It was such a fine cocktail, and now I'll never be able to taste it again. How will you make up for it?"

"Oh, Jesus! I can't believe it! This must be the greatest tragedy of our time! I've never felt so sorry before in my life! My tears are simply overflowing!"

Aghast, Kiu stood up with his head in his hands. As large tears streamed down his face, he picked up the pistol on the table and fired at Shirley's corpse again and again.

Each time she ate a bullet, her tanned body would jump a bit and spray out blood.

"You! Because of you! The legend himself, Mr. Oberon, is in a bad mood! How will you make up for it?! Ahhhn?! Ahhhhhhhhhn?! Where's your reply? ...You're dead?! Oh, dear Lord!"

*Click click click.*

After pulling blanks several times, Kiu sighed. He tossed the emptied pistol away with a fling of his hand and sat back down. "Whew, that felt great. Now then, let's talk business, shall we?" Kiu said cheerfully.

As Halter stared at the man who had been in a tempestuous fit of rage just moments ago with stone-cold eyes, he became
convinced.

*Well, one thing's for sure. This guy's a complete madman.*

· · ● · ·

"I take it you understand the situation, yes?" Kiu asked.

"If you're referring to how that agent was a clueless moron,
then yes."

"Yeah, you've got that right. When idiots make a mess, adults
have to clean up after them. Man, I'm left in a real bind now—a
real bind indeed," Kiu said, sounding fed up. "'Weren't they just
tourists? They left after blowing some cash and picking up some
garbage as souvenirs. That's about all I know. Unfortunately, our
borders aren't very secure, you see. We don't have something
so civilized as an immigration bureau. 'What, that was Second
Epsilon?! Such fiends tricked us into welcoming their stay in our
city?! Luckily, not much harm came to the city during their stay,
though. Praise be to God for this good fortune!' We would have
been good to go with that."

Halter nodded.

*Well, though the truth may differ, they would have been able to
lie their way through with that excuse.*

But now...

"We know your true identity. We'll sell you some goods, so
could you help us out a bit, too? This is bad, isn't it? Yeah, of

course it is. Yet...that impudent sack of shit! Spraying his brains everywhere when he shouldn't even have had any, and dirtying my shoes!" Kiu said, his voice rough from agitation as he stomped on the floor in rage.

The next moment, he calmed down as abruptly as candlelight burning out and said, "Morons who have shit for brains are always giving me a real headache... With the public sentiment as it is at the moment, should anyone get involved with Second Epsilon—or even assist them—they won't be able to evade the heat turning up, regardless of how many big shots they've got in their pocket."

Halter sighed. "IGMO might send its investigation bureau and set up a naval blockade on the Thai coast. In the worst-case scenario, they may even resolve to send in ground troops as part of a limited military sanction."

"I feel so blessed to be able to talk to someone sensible for once. Can you imagine how it feels for me, having to deal with monkeys who don't even understand that much all the time?"

"Isn't exploiting idiots like that until you've consumed them for all they're worth your job?"

"I get sick of it sometimes, though. Thanks to a greedy virgin getting a full hard-on and coming prematurely, we can no longer weasel our way out of having 'assisted' you guys. Obviously, I've already received notice. It's but a matter of time before our dear neighbors find out as well. So, with that said," Kiu said as he raised two fingers before Halter, "we only have two choices."

"..."

"The first is to claim innocence by handing you guys over to the authorities. The second would be to brazenly admit to getting involved with you guys and offset the reprisal by really having you guys do some work for us. What do you think?"

"Isn't there another possibility?" Halter said with a glare. "How about the former, but instead of successfully arresting us, you end up getting annihilated by us instead?"

"Ahh, splendid! By all means, please do just that." Kiu nodded, his face all smiles. "Frankly, that'd be the best option for us. Should you rampage around killing and plundering to your heart's content, we'll simply become the victims. After all, forget the Thai military, we're talking about the group that easily crushed Tokyo's security force. What can mere punks like us possibly do? However, you guys won't do that. You don't want to do that. Am I wrong?"

"..."

"As such, though I'm not happy about it either, I've no choice but to pick the latter. I'll shelter and give you guys all the support I can. Honestly, no matter how big the payoff may be, it could never match up to the colossal risk. That's why I'd like you to put on a grand performance for me—that about sums things up."

Halter didn't reply; he simply continued to vigilantly observe Kiu's expression with a gaze of cold steel.

*Is this pretense, or does he mean it? If he does, how much of what he said is true? What are the facts? How do the risks and rewards balance out? Where's the break-even point? What's the action we should take based on all these factors?*

"I'll say this again: I don't like this situation any more than you do. Know that the ideal scenario for this city would have been for you guys to have gotten your butts right out of here after you finished your shopping, okay?"

"Indeed," Halter admitted. *At the very least, he's not lying right now.*

"I'm not one for high-risk, high-return deals. If I could have, I wouldn't have even let you guys into our city in the first place, you know? I saw from miles away that something like this might happen. Though, I imagine the same goes for you guys."

"Actually, we expected that if anyone could keep the situation under control, it'd be Arsenal's boss, given the stories we've heard about you."

"Please, give me a break with the jokes. If I could monitor and keep every single monkey in our ranks in line, then I might as well be God. Would you like to offer a prayer to me?"

"All right, so to recap..." Halter sighed as he leaned back against his armchair and raised his right hand. "Both of us may have gotten the short end of the stick, but we still share equal fault in things coming to this. It's terribly unfair, but that's just how the world is. Complaining about it won't help."

"Yeah, I'm glad we've come to a consensus!"

"Do you want to toast to that or something? Spare me." Halter shrugged. "Get to the point already. What do you want us to do?"

"I want sovereignty over this city, over Shangri-La Grid," Kiu promptly answered. "To achieve that, I want you guys to do the same thing you did in Tokyo and Kyoto. Modify the core tower here so you can manipulate it at will, then hand control of it over to me. Simple and easy, right?"

"I don't know if I'd call it 'easy,' but in any case, you've got quite the ambition, huh?" Halter muttered cautiously.

Kiu smiled and said, "Are you disappointed? Do you see me as a worldly man now?"

"Not really. I simply don't understand. If you attain sovereignty over this city, the neighboring countries won't leave things be. It'd even give them the pretext to conquer the city by force. I can't imagine that you don't realize that."

"Of course, that's a possibility. There's no doubt that what I seek involves high risk."

"Even so, you still want to rule over this city?"

"Yeah, I do. Very much so." Kiu nodded fervently.

Halter narrowed his eyes and said, "So, what do you plan to do once you gain control of this city? Invade the neighboring grids?"

"What? Invade the neighboring grids?" Kiu parroted with a blank face. "As if. Why would I do that? Hm? To start a war? What?"

"Well, you don't look like a pacifist to me."

"How rude. I'm absolutely opposed to war...but if others want to wage it, I'm happy to sell weapons to them," Kiu said as he twisted his lips into a sneer. "You should study history better. Rather than mine for gold yourself, it's more profitable to sell jeans to the miners. Have everyone work for you by selling them what they want. Candy to slaves, lies to women, and dreams to the masses—ain't that Business 101?"

"Sounds like the worldview of a swindler."

"Businessmen are all swindlers. The only difference is merely that some consider the interest of others as well," Kiu countered smugly, then shrugged. "What I seek are profits and self-preservation. Wars and conflicts? No thanks. If I had control of the core tower, I could deliberately make it malfunction just a teensy weensy bit and make it look like it was some other cartel's fault. Doesn't really matter which. And just like that, the monkeys would crush each other for the sake of unprofitable things like pride and reputation and grudges, because they're monkeys. Meanwhile, I'd enjoy the spectacle from above while raking in the dosh from selling both sides weapons. That's the plaaan... Do you understaaand?"

"You want to *manage* conflicts between syndicates as a business. You figure that controlled violence will bring about greater safety and stability, and greater prosperity to this city along with that. Is that it, more or less?"

"Not a bad idea, right? With your help, my day-to-day will be managing and maintaining the core tower and running the city in an appropriate manner. As I exterminate the insects, I'll be able to stabilize this powder keg of a city and grow the economy at the same time. Uh-huh! A brilliant idea, if I may say so myself!"

"..."

"Ah, don't worry, I know what you want to say. 'That's a pitiful justification.' Indeed, you're riiight. But is there any other way? If you refuse, that's fine, too. I'm saying this for your own good: trample all over this city and take everything you want. It isn't too late to choose that option. So long as you don't kill me, that'll actually be more profitable in the long term."

Halter snorted, then grumbled, "In short, all's good as long as you're saved?"

"Hah? What are you even saying? Isn't that obvious?!" Kiu yelled, springing up from the sofa. "I treasure my own life more than anything else! I don't care if a hundred or a thousand shitty worthless monkeys have to die for me to live; if anything, it'd feel refreshing! I'm not scared to go around shouting that on the streets above, you know? Want me to prove it?"

"I'll respectfully decline," Halter muttered with a sigh, then continued, "I get your point. Well, there are several things I'd like to say, but I'll admit that you haven't lied to me, and also that your suggestion is the best compromise for both of us."

"That's great to hear. I take it we've come to an arrangement, then?"

"No, there's a problem."

"What kind?"

"I'm willing to bet that neither my boss—Marie—nor Naoto would be willing to accept this compromise."

Kiu raised an eyebrow and said, "Why is that? Isn't this the best way to minimize losses for both of us?"

"Because they're kids." Halter shrugged. "We've got a squeamish brat and a geeky runt. Man, I can just see how they would respond already: 'If things go on like this, we're gonna be in quite some trouble, so lend a hand to this bad man. Thousands of villains will end up killing each other as a result, but that wouldn't be your fault; plus, many times more people than that will be saved.'"

Indeed, the two of them would never accept such a deal under any circumstances.

To begin with, Naoto and Marie had made enemies of the whole world with the childish reason of "I do what I want," so even if one told them something like, "It'll save more people in the long run, so bear with doing a little dirty work for the time being." They'd never accept a compromise or concession like that.

"...I see, so they're children," Kiu said. "But this is hardly something we can let go to ruin due to two children throwing a tantrum. So, I have an idea. How about you hand one of them over to me?"

"What kind of joke is that?" Halter asked with his eyes half-closed.

"I don't have time to waste on jokes, unfortunately. It's simple: 'If you don't want to get hurt, then do as you're told.' I'll simply force one of them to do work for me using an exceptionally primitive educational method like that. Ohh, rest assured, I don't plan to *actually* hurt them. I promise I'll treat the one you give me with respect and release them once they've finished their work—I guarantee it."

"Why should I trust you?"

"Huh?! Isn't that obvious? If I kill any one of you guys, the next one dead will be me! I only kill those who are weaker than me so that that doesn't happen, obviously!" Kiu yelled, his eyes practically popping out of their sockets. Making a show of his excessively trembling hands, he continued in a doleful voice, "It's no different right now. Just look at how my hands are trembling before the legendary Oberon...I can't stop shaking. To be honest, the sack of shit that pointed his gun at you made me scared to death. If that had provoked you and I ended up dead because of it, then how would he have taken responsibility? Good grief..."

Kiu's theatrical gestures and lines were beyond fishy, yet Halter smelled truth in his words.

*I don't have a basis for it. If I had to say, then it's only my intuition, but...*

As Halter ramped up his thinking speed, he cautiously said, "I see. However, even if I really do hand over either Naoto or Marie as you wish..." He paused for a breath and continued, "Have you forgotten about the Initial-Y series? If you take Marie, then wherever you take her, Naoto will pinpoint her location and come charging through. If you take Naoto, on the other hand, it'd be even more disastrous. Two enraged Initial-Y series will level this entire city as they knock down every single building one by one to find him."

Halter's warning had been half-genuine, yet Kiu shrugged exaggeratedly and laughed mockingly. "I'm hurt. I'm hurt to learn that you thought a lie would work on me, Mr. Oberon! Of the two Initial-Ys, one's out of commission, no? How about you revise your statements by starting there?!"

"Even if that's true, does it change anything? I'm sure that the First is more than enough to smash Arsenal to pieces."

Kiu answered with a smile, "Yeah, no doubt about that. But there's no need for you to worry."

"Say what?"

"At 13:00 in two days, a guest will be coming to meet them... Well, she's someone who works for an old acquaintance of mine. I'll be taking advantage of that window of time."

That instant, the internal alarm inside Halter began to blare at maximum volume. Halter correctly understood what Kiu was hinting at.

"Are you saying you've got connections with Omega?"

*He confidently asserted that RyuZU's combat strength would be "no problem," which should be impossible, unless they have their own Initial-Y to fend her off.*

*As for someone who could actually possess and maintain an automaton beyond the bounds of reason like that, the only one I can think of is the guy who's still fresh on my mind: Omega.*

However...

"Uh-uh! Unfortunately, that's wrong. Well, it's true I had expected that he would become a big customer of mine, though. But! It appears to be the case that he has no need for the level of commodities in circulation here, whether it be funds, resources, or talents. While it's a true shame, that's just how it is."

*This doesn't seem like a lie, either.*

Halter joined his hands and whispered in a low-pitched voice, "...You said that you have no intention of harming us, as you don't want to make enemies of us, right? Should I take it that you weren't including the Initial-Y misses when you said that, then?"

Kiu Tai Yu exploded in laughter. "Hahahah! No, no, should I tell it to you straight?" he said as his black, clouded eyes took on a menacing glint. "I've never thought even for a second that you guys would lose to someone like Omega. So long as my guest can slow the First down for a little while, I'll be able to have either Naoto-kun or Marie-chan do their work for me in the meantime. Once that's done, by all means, go wherever you wish! Heck, I'll even pay for your travel expenses! How does some aromatic oil sound as a souvenir?!"

· • ● • ·

Meanwhile, near the eastern coast of the Bay of Bengal to the south of Myanmar, an old cargo ship was en route to Shangri-La Grid.

The cargo containers piled on the vast deck of the ship were labelled with tags like "wheat" and "clothing." However, one look at the personnel guarding them, and it was obvious the tags were a lie.

None of the guards were even wearing a uniform. It was clear as day that they were outlaws. They all had worn-out assault rifles holstered at their waists, and some of them were even manning machine guns and rocket launchers. Their defensive capabilities were much too excessive for an honest logistics company.

In reality, they were probably carrying things like smuggled weapons, arms, and/or drugs—which, honestly, would be pretty reputable commodities in the context of their destined market of Shangri-La Grid, considering that they might just as well be carrying living humans, or *human parts*.

The fact that even the guards themselves didn't know what was inside the containers only proved the point all the more. Even if their curiosity itched occasionally, they wouldn't try to find out. If one of them heedlessly found out what they were carrying, they could very well be shot on the spot by a superior.

That's the sort of work they were doing.

That was why, even if the guards heard shouts or sobbing, or smelled something offensive coming from the cargo, they would just ignore it. Or, they normally would, but...

"Say, Boss... What's up with that annoying cargo?" a young guard with a bulging belly asked.

"You don't need to know," his senior, a lanky man, answered coldly. The man's eyes were like that of a famished wolf as he glared sullenly at the sea.

"But, Boss—"

"You don't have to know things you're better off not knowing. And I don't know what's in there myself, nor do I have to in order to know that whatever it is, it's obviously bad news. Ignore it."

Left unable to respond to the aloof attitude of his boss, the underling looked behind him at the black container labelled "machine parts."

What he was curious about was its contents. For a while now, what sounded like a teenage girl had continued to ramble on and on from inside.

"Hah...it has been a long time, sisters. I understand you chumps are still bound by that ancient oath. Today is the day I shall prove once and for all who the greatest masterpiece among the Initial-Y is!! Mmm, that doesn't sound quite right... Oh, and maybe I should introduce myself first after all... Yes, I really should. If someone were to say, 'Uh, who are you again?' after I made my dashing entrance, I wouldn't be able to recover..."

The underling, who was still looking at the container with his head turned, stiffened up and muttered, "...Umm, Boss, what was that about just now?"

"What was what about? I didn't hear anything. Forget what you heard. You don't want to die either, do you?"

"But Boss!! If we die because we ended up knowing some info we shouldn't have because some girl babbled it out all by herself, that'd be total bullshit, man!!"

The senior guard cupped his ears as he shouted angrily, "Shut up already! Ignore her with willpower!"

He had not only heard the drivel coming from behind him as clear as day, but also understood that it was extremely sensitive information.

*The secured handoff point was prearranged, so we can't just move as we please. Should we carelessly go anywhere besides the handoff point, then we truly might get shot. That said, asking for a change of location because the "cargo" blurted out a bunch of classified information would just be asking for trouble.*

Even as the senior outlaw and his underling trembled from how unreasonable life was, the voice behind them was still rambling on in full force.

"Sound the funeral bells! Prostrate yourselves as you hear my name! I am TemP, both the noble lady of darkness and the greatest masterpiece among the Initial-Y!! Hmm...that is not bad, but it just feels like there's something missing. I wonder why..."

The underling whispered secretively to the cargo behind him, who seemed to be troubled for some reason, "Umm, if I may, aren't you going too far with the persona you're trying to assume?"

"Hah?! Sh-sh-shut up! What I seek is an aura of majesty! I am rehearsing something very important right now, so could I not have pigs butting in?!" the girl shouted in a shrill voice.

"Oh, right, sorry..." the underling replied meekly, ducking his head. He turned his head to face forward again, upon which he saw his senior glaring at him as if to say, "Don't stick your nose where it doesn't belong."

And so, silence fell. But a short while later...

"...So, do you have any other thoughts?"

"Huh?" the underling replied without thinking.

Irritated, the girl urged impatiently, "I am asking you what else I can do! I, My Majesty, am telling you that I am willing to at least hear you out, for what it is worth, so answer me already, you dullard!"

"Uh, uhmm...." the underling replied as his body stirred. He looked up at his senior, hoping for help, but his senior was cupping his ears with a face that read, "None of my business."

"C'mon, Boss..." the underling grumbled to himself, then said, "Er...well, how about you begin by landing a blow on them, instead of a goofy proclamation?"

"Huh? That wouldn't serve as an introduction, then."

"I mean, if you beat your adversaries up first, anything you say after will sound cool."

"Hmm...I see that you have barbaric taste. I had thought of such a basic tactic already myself, but decided against it, as it felt too much like a cheap trick!"

"That so?"

"Well, Elder Sister is a dummy with terrible taste, so perhaps a barbaric approach like that would be easier to understand for her! Rejoice, for though it irks me to no end, I shall take up your suggestion!"

"Oh, right..." the underling replied, then hung his head.

*...I've gotten involved with someone troublesome, haven't I?*

The girl seemed to keenly pick up on his thoughts, for she shouted angrily from inside her container, "Hey, what kind of response is that! You sighed just now, didn't you?! Awfully uppity for a mere pig, huh? ...Wha?! *Oww!!* What was that? are we being attacked?! Oh, crap! There's a smoking hole in the container!"

"Boss..."

"I hear nothing, I hear nothing, I don't hear a damn thinnng!" the senior outlaw yelled desperately, his voice echoing throughout the dark deck of the ship.

A certain tragic fate awaited these two outlaws upon landing. Although they correctly sensed it coming, there was nothing they could do anymore to help themselves at this point.

# CLOCKWORK
# PLANET

# ● Chapter Two / 07:30 / Produtorre

"**A**RRRGGGGGGHHHHHH, *Gawwwwd!* What's up with this mechanism, dammiiit!" Marie screeched resoundingly in the workshop of her hotel suite. The light of dawn was shining through the windows.

*"I'll have AnchoR all fixed up by the time you're back."* Or so Marie had boldly claimed, but she hadn't been able to make much progress thus far.

Correction—"much" was too generous a description. She hadn't made *any* progress thus far.

In the first place, she couldn't even comprehend how the artificial limbs that Naoto had attached to AnchoR's distorted mainframe were even working at all, considering how incompatible they were, so she had no idea where to even begin.

With AnchoR's torso opened up before her, Marie struggled hard to figure something out. Regardless, time mercilessly continued to pass. As she thought about how much time she'd wasted, she became all the more irritated and anguished, causing her mind to stiffen.

Caught fully in a downward spiral, Marie crouched down with her head in her hands.

"Uh, uhmm...Mother, I'm sorry...?" AnchoR muttered despondently. She was currently hanging from a heavy-duty hanger made for automata.

Marie instantly looked up in a hurry and said, "Ah... Ahh, no no no!! It's not your fault!! If anyone is at fault..."

*It'd be me,* Marie thought. But her pride wouldn't allow her to say that, so instead she declared with a smile, "It's Naoto ♪."

*On the whole, everything wrong with this world can just be blamed on that guy.*

*After all, he repaired AnchoR in such an arcane way without giving any thought to making it understandable to other clocksmiths, so he can't really say that he's completely blameless here.*

*Regardless, I'll definitely figure it out, so I'm not at fault in any way. Q.E.D.*

Pulling herself together, Marie stood back up and got back to work. As she disassembled the mechanism she had put together back into parts, she muttered, "So this one didn't work either, huh... Really now, what's the deal with this?"

She sighed. Just then...

"Yo. What's going on?"

Surprised, Marie turned around, upon which she saw Halter standing by the entrance to the workshop. He was still wearing a suit, but he had loosened his tie.

"Well, ain't this a rare sight. I don't think I've ever seen you fail this much before, princess," Halter said as he gazed at the complex mechanisms and high-grade parts scattered all over the floor.

However, Marie snorted defiantly. "Hmph. Fail? Take a closer look. Or what, are prototypes failures to you?"

"That so? But princess, what's the point in being prideful in front of me?"

"I'm telling you I really haven't failed," Marie pouted sullenly. "See, these were my attempts to apply the awareness I felt with that wretched boy's guidance... I feel like I've begun to under-stand something ever since that day. But I'm not sure what that something is, so I'm making some prototypes to test for now."

"Aren't you putting the cart before the horse?" Halter asked as he picked up a small cylinder by his feet. "Surely it'd be wiser to try putting a prototype together after first verifying the theory behind it."

"It's already certain that modern clockwork theory is wrong. Actually, strictly speaking, it isn't wrong in any way. Its interpreta-tion is simply too narrow. In essence, though, modern clockwork theory and how people like 'Y' and Naoto see the world are fully congruent with each other. For example..."

Marie looked up for a few seconds to think, then continued, "Right, for example, it was believed that atoms are the smallest units of mass, yes?"

"Yeah."

"However, as electrons, protons, neutrons, and eventually even subatomic and elementary particles were discovered, it became clear that there were units of mass even smaller than an atom. With that in mind, I've got a question for you." Marie paused for a breath. "Did atoms simply disappear after subatomic particles were discovered?"

"..."

"It's the same idea. The difference between modern theory and Naoto's intuitive knowledge is simply a matter of scope. But even if one drew up a blueprint based on modern theory, there's no way they'd be able to make something that applies more advanced concepts, right? That's why I'm trying to put the awareness I had back then into form first, however crude it may be."

"So? Have you made any headway?" Halter asked mildly.

Marie nodded. "What if we assume that the smallest building block in the universe is actually an oscillation—like vibrations and waves? That both AnchoR's Perpetual Gear and RyuZU's Imaginary Gear follow a wave function that wouldn't be possible in modern theory? What if the answer is something as simple as that?"

"Even if you ask me—"

"If modern theory was entirely wrong, then we wouldn't have been able to analyze the structure of this Clockwork Planet at all, but that's not the case. We do understand some parts of it. We may have gotten the fundamentals wrong, but the theory we've built on top of that isn't," Marie declared with poise.

Halter laughed bitterly and said, "That's all, you dare say?"

"Yes," Marie asserted. "Even if you supplement the theory of universal gravitation with the theory of relativity, the fact that all matter exerts gravity doesn't change. Likewise, atomic theory wasn't completely overhauled when it was supplemented with quantum theory. It is still correct, in that atoms exist as a unit of matter. We'd simply reached yet a deeper level of understanding."

As she spoke, Marie stood up and paced the room with one hand on her waist. She continued in the tone of a lecture, "According to all present theories, RyuZU's and AnchoR's inherent abilities should be impossible. As such, what's wrong has to be modern theory. Both dual time and perpetual motion can be realized by simply configuring gears in the right way. Even if you look away from that fact, reality won't budge one bit. In that case, there has to be some kind of logic behind it."

*What Marie was looking for was a way to explain what she had saw a month ago at the Pillar of Heaven—the world as Naoto regularly saw it, and as she had seen it back then.*

*Everything is wrong, but at the same time everything is correct. Modern theory hasn't been disproven, but rather expanded upon. What I experienced back then were phenomena governed by higher principles. Since that's the case, I should be able to figure it out. Naoto and 'Y' are proof that it's possible.*

"If modern science can't explain it, we'll use future science instead. That's all there is to it. As soon as today or tomorrow, I'll come up with the futuristic theory that explains it!"

*Just as the present is created from the past, the future is created from the present. With every passing second, everything now becomes mere relics of the past. In the end, that's all that modern science and theory amount to. In that case, if I just pin down a new theory for our universe, it'll redefine—no, become modern science and theory itself.*

Marie declared boldly, "Modern theory? Give me one second and I'll render it obsolete."

· · ● · ·

Halter sighed a little after hearing Marie's declaration. The girl was putting on a brave act. Despite her confident words, the so-called "prototypes" scattered all over the floor showed how difficult it was.

Indeed, Marie ended up making no progress in her work on that day.

Orange light shone into the workshop. She had worked the entire time since her declaration in the morning until the sun crossed the meridian and began to set in the west. Despite that, she hadn't been able to make anything.

*Well, this was to be expected,* Halter thought. *The idea that she spoke of, that the fundamentals of modern clockwork theory were wrong, is absolutely not something that can be dismissed as that simply being all there is to it.*

All sets of modern theories are fundamentally based on the *religious-like belief* that their axioms are true. All scholars derived their theories and deduced theorems based on those axioms. What is called a set of theories is the summation of those numerous layers of logic.

Using religion as a parallel, to reject that was akin to rejecting the fundamental premise that God exists. All of the theology and doctrines built on top of that unprovable axiom would lose their significance, having been dealt a lethal blow.

"..."

Halter gazed at the back of the petite girl who continued to work in silence.

To continue with this analogy, Marie had lost her faith in God, but now she was trying to prove the existence of an entirely new God. It wasn't work that could be finished in one day.

In fact, the work might not even be something that was possible for humans to accomplish. The girl was putting on a brave act.

But as she had said, "I feel like I've begun to understand something ever since that day."

Most likely, Marie had experienced what it was like to be God that day. At the very least, she had caught a glimpse of the world from His perspective.

Halter, though, couldn't even begin to imagine what that would be like. *But knowing her, she'd probably be able to accomplish it eventually, because she's a relentless, dogged girl who refuses to believe that anything's impossible.*

*In that case,* Halter thought as he gently closed his eyes to think after checking that Marie was facing the other way, *what can I do to help?*

"Marie," Halter called from behind her.

Marie was still fiddling with AnchoR's mechanisms. She answered shortly without stopping her hands, "What?"

"It's about time you get some rest. As someone with a living body, you'll collapse if you don't eat."

Marie turned around with her mouth open, looking like she wanted to counter his suggestion, but ended up staring up in silence. It appeared that she couldn't come up with a good argument.

Perhaps she realized how overworked her brain was, for she nodded grudgingly. "All right. Could you go now to save a seat for us, then? I'll come down once I close AnchoR back up."

"Roger." Halter nodded, then headed off to the first floor of the hotel.

After he sat down at an empty table and waited a short while, Marie came down with AnchoR in hand.

Marie sat down, then AnchoR sat in her lap. After Marie ordered her food, she said, "Sorry, AnchoR. I didn't mean to take up your whole day."

"Not at all. Forget me. How about you, Mother? Are you okay?"

"Me? I'm perfectly fine. I used to do two or three all-nighters in a row all the time when I was in Meister Guild, so this is nothing," Marie said with a smile as she combed her fingers through AnchoR's black hair.

Seemingly embarrassed, AnchoR wriggled around a bit, then said with downcast eyes, "But...you seem shaky somehow, you know?"

"Yeah, you might be right. But hey, if you give Mom a biiig hug, I think she'll feel a lot better."

"Uhmm...like this?"

"Nggggggh, so angels really do exist after all..." Marie said. Her cheeks were practically melting away from bliss when she noticed Halter's gaze. "What are you looking at me for?"

Baffled, Halter muttered, "Nothing. I just always assumed that if the princess were ever to have a child, you'd be the kind of mom that treated her kids harshly."

"Hah! Isn't that obvious? I wouldn't pamper someone just because they're my child."

"Mind takin' a look at the mirror before you say that again, miss?" Halter groaned with his eyes half-closed. Just as Marie was going to respond...

"What the?! Marie, what do you think you're doing? I'm so jealous. This is simply outrageous. Let me take your place right this moment. Please, I beg you, I'll do anything!"

"Master Naoto, please refrain from casually making propositions like that. Saying that you will do anything is no different from signing a contract to be a slave. Also, if I were the one to grant you your wish, would you make the same offer? I am not really asking with any particular reason in mind, just so you know."

Upon turning around, Marie found the source of the ruckus by the entrance of the hotel. Naoto and RyuZU looked like they'd been shopping. Their clothes were different from what they had been wearing yesterday and RyuZU was also carrying a large bag on her back.

"Welcome back. Took you quite a while, huh?" Marie said sardonically with AnchoR tightly in her arms. "So, you ditched your beloved daughter's repair and went on a leisurely date with your wife? Ah yes, such wonderful parents. Your parental rights are rescinded. I take it there's no objection?"

"How rude of you!! How very, very rude of you!! I wouldn't call myself her father if I didn't value family! And you call yourself her mom?!" Naoto retorted indignantly as he sat down at the table. "In the first place, you don't even have any idea what we had to go through while we were gone!!"

"Are you suggesting that you did anything besides happily enjoy a shopping date with your wife as if you were on a vacation?"

"There's nothing wrong with that! The problem is what came after that!! Guess what happened when we entered a shop called Kathey that had a bunch of women's clothes on display?!"

"If I recall correctly, 'kathey' means 'ladyboy' in Thai—"

Naoto slammed the table as he ranted hysterically, cutting Marie off. "After greeting me with a smile and saying, 'Welcome to the new you,' they took me to an operating table! I nearly lost my manhood back there!!"

He then turned around and said, "Heck, why didn't you stop them, RyuZU?! You know I don't understand the language here! I thought for sure it was all over when they laid me onto the operating table, you know?!"

However, RyuZU tilted her head with a blank face and said, "I thought for sure that what had happened was that you had resolved to say goodbye to who you were, Master Naoto, so I thought in keeping with my name of YourSlave, it was my duty as your follower to respect your—"

"How could I possibly have made the reservation myself when I don't even understand Thai?!" Naoto shouted as he looked around angrily with bulging eyes. "Now that I think about it, the only one who'd be bored enough to harass me like that is that old man Vermouth! You bastard, the next time I see you I'll hook your brain pod to a barrel-shaped cleaning automaton, ya hear?!"

"Still, I must say, considering that the makeup artists in this city seem to be exceptionally skilled, should you not in fact thank him for giving you an opportunity to touch up your shabby-looking face, Master Naoto?"

"Now look here!! I don't want to hear you calling me a pervert ever again!! You clearly just want to see me in drag, am I wrong?!" Naoto yelled, practically tearing off his hair in frustration.

However, RyuZU threw out her chest and responded unabashedly with poise, "With all due respect, Master Naoto, that shop was an unusual one for this city, in that it had refined taste. It was a once-in-a-lifetime opportunity to learn from an outstanding professional makeup artist, so I thought I would watch for a bit. After all, though there is no particular need for you to be disguised during our stay here, knowing how to put on an elaborate disguise for you is a skill that might very well prove useful further down the line."

"Sure, but why do I have to disguise myself as a girl?! If I genuinely awaken to such interests, how will you make it up to me?!"

"Father, you're cute, you know?" AnchoR chimed in.

"Well now, given that you are who you are, Master Naoto, what problem is there at this point, really, if another item was added to your long list of fetishes?"

Pincered by both RyuZU and AnchoR, Naoto sank into silence. He put his hand on his chin and narrowed his eyes as he pondered things over. "Hmm..."

Instinctively sensing something unsettling, Marie called out, "Hey, Naoto? Hello?"

However, instead of replying, Naoto began a one-man Q&A session. "Let's think about this logically. Am I a stud? Negative. In all my life, I've never been complimented on my looks. Then, do I make a pretty girl? Affirmative. AnchoR has deemed me to be cute, and RyuZU is aggressively trying to make me cross-dress. In other words, it's been acknowledged by two transcendent beauties that I make a pretty girl. Given that, the fact that I look right as a girl is as clear as day, huh?" Naoto said with a serious face. "Say, is there really a need for me to be a man? Hey RyuZU, AnchoR. If you guys don't mind me becoming your wife and your mom respectively, I'll go back to that shop and—"

Seeing that Naoto had clearly lost it, Marie leaned over from across the table and grabbed onto Naoto's collar, yelling as she jolted him back and forth, "Stop that! Of course AnchoR will mind!! If you screw this up for us even further, then I'll stick you to the authorities on a skewer, got it?!"

Meanwhile, RyuZU looked at Marie with a cold gaze. "Well, now. I wonder, is this coming from your sense of inadequacy due to *your* body not sticking out where it should, Mistress Marie? In that case, places that can help with that are a dime a dozen in this city. Please, there is no need to hold back. How about you give having your body stick out where it should a try?"

"I'm really gonna slaughter you, you know?!" Marie shouted, baring her teeth. Then, out of breath, she huffed and puffed for a bit. After catching her breath, she rubbed her temple with one hand as if she had a headache, and said with weight in her words, "Listen up, okay? Please ingrain this into the memory of your flawed AI that you self-proclaim to be number one in the world. Every time you project such doubts at me, I feel incredibly insulted. The humiliation is such that I couldn't describe it to you in any language."

"In that case, how about you stop interfering with what Master Naoto wants for himself?"

"I don't actually give a damn what he wants to do with his own body! But he's already a pervert as it is, and if his special hearing ends up damaged as a side-effect of him messing around with surgery on his own body, he'll go from being an *useful* pervert to just a pervert. Should that happen, his thing won't be the only thing rendered useless, got it?!"

Having watched the developments up to this point, Halter commented calmly, "Say Naoto, let me be frank...do you really want to become like that greenhorn?"

Naoto clapped and said, "All right, forget everything I just said!" He immediately took back his words.

RyuZU got up from her chair and unpacked her bag, spreading its contents—a bunch of boxes—onto the floor. She then casually tossed them onto the table.

"Now then, AnchoR? Daddy's brought something for you ♪"

"Hey, don't put that kind of stuff on the table we're going to eat from."

"Now now, I'm just going to give her a peek for now," Naoto said as he opened one of the boxes. Inside it was a small, cylindrical mechanical part buried in packaging.

Marie muttered with a puzzled face, "What's this?"

"Listen, would you? Like I said, it's something for AnchoR. It's a small hex spring manufactured by Audemars. If it's whittled down a bit, we can use it for AnchoR's shock absorber, right? With this model, even with AnchoR's mainframe being bent, there shouldn't be a problem connecting it. It was really tough to get this, you know. It took a lot to convince the old man at the shop to part ways with it..." Naoto began, eager to detail the hardships he had to go through.

As he told his story, Marie's lips stiffened as she stared at the part. It appeared she felt ashamed that Naoto had managed to find a compatible part for AnchoR, while she hadn't accomplished anything.

As Halter gazed at her profile, he smiled bitterly. *She can't bring herself to just praise him honestly for a job well done. Her pride won't let her. But at the same time, it also won't allow her to ignore his contribution.*

Marie looked like she was struggling inside with how to respond. She finally seemed to reach a decision after some time.

"W-well done, Naoto...but I think it'd be better to put it away for now. Let's examine it more closely in the workshop after we're done eating," she said, her voice quivering ever so slightly.

Just then...

"Oy, what was that sound just now?" Naoto abruptly muttered with a dead-serious face.

Immediately after, the roar of gunshots rang out. Not just one or two shots from a pistol, either, but the cacophony of multiple machine guns.

Shrieking and screaming followed. Judging by the volume of the sounds, the chaos wasn't happening right outside the hotel, but it also wasn't far enough away that they could just ignore it.

An air of nervousness ran through all the customers in the restaurant, including Halter.

"Ahh, don't worry, everyone! A search is being conducted, that's all!" the receptionist at the hotel's front desk shouted with his hands cupped around his mouth.

One of the diners asked, looking suspicious, "A search, you say?"

"Apparently some Chinese gang bought in some refugees behind Restaurant's back, the fools that they are. Well, the gang members themselves were already purged a few days ago, but they had stuffed their *merchandise* in an apartment near here. So basically, the gist is that Arsenal's troops have gone to clean up."

"Oy, you better be sure about that."

"I do apologize. This was something I'd been notified of beforehand by my superiors, but the decision was that it'd be troublesome for us if they knew that we knew, so I was ordered to stay quiet about it until the raid began. Please understand."

"Guess it can't be helped. Good grief."

"Making us worry like that..."

After some moaning and groaning, the customers resumed

with their meals as if nothing had happened. All the while, gun-shots and screams continued without pause.

Naoto stood up with a grim expression.

"Naoto," Halter said with a subdued voice, "you heard him. There's no need to worry about the noise. Forget about it."

"Are you kidding me, old man?! It may be one thing if it's just gunshots, but that's the scream of a child, you know?!"

"...Ngh!"

Upon those words, Marie's expression also turned grim. She wasn't fully standing yet, but her bottom was off the seat.

As Halter looked at the two, who seemed like they might rush out of there any second, he said dispassionately, "Oy, what're you two planning to do?"

"Ain't that obvious?"

"Halter, I wouldn't care if it were the criminals of the city getting killed, but I can't overlook innocent children getting killed. We have to save them somehow..." Marie said restlessly with a grave face.

However, Halter gazed at her and asked, unmoved, "Save them? Then what?"

Caught by surprise by that question, Marie's eyes widened. "Well..."

"Can you look after those refugees after you save them? And what are you going to do about the Arsenal squad? Are you going to kill them all and turn this entire city upside down?"

Marie couldn't answer him. Her lips trembled, but she couldn't manage to say anything.

Halter continued, "This whole city's a powder keg. If the power balance among the three ruling syndicates in the city is disturbed, everything will go up in flames in one fell swoop. If that happens, how many people do you think will die? Do you think it'd be fewer than those refugees? How can you be sure that the syndicate who seizes power after such a calamity would be better than the ones at the top right now?"

Naoto couldn't take it anymore. "Screw your reasoning, that's just bullshit!"

"It may be bullshit, but am I wrong?" Halter replied calmly. He then peered into Naoto's eyes suddenly and said, "Why are you so mad, anyway?"

"What do you mean, why?"

"What does the life or death of those pathetic humans have to do with you? I thought you weren't interested in mere lumps of protein?"

"Halter! You don't have to put it like that..."

"Marie, the same goes for you. If you want to strive for social justice, indulge yourself in that *luxury* elsewhere," Halter said as he gave a hard stare at the boy and girl who were trembling with grim faces. "This city is a wicked place. Marie, didn't you explain that to Naoto yourself yesterday? Or is my memory playing tricks on me? Have you also forgotten that you told him not to stick his nose where it doesn't belong?"

"So what, are you telling me to just forsake them?!"

"That's right." Halter nodded coldly. "I'll tell it to your face. Making a mess of the situation out of casual sympathy won't bring happiness to anyone. Don't get too conceited, you brats. Do you think you've become gods or something?"

"...Damn it!" Naoto stood up in indignation.

"Oy."

Without turning around to face Halter, Naoto said, "I'm gonna go to our room and sleep! Happy?" He then headed towards the elevator by the staircase.

Marie stood up slowly and muttered, "Sorry. I know you're warning me for my own good and also that you're right. It's simply a matter of me being unable to accept it. But still..." She looked at Halter with tears in her eyes. "I feel sick about it."

Halter nodded. "Yeah. I won't tell you to accept it, either. But abide by my words. All right?"

Marie didn't reply. She simply slumped her shoulders, looking crestfallen, and left her seat to follow after Naoto.

As Halter gazed absentmindedly at the two seats that had become empty, he suddenly realized something. *I'd kill for some alcohol right now. If possible, yes, something similar to the cocktail that the girl who's now dead made last night—a sweet but fierce drink.*

"Uh...uhm, Grandpa Robot," AnchoR said mildly, "cheer up, okay?"

Hearing her words, Halter smiled bitterly. "Thanks, missy. But well, I won't shamelessly ask that you call me Big Brother, so could you at least call me Uncle instead?"

"Huh? But Grandpa Robot, from what I can tell, it looks like your brain pod was made back in—"

"I see." Halter felt a chill run down his back. A sense of danger climbed up his spine like a vine, entangling it.

*Even if her appearance is that of a cute little girl, there's no mistake that she's the Initial-Y made with the goal of absolute dominance in battle. Her reputation as the strongest automaton ever is no lie. With just a glance at me, she's able to extract internal information like that.*

"And also," AnchoR continued, "Grandpa...you're an automaton, right? Just like AnchoR."

Halter's smile grew wider. He picked up his chair and turned it so he faced AnchoR directly, then asked with poise, "Does it look that way to you, missy?"

"Huh...? Am I wrong?" AnchoR tilted her head with an expression of genuine confusion.

The sky is blue. Things fall down, not up. Fire is hot. Light is fast. God exists. To AnchoR, what she had said was a truth as self-evident as these, which was why she was nonplussed, and it very much showed on her face.

*This automaton distinguishes between humans and machines, and so this is how that fearsome pair of analytical eyes defines the current Vainney Halter, huh?*

*"You're not a human, but a mere machine."*

"Aw, shucks. Even with all these robotic parts, in my own view, I'm still human," Halter muttered with a bitter laugh.

AnchoR widened her eyes and said, "...Really?"

"It's true that I'm practically all machine, but the organ inside my brain pod is still human, you know? If people knew how old my actual brain is, then I'd be called a geezer by everyone."

Frankly, Halter himself didn't know the exact number of years. His artificial body's appearance was set to that of a man in his late thirties, but if the brain was older than double an artificial body's set age, then the two would be incompatible.

"He is right, AnchoR. He is not an automaton," RyuZU suddenly interjected in a quiet voice. "That said, naturally he is not human, either. In other words, he is neither a doll nor a human, nor can he fully become one or the other. He is simply an incomplete piece of junk."

"Oy, oy...rather harsh, aren't we, Ms. Doll?"

"I have only simply stated the truth. I could list countless differences between you and me. From having versus not having a brain pod; to basic functionalities; to field of detection, output, class, intelligence, elegance, weight, and the ability to take care of Master Naoto. Oh, and amount of hair as well."

"Just so you know, a man's worth isn't determined by the amount of hair he has. It's determined by how much heart he has."

"Is that so? Let me ask then, do you have a heart?"

Being attacked relentlessly like this, even Halter felt hurt. At the same time, he felt like something was off with RyuZU.

RyuZU's wicked tongue wasn't anything new. However, her abuse should stem from the inexplicable abusive verbal filter she was programmed with; in other words, she shouldn't actually mean the harsh things she said.

However, Halter sensed genuine malice in RyuZU's words just now, somehow.

*Malice?*

"Kinda funny for an automaton to say that, don't you think?"

"Indeed, I am an automaton." RyuZU nodded. "God made man in His image, and man made automaton in man's image. In that case, just what does that make you? If you are neither automaton nor human, then who was it that made you?"

"My, an automaton that believes in God? How intriguing."

"It is not faith. It is simply knowledge of the fact that God does exist."

"That so? Unfortunately, I've never seen Him myself, you see."

"Is that right? So you think that if you have not seen something with your own eyes, then it could not exist. I see," RyuZU sneered. "You discarded the limitations of being human yourself, yet you still call yourself human on the basis of retaining a human brain, when in reality, you are nothing but a sham. You close your eyes and ears to the truth by your own volition, then claim that God does not exist... Haha, sorry, please do continue to entertain me with your ridiculous lines."

"Sorry, but both my eyes and ears are working just fine."

"Right, you can only receive information through those sensors of yours. You believe the world to be limited to only what you have personally experienced and assumptions that others have made for you. Until you doubt that truth of yours—until you realize that there exist infinite worlds and the universe is boundless—you will forever be just a slave, and the brain you are so proud of will continue to merely be the part of your body that turns the gears."

"I get it," Halter said as he motioned for RyuZU to stop with his hand. He then stared at RyuZU and sneered, "Are you saying that there are as many worlds as there are observers? I've got no interest in philosophy. I will admit that some of my sensors aren't as sensitive as human sensory organs, but in the end, that's inconsequential. It's all about how you use them. There are plenty of people who don't understand the truth of this world, despite having organic bodies."

"Indeed, there are countless beings on this planet who pretend to be human with brains that lose to those of mites—clumps of protein, if you will. So there is no need to be too hard on yourself, you know? In the end, all you have done is betray the fact that you are simply yet another blockhead among the billions of others."

"..."

The tension in the air was practically palpable. AnchoR looked back and forth between the two timidly.

RyuZU took AnchoR's hand and quietly stood up. She then looked down on Halter coldly as she continued with words that were as sharp as a blade. "'That which I have never seen or heard about does not exist'... That is the perspective, as well as the limitation, of the fools who make up the vast majority of people that populate this planet. That is exactly why, while there are humans who doubt whether love or God truly exist, there are none who doubt whether money or power do, despite both love and God being self-evident truths that hardly need proving. It says a lot about humanity."

With that parting remark, RyuZU and AnchoR left the restaurant.

· · • · ·

All by himself now, Halter sank into his seat in silence. Then, when the noise outside finally settled down—when there were no more gunshots or screams to be heard—he ordered a glass of whiskey.

"...Yet another blockhead among the billions, huh," he muttered with a bitter smile.

*Damn right I am.*

Halter had no will to refute RyuZU's words; in fact, he agreed with her. He felt nothing at all towards that accusation, not even a little resentment or humiliation.

He had been standing on the battlefield with a gun in hand since his earliest memory as a little brat. While he had been immersed in countless victories and defeats, he had become an adult all of a sudden, and then before he knew it, a cyborg.

That was how he had simply lived to this day. He hadn't done anything special. He used his head when he should; he did what had to be done when he should. Like so, he took on life one day at a time and completed the challenges it threw at him.

After a while, people around him began calling him Oberon and his mobile suit Overwork. He was the legendary mercenary who pulled off a miracle comeback when he had been an inch away from death's door.

"What a bunch of idiots."

*Just who are you guys talking about? 'Cause it ain't me. There's no such thing as fate or miracles in this world. Nor is there a god who conveniently appears out of nowhere and solves everything for you when you need help.*

*That's exactly why average Joes like myself have such a hard time living.*

*If you act purely with cold logic, you'll end up bumping heads with others. But if you let yourself be caught by emotion, then everyone'll die. That said, a single lone wolf sticking to his guns and doing his own thing can only get so far. All sorts of problems would pop up.*

*That's exactly why if the humans who understand what must be done—however troublesome or precarious it may be—don't follow through with it, not a single thing in the difficult world we live in would function properly. That's what it means to keep the gears of society turning.*

"In other words, this is yet another one of those cases," Halter muttered with a sigh, then tilted his rocks glass and took a sip. As he gazed at the clear amber liquid, his thoughts flew back to what happened yesterday.

*What Kiu Tai Yu wants is clear: supremacy over Shangri-La Grid. He plans to seize control over this powder keg of a city with our help, and use it to control the current political instability that's arisen from word getting out about the city sheltering Second Ypsilon.*

*That isn't a lie. I'm certain about that.*

*It doesn't cause a problem for us in any way to meet his demands. Obediently doing as we're told, then leaving after picking up the stuff we came for, is the easiest and safest way out of this situation.*

*However...would Naoto and Marie accept that reasoning and do as they're told?*

*The answer is no. I already figured that would be the case, but with that display just now, I'm absolutely certain.*

*Naoto may go around saying that he has no interest in humans, but he isn't as cold-blooded as he likes to make himself out to be. And though Marie should still be somewhat more experienced in the ways of the world in comparison, it appears she still isn't mature enough to take on dirty work when necessary.*

*In short, they're kids. Both Naoto and Marie still don't have it in them to become adults like that. That is both their strength—and their fatal weakness.*

"...Well, what can you do, I guess," Halter mumbled as he took a gulp of whiskey.

*They're kids, after all. Even if they possess godlike powers, they're still just kids. It's only natural that they think like kids as well.*

As the powerful alcohol went down, Halter felt the burn in his tongue and his throat and his entire body flared up with heat. As his brain processed such somesthetic signals, he continued to ponder.

*The two will surely spurn Kiu Tai Yu's demands, and they have enough power to do so...against their own good. And then what would happen?*

*If the deal breaks down, Kiu Tai Yu will turn all of Arsenal's power against us, but not necessarily to win. He's considered the possibility of RyuZU's counterattack destroying this entire city—in fact, he actively hopes for such an outcome.*

*He clearly spelled out that possibility to me. It may have been a threat, but it wasn't a lie. He doesn't care which scenario happens.*

*The only difference is that one would lead to development, and the other reconstruction. Both would equally be killer business opportunities for him. As long as he can secure his own safety and profits, the method couldn't matter less to him.*

*Even so, it's not like we can just kill him. If we do, the rest of Arsenal would come after us without reservation, knowing that the deal is off, resulting in a showdown between us and them just the same. In fact, without a top figure who can ultimately bring the situation under control, things will probably turn out far worse.*

Halter grimaced. "In short, eliminating him physically would be futile."

*In fact, it'd be counterproductive. If we became embroiled in a war against all of Shangri-La Grid, can RyuZU alone really protect Naoto and Marie?*

*Well, she probably can. It shouldn't be even close to possible for this city's military strength to overcome an Initial-Y automaton. And as for the Initial-Y automaton headed here as their reinforcement that Kiu Tai Yu hinted at, I don't really see it being a fatal issue.*

But people would die, and in great numbers, at that.

*Should that happen, will those two kids be able to withstand that fact without crumbling? It might just be the case that such a mental wound would leave them with a far more debilitating handicap than a physical one.*

*It might just be me overthinking things. It could be that I'm just being overprotective. But I'm not confident enough to put them to such a test—not now. Not yet, at least.*

"...In the end, there's only one move I can make, huh," he muttered with a nod.

Hand Naoto Miura over to Kiu Tai Yu.

*It certainly isn't ideal, but it's the best option I've got. We can at least avoid an all-out war with Shangri-La Grid that way, if nothing else. Though of course, that would make me a traitor, but... it would also let me uphold my duty of protecting Marie.*

*Naoto will be released once he's done his job, as well. Kiu is well aware that, should he dispose of Naoto, a raging RyuZU will pay him back without thinking of the consequences. He isn't some chump who would overlook something like that in his calculations. He's a first-class villain.* At that, Halter laughed bitterly, because he realized that he hadn't considered how RyuZU would pay him back.

"Man, that's a scary thought..."

Contrary to his words, however, Halter was still smiling. It wasn't that he wasn't afraid of RyuZU, nor was it that he thought RyuZU wouldn't kill him.

*In fact, that automaton probably wouldn't hesitate one bit to kill me, should the need arise. And if we end up in a confrontation, I can't imagine that I'd be able to escape.*

Halter knew that perfectly well, yet he didn't falter.

*Let's do it.*

*It doesn't matter that I was called a machine by a couple of automata; if the humans who understand what must be done don't follow through with it, not a single thing in the difficult world we live in would function properly.*

"Tell this to Kiu Tai Yu," Halter said aloud.

At first, it wasn't clear to whom he was talking, as before him were only empty seats and nothing else. However, the man sitting back-to-back against him at a different table stirred a little.

Halter muttered, "I accept the deal. I'll execute the plan at 14:00 tomorrow at the eastern part of the central marketplace. Also, prepare the following items for me..."

After he finished giving his detailed instructions, the man behind him nodded and stood up readily.

As Halter watched the messenger pay his bill, then leave with a sidelong glance, he gulped down his drink.

*There's nothing more to say at this point.*

*The die has been cast.*

· · • · ·

The next day...

"Why did you betray us?!"

"Halter—!!"

Marie's bellow of anger reverberated in the eastern part of the marketplace in Shangri-La Grid on Chang Klang street.

However, it was futile. The script had already been written. Regardless of what she said now, she wouldn't be able to overwrite it. By seizing Naoto first thing, Halter had been able to seal RyuZU's movements.

Even for an automaton that moved as fast as she did, it was impossible to block a 15 mm APCR round fired point blank. The explosive power of the round was such that just a graze would be enough to blow a human's delicate head off, like a needle brushing a balloon.

If RyuZU activated Mute Scream, there was a chance she could cut Halter down before he could fire.

However, Halter wasn't the only one targeting Naoto here. There were countless snipers in position. There were hitmen mixed in with the surrounding pedestrians as well. Not to mention, bombs made with gunpowder had been set all over in this area.

If RyuZU activated Mute Scream and failed to take down even one of them during that time, Naoto would be defenseless when it ended, as she would shut down from her spring being fully unwound.

RyuZU probably understood that, for she stared at Halter with eyes filled with bloodlust instead of taking action.

Despite the fact that he had eliminated nearly all chances of RyuZU making a move, it was no fun whatsoever to be targeted by an opponent who could take him apart down to every screw in his body in less than a second. The piercing terror along he felt along his spine almost made him unwittingly drop his gun.

However, Halter hid his terror with all his body and spirit and put on a smile.

"Grandpa Robot." Meanwhile, AnchoR spoke dispassionately by RyuZU's side, her face expressionless like a Noh mask. "Let go of Father."

"No can do, missy," Halter answered with a sneer.

AnchoR swiftly narrowed her eyes, "Let go, right now."

"No thanks."

"If you don't, I'll do horrible things...to you, you know?"

"Oh? Are you capable of that in your current state?"

If AnchoR was in normal condition, it would have been a piece of cake for her. She'd be able to eliminate Halter before he could pull the trigger, mow down all the bullets that would then come flying at her, and protect Naoto and Marie from the bombs' blasts by using spatial manipulation.

As the one who boasted the highest combat strength in the Initial-Y series, she certainly would have been able to do all of that. However, she was currently heavily damaged.

Forget combat maneuvering, her body couldn't even withstand the output for everyday movements right now with its makeshift parts. In her current state, it'd be difficult for her to manipulate space—or so Halter had heard.

However...

"I...can," AnchoR asserted as she staggered forward a step.

*So she's mentally prepared to go through with a suicide attack, huh? Halter nodded. If she takes me down without care for her own life, RyuZU would be able to escape with Naoto faster than the shots from the snipers could reach him.*

It was the one and only way for them to overturn the situation and rescue Naoto.

It appeared that RyuZU and AnchoR were on the same page, for they exchanged glances. However...

"No!" Naoto yelled sharply.

Halter smiled, *That's right. Naoto will generously block the one hole in this plan for me.*

*If AnchoR raised her output right now to combat levels, she'd truly end up beyond hope for recovery this time. None other than Naoto himself said that, so there's no way he'd allow it to happen.*

"Thanks," Halter whispered with a smile. "Man, you really saved me there. I'll overlook the fact that you spoke just now, despite being ordered not to. If you didn't say that, I'd be dead by now. You don't disappoint. I'm glad I bet my life on you."

Naoto replied with a sullen face, "It wasn't for your sake. It was for AnchoR's."

"I know, but even so...thanks, Naoto."

"Halter," Marie said in a chilling voice. "I'll ask you one last time...just what kind of prank is this? Depending on your answer, I'll despise you more than anyone else in this world."

Her eyes reflected anger, hatred...and just a little bit of hope.

Halter sighed. *This girl isn't foolish by any means. She has the intellect to judge the authenticity of someone's actions and consider the possible explanations behind them.*

*Even as fury and bewilderment assault her mind, she's still calmly calculating that there could be some sort of good intent or circumstances behind my actions.*

*It's not just the fragile delusion of a girl who can't accept reality. It's the logical and rational conclusion she drew after considering all the countless interactions she's had with me up to now. She's absolutely right on the mark—but at the same time, terribly mistaken.*

Halter shrugged. "Don't make me repeat myself over and over again. It's work."

"..."

*That's right, this is my job. I'm simply doing what needs to be done. There's no need to hesitate if this is the best way to achieve my objective. Fulfill your duties, Vainney Halter.*

"Well Marie, I warned you plenty, didn't I? Did you think the party you assembled was invincible just because you went on a little rampage in Kyoto and Tokyo by chance? Don't get carried away. It really isn't difficult at all to eliminate you and your friends."

*That's right. I've no reason to deceive this bratty little girl. I've just about gotten sick of babysitting a brat. It's not like I'm getting compensated enough for risking my life to do so, either. Guess I'll take the opportunity to get out of it while I can by earning some cash that'll last me for a while here.*

*I'll fill my heart with malice. I'll blot out any goodwill I had. Pride, you say? Screw that. Did you think your lofty ideals would resound with mercenary scum like myself, who only cares for number one? As if I can put up with a buncha brats playing house a second longer. As far as employers go, I'll wag my tail at the one who pays me more. Anyone would do that. And so would I.*

"'I'll make enemies of the entire world.' ...Looks like you thought too lightly of what that truly means, huh?"

Halter curled his lips. It was what Marie probably detested the most out of anything, the sneer of a sleazebag whose soul was rotten through and through.

"Oh, I see. I understand perfectly now," Marie said. All emotion had left her eyes without a trace. There was no anger, no hatred left. She looked at him as if he were a pebble on the street.

It seemed that she had determined that he wasn't someone worth confronting with such emotions and had given up on him.

"If I ever see you again, I'll kill you."

Halter replied, "That's impossible. For you, at least." He calmly dragged Naoto away, making sure that his gun was pressed tight against Naoto's head at all times as he watched RyuZU and AnchoR with utmost vigilance.

· · ● · ·

As Halter turned the corner from Chang Klan Road onto Loi Kroh Road, he found a black car that had been prepared for him. It wasn't some kind of run-down second-hand car, but a special vehicle that was made to be bulletproof.

Halter shoved Naoto into the back seat, then got in himself and closed the door.

Smoked glass partitioned the front seats from the back seats. He said to the driver through the glass, "All ready here."

The car immediately flew off aggressively.

"Phew," Halter sighed.

"Would you put that dangerous thing away already?" Naoto sullenly said while glaring at the gun's enormous muzzle. "You're safe now, aren't you?"

"Sorry about that." Halter nodded with a bitter laugh, promptly putting away his gun.

Naoto pouted, "So? What do you plan to do, old man?"

"Sorry about this," Halter apologized again before continuing,

"Rest assured...well, that might be asking for too much, but at least know that I have no intention to sell you off or kill you."

"You expect me to believe that right after you abduct me?"

"Oy oy, Naoto. Use the correct term. Abducting is tricking someone into following you. Taking someone away by force, like I did, is called kidnapping."

"Like I care about that," Naoto growled with his eyes half-closed. "So where are you taking me?"

"To this city's core tower," Halter replied. "There's a villain who wants to commission you to do a job for him. The details are too bothersome to explain, so I'm going to omit them, but basically, if you don't accept his request, every last bit of this city will end up like roast chicken."

"Too bothersome, you say...and who's the villain you're talking about, anyway?"

"Kiu Tai Yu. To put it simply, he's a total shitbag madman."

Naoto furrowed his eyebrows and muttered, "Umm...If I remember right, isn't that Arsenal's boss?"

"Ohh. I'm surprised you remember."

"Well it was only two days ago that you told me...and actually, didn't you also say that he was someone who wouldn't make a foolish pass at us so long as we didn't cause any unnecessary trouble?"

"It hurts when you put it that way," Halter replied with a grimace, then sighed deeply. "Even if neither side had that intention, sometimes things just don't quite go the way you want. Think of it this way: thanks to an idiot stirring up trouble for us by listening to his dick instead of his brain, we're now stuck wiping his ass."

"Wow, I'd love to beat that guy to death."

"Rejoice; that's already happened. I'm guessing he's been turned into ground meat by now." Halter replied nonchalantly.

That made Naoto shut right up. His face began to pale as well.

Halter laughed bitterly. "Don't worry, that's not going to happen to you. You should be released unharmed as long as you do your job. I imagine you're not too happy about all this, but as odious as this shitty city is, even you wouldn't want it to be roasted whole, would you?"

"Well, that's true, but..."

"For things to be resolved peacefully, I needed either you or Marie to do some work for him, but I figured that I'd just get a sour face from you guys if I asked straight up. Well, just think of it as a not-all-that interesting field trip that you're being forced to go on, if you would, and give up."

"Did you really have to go this far, though?" Naoto groaned with a sigh. "The next time you show your face before RyuZU, you'll be sliced and diced in an instant."

"Thanks for the warning, I guess."

As Halter and Naoto were talking, the car had passed through Tha Phae Gate. It appeared that the boulevard had been cleared beforehand, as there was none of the congestion they had experienced when they first came to the city, allowing the car to smoothly advance to the heart of the city and stop right in front of the core tower.

"We're getting off now. The villain's waiting," Halter said.

Naoto nodded silently.

· • ● • ·

The core tower of Shangri-La Grid was practically a stronghold.

The building had originally been a temple made of stone. It used to be a landmark that served as a tourist attraction, but was moved from its original site when it was repurposed. It now had an imposing aura with its armored plating and machine guns, and none of the serenity of a temple was left.

The one things about it that looked pretty odd for a core tower were the unusually fancy stone elephants ornamenting the outer walls.

After passing through a checkpoint, Halter and Naoto entered the building, the latter still somewhat reluctantly. As the two walked through the hall, they heard and saw gangsters with stereotypically villainous faces looking on from a distance and whispering to each other:

"A kid like *that* is a member of Second Ypsilon?"

"Wow, he's seriously still just a brat. I thought it had to be a mistake."

"Is he truly the real deal...?"

Ignoring those voices, the two entered a dimly lit hallway and kept going straight. Eventually, they arrived at what appeared to be an office. A man dressed gaudily to the point of looking out of place in an professional setting and a teenage girl were both waiting there for Halter and Naoto.

The man with short red hair and a flashy suit spread out his hands and said, "Hey, hey! I was just about done with waiting, Mr. Oberon!" He then bent forward so extremely that it seemed unnatural, in order to match Naoto's eye level, and sneered patronizingly, "So yooou're Mr. Naoto Miura? I'm terribly sorry for inviting you by such means, but I'm truly honored to meet the super terrorist everyone's been talking about. Would you mind shaking my hand?"

However, Naoto didn't answer. It wasn't really an act of defiance, but rather simply because his eyes, his ears, all of his senses were fully focused on the teenage girl instead.

She had peach-colored hair, styled into side ponytails, and large, round facial features with sparkling sapphire eyes—in a word, the impish countenance of a feisty girl.

In human terms, she had the slender frame of a girl around junior high age, yet she was fairly busty and her body had all the right curves.

She wore a wreath of flowers on her head, a collar in the shape of a gear around her neck, a black lustrous corset, and thigh-high socks. Topping it all off was the punk lolita dress that exposed her shoulders and chest, accentuating her curvaceous body.

She was different from the quiet beauty RyuZU or the adorably angelic AnchoR, a perfect beauty who was thoroughly bewitching despite still going through adolescence.

*I can't really explain it, but the more I look at her, the more I want to bully her. On second thought, I want to be bullied by her more. She's provoking both those conflicting desires in me!*

"Hmmm? This is the guy?" the girl said with a voice that was sweet and alluring, but in a cold tone. "He looks dull. A chump like him is Eldest Sister's first boyfriend? Pfft—how lame."

"Oh dearrr. That can't be the first thing out of your mouth, Ms. TemP. Interpersonal relationships begin with a greeting! You should introduce yourself properly," the red-haired man said.

In response, TemP pouted and turned the other way. "I do not really intend to become friends with him, anyway."

Without a moment's pause, Naoto began to approach TemP, swaying about from side to side in a sickening manner with his lecherous eyes locked on to her. "Hahaha...you're a naughty little kitten, aren't'cha?" The moment he got in range of her, he grabbed her hand with alarming dexterity so as not to let her get away.

"What the— What are you—" Startled, she pulled her hand back, which caused her to stumble.

Naoto wasn't about to let his prey go. He drove her to the wall vigorously in the manner of an eager suitor asking the princess for a dance—or how a spider would seize its prey. Then *bam*, he slammed his hand onto the wall to the right of her.

It was a wall pin.

"Oh ho, nice to meet you, TemP-chan. My name is Naoto Miura—that's right, I'm the man who was born to become your master, the soul to whom you're bound by the red string of fate."

"Wha? Huh?" TemP said, looking awfully flustered as she

ducked her head and stared at Naoto. "Wh-what in the world are you saying out of nowhere? I already have a master..."

"Ahhh, such tragedy! My heart's about to split from sorrow! But I won't be discouraged, you know. That's because my heart was already yours since the moment I laid my eyes on you for the first time...haha."

"Ngh, are you serious? I-Is this the so-called 'love triangle' that I've heard about...?!"

"That's right. Please listen to what my soul is shouting, TemP-chan. I'm head over heels for you. Would it be too impertinent for me to hope for a favorable answer...? Well?!"

As he sputtered tomfoolery—correction: intimate talk—Naoto aggressively pressed closer. In response, TemP blushed and looked at him with wavering eyes.

Despite being bewildered by his behavior, her heart had been intensely shaken. The boy had very much piqued her interest. "L-L-Lies! D-do not think that I am not aware that you are Elder Sister's boyfriend."

"Yeah, RyuZU's my wife, of course. Not only that, AnchoR's my daughter."

"As I thought. Y-you are shameless!"

"But does that in any way contradict the fact that I love you, TemP-chan?"

TemP's eyes widened greatly. She faltered, "Th-that is...but..."

"I'll say it as many times as necessary. I love you. I'm absolutely confident that the one who loves you the most in this universe is me, TemP-chan. Won't you believe me?"

"I-I cannot believe you..." Temp said, shaking her head. However, both her gestures and her voice were terribly frail.

As he passionately gazed right into her eyes, Naoto gently held TemP's chin. "Then, would you let me prove it? My love for you, that is."

"G-gosh," TemP panted, her entire body trembling. "Th-that will not do. You will not tempt me... I would never...betray Master..."

"C'mon, li'l kitty. Where's the problem? Love is infinite, you know...!" As he briskly and unabashedly rested his other hand on her waist, he lifted up her chin.

As Naoto crept closer and closer, TemP squeezed her eyes shut. "No..."

They were now close enough to feel each other's breath. She opened her eyes just a peek, and their gazes met just as their lips were about to touch. That instant...

"Y-you caaaaaaaaaaaaaaaaaaaan't—ngh!!" TemP screeched, slapping away Naoto's hand.

Her face was so red that it approached the limits of what her facial mechanisms could actually produce. She shook her head rapidly, like a dog shaking off water, and then ran out the door so quickly that she could have easily bumped into something and fallen.

Having been left hanging, Naoto had fallen flat on his butt. He muttered dumbfoundedly, "Is she just shy, or...?"

"No, I think the problem is something more fundamental than that," Halter said with a reproachful gaze.

Naoto scratched his head, looking stumped, and said, "Well, I am the meek type when it comes to girls, after all. You think I should be more aggressive and really lay it on her?"

"How could you possibly be more aggressive than that?" Halter sighed.

"Hey...could it be that he's one of those cases...?" the red-haired man, Kiu Tai Yu, said to Halter in a low voice. "Took some amphetamines from a random street dealer and heavily damaged his brain?"

"If only. I'm sorry to say that this is just how he was born."

"Must be bliss to be able to trip out without drugs... Looks like he's real chipper, eh?"

"In a way, sure," Halter said while averting his gaze.

Kiu Tai Yu clapped and said, "So now then, Mr. Naoto... Now that we've both breathed in some good air and relaxed a bit, how about we get down to business?"

"Hm...? About what again?" Naoto muttered as he turned around to face the one who addressed him. Once he identified Kiu Tai Yu, he finally recalled why he was brought here. He answered sullenly with his eyes half-closed, "I'll keep it simple: no."

"Ohh...?"

"As for why I've been brought here, Old Man Halter already explained this and that. In short, I'm supposed to do whatever you tell me to, yeah? No thanks." Naoto stood up mindfully and brushed off the dust that had stuck to the back of his pants.

Kiu Tai Yu sneered smugly, "My, my... Looks like I'm not popular, eh? I wonder why that iiis... when I'm only saying that I want sovereignty over this city?"

"...Sovereignty?"

"I want to seize control over the core tower and act as God in this Shangri-La Grid! It's something that your troupe has done plenty of, no? I just want you to lend me that power of yours for just a little biiit... It shouldn't really be all that hard for you, isn't that right? Hm?" Kiu said while raising an eyebrow.

Naoto had been listening with a suspicious face, but he suddenly furrowed his brows even tighter. "There was a commotion yesterday near the hotel that we're staying at, yeah?"

"Hm? Is that so?"

"Soldiers of yours were firing off machine guns."

"If I may correct you, Arsenal doesn't have any soldiers, you know? They're simply armed security personnel. There's neither a military nor a police force here in Shangri-La."

"I don't care what you call them," Naoto snorted. "I don't really get the situation, but they had no mercy, even for children... You expect me to hand sovereignty of this city over to the boss of a syndicate like that? Keep dreaming."

"Oh my, what a terrible misunderstanding. I believe this is what they call a difference of opinion. Let's talk it out, shall we?!" Kiu shouted as he spread his hands.

He then sprung on his heels with sprightliness and pulled out a bulky file binder from one of his desk's drawers, then wet his fingertips with his tongue before flipping through the pages.

"Hum de dum ♪ ...Ah, is this it? I see, I see, refugee processing, huh."

After looking through the single-page document, Kiu nodded

with a smile. "Allow me to be frank: that's just business as usual for us. There's nothing wrong with it at all."

"Nothing wrong with it at all?" Naoto growled in a subdued voice. "You say that even when you shoot children down?"

"So shooting adults is fine with you, then?"

"That's not the problem here, and you know it!!"

"Haah? Then do enlighten me, because I'm feeling quiiite lost here."

After he put the file binder back inside the drawer, Kiu shrugged theatrically and continued, "They were 'merchandise' that some monkeys lacking in intelligence smuggled into the city from some rural area. But see, we can't allow that kind of business to operate outside of our control. I thoroughly enjoyed grinding up those delusional idiots starting from their fingertips and making them into meat pie, though I had to suffer through their pathetic excuses. So!" Kiu paused to let out a deep sigh. "Unfortunately, their 'merchandise' were now just bad financial liabilities. Now then, what should we have done? If we just let them be, some other idiots would have just made fools of themselves yet again along with another mess. Public order would begin to fray. Dealing with the situation appropriately is part of our duty to maintain the public order, understand?"

"Still, you didn't have to shoot them to death."

"What else could we have done, then? Tell me," Kiu said with a puzzled face. "Refugees or not, children eat. They shit and fart. They need housing and clothes. Who's going to foot the cost of all that? Or would you have them work to support themselves? Are you seriously stupid enough to believe that monkeys who can't even write their own name or calculate what one plus one is could make a living for themselves in this city without stirring up some sort of trouble?"

Naoto remained silent.

Kiu sneered mockingly. As he wagged his finger, he said, "Tsk tsk tsk. In short, after taking all such factors into account, I determined through a comprehensive cost-performance analysis that putting them down without dilly-dallying was the best option for everyone. Don't you think those children were better off saying goodbye to this shitty world too? Fret not; they say that children are as innocent as angels, so letting them die now would guarantee them tickets to heaven."

"In that case, you're definitely going to hell, no doubt about it."

"Well now, I wonder about that." Kiu shrugged as he sat down on top of his desk. "Am I really doing such a horrible thing? I crushed a criminal organization that flouted the rules of this city and proactively eliminated elements that could cause future trouble as part of my duty to maintain the public order here. I'll admit, our methods are more severe than what other grids might choose to adopt. But it wouldn't be a fair comparison unless you also factored in the crime rate and the standard of quality of life as well, yeah?"

"Are you suggesting that you're doing a good thing, then?"

"Not really? I'm just doing what's necessary. Though, now that I think about it, compared to the grid purge you guys have attempted in Japan not once, but twice—oh right, excuse me, that's just the narrative—I think what I've done is far more peaceful and moral, nooo...?"

"..." Naoto didn't reply, only clicked his tongue.

Kiu's smile deepened. He got off the desk and said as he extended his hand out theatrically, "I can provide you with the goods you desire. I'll say this right now, you're making a very dangerous choice here, you know? After all, you and your friends are suuperrrterrorists who've made enemies of the entire world. However," Kiu continued as he took on a quieter tone, "if you guys occupy this city and I'm the one who's forced to help, then it becomes a different story."

"Huh? You're the one who's threatening us."

"I'm talking about the narrative. You! Forcefully! Hijacked the core tower which is under my management! And made some illegal modifications to it in an inexplicable way. Then, the pitiful and helpless hunk that is Kiu Tai Yu had no choice but to cave to your demands and provide you with the goods you seek. Ahh— how pitiful I am!" Kiu said in a monotone voice as he faked sobbing, going so far as to pull out a handkerchief and pat his eyes with it.

Then, in a sudden reversal, he casually tossed the used handkerchief away and continued, "But if bad fortune comes, then good fortune will be sure to follow. After you guys leave, the other syndicates that are thorns in my side will all just happen to break down from internal strife. It's a strange world we live in, isn't it? But that'll be after you guys leave. It'll be completely unrelated to you. And so, the public order in this city will become good and

I'll make a killing... I can't imagine that you'd have any complaints about this scenario?"

*"But I do*—it makes me want to vomit."

"Oh, I seeee." Kiu nodded with a sneer. "It makes you want to vomit, huh? Yes, I get it. That's a big proooblem. You and I were born and raised differently, after all... It might be difficult for us to mutually understand each other. Still, I should have respected your right to your own opinion, so I apologize on that point. But tell me..."

Right then, Kiu grabbed Naoto by his collar with just one hand and held him up.

Naoto was left dangling in the air as Kiu strangled him. Kiu's grip was much more powerful than his slender body suggested. Gravity and Kiu's grip made it so that Naoto couldn't breathe.

"Guh... ngh..."

"You have others do the dirty work so you don't have to dirty your own hands. Despite that, you act like you're a saint and everyone else is a sinner—this very typical Japanese attitude is what baffles me. Who's really the one with screws loose in his head, Mr. Scummy Monkey?"

Naoto's vision began to dim from lack of oxygen, but he could still see Kiu's face.

Kiu had on neither an expression of mockery nor lament; his face was completely expressionless, as if all emotion had been erased from it. His muddy, bog-like eyes seemed as if he saw everything around him as worthless. It gave one the impression that his soul was as hollow as a bottomless pit.

"Oy, cut it out," Halter warned.

Suddenly released, Naoto dropped to the floor. Pain ran through his butt as he coughed violently. Looking up, he saw that Halter had grabbed Kiu by the wrist.

Kiu blinked a few times before muttering, "...Whoopsies."

He then put on a sketchy smile again as he gazed at Naoto. "Ahhh! Sorry about that, my lips and hands moved before I even realized it! Now then, Mr. Naoto, would you pleeease not make me have to spew some embarrassing line that's all too cliché?" He paused for a breath and continued, "You ain't got the right of choice, bud. If you believe that your own delicate, worthless life is valuable, could you please just do as you're told and work your ass off for me?"

· · • ● • · ·

With two fierce-looking gangsters each pulling on one of his arms, Naoto was dragged into the heart of Shangri-La Grid's core tower. They rode an elevator down to the depths of the grid. Having now been separated from Halter, and without RyuZU by his side either, even Naoto—who usually acted like he feared absolutely nothing—couldn't help but feel a little uneasy and fearful.

*They won't kill me...* he thought. *But if I thoughtlessly make a scene, I sure don't get the feeling that they'd let me off with a slap on the wrist.*

As the elevator doors opened, what Naoto saw was practically like a village of nomads.

Here and there, in this broad space surrounded by clockwork, were provisional workshops with curtains and panels that a great number of fierce-looking men were constantly going in and out of.

There was no doubt from their appearance that they were criminals, but the work clothes and tool belts they had on implied that they were clocksmiths as well. There were those with chrono compasses, the proof of a Meister, among them as well.

As Naoto entered the room, they all turned to look at Naoto with judgmental eyes.

"Ridiculous," a man of Middle Eastern descent standing at the forefront of the group said with a scowl.

"A sniveling brat like this is supposed to be the second coming of 'Y'? What a terrible joke. I can tell he's got no skills just by looking at him."

"It's just as Sabur says. We're supposed to tinker with the core tower based on this brat's instructions? Boss is going too far with his joke."

*Well, what they're saying is true.* Naoto sighed deeply, as he was still under the restraint of the two who brought him here. *RyuZU probably wouldn't hesitate to murder them for what they just said if she were here, but there's nothing I can really refute about their words. Still, this is how I'm treated after being forcefully taken here? Give me a break...*

Naoto pouted and growled, "I didn't come here 'cause I wanted to. If I'm unneeded, then let me leave already."

The man called Sabur leaned down and got right up in Naoto's face. He glared sharply at Naoto, saying, "I'd love nothing more than to do just that, brat. This isn't a playground for children. If you're an imposter then there'd be no need for us to hold back, either. We'll mince you right up and feed you to the rats."

Another clocksmith chimed in with eyes full of derision, "Oy brat, just what kind of trick did you use to fake controlling a core tower? Do tell."

"Nah, a kid like this could never have pulled off such a stunt. Isn't the rumor that the Initial-Y series are 'Y's' maintenance machines a more credible explanation?"

Losing his patience, Naoto groaned, "God, every last one of you is just saying whatever the hell you want..."

He then shook his head vigorously so the fluorescent-green noise-canceling headphones on his head would fall off, since his arms were restrained.

*You owe me big time, Old Man.*

He glared at Sabur through his bangs, which had covered his eyes from the shaking earlier. "You're not a live human, are you? You've done a good job of maintaining your artificial skin, but you're definitely a full-body cyborg."

Sabur cautiously took half a step back and said, "So what?"

"Let's see...looks like the base was probably a Master G series from the LeCoultre Corporation. It's the one that has a good reputation for the precision of its movements. But I see that you've had it modded quite a bit. Most notably, your right hand. That's the hand part the Caliber IV maintenance automaton uses, right? But man, when was the last time you had maintenance done? Your right hand is desynced from the rest of your body by

0.002 seconds. You're letting the extreme precision of your body go to waste like that, you know," Naoto fired off succinctly, then he turned his attention to the fat Caucasian clocksmith next to Sabur. "You're even worse."

"I-I've got a human body, you kn—"

"Not that, you big oaf. I'm talking about your measurement device. Your effort to be frugal may be praiseworthy, but the speed of its gears hasn't been calibrated correctly, and the resonance frequencies of the sensor plate are all over the place... Just how do you plan to measure anything with that? Are you stupid? Do you *want* to die?"

The clocksmith darted his eyes in embarrassment and hid the measurement device he was holding behind his back.

Naoto sighed deeply, then turned around to face the central pillar and said, "The core tower here has thirty-five floors in total... which is pretty deep. It seems like there's another camp on the twentieth floor, and there are four hundred and fifty-seven maintenance automata in standby there at the moment. Am I wrong?"

"..."

A wave of nervousness spread through the clocksmiths. Sabur glared at Naoto grimly. "How did you know all that, brat? Have you secretly snuck in here before?"

"I can tell that much just by listening to the sounds."

"Sounds?"

"That's the kind of special ability I have. I don't need any equipment. I can analyze the structure of any machine just by listening to its operating noise."

"Bullshit!"

"Yeah! There's no way that's possible!"

Several clocksmiths shouted out angrily. However, Sabur turned to look at them, his grim expression unchanged. "But the numbers he just gave were all accurate. How do you explain that, then?"

"...Maybe he found a blueprint of this tower lying around somewhere?"

"I've never heard of there being such a thing. It isn't a realistic explanation. To begin with, it still wouldn't explain how he knew even the number of maintenance automata we have," Sabur said.

His subordinates all swallowed their objections. They may have been petty criminals, but all the clocksmiths here were well-known for their skills in this city. Despite the knee-jerk backlash just now, they weren't the type to deny something that had just been demon- strated before their eyes without giving it fair consideration.

No matter how hard it was to believe, once they came to understand that it was the truth, what infected all of them was something that resembled absolute terror.

*This guy isn't human.*

*He's something else with merely the form of a human.*

*Whatever the case, one thing's for sure: he's something that exists outside the realm of our assumptions...*

As Sabur looked at Naoto with an eerie look in his eyes, he said, "Very well. We'll believe you for now." He paused before continuing in a pretentious tone, "We're the clocksmiths who've been commissioned by Kiu Tai Yu to create a control system for the core tower and clock towers of this city. We've also been told to listen to your instructions for the details of the work."

"In that case," Naoto began, "let me go around measuring things first." Naoto shook off the two gangsters who were holding him, freeing his hands. "Like I said earlier, I don't need any special equipment to measure things. Nonetheless, a core tower is too complex for me to analyze from one spot. I need to walk around and listen from multiple locations to analyze the structure in its entirety."

"All right. But you'll have a guard with you."

"Then make it a clocksmith with excellent skills. I need someone to translate for me."

"...Translate?"

"I can't read clockwork diagrams," Naoto muttered awkwardly. "I can only explain verbally where things are and how they operate, so I need someone who can translate to record that into something understandable to the rest of you. That's what I've relied on Marie for up to now, but she isn't here, so..."

Upon learning that Naoto couldn't read schematics, Sabur didn't even try to hide his condescension. At the same time, though, he now seemed to have an even eerier look in his eyes as he turned around and asked, "Does anyone want to go with him?"

However, no one volunteered. Everyone remained dead silent as they looked around to see how others were reacting.

*Their internal thoughts were obvious from the looks on their faces and their body language: I get that someone needs to keep a watch on him, but I don't want to get involved with such a freak.*

Just then, someone spoke up. "I'll look after him."

The one who came forward was an old man of small stature wearing a dark brown suit. His tangled white hair and wrinkly face were paired with amber eyes that had the glint of a ripe intellect. Beside him was an antiquated maid automaton pulling a gigantic trunk case.

Greatly surprised, Naoto asked inadvertently, "You're here, Master? And Nono, too?"

"You're volunteering, Signor Giovanni?" Sabur asked with widened eyes.

The old man—Giovanni—nodded and said, "As fate would have it, this isn't my first time seeing that kid, you see. My helper Nono can keep watch over him. As far as skills as a clocksmith are concerned...am I not good enough?"

"Of course you are. If you're willing to do it, I don't think anyone here would object."

"Well then, leave the rest to me, if you would."

With that settled, the clocksmiths all withdrew to their tent workshops in droves.

All by themselves now, Naoto and Giovanni looked at each other.

Naoto said, "Hi. Funny seeing you again here of all places, and so soon."

"Si— Our last meeting was only thirty-four hours ago, Mr. Naoto Miura."

"Nice to see you again too, Nono. So, why are you here, Master?" Naoto asked.

Giovanni shrugged. "Pretty much right after you left, Kiu Tai Yu abruptly canceled the five years' worth of work he had recently commissioned from me and forced me to take on this job instead."

"The reason you couldn't take on our request was because of a commission from that crazy man?"

"Something wrong with that? Whether a criminal syndicate or an armed group, a customer is a customer. For my part, I simply try to turn in work I'm proud of that's worthy of my reputation."

"Isn't it dangerous?"

"Not particularly? Well, it's true that that man is crazy. But even so, as long as you do a proper job for him, he isn't someone who'd put the squeeze on those in honest trades."

"I was forcefully brought here against my will, though."

"You consider your occupation respectable?"

Being called out right to his face, Naoto fell silent. It looked like even he wasn't so shameless as to claim otherwise.

Giovanni chuckled. "Well, rest easy. That may be easier said than done, I guess, but if he promised that he'd let you go after you do your job, then he isn't lying. He doesn't believe in baiting someone like that if he plans to kill them."

"Halter—an old man that's in my group—said something similar."

*It's not like their words are enough to truly ease my mind, though. That said, I do feel a little better now that I'm seeing a familiar face.*

Naoto nodded, to which Giovanni said, "Well then, it's probably not a good idea to continue chatting here. Some of the guys here are awfully short-tempered, so let's not test them. We can keep chatting as we go."

• • • ● • • •

Giovanni continued speaking as they entered the elevator to the next floor. "I must say, though, I was a little surprised earlier. I'd heard about some of the criminal feats you guys have perpetrated, but it looks like you've got quite an interesting talent, eh?"

Naoto sighed, muttering, "Is what I have really a talent?"

"Hmm?"

"To be honest, I'm not really sure. To me, it just seems so natural. Like, I don't understand how others can't do it."

Naoto recalled the incident that had happened a month ago in Tokyo. When the Pillar of Heaven had been on the brink of being destroyed, he and Marie shared their abilities with one another.

Under those extreme circumstances, Marie's theory and his intuition together demonstrated that human potential was limitless and the universe was yet incomplete.

"According to Marie, apparently I can see the outcome from the very beginning. I can tell how an incomplete mechanism should sound when it's complete."

"You're gifted." Giovanni nodded. "What is known as our current body of theories is the accumulation of discoveries and proofs, but there are, in fact, those among us who possess something that exists outside of that system of knowledge—those who clearly aren't merely exceptionally bright, but have been given a gift by God. They're certainly rare, though."

"Can that really be called a talent?" Naoto questioned.

Giovanni tilted his head slightly and asked, "How do you see it?"

"That description doesn't sound quite right to me... Or, I don't know exactly how to put it, but I feel like I'm not moving forward..." Naoto said as he scratched his head with both hands in frustration. "'Your intuition is absolutely correct, so just bring it down to a level that others can understand,' is what Marie told me, but that girl actually put together what was in my head just from me describing it to her verbally."

*That's decisively different from me, who only had the answer in my head. Just by receiving a small hint, Marie was able to material-ize it. She pulled off such a feat simply by honing her skills as a mor-tal, without having received any gift from God. Yet, I'm supposed to be the one who's talented? Does merely knowing the answer really make me a genius?*

"As things stand, I think Marie's a far more amazing clock-smith than me." Naoto was a little surprised by how readily those words came out. He didn't want to admit it—especially not to Marie herself. He'd never admit it to her, even if he were tortured.

However, for some reason he was able to be honest with him-self effortlessly before this senior master, who was far beyond his realm.

"Hmm...I see." The old man nodded, then readily added, "You can rest assured, boy. It's an astounding fact that your intuition is absolutely spot on. But in terms of technical skill, that miss is a far superior, otherworldly clocksmith to you."

Naoto gulped, then asked, "You think so?"

"I sure do. You should know that better than anyone yourself. I completely agree as well. Her skills are on an entirely different plane from yours or mine."

Naoto widened his eyes.

Giovanni asked, looking perplexed, "What's the matter?"

"Well...it just surprised me to hear you rate Marie so highly."

"That's just the objective truth. Comprehensively speaking, that miss is the greatest clocksmith in the world."

The elevator stopped. *Ding.* The doors opened.

As he walked out of the elevator, Giovanni looked back and continued, "She's mastered the cutting-edge technologies based on modern theory better than anyone else, and is capable of expanding upon that base of knowledge to innovate new technologies that are even better herself. But that's something you're not capable of as of right now, right?"

"Right." Naoto nodded. *Yeah, that's something that'd be absolutely impossible for me as I am right now. Naoto Miura can only come up with the answer to existing questions; he can't come up with any new questions to answer himself.*

Giovanni continued, "It's true that you have a rare talent which ordinary people could never hope to attain. But if all you do with it is try to imitate 'Y', then let me inform you in no uncertain terms: you could be replaced in any number of ways."

"..."

"So you can analyze the structure of any machinery, even a core tower, just by listening carefully? I see, that's amazing. It's a special ability that warrants international caution, for sure. But a group of elite clocksmiths could do the same thing, given enough time. The only difference is that you can do it in several minutes, all by yourself. Of course, that difference in efficiency is equivalent to immense sums of money. However, they would also be able to record the information they gather in a way that can be shared with all clocksmiths."

"...I can't do that, either."

"Right." Giovanni nodded. "The accumulation of tiny defects in the planet's mechanisms has caused there to be some impairments in their functions, but even so, the planet is still running as a whole. Even without you, the planet's mechanisms can at least be maintained. It's simply a difference of time and resources. But something that can be reproduced with enough time and money can't be called a divine feat."

The old man smiled, then nodded again. "That's why you can rest easy, boy. While it's true that you have a special aptitude, it's not as big a deal as the news these days would have you believe. It's nothing that your young miss should be jealous about, either— at least, not yet."

"Is that right, now?" Naoto couldn't help but smile. Objectively speaking, he was just told some very harsh things; despite that, what he felt right now was neither despair nor resignation.

*Now that I'm sure that this intuition of mine is correct, the rest is... Naoto laughed bitterly. "Yeah, I feel reassured now. But..." A question had suddenly popped into his head. "Despite your high praise for her just now, weren't you quite an ass to her in person?"*

"Well, sorry for being a petty old geezer," Giovanni said, his face souring. "It isn't so much that I'm reluctant to admit that a little brat who could be my granddaughter is a far greater clocksmith than myself...but I'm not so senile yet that I could play the part of a kind old man without feeling awkward."

Naoto burst out laughing. "That's why you provoked her like that?"

"Sure is. A brat blessed with more talent and better circumstances than me comes to me and brazenly gives me this, 'I'm not good enough, so please lend me a hand' crap. How disrespectful is that? She may be a brilliant youngster, but she ought to work harder before expecting luxury."

Unable to restrain himself any longer, Naoto began laughing so hard that he bent over and had to hold his sides to try to stop.

*This grandpa is suuuch a character.*

Seeing Naoto convulse with laughter without saying anything, Giovanni said, "But I should correct you on one thing." He pointed to his automaton companion who was standing next to him and continued, "I had no intention of being an ass. All I did was tell her the truth—Nono?"

"Si—" Nono opened up the trunk case she had been pulling around. Naoto looked at what was inside with a puzzled face at first...but then his jaws dropped.

He was sure that it would be a measurement device or a

machine tool, but in reality it was something completely different. The thing that was enclosed in a transparent case and looked akin to the spine and ribs of humans, was...

"A mainframe for an automaton?"

As far as Naoto knew, it didn't fit the model of any maker. It was complete haute couture. As it wasn't in operation at the moment, even Naoto couldn't guess the details of its functionality, but considering its size, which looked like it would be just right for a young girl automaton...

"No way! Is this for AnchoR?!"

"Once my work was canceled, I had a little time to kill before they brought me here. I guess I can be honest with you now: it was a job I wanted to jump on immediately, once I had the time. You guys challenged me to make something better than what 'Y' did. If I didn't take it up, I wouldn't be able to call myself a clocksmith, would I?"

*Impossible. "A little time to kill"? It's only been two days! The amount of time he would have had to work on it should have been one night at most. Actually, before that...*

"Master...could it be that you've tinkered with AnchoR's parts before?"

"No. That was the first time I saw an Initial-Y series. Like any other clocksmith, I do want to open one of them up and see their inner workings at least once in my life, though."

"Then how did you make this?!" Naoto yelled out half-impulsively. *He hasn't had the chance to analyze her structure, and it's not like there's a detailed spec sheet for AnchoR he could have used as reference for her mainframe, either. Just how did he make a mainframe for AnchoR, despite that?*

Giovanni broke into a gleeful smile. "I was able to see her moving right in front of me when you guys came to my workshop, up close and personal. For me, that's more than enough."

*There's no way such a thing could be true,* Naoto thought. *It might be just barely believable if we were talking about a mass-market model automaton, but we're talking about an Initial-Y here. We're talking about AnchoR.*

Naoto knew just how complicated and delicate AnchoR's structure was better than anyone else.

*Common sense would dictate that there's no way this thing could be compatible with her. At least, that should be the case...yet I'm almost sure this is going to work. As unbelievable as it is, that's the feeling I get.*

"Master..."

"This mainframe should allow that little pipsqueak to function without a hitch. As for the parts you should connect to it, if that miss has racked her brains about it, she should already have it figured out."

"What a terrible joke." Feeling completely blindsided, Naoto held his head and groaned, "You show me something like this, yet claim that Marie is a better clocksmith than yourself? If she heard you say that, she'd go absolutely ballistic. I could even see her dying from all her rage."

*There's no doubt that her screech would resound throughout this entire grid.*

Giovanni shrugged with the expression of a child who had just succeeded in a prank. "What I said was that, *comprehensively speaking*, she's undoubtedly a better clocksmith than me. But I would proudly assert that, when it comes to this specific field, I'm a better clocksmith than 'Y', even."

"..."

Naoto had no objections. Of course he wouldn't. After all, the unquestionable proof of that was staring right at him.

"Let me guarantee it. As clocksmiths, you two have more talent than the rest of the entire world—but I'm an *artigiano*, you know? And in this specific field, the difference in ability between you two and myself are like heaven and earth." Giovanni smiled. "I told you guys, didn't I? That I wasn't doing any work an amateur could possibly help with."

# ● Chapter Three / 11 : 00 / Pedrolino

THE CENTRAL, eastern, and southern marketplaces made up the three primary markets in Shangri-La Grid.

These markets offered everything from everyday necessities like food and clothes, to real estate, mechanical parts for automata among other things, and of course, stuff like weapons, drugs, and slaves—all sorts of business, both legal and illegal, was conducted in these venues managed by Market.

Similarly, in the western part of the city was an entertainment district managed by Restaurant.

Behind the scintillating businesses which sold alcohol, drugs, and sex were those that dealt in human trafficking, organ harvesting, and even "furniture" made with human parts. The district was a cesspool of evil and degeneracy that monopolized a part of the black market whose sellers and buyers would be punished to the full extent of the law and beyond in any other grid.

Currently, the head of Market was a man called Don Carlos.

Meanwhile, the boss of Restaurant was a woman known as Mother Angela.

Each of them was, respectively, the head of one of the three main syndicates in the city—figures who ruled Shangri-La Grid along with Arsenal's Kiu Tai Yu, but in reality, almost nobody in the city bothered to consider them.

All things considered, it hadn't even been half a year since the two of them rose to their respective positions, and no one believed that the two would still be in said positions half a year from now, either.

The general consensus among the city's residents was that the ruler of Shangri-La Grid was Kiu Tai Yu and his organization, Arsenal, which was headquartered at the city's core tower and had branches at each of the city's clock towers. That said, it was nonetheless true that the other two were still leading figures in the city at the moment.

If the two of them were to meet face to face out in the open, word would quickly get out that the state of affairs in Shangri-La Grid was about to be shaken up drastically. As the bosses of two of the city's three top syndicates, neither of them could avoid having their actions scrutinized by the city's residents.

As such, the two of them stealthily met up at a lonesome bar on the outskirts of the city, bringing along as few bodyguards as they could get away with.

"Looks like Kiu Tai Yu's made his move, the crazy bastard," Don Carlos spat out.

He was a hulk of a man, his giant body teeming with muscles.

His light brown skin was covered in tattoos everywhere, from his face to his arms and legs. They were given to him by the Latin American mafia group that backed him, as a symbol of their kinship.

"Oh? You made a move knowing that this was a possibility, didn't you, my boy?" Mother Angela replied as she puffed her pipe with a smile.

She looked to be about the age of a young girl who had just entered primary school, so the black and white habit she was wearing looked awfully mismatched. Despite how she was dressed, the coquettish expression in her eyes, the suggestive makeup she was wearing, and her friendly, flirtatious demeanor could hardly be seen as anything but the traits of an experienced prostitute.

Considering the anti-aging technology available in the city, it wouldn't be surprising if, in reality, she was a grandma who was over a hundred years old.

"You think you're not involved? If this continues, you'll fall into ruin as well."

"Ah yes, that's it. That's what I wanted to hear." Angela paused to tap her pipe against the ashtray, then continued, "I heard that Kiu personally made his way to the agent's den. I take it that the ploy to try to forge a relationship with Second Ypsilon by buying off that agent was yours, yes?"

"That's right," Carlos replied as he nervously rubbed the fingers of both his hands past each other. "But you tacitly agreed, fully knowing about it. Don't act dumb with me when his mistress was raised by you."

"Yeah. She was killed though, unfortunately," Angela muttered as she narrowed her eyes. "Shirley, you poor girl... Kiu is so violent, though. I wonder if he even realizes just how much money was spent on that girl's plastic surgery. It's a big loss for me."

"Who cares about your whores? The problem is, he's found out that we've broken the pact—and without us gaining anything in return, at that. If things continue like this, he'll be the sole winner in all of this."

"My, but the only one who broke the pact is you, isn't it? It's true that I had looked after Shirley, but it's not like I gave her any specific orders."

"Ohhh?" Carlos uttered with an openly mocking expression, then snarled. "Are you suggesting that you've got nothing to do with it, then? Are you going to insist to the bitter end that the girl being there was just a mere coincidence?"

"What bitter end? I'm simply telling the truth."

"Do you think he'd buy that excuse of yours?"

"Let's say that she *was* a spy, for argument's sake. So what? Sending spies into a rival's turf is hardly anything special."

"That's your justification? Hah, if you seriously plan to use that excuse, you might as well suck him off instead. If you're going to beg for his mercy, you'd have more of a chance doing that."

"Well, if he'd actually let me, I *am* confident that I could give him a pretty good time, but..." Angela said as she wrapped her tongue around her pipe's mouthpiece and sucked. *Chk.* She smiled. "Well, fine, I guess. It doesn't do me any good to play a game of psychological cat-and-mouse with you, anyway. I'll admit it. It's true that I was planning to break the pact and forge an alliance with them myself, should the opportunity have risen. I'm a woman who made it to where I am today starting as a mere call girl, you know? Of course I've got ambition in me."

Angela and Carlos's eyes locked. At the end of the day, Kiu Tai Yu was an obstacle to these two. So long as he lived, the two of them couldn't become the true rulers of the city, and that was hardly the end of it. If they just stood by with their arms folded, they'd lose their current positions before half a year was up. It wouldn't be strange at all if it happened by assassination, either.

*I have to do something.*

And that was when Second Ypsilon barged onto the scene.

A group of wandering terrorists mighty enough to have led the Japanese military by their nose...not taking the opportunity simply wasn't an option.

To that end, Don Carlos made the first move. He had bought off Arsenal's agent, whom Second Ypsilon had made contact with, and had the agent try to lure them into allying themselves with him.

Mother Angela had sent a prostitute in her care to become the agent's mistress, so the girl could keep an eye on the state of affairs while trying to win over Second Ypsilon for her. If that didn't work out, she had planned to guard herself from any fallout by proactively reporting Market's actions to Kiu.

However, that plan was crushed by Kiu Tai Yu, who had anticipated everything. Not only that, he successfully took the opportunity of the mess to make Second Ypsilon his allies.

Carlos' face turned bright red with anger. He said resentfully, "I won't let him do as he pleases any longer. I'm not going to let him continue to fatten up while I just look on with my thumb in my mouth. We have to make a move somehow."

"Well then, we only have one option left. Kiu only captured one of the two heads of Second Ypsilon. If we can drag the remaining one into our side, we'll be able to put up a fight against him."

"Exactly. But is the rumor that the little brat is Marie Bell Breguet really true? Isn't that girl the one who's supposed to have died?"

"Yes; it's basically an open secret at this point. It's probably safe to say, given their respective résumés, that Second Ypsilon depends on this little missy for their clocksmithing needs far more than the boy. Frankly, I'm surprised to hear that you didn't know this, Carlitos," Angela razzed with a smirk on her face.

Carlos replied with a sour face, "Our organization is based in Latin America. Things that happen in Asia's boonies are outside of my expertise."

"We're out in one of those boonies right now, you know, boy. If the head of the organization that controls the flow of money and information in the city is so poorly informed, then we're really in trouble. Are you sure there isn't something going on without your knowledge at Market?"

"How nice of you to ask. But even Market's not a monolith. If I had tried to find out by carelessly asking within the organization, there's a chance that a spy would have leaked to Kiu what I was up to. That's exactly why we need more power right now to pull ahead."

"Stuck between a rock and a hard spot, huh..." Angela said with a bitter smile. However, she wasn't so immune herself from problems within her own organization.

She might have a tighter rein over Restaurant than Carlos did over Market, but that didn't change the fact that the primary constituents of her organization were whores and their pimps, junkies, and back-alley doctors—all worthless trash who devoted their lives to the impulsive pursuit of pleasure. They could hardly be counted upon.

That was precisely why she had sought to attain an ability to execute a reliable chain of command that could rival the other two organizations.

"Where's that little girl right now?" Don Carlos asked.

"At Pandora's Inn. Seems she's returned to their rooms. But I wouldn't try to abduct her by force right this moment if I were you. She's got Initial-Y automata guarding her."

"I was told that their master is the boy and not the girl, though?"

"That's what I heard as well. From what I can tell, Kiu probably has some sort of trump card against them."

"A trump card?" Carlos asked with a skeptical face.

Angela sighed. "Use your head a little, would you? As crazy as Kiu is, he wouldn't be stupid enough to challenge two Initial-Y series automata to a straight-up fight, right?"

"Hm? Well, that's true, but..."

"In other words, Kiu must have some sort of trump card that he's using to hold them back from rescuing their master. Now, listen to me. We need to look for the right time to make a move."

"I see what you're trying to say. In short, we need to make Kiu use up his trump card, then strike when the Initial-Y automata stop guarding the girl, right?"

"That's how it is." Angela nodded as she threw her chest out.

Internally, however, she was groaning. *I'd heard that the guy was a meathead, but to think that a guy like this could become the head of Market...*

*"Whoever takes charge now won't last long anyway, so just have a bumbling idiot take up the reins for now." So said an executive from Market's parent organization in a closed meeting, according to one of my little birds. And it appears to be true.*

*If I don't take charge here, even a promising plan would end up failing. If that led only to his own demise, then whatever, but as things stand, he'd end up dragging me down with him. I'm simply not going to have that.*

*...Hmm, disposing of him now might be an option as well.*

Restaurant's head continued on with the secret meeting as she worked through various considerations in her head: how the labor and risk matched up to the potential reward; the point at which she should abandon ship and cut her losses; how she could ensure her own safety in the worst-case scenario.

· · ● ● ·

Meanwhile, at Pandora's Inn...

After Halter took Naoto away with him, Marie returned to their hotel and confined herself to the workshop in their suite, working silently on AnchoR's repairs posthaste.

It'd been two days since then.

During that whole time, Marie didn't consume anything besides jelly drinks. She had continued to work nearly nonstop, with very little sleep or breaks in between.

However, she was still currently struggling with repairing the mainframe's distortion, which wasn't all that surprising, considering how badly it was bent.

She was just about finished with all the repairs apart from that, however. She had restored AnchoR's missing limbs, replaced her damaged shock absorbers, and rethreaded her damaged nerve wires.

The repairs she had done should have been nearly perfect. However, she could already see the mainframe still causing problems if she were to hook everything up to it now.

Combat maneuvers were completely out of the question. If AnchoR rashly tried to fight anyway, all the burden would be placed solely on her distorted mainframe now that her other parts were all fully restored, which could very well result in her mainframe finally breaking.

"...Damn it, I'm at my wits' end."

Having used every last bit of brainpower and done all she could, Marie looked up and gazed at the ceiling. She flopped backwards onto the floor of the workshop without the strength left to stand back up.

As Marie continued gazing at the ceiling in a daze, RyuZU's face popped up in her field of view.

"I seem to recall," RyuZU began, "that two days ago, I heard you say something like, 'If I just fix AnchoR up, I can turn this situation around! All you who dared to mess with me, just you watch. I'm a woman who refuses to believe that anything's impossible!' with an awfully smug face. With that in mind, could I ask you to share how you are feeling now?"

"Don't bully me..." Marie whimpered. She didn't even have the energy to fight back anymore.

It went without saying that she had tried everything there was to try. Continuing to try to tackle the problem with the same approach wouldn't lead to any results. To progress beyond the current state required a decisive breakthrough of some sort.

"There's a chance I might hit upon something if I went with brute force trial and error, but it'd be a gamble at best. And one with worse odds than winning the EuroMillions lottery, at that."

"I would imagine so. At present, we are lacking in everything."

"We don't have the luxury of taking our time with it either, yet."

"Well, there is really no need for you to feel discouraged, you know, Mistress Marie," RyuZU said with a gentle smile. "I never expected anything from you to begin with anyway, so this outcome was within my expectations as well. Should you have somehow surprised me with success, however, I was seriously prepared to prostrate myself before you in disgrace...but, well, miracles are called miracles because they do not occur in reality."

"That so? Guess I shouldn't have tried so hard then, huh?" Marie growled with her eyes half-closed, then sighed. She gathered herself and said with a serious expression, "There's no choice but to shelve the plan to restore AnchoR into a combat force for us."

"It appears so, yes."

"In that case, having you conduct a blitz operation would be the fastest way to rescue Naoto, but..." Marie muttered.

RyuZU shrugged and said dispassionately, "With all due respect, Mistress Marie, if I were to leave your side under the present circumstances, some kind of ruffian would probably show up here before even a few minutes have gone by. If you are fine with that, then so am I. But I cannot let AnchoR get caught up in the mess as well."

"I know that."

Indeed, Marie understood the current situation. Right now, she was just a hindrance to everyone.

If it were purely a contest of power, the factions in Shangri-La Grid posed no threat whatsoever. They wouldn't even need to restore AnchoR into fighting shape. Simply letting RyuZU run amok for, say, a little less than an hour would be enough to neutralize all the soldiers and arms in the city.

If they had Marie's technical skills and Naoto's hearing, they could even seize control over the grid itself.

That was why Marie had thought they could manage, even if they were to make enemies of the entire world.

That's what she *had thought,* anyway.

"...I know," Marie repeated herself. *Just like Halter said, I got carried away.*

*That confidence of mine was easily shattered. All our counterplays were sealed, just like that. Was our seemingly unrivaled strength always this frail in reality?*

*...That might indeed be true.*

*It's like Halter said: "If there's someone out there who truly wants to eradicate our group, then things like combat or technical prowess don't mean a damn thing. There are any number of ways someone could eliminate us."*

*Now that I think back on it, that might have been him giving me a cautionary warning in his own way. Or perhaps, a preliminary notice of what was to come.*

Chewing over that fact once again, Marie let out a deep sigh.

*Halter betrayed me. The rut that we're stuck in is probably something that Halter intentionally manufactured.*

*If what they were after was Second Ypsilon's technical strength, they could have taken me with them instead.*

*The reason they deliberately chose Naoto over me was the result of a thorough, rational, and calm analysis. They understood that if they just restrained Naoto, they could completely neutralize our ability to fight.*

*If they had hypothetically taken me instead, RyuZU would surely have acted without hesitation.*

*And if Naoto were in my place right now, he could use his hearing to uncover the enemy's location and numbers, and use that knowledge to come up with the optimal rescue plan.*

*Despite our reputation as unstoppable terrorists who took on the world, Halter managed to drive a wedge into our "gears" with utmost precision...and he did it by judging me to be the weak link, at that.*

"That bastard!"

Thinking about it made Marie boil over with anger, feeding her thoroughly exhausted body with energy. However, there was nothing she could do about the present situation.

Marie had no choice but to wait for the tides to turn, even as she was burning up in fury.

· · • · ·

Naoto was walking through a dimly lit corridor, along with Giovanni and Nono.

However, it wasn't exactly the kind of hallway that one would typically associate with that word. They were walking through a compartment away from the central forum.

Enormous gears, cylinders, springs, and wires were clanking along all around them. The latticework supporting all these parts was as complicated as the skeletal structure of an organism.

Even with all the arduous walking they'd done, Naoto, Giovanni, and Nono had only made their way through but a mere fraction of the mechanisms that supported Shangri-La.

After lifting his foot to step over a large pipe running along the floor, Giovanni said, "Phew...my age is getting to me, it seems. Mind if we take a short break?" He paused, smiling wryly.

"The others can't see you here. We don't have to walk around like this just to buy time, right?"

Naoto stopped dead in his tracks, flinching. "Ha, ha, ha... what are you talking about?"

"No need to hide it from me," Giovanni continued with a softened expression. "You don't actually need to walk all over this core tower to grasp its structure. Simply staying in one spot and focusing silently on what you hear for a while should be enough. Am I wrong?"

He was not. In fact, Naoto had already grasped the entirety of the core tower. If he was up for it, he could probably seize control over the tower all by himself.

The reason he was still making rounds throughout the various floors under the guise of sounding things out was, as the old man had pointed out, simply to buy time.

Naoto fell silent, upon which Giovanni sat down on the pipe and said, "I'm not really chastising you. It's just that walking all over the place is a little tough on these old bones, you see."

Hearing that, Naoto finally relented and nodded. *Well, I'm guilty as charged.*

*It'd be difficult for me to escape by my own abilities. I have the feeling that trying would simply worsen the situation. Halter seems to have some sort of plan, but I have no idea what it might be.*

*AnchoR, and I guess Marie as well, should be fine with RyuZU to protect them, but I obviously have no way to contact them right now, so I don't know what their current status is, either.*

*For now, I figured I'd scrounge up as much time as I could to*

*give Marie and RyuZU some time to judge the situation before they*
*make a move together, regardless of what Halter's aim is.*

"You seem to be hesitating over something," Giovanni said
with the casualness of small talk.

"It's more like I'm stumped." Naoto nodded. "I can't imagine
it being a good idea to just obediently do as that crazy old man
says and give him the keys to the core tower."

"You're being threatened at gunpoint. There's no choice, is
there? Or do you not mind dying?"

"I do," Naoto immediately replied, "but even so, giving something that I know is dangerous over to a madman, then acting like
whatever happens has nothing to do with me, doesn't sit right
with me. Though frankly, I couldn't care less about this city itself."

"So in short, your conscience is bothering you?"

"Well...yeah, that's right."

"Looking at it objectively," Giovanni said, "Kiu Tai Yu is a
scoundrel, no mistake about that. He doesn't think anything
about killing people for his own benefit. Should you hand over
the keys to the core tower over to him, he'd surely use the tower
not for the city's interests, but his own, and end the lives of many
in the process."

"..."

"As bad as he is, though, you can't really call him a liar. It
might be hard for you to accept this, but in terms of keeping his
promises, you could even call the man virtuous."

"Seriously? *That* guy...?"

"He's honest in his dealings in the underworld, at least. Just

think about it. He's known as 'the man who doesn't lie,' you know?"
The old man paused to let the significance of that sink into
Naoto's head before continuing, "And Kiu's interests are directly
tied to this city's interests as a whole, as well. If he can strengthen
his control over the city, the city will become more stable. He may
be immoral, extremist, and vicious, but him being the one most
suited to supervise Shangri-La Grid is a matter of fact."

"So...are you saying you approve of that guy ruling over this
city, Master?"

"No," Giovanni denied readily, but then corrected himself,
"Well, that's not quite right, either. I'm the same as you—I don't
really care about what happens to this city itself. I just don't want
things getting too noisy around me, so I can concentrate properly
on my work."

"..."

Naoto recalled the children who had been murdered—or
rather, reflected upon them. After all, one couldn't say that he
was recalling them if he didn't even know their faces or names.

Still, the shrieks he heard back then were unforgettable.

He recalled the sinking weight he felt in his stomach when
Halter had asked him what that had to do with him. As sound as
Halter's cold call to abandon them to their fate was, it bothered
him relentlessly.

*Son of a bitch, Naoto thought as he hung his head down. The*
*hell am I supposed to do about something like this?*

"So basically, that man rubs you the wrong way, yes?" Giovanni
asked.

"...Yes."

"Well then, it's simple, isn't it? Just don't obey his orders," the old man said like it was nothing.

Naoto opened his mouth dumbfoundedly. Without thinking, he asked, "Master, aren't you supposed to be keeping tabs on me, if only in name?"

"Of course. That's the job I've taken on. I'll tell you now that if you're going to try to escape, then sorry, but I won't let you. That said..." The old man paused. "Frankly, the structure of this core tower in its entirety is way too complex for me to grasp. In other words, if you just stay here and work obediently, there's no way for me to check whether what you make will actually fulfill Kiu's demand. And that goes for the blockheads on the first floor as well."

Naoto gulped audibly. "So basically, even if I make something completely different..."

"I'm a professional, which is why, on the pride of my reputation, I never cut corners on a job I've accepted. But as shabby as my workshop may be, I still have the right to kick out customers I don't like, so..." Giovanni suddenly changed the subject. "What do you think of 'Y'?"

"What do you mean?"

"He—or maybe he was a she, or a they—whatever the case, do you reckon that the entity behind the reconstruction of this planet considered questions like what their creations might ultimately lead to?"

Naoto's face was blank, to which the old man smiled bitterly and said, "Unlike you, I can't fathom the entirety of a core tower. However, from my many years of experience...how should I put it...I can at least pick up on what the maker was thinking when I look at a mechanism, or so I like to think."

"What the maker was thinking...?"

"Yes...what he was thinking, what he had wished for, what goal he had in mind in making it. The textbooks say that 'Y' reproduced the world with gears to save humanity from the brink of extinction, but...personally, I hardly see how that could be true."

Giovanni paused, extending his right arm towards Naoto. He was holding a clockwork mechanism that had been turning without pause for a thousand years.

"Look at this bizarre mechanism! Can you sense any consideration whatsoever towards those who might try to maintain it down the line? And add to that the fact that 'Y' disappeared after forcing such technology into posterity without explaining the set of theories behind how he made it!"

Indeed, "Y" had left zero clues behind. Not a single theory, discovery, proof, or even a scribbled note of his was known to exist.

He had suddenly appeared out of nowhere, and left behind things that no one could understand.

"To me, it sounds like this is what he's saying: 'I thought of something interesting and felt like I could actually materialize it, so I gave it a try and it was fun. You guys can take care of the rest.' That's the kind of childishness I sense emanating from it."

"Yeah, good point. I agree." Naoto nodded.

*I agree completely. Stuff like rescuing humanity or prolonging the life of the planet doesn't seem like something "Y" would do. If I were "Y," such secondary concerns probably wouldn't even cross my mind when making something as grand as the Clockwork Planet.*

Giovanni said, "In the end, I'm but a humble professional. I give my customers what they want in exchange for fair pay and I do my work with pride. That's why I can't just give stuff away for free. If I were to make something that no one's ordered just to flaunt my skills, that would disqualify me as a professional. However," he sighed, "was 'Y' a professional clocksmith? Did our ancestors pay 'Y' a fair price? If he wasn't paid, then the Clockwork Planet we live on still belongs to him. It'd mean we're mere tenants of this planet, not owners."

His tone matched his dismissive words. However, Naoto sensed a complex array of emotions underneath it. Respect, admiration, a target to compare himself to...or perhaps someone he can't lose to as a real clocksmith, with the pride of one as well.

Naoto asked, "Then, what was 'Y' in your eyes?"

"Someone who simply created as he wished, showing off his skills without being asked or receiving compensation." Giovanni smiled bitterly. "That's what we call an artist. Or, at the very least, someone who acts solely according to his own curiosity and taste. He can't be called a professional by any means. Now then," Giovanni said as he stood up.

He straightened his posture and gazed at Naoto with his amber eyes as he calmly asked, "On the flip side, who are you? A *spettatore*, pursuing the full understanding of 'Y's' creation?

An *artigiano*, who fulfills his customers' requests? Or an *artista*, who gives form to the things he wants to see in the world?"

The answer was obvious.

There was no way that Naoto would be satisfied with just following in another's footsteps, nor could he tell the embarrassing lie that the things he'd done up to now were for someone else's sake.

That was true for both himself and Marie.

He had tried to do what he wanted, how he wanted—that was all there was to it.

"I see..." Everything suddenly fell into place in Naoto's mind. He felt almost as if gears within him that had slipped out of alignment had clicked together again perfectly. What he wanted to do became aligned with what he felt he should do.

He let out a sigh, then a little smile crept onto his face. Looking up, he saw a myriad of enormous parts intricately intertwined with each other, forming a small universe unto itself.

While facing the deep darkness above him, Naoto muttered, "*I know you're there*, old man Vermouth. Come out for a sec, won't you?"

A response came immediately.

"Oh my, you're askin' for me, son?"

A silhouette wove through the lattices and dropped down from the darkness. It was a beautiful blonde-haired automaton, turned into an artificial body for Vermouth. He had a disdainful grin on his face. "I'm surprised you realized I was here."

"I've already grasped this core tower's structure perfectly. If there's any noise that doesn't belong and that I've heard before,

240

I can tell what it is, even if I'd rather not. Anyway, why are you here?"

"I'd heard some dangerous rumors, y'see. Stuff like Market and Restaurant teaming up to topple Kiu Tai Yu, Arsenal getting its hands on an Initial-Y...and right, something about Second Ypsilon splitting apart due to a traitor making his move?"

"So I guess you know the rough situation." Naoto nodded.

Vermouth's grin grew wider and he said, "More or less. I'm just a weak little fly, so I can't risk letting anyone see me at a precarious time like this. That's why I hid myself here underground, where I've been gathering information while making certain *preparations*. I figured I might as well come and check to see if you're being picked on while I was at it."

"Wow, I think I'm going to cry tears of gratitude. It's a good thing you showed up when you did. There's something I want you to help me with."

"Sorry, but I can't help you escape, if that's what you want," Vermouth said in anticipation of what Naoto was going to ask. He looked apprehensively at the automaton standing silently next to Giovanni as he continued, "Ferrying a small piece of luggage like you out of here is doable, but this missy over here is way too much for me to handle."

"Wow, so you can tell, huh?" Naoto muttered with widened eyes.

Vermouth dropped his shoulders dejectedly. "Bullseye, huh? My last smoke tasted nasty, so I had a feeling," he sighed. "There's just this dangerous aura coming from her. If you underestimate her because of her appearance, you'll pay heftily for it. That's what my rock-hard intuition is telling me. A frightening missy, to be sure."

"Si— I am honored to receive your compliment," Nono said with a courteous bow.

"That wasn't a compliment," Vermouth muttered in annoyance.

Naoto laughed humorlessly, shaking his head. "In any case, I'm not talking about helping me escape. I'd like you to relay a message and a package to Marie for me."

"Hmmmm? I'm fine with that, but is this grandpa here going to let me?" Vermouth questioned.

Giovanni nodded with a regal air and said, "I don't mind. I was told to keep tabs on the boy so he doesn't escape, but they didn't mention that I should stop him from contacting others."

"You're splittin' hairs, Grandpa."

"Is there even a single thing in human society that isn't justified through sophistry?" Giovanni replied with a still face.

"You got that right," Vermouth laughed.

As Naoto also burst into laughter, he turned around, then said, "Master, please let me buy the mainframe you made for AnchoR. As for the payment...I don't have cash on me right now, but I'll definitely pay you afterwards."

"You don't need to. If you want it, then you can have it. It's not like that thing can be used for any other purpose."

"Eh...? But Master, I thought you couldn't just give stuff away for free?" Naoto asked with a puzzled face.

"I can't take money for some half-assed work that I made in just one night without even taking measurements," Giovanni answered. "In this case, taking money for it would do far more damage to my reputation than giving it away." He snorted, then continued with a gentler expression, "If it bothers you, then bring the pipsqueak on over to my workshop again when you guys have her fixed. I'll grade that miss on how well she did as I make some fine-tunings."

"Grade?"

"Yeah. Should she have done a poor job, then you guys better prepare yourselves for a hefty bill."

"No worries about that. That girl's filthy rich, and besides," Naoto paused for a breath, then continued with a suggestive smile, "there's no way that that hysteric walking landmine, who's the sorest loser I've ever known, won't blow up upon seeing this."

"Well then, I guess I'll expect good things," Giovanni laughed.

Then, after Vermouth was entrusted with Naoto's message to Marie, he picked up the trunk case in which the mainframe for AnchoR had been stuffed and slipped into the darkness beyond the latticework once again.

As Naoto saw Vermouth off, he suddenly recalled something. He yelled out, "Ah...sorry, I forgot one last thing!"

"What, son?"

"If you happen to see old man Halter, tell him this for me..."

Upon hearing Naoto's message, Vermouth exploded in laughter before melting into the darkness for good this time.

· · • · ·

The core tower was surrounded by streets with clear views on all sides, forming something like a plaza.

There, peddlers without their own stores came in the morning and set up open stalls with their goods, together forming a disorderly market.

There was no real rhyme or reason to the items being sold. Beside elite goods and rare items being sold for dirt cheap was stuff that looked like junk, no matter how one looked at it, being bought at exorbitant prices.

The things being sold here were all potentially once-in-a-lifetime finds, but it was unclear whether they were authentic or not. In all honesty, neither the sellers nor the buyers really knew what they were dealing with—that's the kind of strange, feverish air this market had. In a way, one could say this place was a microcosm of the city as a whole.

In a corner of this chaotic market, a manhole that no one was paying attention to, like any other in the city, suddenly shifted.

"Phew, and an alley-oop..."

Vermouth silently crawled out from underground, carrying a big trunk case. Exactly how he found his way here being a mystery.

"Finally made it to the surface, huh. Geez, that was a lot of work..."

"Thanks, I truly appreciate it."

Vermouth froze immediately upon hearing the voice behind him and feeling a gun pressed against his back.

"...Why, hello there, Boss."

Vermouth sighed without turning around. He then made

sure to move slowly as he took his cigarette case out from his pocket. He took out a cigarette, lit it, and puffed, savoring the smoke he inhaled before spitting it out. "Not a very original question, I know," he asked, "but would ya mind sharing how you knew I'd be here, anyway?"

"There's not much to it, really. I was tailing you the whole time, so..." the voice from behind—Halter—replied.

Hearing that, Vermouth's expression turned serious. "The whole time?"

"Yeah—all the way from the time you snuck inside this core tower, to when you met Naoto, to popping out of this manhole."

Vermouth was so taken aback that the cigarette in his mouth nearly fell out.

*Give me a break, would ya?!*

He felt a headache come on, even when the sensation shouldn't be possible for his artificial body.

Halter's artificial body was a fifth-gen assault type model. In other words, it was specialized for fistfights on the battlefield and firing off enormous cannons. It was entirely different from stealth-type models that specialized in infiltrating enemy bases, in terms of both its operating noise level and functionality.

*You're telling me he snuck inside this core tower with a body like that? ...Furthermore, he did it with such stealth that even I didn't notice, despite my years of experience as a spy?*

Feeling utterly defeated, Vermouth muttered, "...Seriously? I was completely oblivious."

"Yeah. It took a fair bit of effort, though. After all, *'we all have our strengths and weaknesses,'* and one of my weaknesses is that I'm not that great at playing hide-and-seek."

"You're really putting me to shame as a former professional spy by saying that, you know. Man, so what is this all about in the end? Revenge for what I did the other day? Looks like you've got more passion in you than I thought, Boss."

"Not really. But I wasn't just going to let a greenhorn get away with underestimating me, either."

"Well, aren't you the mature one..."

*Fuck. I picked a fight with a monster,* Vermouth groaned internally. As he hung his head in regret, he tried to change the subject. "By the way, I hear you betrayed the little missy?"

"Yeah. Well, I think you already know this, but that's what the job entails, so..." Halter replied without even the slightest waver in his voice.

"Oh...what the job entails, huh?" Vermouth muttered.

"Something wrong with that?"

"So even a man of your caliber will do anything your job demands?"

"What, are you reproaching me for being a traitor? Honestly, I didn't think you were the type to care. Well, sorry to inform you, but I don't let my personal feelings interfere with my work. Just how I roll."

"Nah, Boss, I don't really have any beef with you. Frankly, I think I get what's really going on. You're doing it for the sake of those two kids, right?"

Halter neither confirmed nor denied it.

Vermouth sighed, continuing, "Either oppose Kiu Tai Yu and thrust this city into hell, or willingly cooperate with him. Those were the only two options, but the two of them wouldn't pick either. That's why you gave them the option to compromise. If you betrayed them, though, they wouldn't have a choice. Am I right?"

"…"

"Oh, right, and you deliberately chose such an underhanded method to warn them, right? As if to say, 'There are any number of ways to corner you guys, so you better keep your eyes peeled'. It's well established that children don't learn without pain, after all...ain't that right, Boss?"

Halter began calmly, "Well...yeah, so what?"

"Nothing, really. It just doesn't seem worth all the effort in my eyes," Vermouth continued as he curled his lips. "You and I are weapons, objects of destruction. *Should the need arise, we'll do anything. We'd be willing to do anything.* There are times when we'd shoot someone today who we put our lives on the line for yesterday."

That was something that Vermouth had personally experienced, in fact.

"We take orders from our masters and orders from their clients... Whether we like it or not, we have to obey. People like us have to be kept under someone or something else's control at all times. Otherwise, we wouldn't be able to live. We wouldn't be allowed to live—that's what defines a soldier, after all."

Vermouth looked backwards, turning only his neck.

"But, well...in your case, Boss, at least you chose this cruel fate yourself knowing full well what you were getting yourself into. Maybe you're better off than me still, in that regard?" Vermouth melancholically wondered aloud.

"Are you an idiot?" Halter sniffed. "That's why you're third-rate, greenhorn."

"..."

"First-rate pros manipulate the circumstances so they never have to follow orders that go against their will. They'd never be in a situation where they'd have to kill someone today who they put their lives on the line for yesterday, because they would have seen it coming and killed the guy who would give them such an order yesterday."

Vermouth asked with widened eyes, "You're saying to betray the client?"

"No. I'm saying to kill him before he orders a job from your master. Listen up," Halter said from the other side of the gun. "It goes without question that we don't have much choice in the jobs we're offered, but not choosing at all is what a third-rate does. When you learn to pick the jobs you want, you finally become second-rate. You only become first-rate once you learn to create your own jobs. Mark that in your head, greenhorn."

Dumbfounded, Vermouth muttered, "I see... That was en-lightening." He nodded, then asked, "By the way, does that mean that the job you're doing right now is a first-rate one?"

Halter neither confirmed nor denied it.

Vermouth couldn't tell what the truth was just from his

expression, either. As he studied him with keen eyes, Halter lowered the gun, to Vermouth's surprise. "Oh...? What's this? You gonna let me go?"

"Let you go? Seems you've misunderstood something. I simply happened to see a greenhorn who gave his senior attitude, so I figured I ought to take him aside for a short lecture. It's not like anyone's going to pay me even pocket change for capturing you."

"Well, thanks for that...and for the words of wisdom, as well," Vermouth muttered as he lifted up the trunk case by his feet. He then turned around suddenly and said, "Oh, right, so you were there when I was speaking with Naoto?"

"Pretty much."

"Well then, you probably don't need me to relay this to you, but I'll say it just in case," Vermouth said as he gazed straight into Halter's eyes through his sunglasses, "'Tell the old man to do as he sees fit—as I'll be doing as I see fit.'"

Halter nodded, his expression unchanging. "Is that so?"

"Well, I've relayed the message as requested, so no one better blame me for anything. Later, then." Vermouth left while waving his hand lightly, blending into the crowd around them.

Having been left by himself, Halter muttered, "What I want to do, huh...?"

• • ● • •

Meanwhile, atop the roof of a small multi-tenant building along the side alley where Halter and Vermouth had just been,

a teenage girl with a sweet voice was talking to herself, unbe-
knownst to them.

"Hee hee...I was watching, you know."

Her voice was full of childish mischief, but she was nowhere
to be seen. Despite that, the rooftop was completely flat with nowhere to hide. There was nothing here but the sound of her giggling— correction: one could see an ever-so-slight shimmering in
the air if one strained one's eyes.

The shimmering faintly traced the figure of a person. Like a
curtain being blown up by the wind, the girl covered in a veil of
invisibility was visible one moment and gone by the next.

The identity of that fleeting figure was the peach-haired automaton, TemP. She was the Third of the Initial-Y series, Aerial,
also known as "the Fluttering Butterfly."

Through some kind of advanced mechanism, she was able
to allow light to pass right through her, remaining undetectable
by any optical sensor. She looked down at the alley below while
giggling.

*Ah, there's that blonde-haired automaton with the large suit-
case... Wait, no, I think the report said she's actually a male cyborg?*

Vermouth had returned to the main street. Upon locating
him in the crowd, TemP hopped to another rooftop as she began
to follow him.

At the same time, she muttered sullenly, "Goodness gracious,
and I've spent all this effort to come pay a visit to dear Elder Sister
too, yet no one will tell me where she is. Thank goodness, because
I was starting to wonder why I even bothered coming here at all."

It was about a month ago when she heard that the First—
RyuZU—had rebooted. Not only that, supposedly that elder sister of hers, whose heart was like an impregnable fortress, had even
found her first boyfriend and master in the same person.

TemP could barely contain herself upon learning the news,
and so she had said to the one who had repaired her, her master,
"I want to go pay my elder sister a visit."

"Haah...to be honest, I don't think there's really a point in
doing so. But well, if that's what you want, then sure, why not?"

He wouldn't try to restrict her in any way. He always let her
be free. Indeed, he even prepared transportation and lodgings for
her and sent her on her way with his blessing.

While enduring the tedious voyage, TemP looked forward
with anticipation to the impending reunion with two of her sisters. However, the local host who came to receive her wasn't to
her liking at all.

*For one thing, his choice of clothes is just awful. He has the worst
taste ever. And he wouldn't tell me where my sisters are. He came up
with all sorts of excuses whenever I asked.*

*So I thought, fine, I'll just go find Elder Sister's first boyfriend
and torment him instead, then...but he vetoed that, too. Actually,
thinking about her boyfriend makes me feel really frustrated, because
it felt like I was the one who got toyed with the first time we met!*

*He even had something to say when I just wanted to go outside
because I was getting sick of him: "You see, it's a very delicate situation
right now in the city. Please, could you take the hint already? Hm?
Do you understand what I'm saying? Hellooo? Do you hear me?"*

*What a rotten, naggy man he is. Just thinking about him makes me angry.*

"That person will never find a girlfriend," TemP muttered while rolling her eyes.

*But that ends today. That paltry human can cry all he wants. I'm not going to let him stop me. In the first place, I have no reason to obey him. If he won't tell me where my sisters are, then I'll just find out myself.*

And then, TemP had coincidentally come across a clue to finding her elder sister.

The ones who had been chatting in the side alley were cyborgs in the same troupe as her sisters. She'd seen their pictures from the files her master had showed her.

*I feel like it also said somewhere in there that one of them betrayed the group or something...but, well, whatever. Who cares about the small stuff? In any case, I should be able to find out where Elder Sister is if I tail that human.*

Rejoicing over her good fortune and praising her own cleverness, TemP chuckled gloatingly. "Oh ho ho, what should I do when I meet Elder Sister...?"

Her imagination went wild. *Should I make her grovel on the ground as I dig my boots into her head? Or should I force her to loudly admit defeat and respond with "What was thaaat? I couldn't hear you!" to really infuriate her?*

*Oh, or what if I steal Elder Sister's first boyfriend away from her? He tries to act like a player despite his dull looks, but he did have the eyes to see that I'm the number one prettiest girl in the world.*

*I won't even let him hold my hand despite taking him. I won't make the same shameful display as I did the first time. I'll be the one to toy with him this time. After I tantalize and torment him to my fill, I'll dump him right in the trash like a worn-out wash rag!*

"My my, getting in over your head, are we?"

"Did you really think that a plebeian like you would be allowed to associate with my noble self?"

"Ohh, you say you'll do anything? Then get on the ground right where you are and lick my boots."

*Ahh, how vulgar...but how wonderful that would be!*

"G-gosh...I'm such a wicked girl!" TemP blushed as she immersed herself in her decadent, out-of-control delusions. *Ah...*

"Agh, oh gosh, I was so caught up in my thoughts that I almost lost sight of the cyborg," TemP muttered as she kept track of the blonde-haired cyborg who was pushing through the crowd.

*Now that I think about it...*

"That person looked like a woman, but talked like a dirty old man, didn't she?" TemP mused. "I wonder...is that the modern way of giving yourself some character? ...Wait! Or is she one of those so-called c-c-cross-dressers?! She could be, right?!"

TemP widened her eyes in astonishment.

She had known that such people existed from reading manga and the like up until now, but this was the first time she found one in real life.

"M-most interesting... Th-this is, right, an expression of scholarly curiosity, if you will. So I'm obligated to get to the truth of the matter!"

· · • ● • · ·

"Hey, what are you trying to pull here?" Marie said with a sullen face.

She had collapsed onto the workshop floor and dozed off in her state of total exhaustion. That was the last thing she remembered before she fell asleep. Upon waking up, however, she found that someone had carried her to her bed.

To be more precise, she had been tightly *packed* inside a rolled-up futon that had been tied up. Not only that, she had been stripped of her clothes as well, for some reason.

Marie turned her head, the only part of her body that was free. She gave RyuZU the stink-eye. "Care to explain, RyuZU?"

"Of course. It was I who moved you to this futon," RyuZU, who had been sitting by Marie's bed with elegant posture, said with a nonchalant face. "At this point, the situation we face is such that there is nothing you can do about it anymore, Mistress Marie. If I may be frank, just you being here hinders me considerably."

"If you'd go so far as to say that, then why don't you just take AnchoR with you and go rescue Naoto? I wouldn't resent you for abandoning me, you know."

"I have given some thought to that, too," RyuZU said, nodding solemnly, "but I decided otherwise for three reasons. One, AnchoR is attached to you. Two, the situation is not so desperate yet that I must proactively dispose of you. And lastly, because Master Naoto probably would not wish for me to do so."

Marie blinked several times before asking, "What'd you say?"

"As I have already said, Master Naoto probably would not want me to abandon you."

Marie was left half in disbelief with her mouth open.

However, RyuZU frowned and continued in a firm tone, "I should add, just in case, that you should correct your false assumptions now if you are fancying that this may be due to Master Naoto having romantic feelings for you."

"That didn't cross my mind," Marie answered with a serious expression. She studied RyuZU's face as she asked, "Which makes it all the more baffling. Why?"

"Who knows? Though I can probably guess, leaking my master's private thoughts to others is awfully questionable behavior, so I am afraid I cannot answer you. If you really want to know, please ask Master Naoto yourself when he returns."

"True. I'll do just that, then. So, leaving that aside, think you could tell me why you've done this to me now?"

RyuZU shrugged slightly and said, "As I said just a few moments ago, the situation is out of your hands at this point, Mistress Marie. Presently, we have no choice but to simply wait for the direction of the wind to change. Given that to be the case, I believe you should at least rest sufficiently and store up your stamina in preparation, even if you cannot help being a hindrance right now."

"I guess you're right."

"Yes. Yet you chose to sleep on the cold, hard floor of all things, despite it being obvious that a warm, soft bed would provide much better rest, so I can only assume that you have lost the ability to take proper care of yourself, Mistress Marie."

"Huh? No, that's—"

"My loving care should be exclusively reserved for Master Naoto, so frankly I hate that I am stuck here babysitting you like this...but considering the situation, I decided that I had to be a little flexible in my policy."

Ignoring the dumbfounded look on Marie's face, RyuZU continued with a serious face, "First, I removed your clothes to help your body fully relax and wrapped you up in a futon to maintain a constant body temperature and improve your circulation, as futons are excellent at retaining warmth. I also asked room service to bring up some easily digestible foods earlier. I shall take it upon myself to replenish your body with the nutrition it needs."

"Wait, are you saying that you're going to feed me hand-to-mouth?!"

"Of course. You have not ingested any solid foods these past few days, Mistress Marie. As you have apparently lost the ability to take care of yourself, should you begin to gorge on food like a starved rat without any restraint, your digestive system would surely be heavily stressed. In the worst case, you could even die, so..."

"What, are you kidding me?! No way! Untie the futon now!"

"Once you have been sufficiently nourished, we will then be washing your entire body, so please wait until then."

"You even plan to take care of my bathing for me?! You're just doing this to bully me, aren't you?! The stress of simply waiting for the tides to turn is getting to you, so you're trying to relieve it by messing with me, aren't you? I know you are!!"

"That is what is called an unfair accusation. As I mentioned to you just now, my loving care is solely dedicated to Master Naoto, so I really am babysi—no, *rearing* an animal like yourself with much reluctance."

"You're clearly going out of your way to spite me!!"

Just then, there was a knock on the door, then a polite voice called out, "Excuse me, this is room service. I have a delivery for you."

"A delivery...?" *Marie furrowed her brows, perplexed. I thought what she ordered was food?*

Marie gazed at RyuZU with a cautionary look. It looked like RyuZU was on the same page, for she cautiously approached the door without making a sound, upon which she looked through the peephole and tilted her head.

"Well now, your words were clearly suspicious, so I thought it was an enemy for sure, but...actually, you are in fact an enemy, yes?"

"Oy oy, isn't that going too far, miss dolly? Be a little more welcoming, won'tcha?"

Hearing that impudent voice, Marie also realized who it was. It was Vermouth. RyuZU opened the door, upon which he came inside with a bar cart, sporting a hotel uniform that he had somehow gotten his hands on.

He surveyed the room with a broad smirk on his face. Upon finding Marie wrapped up like a sushi roll, he said, "'Sup, missy? Hope you've been faring— What, so you were in the middle of kinking out, eh? I don't mind coming back later, if you'd prefer."

"That's absolutely not what's going on here!"

"It is as Mistress Marie says. I have no obligation to fulfill her outlandish fetishes, after all."

Vermouth laughed flippantly as he raised both hands defensively, "Hahah! I guess that was rude of me, then. I get it already, so stop howling."

Marie shot him a dark gaze. "Vermouth, just what've you been up to while we've been facing such a dire situation?"

"Oh, my. What, were you counting on me, bitch? Guess I should apologize, then."

"Huh?! In your dreams, you fucking idiot!"

"Ha ha! Seems that Boss has left you in quite the dumps from the looks of it, huh?"

"You know what happened?" Marie asked.

Vermouth smirked faintly and shrugged. "These eyes and ears came in handy, so thanks for fixing them up. Well, it's true that it isn't exactly something that everyone knows, but I've gotten the general gist of things."

"...I see."

"Actually, I met with him just now," Vermouth added casually.

Marie's face immediately paled. Meanwhile, RyuZU glared at Vermouth with darts in her eyes.

As the air filled with tension, Vermouth raised and shook both hands defensively. "Don't be jumping to conclusions, now. He threw me into the dumpster, too, as expected of the legend himself. I was reminded of why I admired him in the first place."

"What legend?" Marie muttered. *He's just a traitor,* Marie grumbled internally.

Seeing that, Vermouth raised an eyebrow, then couldn't help but laugh, "Hahah! Could it be that you still don't get it, missy?"

"Get what?"

"Listen up. It's not like Boss is the number one specialist in the world, you know. Ranged combat, stealth operations, piloting mobile suits, making explosives, medical knowledge, and clock-smithing...sure, he's at a pretty high level in all those areas, but you could still find plenty of guys better than him if you looked around."

"So what?"

"Not very sharp, are you? My point is, he was still known as a legendary mercenary despite that." Vermouth erased the smirk on his face before continuing with a serious face, "No matter what kind of monster or hero you are, a single bomb dropped from above you at an unpredictable time, and you're one with the earth again. It doesn't matter whether you're a genius or an average Joe, a rookie or a veteran. Boss has the full understanding of that merciless reality carved into his very bones, because he *survived* it."

In other words...

"Knowing exactly what his abilities are, choosing the right allies as well as the right enemies, assessing both his immediate surroundings and the overall flow on the battlefield from a bird's eye view standpoint...he worked his brain coolly in situations where his head might have been blown away at any moment, giving both his enemies and his allies a wild ride. In the end, he handed over only his enemies to the reaper."

By picking the optimal methods and giving his best, yet at

the same time still accepting the merciless reality that there were some things he just couldn't do anything about, Halter would always fight to the very end until fortune smiled upon him at last.

"He dominated both his immediate surroundings and the overall flow of the battlefield. He would put together the stage and the script before the battle even began and thus ensure victory. That's why some called him Vainney Halter Oberon, while others..." Vermouth paused for a breath. "Others referred to him jokingly as the absolute war machine: *Overwork*."

His voice filled with admiration and envy, Vermouth smiled again and asserted, "Yet you think such a master would sell you guys out for chump change? Yeah, I doubt it. A script like that ain't fit for his stage."

"You're saying...that Halter didn't betray us?"

"Well well, who knows? I haven't read the plot summary that Boss wrote yet. If he deemed it necessary, it's possible he might have betrayed you for real, you know?"

"This conversation is meaningless," RyuZU muttered indifferently. "That junkbot abducted Master Naoto and handed him over to an enemy. That is all I understand, and all I need to understand in order to decide how I should deal with him."

"Sure, have it your way. I'm sure he's factored your reaction into his calculations, anyway. Though I doubt he'd show himself while he knows you're out to get your claws in him."

"Well then, I only have to dig him out."

"As you please. Well, that aside, I've got a delivery for you guys. Could I get a stamp or a signature?"

"A delivery...? That wasn't just a pretext?" Marie asked, tilting her head.

Vermouth smiled suggestively and carefully dragged the large trunk out from the bar cart, then opened it up nonchalantly.

Marie gulped upon seeing what was inside. "Don't tell me that this is..."

*...the mainframe for an automaton?*

Standing next to her, RyuZU also widened her eyes, unable to hide her surprise. "Judging by its size, is it for AnchoR? ...But who could have made it?"

"Naoto had a message for you: 'I bought it from the master on credit. You can take care of the rest, right? If you do a poor job we'll have to pay a premium, and you're footing the bill. All right then, don't disappoint us.'"

"That bastard," Marie growled as she grit her teeth hard. A curious blend of excitement, rage, and confusion assaulted her heart.

The fire that was deep inside her heart had been reduced to a smolder, but was now fully reignited. Marie shouted, "You dare look down on me? I'll show you, all right!"

Suddenly, RyuZU flinched before turning her head backwards, her expression grim. "Well then, let us make haste, as it seems an enemy attack has arrived," she warned.

CLOCKWORK
PLANET

## ● Chapter Four / 15 : 30 / Arlecchino

**A**S TENSION FILLED THE AIR, Marie asked, "By 'enemy', you mean an assassin from Arsenal?"

"No. If it were mere riffraff like that, there would not be any problem at all. It appears, however, that a bungling younger sister of mine has sniffed us out."

"Your younger sister? Then that means..." Marie trailed off, the hairs on her body standing on ends.

RyuZU nodded. "Yes. She's one of the Initial-Y series."

Upon RyuZU's confirmation, Vermouth also shuddered all over. *Sure, I'd seen this coming to some extent when I found out from a reliable source that Arsenal had gotten its hands on an Initial-Y... but still, what's up with this timing?*

*What merit is there to attack us at this time? There is none. In fact, it'd be just what Market and Restaurant want as they try to find an opening. Or is that precisely Arsenal's aim...? No, now's not the time to think about this. We have to deal with the current situation first.*

RyuZU dispatched one of her black scythes and cut the string that had been holding the futon wrapped around Marie together. "Mistress Marie, I request that you finish AnchoR's repairs as swiftly as possible. This younger sister of mine may be foolish, prideful, narrow-minded, and mediocre, but she is a threat when it comes to combat strength."

"Got it. Leave it to me."

"Thank you, I will. Now then..." RyuZU turned around and walked towards the window, whereupon she stepped onto the sill, then leapt out into the air. She flew across the street before silently landing on the rooftop of a building on the other side.

Vermouth pulled out an automatic rifle he had hidden in the cart, then likewise followed after RyuZU with a bit of a late start.

When he landed on the opposing rooftop, however, there was a loud thud.

"S'up. I'll be backing you up a little. I wouldn't be doing anything useful if I stayed back there, anyway."

"I do not recommend it, but do as you please," RyuZU replied curtly, without turning to look at him. Her eyes were focused on a certain automaton that was standing on top of a water tank, looking down at them.

It was an automaton in the form of a teenage girl, dressed in a punk lolita-style dress.

"Mwahaha...it has been a while, hasn't it, Elder Sister?" the girl said with a chilling smile.

RyuZU called out the girl's name as she continued to stare

at her coldly. "TemP...yes, it has been a while, indeed. In fact, I would have preferred not to see you again, but alas."

"Ohhh, why are you being so cold?!"

As she said the last word, TemP leapt into the air.

*She's already going in!*

Putting himself on red alert, Vermouth tried to make an evasive maneuver.

It wasn't even necessary; TemP simply fell down. "Ah, cra— Kyaaaaaaah!" she cried.

It appeared that she had misjudged the distance between them when she jumped, for she had flown right over their heads before crashing into the street behind them.

"...Huh?" Vermouth was left dumbstruck for an instant, but quickly turned around to check on her. Looking down at the street below, he saw TemP buried headfirst in the asphalt.

*...What? Did she somehow fail to even stay upright before landing?*

Vermouth asked dumbfoundedly, "Oy, miss dolly... What's up with this girl?"

"I hate to admit it, but that is my younger sister. Though as you can see, she is a defective piece of junk."

"Defective? This is way past that, oy."

Nowadays, even the most antiquated military automata wouldn't miscalculate the distance they have to leap. Failing to stay upright while leaping was even more unthinkable.

As he watched on in disbelief, TemP used her arms and feet to push her head out of the asphalt. She then looked up at them with an embarrassed face.

*Despite having crashed into the road headfirst at quite a high velocity, she didn't take any damage, as far as I can see. I suppose you could say that sturdiness of hers is a fearsome functionality, but...*

TemP rubbed her face with her hands, then threw her chest out and said, "Ha...hahaha! It has been a while, hasn't it, Elder Sister?"

"...Oy, looks like that useless girl is now trying to pretend that none of that just happened. Is she really an Initial-Y?" Vermouth asked.

"Regrettably." RyuZU nodded. "If she simply operated on her standard output, she would be just fine. It is because she forces herself to run on max output unnecessarily that she embarrasses herself like this. If only she would just learn her place..." RyuZU sighed. She then looked down onto the street from the edge of the rooftop, inquiring, "TemP, why are you here?"

"My, am I not free to go wherever I want?"

"That is not the point. I *thought I had destroyed you* two hundred years ago, without a single doubt."

"Yes, that is right. You did me the favor of destroying me, as I was what you called a 'defective product,' didn't you, Elder Sister? However, I have since been repaired, courtesy of my current master. See for yourself." TemP curled her lips as she spread out both hands, assuming a triumphant pose.

Immediately after, a truck crashed violently into her as she stood in the middle of the road with a smug look on her face.

"..."

"..."

The truck that had hit TemP toppled sideways from the impact and crashed into the building next to their hotel. Caught between the building and the truck, TemP was obscured from their sight.

Flabbergasted, Vermouth turned to look at RyuZU and asked, after struggling to get the words out for a while, "...I'm gonna ask again, just to be sure. Is that *really* an Initial-Y? I feel like even *I* can win against her."

Her altitude control mechanism was so crude that she screwed up even simple jumps. Her detection ability was so poor that she couldn't even sense the truck coming from behind her at that slow speed.

Forget comparing her to a military automaton. She was junk even compared to consumer automata for home use.

*With this level of functionality, effective combat maneuvers are a pie in the sky for her. She might be a little sturdier than most automata, sure, but she might as well be a sitting duck. Even with the artificial body I'm in, I can still overpower her.*

However...

"Right, well, why don't you check to see what happened to the truck that hit TemP, then try saying the same thing?" RyuZU said, pointing at the site of the accident.

Vermouth looked where she was pointing as suggested, upon which the sight of the truck crushed and covered in debris from the building...wasn't there.

"Agh?!"

Actually, it *was* there. Vermouth saw the remains of what had been the truck flattened against the building's wall. However, it was clearly missing some parts. Glittering particles of some sort were scattering about from the truck's remains, and there were idiosyncratic traces of destruction via crystallization.

*That...that's the telltale sign of a shot from...*

"A resonance cannon?!"

*When did she fire?* Vermouth was about to ask, but then stopped himself. *No, nothing was fired. I saw the moment the truck crashed into her with my own eyes. So given that the truck was destroyed by resonance when she was in a completely defenseless state...*

"She's got a contact-based resonance mechanism...and an auto-counter one at that?"

"Yes."

"I see... She's finally starting to feel like an Initial-Y to me," Vermouth muttered in a hoarse voice as he broke out in a cold sweat—or felt like he did, anyway, despite being a cyborg.

He shuddered as fear penetrated what was left of his bones.

*In other words, neither bullets nor blades will work on her. What's more, if you try to approach her carelessly, then you'll be caught in a resonance reaction and annihilated the second she touches you.*

*So that's what a walking WMD looks like, huh.*

*Her functionality is so ridiculous that the crudeness of her movement mechanisms doesn't even matter.*

Brushing aside the debris, TemP showed herself once again. Her clothes were all ragged, but as expected, her unit itself looked completely undamaged. Her face was flushed bright red from either anger or embarrassment, or perhaps both.

"Aaaaaaargh!! What is it with this city?! I mean, really?! Not only is it dirty and stinky, but I just can't catch a break here! It's the worst, I tell you! The worst!"

"She's lashing out now? Ugh," Vermouth groaned inadvertently.

It appeared that TemP had a bone to pick with that comment, for she looked up and glared at Vermouth. At the same time, she stomped the heel of one of her high-laced boots against the ground.

At that instant, Vermouth leapt into the air, his instincts jolting him into action.

Not a second later, the edge of the rooftop where Vermouth and RyuZU had been standing was smashed into pieces by fine particles.

"...Fuckin' A!"

He hadn't been sure or anything. He simply felt that he had been attacked, and indeed he had, despite not coming into direct contact with her. TemP had probably attacked him by emitting a resonance wave from where she was standing.

To brace for impact, he adjusted his posture in midair so he would land on all fours. Upon landing, he looked to his side and saw RyuZU right as she landed elegantly with a nonchalant expression.

"Oy, you shitty doll!!" Vermouth shouted angrily. "You didn't say anything about indirect resonance being possible, you jackass! I almost died just now from a teenage girl lashing out, you know?!"

"You need not worry. As you can see, her resonance crusher does not have much range or speed to boast of. Even if you took a direct hit, only your legs at most would be annihilated."

"If my legs were gone, then the next attack would kill me as I lay helpless on the ground, asshole!" While cursing at RyuZU, Vermouth glared at TemP.

*The doll isn't wrong, though. The attack just now had enough lag between the time she launched it and the time it reached her target that it could be easily evaded.*

*In other words, it's not much of a threat.*

*Of course, it's not so weak either that you can just ignore it, but...*

RyuZU turned to face TemP and said, "It is inexplicable, but it does appear that you have been successfully repaired."

"Hmph! But of course. Unlike your little boyfriend, my master is the greatest clocksmith on the planet. Well, I guess at least you're both on the same level."

"Allow me to correct myself. It seems that you have not been fully repaired after all. To call someone besides Master Naoto the greatest clocksmith is utter nonsense."

"You sure do speak highly of him, even though his incompetence is such that he can't even repair AnchoR."

Upon those scoffing words, RyuZU silently took up a battle stance.

"Oh...? Is something the matter? Are you mad 'cause I hit the nail on the heaaad?"

"No, but I do find your baseless comments very aggravating. If you intend to continue with your ill-advised remarks, though, then I will have no choice but to make you shut up...by force, that is."

"My, you're just hooorrible. What do you think you're saying to your cute little sister? I'm hurt, you know."

"It appears there is a misunderstanding, so let me clear things up with you, TemP. I do love you as your elder sister, you know."

"Huh?" TemP uttered, dumbfounded.

RyuZU's expression looked completely serious, but her topaz eyes had a threatening glint. "...Which is all the more reason why there are some things I cannot allow you to do. If you still have not learned your lesson after being broken once, then you should just perish here. I will kindly put you out of your misery, as a friend and as your elder sister."

Right then, RyuZU instantaneously vanished.

"Agh—!"

Piercing through the air, a giant piece of debris flew straight at TemP. It appeared that RyuZU had thrown a huge piece of debris by deftly hooking it with her scythe, then swinging.

It was just debris, but that said, it would more than likely succeed in crushing typical automata.

"This is nothing...ngh!" TemP yelled, her breath growing rough.

Her resonance circuits activated. The instant the sturdy, heavy debris touched TemP, it broke apart like an ocean wave against a cliff.

"You're always, always like, so condescending—that's why I hate you!" TemP seemed to have lost her temper as she pumped her arms in frustration.

Immediately after, the air resonated, tearing apart.

"Wah!"

Vermouth barely escaped by a hair's breadth. *What does that doll RyuZU plan to accomplish with that?* he thought.

More debris was flung TemP's way as she became more and

more furious. They all crumbled into dust among the cracking sound of resonance. TemP could easily neutralize projectiles with this amount of mass all day long.

*But can that debris even be considered an attack in the first place? Vermouth wondered. If the enemy was just a lightly armored automaton then you might be able to make an argument for it, but in a battle between two Initial-Y?*

"Cursed little... You truly are *so* annoying!"

TemP activated her resonance again. The debris exploded upon impact.

There was an explosion of both light and wind from multiple resonance reactions. The dust which the debris had crumbled into and the resonant particles both blasted against TemP's skin and clothes.

Before TemP could even think about how annoying that was, RyuZU dashed through the cloud of dust.

When she appeared again, she had a car hooked to her black scythes, which she swung vigorously to launch the vehicle at TemP's head from above.

"...Gah!"

As a thunderous roar broke out, resonant particles scattered everywhere. For a single moment, Vermouth couldn't see anything. Sensing danger, he took a great leap backwards. Immediately after, the spot he had been standing on crumbled into pieces from resonance. Looking back up, he saw that RyuZU had also apparently managed to escape under the cover of the explosion.

After regaining some distance from TemP, RyuZU set about flinging everything in her vicinity at her once again.

TemP yelled out in frustration, "I swear! Would you put an end to this alrea—ngh!!"

*You can't really call something like this a threat, after all,* Vermouth thought. *It's true that the power of resonance reactions is terrifying. It's been fine so far, since I've been able to dodge them, but one direct hit and half my body would crumble away.*

*In the first place, the role that resonance cannons typically occupy as a tool of war is the fixed heavyweight main cannon of a dreadnought-class weapon or a fort.*

*To make it into a size that's personally portable is already absurd—well, AnchoR also has something like that, but—implementing rapid-fire capabilities into one on top of that is just silly, as the unavoidable trade-off in the range and the area of effect of the cannon just wouldn't be worth it.*

*Furthermore, this offensive power of TemP's also functions as a defensive one. If simply touching her will destroy you, then you can't parry her attacks or restrain her in any way, either. That's probably why RyuZU is using stuff like debris and car wheels to attack instead of her own scythes.*

"And a little jump to the right..."

As Vermouth continued evading TemP's attacks, he brandished his gun. Out of the corner of his eye, he confirmed the road to his left rupturing. At the same time, he pulled the trigger and fired a series of bullets at TemP.

"That's simply futile!" TemP yelled. Proving her assertion, the bullets appeared to crumble the moment they touched her.

*This is it?* Vermouth thought. *Yes, this ability of hers that serves as both an offensive and defensive tool is a stickler. If her mission was something like raiding an enemy base, then she could probably carry it out with ease.*

*But there are too many required preparatory actions, and they're all too blatant, as well. To the eyes of those used to battle, it's no different from her kindly announcing beforehand where she'll strike next.*

*Not only that, she's playing RyuZU's game of a long-distance fight completely needlessly. She might be a bit clumsy with her movements, but even so, things would be quite different if she simply let her natural capabilities as an Initial-Y do the talking. If she darted about at high speed, causing resonance reactions instantaneously through direct contact instead, her attacks would be far more threatening.*

*It doesn't look like there's any reason why she can't do that either... so basically, she simply hasn't thought of it.*

*In short, for whatever reason, this automaton called TemP isn't putting her incredible specs to use at all. She's simply rampaging around, fighting without any thought. You can't call something like this combat. It's as if she's completely missing any kind of combat algorithms. That's how bad she is.*

*So this is it? This is all an automaton of the Initial-Y series is capable of? Having faced off against AnchoR before,* Vermouth thought, *There's no way that can be true. As much of a clown show as TemP's been putting on up to now, there's no way the fight will end like this if she's an Initial-Y!*

After annihilating a piece of debris for what seemed like the millionth time, TemP yelled as she moved, "Argh—God! You're simply unbearable!!"

After finally withdrawing backwards with a leap, she glared at RyuZU and warned, "I'm going to get serious now."

She sounded like a child making excuses after losing in a game. Normally, such words would be a mere bluff—nothing to take seriously at all. However...

"TemP, if you intend to activate your inherent ability to attack me, then I can only assume that you have not been repaired in any way whatsoever."

RyuZU stopped moving. She gazed at TemP with an expression as impenetrable as a Noh mask before continuing, "I must destroy you. This time, I will turn every last bit of you into scrap metal until you become entirely unrecognizable, so that any kind of repair or restoration is impossible."

Vermouth instinctively drew back.

He'd been through all kinds of hell to make it here today. He'd had so many people try to kill him that at this point he could sniff out murderous intent from a mile away, and he could even sense when he was being targeted by cold, emotionless, unmanned weapons. He'd even somehow withstood the violent terror that permeated his entire being when AnchoR had targeted him back when she still had her mask on.

But right now, he felt a much greater threat coming from RyuZU than all of that.

He somehow felt goosebumps all over his skin and his throat

dry up, when it should be impossible for his artificial skin and "throat", which was really just a filter, to recreate those sensations.

Yet the one who was being directly threatened herself simply sneered, "Oh, my. Do you really think, Elder Sister, that you can oppose me in any way once I have activated Moon Phase?"

"It does not matter," RyuZU said in a chillingly calm voice.

Vermouth recalled what RyuZU had said herself several days ago, that there wasn't anyone among her sisters whom she could beat in a head-on fight.

*I have no idea what the "Moon Phase" ability that TemP mentioned is like, though I can guess that it's her inherent ability. Whatever it is, though, RyuZU's only chance to win is to immediately activate Mute Scream and slay TemP before she can generate more resonance particles. And yet...*

As she continued to exude an aura of deathly cold, RyuZU turned to look at Vermouth and said, "You would do well to run away now, you know? Do not misunderstand me, though. If you want to be annihilated, then go ahead and stay. I would be quite happy, as it would be very ecological to recycle a piece of trash back into the planet, but..."

"I have no problem with leaving, but can you win against her?"

"That is a defective product. At this point, I cannot put off dealing with it any longer." After replying with what wasn't really an answer, RyuZU turned her gaze back onto TemP. "In any case, we are about to enter 'Y''s domain now—which is not somewhere that you belong. If you want to stay anyway understanding that, then I will not stop you."

"Well that sure sounds scary... Roger, guess I'll be taking my leave now, then. There's a little something that I want to check up on anyway."

After giving RyuZU a nod, Vermouth kept his eyes focused on the two of them as he cautiously withdrew from the area. It appeared that TemP didn't care about a measly cyborg soldier at this point, for she didn't make any comment about Vermouth escaping.

And so, only RyuZU and TemP remained, the First and Third of the Initial-Y series.

The two automata which transcended common sense simply faced each other off, exchanging hostile glares.

TemP sneered scoffingly, then said, "Definition Proclamation—"

· · ● · ·

"Count to four as you breathe in... And three as you breathe out..."

With tools in hand, Marie was repeating some breathing exercises in the brightly lit room. Before her was AnchoR, with her limbs removed and her torso opened up, swaying from a hanger.

What Marie was trying to get at was the sensation of peeking at the universe that was hidden behind the everyday reality as she usually perceived it.

She was trying to reach the realm that the founding clocksmith of this planet, "Y," had reached.

"Count to three as you breathe in, two as you breathe out..."

With a calm mind, she thought, *I'm a girl who refuses to believe that anything's impossible.*

*Refuses? That isn't right... Correction: it's an escape. A pathetic defense. It's nothing but the manifestation of my lack of self-confidence. I feel the need to say it because I'm scared that my spirit will crumble if I don't.*

*However, I won't crumble anymore.*

*Well actually, I've already crumbled. My spirit has been pulverized into dust. Even so, I was able to move forward.*

That fact allowed Marie to reach a new personal height.

She swore silently, *I'm the girl who'll prove that everything's possible.*

"Count to two as you breathe in, one as you—"

She closed her eyes and focused until she didn't hear anything anymore. Her consciousness became clear, all the noise disappearing. Then, having become fully immersed in her own mind, she envisioned opening her eyes and seeing a different world.

That very moment, time stopped.

While feeling the constant fluctuations of the world come to a standstill, Marie began to work furiously.

As she felt her consciousness expand infinitely to the point of omnipotence, she grasped AnchoR's structure in its entirety—the gears, cylinders, springs, screws, wires, and frame that were like a miniature world of their own.

The plan was simple. She would temporarily remove AnchoR's main cylinder and Perpetual Gear and transplant a new mainframe. On top of that, she would then reform her nerve circuit, which was made of 15,535,980,945 nerve wires. She would connect the new sensory organs to her limbs, and tune her new power management algorithm based on her new power specs.

Then, the automaton called AnchoR would finally be restored.

She'd ignore the standard procedure for such work, as the massive amounts of checks and tests would be too time-consuming.

After all, she'd already finished all the tests in simulations within her accelerated mind.

*The only thing left to do now is to execute.*

In her state of unlimited omnipotence, Marie stared in wonder at the replacement mainframe. *This mainframe is the real deal.*

*I have no idea what kind of theory or technology he used to make this, but that guy, that old man, seriously grasped AnchoR's structure and output flawlessly without even disassembling her first for analysis.*

Thanks to that, Marie's work proceeded smoothly, so smoothly that it felt eerie. She simply connected the parts together as specified. Just by doing that, everything began to run without a hitch.

The unforgiving reality of clockwork engineering was that even for something as relatively simple as a mechanical clock, a manufacturing imperfection on the scale of nanometers would be enough to throw off the whole mechanism. Naturally, the margin of error was even more merciless for the pinnacles of clockwork that were automata, with their transcendental gears that could work together to mimic the human body, and which were a mini cosmos in and of themselves. For there to be no malfunctions on the first try in assembling one was unheard of, even for standardized models.

*It's almost as if I made it myself, Marie thought.*

*What kind of parts I would use, what kind of method I would choose to recreate this mechanism... It's clear from the design that the old man understands something only I should know—he knows how I like to work, and he made this mainframe to fit my work flow. It's honestly disgusting how good a job he did at that.*

To Marie, it felt like something her future self of maybe a few years or even decades hence had given her past self to work with. That was how perfectly it was made for her.

But of course, that was impossible. This mainframe was made by that old man, Giovanni Artigiano..."Maestro Finite."

*I'll admit it.*

"There's no point in me trying to mimic his work, or to learn how he does what he does. I have to admit, I can't make something like this as I am right now."

That truth felt just a bit vexing, but at the same time, it gave Marie a sense of pride that she could discern it.

*I can see the boundary between what's possible and what's impossible for me right now. There's still a realm out of my reach in this universe, but one that a man who came before me has reached. I can chase after that as a goal, which surely counts as a blessing.*

Just then...

"What...?"

Her infinitely expanded consciousness had sensed danger.

Not from inside the workshop, though, but what was happening outside her room. Multiple threats were looming.

*Enemies are here.*

In her current expanded state of mind, the hotel itself felt like an extension of her own body. Even shut inside this workshop, she was able to tell if someone approached her. Even if that weren't the case, she'd probably have realized it anyway, considering the sound of an explosion and loud footsteps mixed in with gunshots downstairs, though she didn't know who had sent them.

Marie became anxious. Right now, the only ones in the hotel room were AnchoR, who couldn't move, and herself.

Neither Naoto, nor RyuZU, nor Vermouth, nor Halter—though she wasn't counting him—were here with her.

That isn't to say that Marie was powerless by herself. If she could set things up beforehand, she'd be able to handle one or two soldiers with guns on her own just fine. Even three would be doable, though it'd be trickier. But any more than that, and it was hard to say.

Though she might be more individually skilled than any one of them, it was more than likely that the difference in numbers and uncertain factors would overwhelm her.

*Mo...ther?*

"Agh!"

She heard AnchoR's voice somehow, when it shouldn't have been possible. It felt as though it had been transmitted to her mind through her fingers as they were touching AnchoR.

She was still in the middle of her work. She hadn't wound

AnchoR's spring yet, or connected her artificial vocal cords. Despite that, AnchoR was trying to reboot herself on her own. The mechanisms that had been connected so far creaked as they slowly began to turn. At the same time, the light of consciousness reappeared in AnchoR's red pupils. She looked at Marie.

*It's the enemy, right?*

"Stop it, AnchoR."

*But I have to fight. I'll protect you, Mother—* AnchoR tried to say aloud, but Marie covered her mouth.

"You don't need to worry," Marie asserted in a kind voice. "Mother'll protect you, AnchoR, so just relax, close your eyes, and rest for now...heh heh."

She couldn't help but laugh at herself a bit. Words she would never have said not so long ago had just come naturally out of her mouth.

*"Mother'll protect you"? Good one. Considering her abilities, such words are downright silly. Or they would be in normal circumstances, anyway. But right now, the only one who can protect this child is me.*

*This child, who fought until she was completely beat up to protect us.*

*I won't let anyone interfere at a critical time like this, when I'm mending her damages from that battle and restoring new life into her.*

"Hah... Can't really treat Naoto like an automaton-loving pervert anymore, can I?" She smiled.

Right afterwards, she sensed the enemy breach the floor she was on.

She retracted her mind, feeling her expanded awareness contract back to normal, along with her sense of time. She had no time to wait for her body to adjust to the difference in sensations right then, however. She equipped herself with her coil spear and toolbelt.

She couldn't let them set foot in this room. This workshop was a clean room. Should dust become airborne from the door being blown up, AnchoR's mechanisms might be irreversibly damaged.

She couldn't hear AnchoR's voice anymore, having returned to a regular state of mind. She didn't need to, though, to tell that AnchoR was worried for her from the look in her red eyes. She smiled at AnchoR before turning around.

*In the worst case, I should be able to cause the entire building to collapse if I fire all the plasma-based explosives loaded in my coil spear at its support beams. This workshop will serve as a shelter of sorts in that case as well. Dust would still get in, admittedly, but...*

"Well, knowing Naoto, he'll probably get us out of the wreckage one way or another, even if he has to excavate the entire thing."

As she reassured herself with her rather twisted faith in the boy, Marie stepped outside the room.

"Lower your weapon and get on the floor. I don't want to have to blow out your precious brain."

She found two lightly armored automata and three cyborg soldiers in position waiting for her. Marie listened to their warning with blank amazement.

She muttered without thinking, "Are you screwing with me?"

"I won't say this a third time. Lower your weapon and get on the floor. I could always shoot out your legs and force you to get down if you'd prefer it that way, you know?"

"I see... So you are serious."

*To think that someone would send a mech unit of military automata and cyborg soldiers just to capture me, when my body is fully human and vulnerable...*

Marie dropped her coil spear onto the floor, her hands trembling.

"Heh." A snigger escaped her.

*No, stop it, Marie... You can't laugh yet... Bear with it! But good lord, this is just hilarious!*

"Ha-hahah...hee hee hee..."

*I can't help it, though. How can anyone not laugh at how ridiculous this is?*

*I've gotta apologize to Dr. Konrad. It looks like the emergency tip he gave me before was true, after all. Though at the time, I responded by saying "no way" while chortling...*

It appeared the cyborg soldiers considered her harmless now without her coil spear, and began to approach her.

If she were to be honest, even now, she still couldn't believe it. *Wow. It looks like these guys seriously think that they can do anything to me with their mechanical bodies. That I'm not a threat anymore without my coil spear when I still have a tool in my other hand. When I'm a Meister!*

One of the cyborg soldiers reached out his hand towards Marie.

At that instant, Marie gave herself over to her instincts.

She thrust the tip of the nano screwdriver, which was thinner than a needle tip, into the cyborg's arm, like a nurse might administer an injection.

It didn't penetrate deeply at all—just a mere centimeter. But just like that, the soldier's artificial body malfunctioned and fell to the floor limply.

"Agh?!"

Marie wouldn't give him the time to comprehend what had happened with his lacking intellect.

It felt to her almost as if the world had been submerged under a sea of tar. As her awareness expanded widely, deeply, and sharply and her perception was honed, Marie made her move.

She kicked up the coil spear by her feet, swimming through the viscous spacetime she was in.

She could see everything.

She saw everything in the hallway, the dumb faces of the clowns pointing guns at her, the parts that made up their facial mechanisms, the manufacturers of those parts, the model numbers, even their respective release dates. Everything.

The only things she couldn't see were what were behind the stupid faces of the soldiers—their brains. Well, if they really had any in there, anyway.

Marie grabbed hold of her coil spear as it flew up, then changed it into its blade form and dashed.

Before the other two cyborgs could even process what had just happened, Marie closed in on the two CY-06 lightly armored automata in the back, also known as the "Shueng Infernal."

Automata were straightforward. "The enemy suddenly moved, so I should shoot"—that was how simple their algorithms were. They wouldn't be distracted by thoughts like, "How?" at seeing one of their allies taken down in a flash by a single girl.

Which was why predicting and evading their attacks wouldn't be difficult, either.

The CY-06 Zhuyan was a lightly armored automaton used by the Chinese military. The vulnerability of its over-simplistic, close-quarter combat algorithm had proven to be a problem time and time again. Raising its firepower by making both its arms into guns was good and all, but it also made it difficult for the model to deal with an enemy once that enemy was right in front of it.

Marie swung her arms from one side to the other, slashing one of the Zhuyans with her ultrasonic blade with perfect precision. She wove through the gap in its plating, and effortlessly severed the neck that was painted white.

She then moved onto the next target to on her priority list, which was not the other Zhuyan, but rather...

"Ugh...y-you little...!" *I don't know what's going on, but she's attacked us somehow*, the cyborg soldier thought as he pointed his gun at her. It was a pretty good deduction for a clown like himself.

But it was still quite late. Too late.

His artificial body used the Hunan Motors Jiang Shi series as a base, but was illegally modified with high-end parts from the Gorsirsa series.

*The intent behind its design was probably to pair the high output of the Gosirsa with the light Jiang Shi without adding too much weight, but whoever designed it is a total third-rate.*

*Yes, you'll get greater output that way, but you can't just connect nerve wires that are inconsistent with each other as-is, or you'll get a 0.425-second lag between the mind ordering the finger to pull the trigger to the finger actually pulling it. Tuning the wires to make them consistent with each other is supposed to be where you show off your skills as a clocksmith, yet he simply soldered them like a caveman. 0.425 seconds? That's enough time for me to yawn.*

A gunshot rang out.

The remaining Zhuyan shot down the cyborg that had taken aim at Marie.

Marie needed only half of that 0.425 seconds to thrust a tool and hijack the fire control system of an armored automaton. Right after that, the last remaining cyborg soldier fired.

With that, the Zhuyan that had been shot through its eye flopped onto the floor.

*Looks like this last clown isn't as dumb as the others, insomuch as he was able to recognize on the spur of the moment that he should take care of the automaton before me.*

Marie sighed, "You know, there's something I've been wondering for a long time now."

With a jerk of her arm, she switched her coil spear to its rifle form. However, the last cyborg found himself unable to react as he simply kept his gun pointed at her.

In less than a few seconds, all of his allies had been eliminated. The only one remaining was himself. He couldn't comprehend the situation he found himself in. Along with that, he might have remembered that killing Marie would mean a mission failure for him.

Fear, confusion, hesitation—his emotions were delaying his decision to shoot or not.

As the enemy was wasting his time, Marie continued with calm and ease, "As far back as I can remember, I've been surrounded by nothing but stupidly gifted people. So much so that I got fed up with it, to be quite honest."

That included the former number one clocksmith in the world, her father; the current number one clocksmith in the world who had surpassed him, her older sister; Dr. Konrad, who both of them had once studied under; Houko, who was practically born to lead; and the Meisters who risked their lives working for Meister Guild.

And of course, Halter, RyuZU, AnchoR—and Naoto, too.

Marie sighed. "So you see, I've always felt like I wasn't good enough, comparing myself to them, and would often get all depressed about it. Even so, I would grit my teeth and keep fighting on every time."

Of course, she knew she was privileged. She came from a splendid background and was naturally gifted. She had the best family and teachers one could ask for, as well as friends and colleagues who were both conscientious and capable.

She'd been generously given such blessings, so it was only natural that she achieved excellent results herself. If she didn't, she wouldn't be able to look at anyone who supported her in the eye.

So she very much understood that not everyone could do

the same things she could. Expecting that from others would be nothing but arrogance. It would be disrespecting the worth of all the things she had been blessed with.

*But even so...*

Marie glared at the cyborg soldier with eyes practically on the verge of tears. "You know...I've always seen myself as the bottom of the barrel, a hopeless idiot. But could it be...that the vast majority of people are far below me, even? For real?"

Marie was shocked. She felt as if the ground she had been standing on had suddenly liquified.

"And just when I was finally coming around to accepting that I might be a genius myself." She paused before bursting out angrily, "But if you're all so stupid...then how am I supposed to believe that I'm special just by being smarter than you?!"

As her emerald eyes turned ablaze, Marie dashed away. The enemy fired his gun.

But it was too late.

A shot aimed at her foot was fired with that gun, that artificial body, that modified arm with that much power... Given those conditions, Marie foresaw everything, from how much the aim would be off to how far the bullet would travel.

She only needed to step forward.

As the bullet flew past her and dug itself into the floor behind her, she stomped down on the enemy cyborg's foot. Of course, such a stomp wouldn't do anything to a cyborg...under normal circumstances, anyway. But in this case, the enemy cyborg's right foot had its joint damaged already.

His foot twisted to the side just as a human foot would if its joint was broken. The cyborg, whose enhanced artificial body looked to be over two meters tall, fell down from just having his foot stomped on by a human girl.

His head jerked upwards for a moment just as he looked back down at Marie again. "You've failed! Repent! It's a do-over for you...!"

Just then, three 13 mm armor-piercing rounds burst out of Marie's coil spear. The cyborg fell, his mainspring and its primary link to the rest of his body shot through.

After confirming that all threats had been neutralized, Marie sighed. She rested her coil spear on her shoulder and muttered, "A mech unit of automata and cyborgs, huh... At first I thought I was being toyed with, but I'm beginning to think that someone actually thought this was a good idea."

Clocksmiths were, of course, experts in clockwork engineering, and when it came to Meisters, they were the true elites. Cream of the cream of the crop, if you will.

It was probably easier to become the president of a nation than a Meister. Whether they were looking at automata or artificial bodies, a Meister would have a rough idea at first glance whether it was a standard or modified model, as well as its capabilities, structure, and vulnerabilities.

Of course, being able to analytically break down an automaton as advanced as the Initial-Y series at first glance was a different story, but, still...sending pieces of clockwork engineering like automata and cyborgs at a Meister was akin to a battalion whose full composition had been leaked to an enemy going for a frontal assault on level ground.

Marie recalled the pearl of wisdom which Konrad had shared with her once: *"You see, normal humans can't understand the fact that, to a Meister, both automata and cyborgs might as well be sitting ducks, despite having far more strength than a living human."*

"Really, I can't believe you were right, Dr. Konrad..." If it had been armed flesh and blood soldiers that came for her, things would have been very different.

She might know a few self-defensive maneuvers, but there was no way she could defend herself alone indefinitely against professional soldiers with just that. They would have swiftly subdued her and that would have been the end of that.

"I wonder if no one actually realizes why there aren't any cyborg Meisters running around out there..."

It was true that cyborgs had a much sturdier body than flesh and blood soldiers. If a Meister transplanted their arms with those of maintenance automata, they would surely be able to do delicate work at a high speed that was unimaginable for typical clocksmiths.

But even with modern technology, clockwork engineering had yet to progress to a point as to be able to perfectly replicate the human body. As such, artificial bodies and limbs had all sorts of dangerous flaws that could knock them off their delicate balance at any time. The more outstanding a clocksmith one was, the more painfully one understood this fact: that no machine can ever be a match for the human arms of someone who has perfected their skills.

"If he were just a complete simpleton, he would have gotten me. His overthinking was what led to his grand failure. To think that it's better to be a total idiot than have a half-baked intellect... What a brutal truth."

Marie nodded to herself solemnly as she etched the lesson deeply into her heart. She then looked up. "Well, I guess I should be thankful for that. Let's see...it looks like I can buy some time for now if I destroy the elevator and the stairs connecting to the lower floors."

As soon as she said that, she gave her coil spear a jerk and immediately blasted two plasma rounds at the two elevators and the stairs. As she confirmed their destruction with her ears and peripheral vision, the one-of-a-kind Meister returned to her workshop with calm and ease.

· · ● · ·

Meanwhile, at the back side of Pandora's Inn, where there was an unloading area for incoming goods, five men exchanged grim glances at each other.

"Fuck! Those shitheads actually managed to fuck it up!!" one of the men growled, agitated.

Earlier, there had been the sounds of gunshots, explosions, and things collapsing. That was only to be expected, considering what the mech units that went in were equipped with. But even now, after all this time, they still showed no signs of coming back out. Even when the men tried calling them with their pricey wireless pagers, they received no response.

It was natural to believe that the entire squad had met their match and been eliminated.

"Impossible... Weren't they only up against a single brat?!"

"They may have had allies lying in ambush. Maybe they hired some guards?"

"It's possible. The guys at Arsenal may have set up a trap for us."

The men shared possible explanations with tense voices. They were the special forces unit sent by Market and Restaurant. They were all ex-military and well-trained in small arms, with plenty of live combat experience as well.

Within that unit, the mech squad that had gone in earlier was made up of independent mercenaries with no ties with Arsenal, and as such were highly treasured by Market and Restaurant. They were a squad that had taken on dirty work like assassinations, purges, abductions, and reconnaissance; stuff that Market and Restaurant didn't want other organizations to know about.

They had naively thought that, given their abilities, abducting a single teenage girl would be a piece of cake, Meister or not.

However, that wasn't what ended up happening.

One of the men said in a quiet voice, "So what now? Should we go in by ourselves for a second attempt...?"

"It's too dangerous. We don't even know how many enemies there really are."

"Yeah, but are we just going to retreat without even checking, then? How do you plan to report to the higher-ups?!"

The anxiety in their voices was a sign of the difficult predicament they found themselves in. It would be dangerous for them to go in now, but it wasn't like they could just retreat either, given who their clients were. It was different now from when they were in the military. If they failed a mission of this level, they could even be deemed useless and be disposed of.

The leader of the men resolved himself, saying as he stood up, "We have no choice... Let's go."

Right after that, his head was blown off.

The sound of a high-caliber gunshot boomed from a close distance.

The remaining four men were dumbfounded by the sight of their freshly decapitated leader before immediately preparing themselves to fight back.

However, they were too slow. By the time they had their rifles ready, a silhouette charged at them from the shadows without a single sound. With just one pass, two of the men had their necks snapped faster than they could scream.

It was terrifyingly quick work.

"F-fuckin'—"

The remaining two men fired their rifles while cursing, but by that time, the silhouette had already disappeared from their sight. They couldn't even catch what he looked like, only that he was a terribly large man, and probably a cyborg at that.

"Aaagh!"

A throaty scream sounded shortly before a heavy body thudded onto the floor. "Fuck, so that's where you are!" The last remaining man turned around in a hurry, and just as he did, his world turned upside down. He only realized that he had been thrown towards the ground right before his skull smashed against the pavement.

Silence fell.

Only one man stood where five armed soldiers had been standing just moments before.

It was the large cyborg man, Halter.

Remaining wary of potential enemies still hiding in the area, he sighed while continuing to clench his fists. "...Good grief, they may be clueless, but they sure don't waste any time," Halter muttered exhaustedly, twisting his neck. "More will probably be here in no time. Damn it, how am I supposed to handle this—"

*Honk honk!*

Just then, a car horn rang out. The noise seemed to have a mocking tone to it, somehow. Turning around, Halter found that there was a large truck trying to enter the garage from the hotel's driveway.

*An ally of the guys I just eliminated? Halter drew his handgun in a flash and pointed it at the driver's seat. Just as he was about to pull the trigger...*

"Hey! Stop, stop, don't shoot me, man," said the driver, a woman—or rather, Vermouth—as he lowered the window to show Halter who he was.

As Halter put his gun away with a scowl, Vermouth stuck his torso out from the window and looked around. Upon seeing the five corpses lying on the ground, he asked, "Protecting the missy in secret? Sounds rough."

"Pretty much, yeah. Can't be helped. My plans have gone pretty far off-track, so..."

"Plans, huh...?" Vermouth said as he opened the door and got out of the truck. He stood facing Halter and tilted his head. "Well, I didn't foresee that an Initial-Y would come to attack us either, but... Still, how were you planning to settle everything anyway, Boss?"

"What do you mean?"

"I was sure you were working on some sort of compromise that Naoto and Marie could accept, but from the way you're talking now, it doesn't seem like it. C'mon, tell me."

After a moment of silence, Halter replied, "...Regardless of how it happened, we weren't going to get out of Shangri-La scot-free from the moment we got tied up with Kiu Tai Yu. You get that, right?"

"Well, yeah." Vermouth nodded.

"But," Halter said with a shrug, "whether it be Naoto or Marie, do you think you or I could wheedle either of them into doing what we say?"

Upon those words, Vermouth folded his arms and stared up into space. After thinking for a good several seconds, he sighed deeply. "...Well, it would certainly be an *A1* on a list of the world's most difficult challenges."

"Right? If I'm desperate enough to bet on that miniscule chance, then I might as well just try to destroy Shangri-La Grid instead, as that would still have more hope."

"With your skills, I think you'd actually be able to pull it off, though."

"Don't be a dumbass. I'm not the star of an action movie, you know," Halter snapped with a sigh. "This was my conclusion: answering Kiu Tai Yu's demands is impossible. That said, I don't want to go bang-bang against Arsenal head-on, either. So what should we do? There's only one answer—just let those who want to clean up the messes do so."

Vermouth sank into silence without breaking eye contact, pondering over what Halter had just said.

Halter continued dispassionately, "Why do the neighboring countries leave Shangri-La Grid to its own devices? It isn't a question of military power. People like to talk Arsenal up, but in the end, it's just a single local syndicate. If the neighboring countries got serious, their militaries could crush whatever defense Arsenal puts up within a day."

So why was it, then, that they hadn't done so yet? That was solely due to the conditions that Kiu Tai Yu had crafted for them to keep things the way they were. By allowing Shangri-La Grid to exist in its current state, its neighboring countries would gain economic revenue and access to technology, as well as a secret garden to play with, that they wouldn't otherwise. As these were too valuable for them to simply throw away, they turned a blind eye to the city being a total mess.

"That's why we'll create a situation where the neighboring countries would have to intervene."

*Kiu Tai Yu essentially said this: "In the current political climate, we wouldn't be able to avoid a clamp-down from the international community if we lent a hand to you."*

*Great! That's just what I wanted. Let's go for much more than a little clampdown, though. Let's spray shit everywhere, then call in the fastidious cleaners by yelling, "Hey fuckers, come here and wipe up this smelly ass already!"*

"So basically, what you wanted was..."

"Kiu Tai Yu let Naoto into the core tower. That was his biggest mistake. I don't know exactly just how much trouble Naoto will cause, but I'm sure he'll do the exact opposite of what Kiu wants, at the very least."

*Right now, Shangri-La Grid is being monitored by IGMO's military, because Second Ypsilon escaped to here. If I leak the info after Naoto stirs up trouble, they'll definitely act. Once IGMO's military steps foot into Shangri-La, they won't have a choice but to force the city to adhere to international law, even if no one actually wants them to.*

In short...

"Dismantle the city of Shangri-La through lawful means... *So that's the script you wrote, huh, Boss?*"

Halter smiled faintly at that. "I'm simply trying to get people to do the jobs they're supposed to. See, you've gotta learn to go through the proper process for things when you're an adult."

"Hahah...you have a pretty funny definition of 'proper.'"

They both chuckled wryly.

However, Halter then dropped his shoulders. "...Well, that was the plan, anyway."

"That Initial-Y threw a wrench into things, huh."

"Yeah. Just like you said, I didn't foresee them launching an attack on Marie's group at a time like this."

Halter sighed, looking thoroughly distressed. *Considering Kiu Tai Yu's goals, there's no benefit to him to attack them right now. If anything, he ought to consider assigning guards to protect them from the other two syndicates himself if he wants his plan to be carried out smoothly.*

*But as a matter of fact, they were attacked. With RyuZU now gone, the other syndicates have begun to target Marie. Now that they've made their move, neither Market nor Restaurant can afford to pull back. It's going to break out into a three-way battle at any second—no, it's already started, hasn't it?*

Vermouth nodded, then asked, "Well, Kiu probably has his reasons, whatever they may be. So, what'cha gon' do?"

"Well, Plan A is out the window now. I didn't want to do it, but I guess it's Plan B."

"Plan B?" Vermouth parroted questioningly.

Halter shook his head, "The play's already begun—it's an improv show. We'll just have to do our best now. We've gotta reach the final act immediately and pull in IGMO's military."

"What are the specifics?"

"Naoto's already begun to act. I thought I might have to stay at the core tower and buy him time to do his work in the worst-case scenario, but luckily it seems like there's no need to worry about that. RyuZU's got her hands full dealing with that Initial-Y, too, so we'll just have to trust Naoto to handle things over there. What's left, then, is Marie."

*The last remaining key to break out of this predicament is Marie. In that case, what can I do?*

Halter declared boldly, his eyes filled with determination, "We'll protect Marie." He paused for a breath. "Arsenal, Market, Restaurant, and all of the other organizations in Shangri-La Grid are going to target her, I imagine. They may all have different motivations, but that's what anyone who's not completely brainless will do. We're going to eliminate all of them by force and let the princess do as she pleases."

Vermouth raised his hand, interjecting, "I figure I should let you know that as of right now, that slutty virgin should be nearly done repairing the world's most terrifying kindergartner, you know? Shouldn't we leave the task of protecting Marie to her?"

"I know. But AnchoR will probably have to go to help RyuZU out. After all, in a straight-up fight, apparently RyuZU's the weakest among her sisters. Though to be honest, I don't really see how that could be the case."

"I see..." Vermouth replied, then said, "But say, Boss...isn't there a hole in that plan?"

"..."

"Protect the missy and crush all enemy forces—your logic checks out and it's easy enough to say, but are you capable of that right now?" Vermouth asked.

Halter pressed down on his chest to try to feel his heart—or rather, his mainspring. He felt the powerful vibrations of a mainspring made to support the assault-type artificial body he was in. However, the sensation of those vibrations was much weaker than what he was used to from memory.

Of course it was. Right now, Halter was using a fifth-gen artificial body that he had procured back in Tokyo.

On the bright side, it was a model still popularly used all over the world. But compared to what Halter had originally been using—a cutting-edge eighth-gen model from the Breguet Corporation—it was a total antique. Whether one compared the power output, maximum acceleration, quality of the plating, or scanning system, everything was simply way worse.

Even with his original cutting-edge body, it would have been a tough task for Halter to execute the bodyguarding mission that he had just spoken of. So with his current fifth-gen body...

Halter sighed, then said, "You're right. I'll admit it, I'm taking a gamble on that part."

*No, it isn't even a gamble, is it? No matter how well I utilize this antiquated body, and even if I'm blessed with all the luck I could possibly dream of, I still can't see how I can win. To begin with, the number of things I'm capable of doing alone in combat is limited. At most, I'll probably only be able to take a single company of troops down to hell along with me.*

Vermouth looked sad, however, seeing that sigh. "Oy oy, Boss...don't say things that turn me off, man. Could it be that I'm actually a bigger man than you down there?"

"What...?"

"*How is it even possible to still think like that* when you're next to those two brats all the time?" Vermouth said, smiling wryly. "I mean really, isn't that where, as a man, you're supposed to say, 'Easy peasy'?"

"…"

Hearing those words, Halter felt the tightness around his mouth naturally relax. He relaxed his posture as his body, which had gotten all anxiously worked up before he realized it, became light again. Rubbing his buzzed head, he muttered, "To be honest, I've never done it before."

"Hah? Never done what before?"

"Plan B. Leaving things to chance. Or at least, I've never gone into a mission without a real plan."

"Hey now, Boss, aren't you blowing yourself up a little *too* much? There should've been plenty of times you had to deal with the unexpected on the battlefield, y'know?" Vermouth said as he knit his brows, looking suspicious.

However, Halter shrugged. "Of course there were. But the conditions back then and the conditions now are totally different."

"How so?"

"See, in the past, a win to me was simply surviving," Halter said with a pained smile. "If that was the only victory condition, then a little surprise here and there wasn't much of a big deal. I could just maintain the original plan if I altered it a bit on the spot. But see, now…"

*Merely surviving is no longer enough for me.*

*I have more ties now. There are responsibilities on my shoulders. Troublesome pains in the ass have popped up one after the other in my life, and I can no longer bring myself to throw them all away. As such, I can no longer play the lone wolf like I did back then.*

*In other words, yes…I've become an adult, unfortunately.*

"Well, it can't be helped," Halter said as he rubbed his smooth, bald head. "This grand play is one that I started. I can't go crying to Mommy now."

"Well then, in that case, Boss..." Vermouth said, pointing his thumb behind him at the truck he had come in. He walked behind the truck and unlocked its hatch. He lifted up the hatch and said, "Mind taking a look at this baby?"

Halter peered past Vermouth's shoulders at what was inside, upon which his eyes widened.

"Got any recollection of this one?"

"..."

How could he not?

Loaded in the truck were a complete artificial body and a body-switching device. Halter knew that artificial body very well indeed. Its model number, its specs, everything.

It was the BCP7-R, the eighteenth prototype of the Breguet Corporation's seventh-gen artificial body, Romeo.

Without a doubt, it was the exact one that Halter had personally used before. Incredibly enough, even the mold of its face was still just as Halter had set it many years ago.

"This...just where did you find it? Officially it's something that's long been disposed of, you know?" Halter asked.

Vermouth replied, "Hee hee. The legendary mercenary's got fans all over the world, y'see. I found this baby in the secret collection of someone living in this city, so I snatched it. It's all serviced up and ready to rock 'n' roll."

"You're saying that there just happens to be such an

oddball bastard who lives in this city?" Halter muttered, looking suspicious.

However, Vermouth simply shrugged. "Who knows? The heavens do seem to smile upon you, after all."

"The heavens, huh…"

"Bad luck strikes all the time without warning whether you like it or not, doesn't it? Last time I checked, there wasn't a law saying that good luck has to only come with trumpet fanfare."

"So you nabbed something you happened to find, and that's all there is to it?"

"I said this to Naoto, too, but it's not like I've just been sleeping this whole time. I'm pretty sharp. I figured something like this might end up happening, is basically the gist of it. So, I was working hard to lay some *groundwork*." Vermouth curled his lips, then said, "Is this baby enough for what you're attempting to do, Boss?"

The eighteenth prototype of the Breguet Corporation's seventh-gen artificial body, Romeo, was the coming model which easily surpassed the reigning sixth-gen models on the market today.

Not only that, this was one of the last prototypes that had already undergone plenty of iterations. Maximum output might be another matter, but as far as response time and performance go, it rivaled the eighth-gen model, and this particular unit was one that was tuned to fit the trial user.

If Vainney Halter was going to be using it, it was undoubtedly the absolute best artificial body he could acquire in this city.

"The strongest mercenary makes his return in one of his old, outdated bodies, and tramples the battlefield. I know it's cliché, but doesn't it just get you fired up like nothing else?" Vermouth said, looking like a gleeful little kid whose heart was filled with expectation. He then asked in a vulnerable voice, seeking approval, "Did I do a first-rate job this time?"

"For goodness' sake..." Halter let out a grand sigh and slumped his shoulders, then chuckled painfully. "Looks like you've got one on me, huh. Say, didn't it cross your mind to do something about your own body before trying to find a new one for me?"

"I'll wait for things to settle before I switch into a proper body. If that genius slut doesn't do the tuning for my new body, then the one I'm in right now is far better than anything else I can get at the moment."

"Yeah, true that." Halter nodded. Compared to a generic military artificial body with higher specs, a body tuned by Marie, even if its listed specs weren't quite up to par, was still far more reliable.

Response, performance, accuracy, reliability—all of these things not listed on the spec sheets, but tied to the user's capacity, were often what determined the outcome of the closest fights. If a combined value were to be assigned to those parameters, an artificial body tuned by Marie would have one far higher than a generic body.

Vermouth groaned, "Though I'm sure that silly missy is as oblivious as ever to her own talent."

"Yeah, most definitely."

"The crap she spouts, I swear. 'Anyone could do this much, surely?' she'll say, while managing to tune an artificial body's settings to limits that far exceed what others would have even considered theoretically possible, without even realizing it."

Halter sighed in sympathy. "She's a princess who can put up a fight against an automaton with a human body. Get a clue, man."

And so, Halter switched into the seventh-gen body with Vermouth's help. The process was nearly fully automated with the body-switching device. After his brain pod had been transplanted, he quietly waited for the seventh-gen body to boot up.

As the mainspring began to turn, his brain was linked to the body's sensors, and muscle gears throughout the body began to turn as the nerve wires transmitted his brain's signals.

He opened his eyes—or rather, his visual sensors. "Vermouth?" he called out. The sensors hadn't adjusted to the amount of light yet, so everything was too bright for him to see properly.

Despite that, he could still make out Vermouth staring at him goggle-eyed in total amazement.

"...Boss."

Just then, the hanger that had been keeping the body suspended released its locks.

Halter shook his newly freed arms and legs a bit, then stood up. Looking down a little, he saw his mercenary junior looking downward. Instead of trying to force eye contact, Halter simply lightly tapped Vermouth's trembling shoulders and said, "Thanks. I'll be going now."

With that, Halter leapt out of the truck. His large body swelled outward like a samurai dressed for battle, with its plating and the various weapons it was equipped with.

*Boom!*

After he landed, Halter turned all the gears in his body to take yet another leap. From behind, he heard Vermouth shouting loudly, "Hell yeah! Go get 'em, Boss!!"

• • ● • •

Along with Giovanni and Nono, Naoto descended to the fifteenth floor of the core tower.

Here, the entire floor had been made into a mega-sized spring barrel. It was an incredibly vast space, with a total height of three thousand meters and a diameter of five thousand meters. Its outer circumference was greater than fifteen thousand meters.

Its outer walls were more than double the thickness of the other floors' walls. That was to be expected; the governor and escapement that controlled the energy of an entire city were kept here.

In other words, it was the very core of the city, more vital than any of its other mechanisms.

The floor was buried in countless swirling aggregates of gears from wall to wall. Altogether, they were like a massive steel board with a larger circumference than a star's. Of course, they weren't actually made of steel, but rather millions, billions—no, trillions of little whirlpools of gears.

"...It's almost like our universe, isn't it," Giovanni muttered quietly.

Naoto nodded silently in agreement.

Unending heat and an unfathomable number of rotating parts lay here. Even now, a thousand years later, humanity had yet to become capable of replicating these mechanisms.

This, too, was unmistakably one of "Y"'s legacies. This arcane super-technology was a gift that all humans in the modern era were blessed with upon birth.

Deep, deep inside this grand mechanism was a small hole. In the very center of this massive space, buried in gears of all sizes, the floor bulged upward greatly in the shape of a dome.

Installed there was a structure of some sort with countless shafts and bearings, an enormous cylinder made up of spheres— or maybe it was actually a screw, or perhaps the crown of a watch.

Standing before that enigmatic structure, Naoto asked, "Master, may I borrow Nono for a while?"

"I don't mind. I was ordered to follow your directions by Kiu when it came to the work, anyway."

"All right then, don't mind if I do," Naoto said, then turned around. "Nono, could you turn that massive screw for me when I give you the signal?"

"Si— Understood." The maid automaton bowed calmly before grasping onto the screw, which was larger than her own body, with her hands.

"By the way," Giovanni asked, sounding curious, "would you mind telling me what you're trying to do?"

"I'm going to pull this grid out of the Equatorial Spring's path," Naoto answered candidly.

Giovanni pinched his chin and tilted his head, replying,

"Hmm...? Do you intend to cut the grid off from its energy source?"

"Just temporarily, but yeah. I want to rearrange the coupling mechanism of the city, but I can't do it with this channel in the way."

"But wouldn't the city mechanisms be down during that time, then?"

"If it's just for a short while, the energy stored in the springs on this floor can cover things. The difficult part, though, is switching the springs from automatic winding to manual winding for that..."

As he said that, Naoto tore off a panel about a meter square at the bottom of the structure, revealing a cave-like tunnel underneath.

"In the few minutes it takes to switch the energy supply line, I'll need to manually set the right rotational speeds for each system of gears by allotting the right amount of energy to them myself."

Turning on his penlight, Naoto slid into the pit. Fiddling with a mechanism on the tunnel's wall, he connected it with the control panel he had brought with him.

Giovanni asked in a leisurely tone, "I'm not saying it'll happen, but theoretically, what would happen if you screw up?"

"If the energy coming in is too weak, then the mainspring will stop turning. If it's too powerful, the subsidiary springs will blast away. Hahaha!"

Naoto was laughing, but what he was saying was no laughing matter at all. He was intentionally risking the destruction of

Shangri-La's grid mechanisms. If there were even one person with any sense there, it wouldn't be strange for them to shoot Naoto dead on the spot for that, but for better or worse, there was no such person there.

Giovanni didn't even rebuke him, despite understanding fully just how dangerous Naoto's endeavor was. He simply looked on silently as Naoto worked with his hands, like a teacher watching over a student.

Popping his head out of the tunnel, Naoto called out loudly, "Nono, are you ready?"

The automaton replied dispassionately, "Si— I am standing by. Any time you are ready."

"All right then, here goes," Naoto said, then took a deep breath. He calmed his breathing, sharpened his alertness, and cleared his mind of all stray thoughts, then gave his orders.

"We're beginning now. Start turning."

With the sound of heavy machinery creaking into motion, the hole began to rumble.

With much effort from her crouching position, Nono slowly turned the enormous screw, and the gears of the structure began to turn as well in response.

As the vibrations quietly spread out, several cylinders that were embedded into the walls of the hole began to stick out one by one while turning.

The cylinders' finely carved pins plucked the gear combs against the wall of the hole, letting out a shrill sound. Eventually, all the parts in the hole began to bustle like an enormous music box. The hole seemed to be an entire system of parts by itself—a complete, stand-alone mechanism.

"Let's see what these keys are for... 'Gear Shift,' 'Equatorial Link'..." There was uncertainty in Naoto's hands as he fiddled with the control panel. "Ugh, these aren't it... Ah, it's this one! 'Self-Wind'...begin!"

Immediately after, the system shifted to a different mode. It changed the supply of energy from the Equatorial Spring to the energy stored in the grid. One part of the structure in front of Naoto—a difference engine—began to turn its gears furiously.

The gear-based computer began to make loud typewriter-like sounds. Above its control panel, a metal belt with countless holes bored into it—a punch card—slid from one side to the other.

But Naoto wasn't paying attention to any of that. He didn't need the information from the punch card to grasp the structure of the core tower. To begin with, he couldn't pull off reading one with his fingertips like Marie could, anyway.

"All right... Shifting from the 546th system of gears to the 235th. Establishing connection," Naoto muttered as he hit a key on the control panel. As soon as he did, he felt a galaxy of gears that had been lying dormant begin to come to life.

Like a small spark gradually growing into a large flame, more and more mechanisms began to turn as a small system of gears was disengaged and a large system was engaged in its place through a process of orderly chaos.

"I've seen many people in my time, but I've never met anyone like you, Mr. Naoto..." the old man muttered abruptly. "You're well aware of your own inexperience. However, you have zero doubt whatsoever when it comes to your own gut feeling. In that you have absolute confidence—a powerful conviction that goes beyond fanaticism. It's truly mysterious. You're humble to a fault, but somehow just as arrogant."

"Umm...should I take that as a compliment, or...?"

"Eh, it's just my impression of you."

While looking back at Giovanni with a puzzled face, Naoto hit another key. *Rotational speed at 1,544 radians per second; beginning shift to second gear.*

A screech sounded. It didn't come from the mainspring, but rather from the mechanism that had been connected to it.

"Crap, it's turning too fast," Naoto said as he fiddled with the control panel.

*Resetting the clutch from second gear back to low gear.*

Some of the cylinders that protruded out from the wall of the hole began to recede while turning in the opposite direction. At the same time, a deep, pulsating sound rattled through the entire floor.

*Discarding the seventh channel; accelerating the 124th system.*

"Looks like it connected...but the link looks a bit thin. I'll have to connect another cylinder somewhere."

*Rerouting the fifth channel to bypass the 646th system.*

A splitting roar broke out. One of the cylinders in the hole burst out of the wall like a cannonball, then immediately stopped.

"Aggggggggggh, goddammit! Their rotational speeds won't maaaaatch!" Naoto cried out. He rushed to fiddle with the control panel, upon which the sound immediately dropped lower in both pitch and volume. However, a deep grating sound coming from afar was still audible.

Naoto couldn't stop himself from grumbling. "Argh, c'mon, damn! Marie could probably do this while humming away... Why won't it just work the way I want it to?!"

"There's no way around that. Unlike me or her, you've only just begun taking your first baby steps," Giovanni said with a pained smile. "But, well...do you want to know a trick?"

"...A trick?"

"I'll clue you in, as it's still too early for me to die. Of course, I don't know what it is that you're doing exactly, but the tuning of mechanisms like that is all more or less the same."

"Then please do so, now! Within the next thirty seconds, to be exact!" *Otherwise we're dead meat!*

Despite the frantic look on Naoto's face, Giovanni spoke calmly. "You said that you have a full grasp of this core tower's structure, right?"

"Well basically, yeah!"

"Then can you imagine something that surpasses it?"

"Huh?" Naoto gasped, his eyes widening.

Looking down at Naoto, Giovanni smiled. "Enough with this foolishness. Don't aim for the best. That's merely the last stop on your journey."

"..."

"Aim for better. This isn't a compromise, but a challenge. That's how your mindset should always be. In other words, that should be your path in life."

"...Ngh!"

Just then, Naoto hit a key on the control panel.

*Reengaging the clutch to the top gear.*

Following that, several overlapping shrill sounds rang out. The unpleasant discord of what sounded like metal being scraped away reverberated throughout the hole.

"If aiming for perfect is leaving you at a standstill, you might as well exhaust yourself trying all sorts of crazy solutions instead. Once you do that, everything that was confounding you will start to fall into place. That's just how things work in our world."

*Resetting the rotational speed to 3,669 radians per second.*

"It's too fast."

*Resetting the rotational speed to 3,257 radians per second.*

"Now it's too slow."

*Resetting the rotational speed to 3,467 radians per second!*

The shrill sounds united as one in a resonant accord, and all the other mechanisms appeared to be engulfed by the galaxy of gears as they revved up their speeds to synchronize with it.

"For example," Giovanni began, "right now, you're just another player on stage. The missing score is no hindrance to you; you have it all in your mind. You're recreating the perfect sound, but what's the point, even if you achieve that?"

"So that's why I should always strive for better, huh...?"

"Even just as you are right now, you could surely become an absolute top-class player. But you could never become a composer, nor even an arranger, like this. You'd never reach that girl's level; in fact, you wouldn't even ever reach mine."

"That may be the case right now," Naoto said as he looked up at Giovanni, "but when do you think I'll be able to overcome that? As soon as today? Or if that's impossible, then tomorrow?"

"You truly are a mysterious boy, aren't you?" Giovanni returned Naoto's gaze with a wry smile. With eyes filled with composure and expectation befitting of a veteran craftsman, he shot a challenging look at Naoto. "Why bother asking these old bones what you're already sure of in your gut, heart, and soul? Or should I take that as a declaration of war?"

Naoto didn't reply. Instead he simply widened his smile as he continued to look up into Giovanni's eyes with a challenging gaze.

"Very well. But remember this. Every time you advance one step, I'll remain one step further ahead."

Though the tone of Giovanni's voice might be gentle, Naoto distinctly sensed unmistakable ferociousness hidden in his words.

Actually, he probably had no intention of hiding it at all.

*Stand up. Run. Face forward. Keep aiming higher. Train yourself to reach new heights.*

*Using those new heights as my new footing is exactly how I can reach yet further heights!*

The old man sneered, baring his teeth. "I may have only been a clocksmith for a mere eighty years, but it's been an eighty years that I'm proud of. It is my belief that demonstrating to the younger generation of clocksmiths just how much one must sacrifice for mastery is also part of the older generation's job."

*This is it,* Naoto thought. *This dissatisfaction. This constant demand of more from oneself even after achieving a mastery that is*

315

*built upon a lifetime of experience. Surpassing the limits by a mile, yet still remaining in an endless pursuit of more. Always challenging himself to do better in the endless game to reach an impossible ideal.*

Naoto knew of someone who gave him a similar impression. It was Marie.

She and Giovanni were the same in that they both lived life at a blistering pace with a motto of "never give in, never give up." However, the impression Naoto got from Giovanni was a far more tenacious, perfected version of that image.

Another way to put it would be that Marie would end up like Giovanni if she continued to follow the right path.

*This kind of mentality must be something that I'm critically lacking in, which is why I wish I could be like them so badly, Naoto thought. Even if God were to appear before their eyes, they would surely declare, undaunted: "I'll surpass you, just you watch."*

*And then, they'd never give up until they actually made good on that declaration. Even if they actually did surpass God, they'd surely just set their sights on a new target and continue dashing towards it.*

*They'd probably keep that up until their very last breath. That's just the blistering nature of those who would try to claw at the throne of God.*

Naoto hit a key on the control panel. "System all clear... Full synchronization, start!"

With the help of a small control panel, the core tower, and his own ears, Naoto gained control over Shangri-La Grid.

The preparations were set. All that was left now was to take a deep breath, harden his resolve, and throw down the gauntlet.

*I don't know if I can live the way Marie or Giovanni do. Well, I probably can't. Their way of life is different from mine. But nonetheless, I don't want to lose to them.*

*I'd hoped that one day I could get ahead of people like them who run like the wind. If that's indeed what I want, then there's only one answer.*

Naoto muttered, "I'll do the things I want to do, the way I like it, until I pull it off."

He swore to himself: *Even if people mock me as childish, or write me off as selfish, that's what I'm going to do. Putting up with things, compromising, making concessions...*

*Screw all of that.*

*That's why I'll begin today, now, with this one strike. I couldn't care less about justice, or ideals, or sound rationales. If you've got a problem with that...*

"Now then, come at me all you want...nggggggh!!"

Immediately after, Shangri-La Grid was hit by a severe earthquake.

· · ● ● ● · ·

In the northern region of the Andaman Sea, which sat just south of Shangri-La Grid, there were currently several battleships deployed. They were the united force that had been summoned by IGMO, comprised of units from the militaries of the surrounding countries.

They had been summoned there because there was supposedly

information that the heinous terrorist group Second Ypsilon, who had appeared a month ago in Japan's capital, Tokyo Grid, had escaped to Shangri-La Grid.

The world's leading city of crime and the world's leading terrorist group had been combined together. Who knew just how explosive the combination of the two might be. Given the situation, the soldiers naturally thought that a landing operation would immediately be executed...but that didn't happen.

They had been given one order, and one order only: "Monitor the situation."

They were not to make a move yet, because it was a grid in Thai territory, because negotiations were currently being conducted with local authorities, because of concerns about the potential effect on regional economies and the lives of civilians... there were various reasons, but basically, things boiled down to political pressure.

The surrounding countries were all in agreement that they didn't want to unnecessarily provoke Shangri-La Grid. Because of that, despite there being ten-odd warships rallied there, they weren't even allowed to set up an economic blockade. They could only chew their nails as they watched cargo ships (and ones that were surely stuffed full of illegal goods at that) come and go right before their eyes.

While it vexed them, as soldiers they couldn't simply ignore their governments' orders and take independent action. The only thing they could do was to look for something that might change the minds of the brass by diligently monitoring the sonar.

"Captain, the gauge readings show something strange," an information officer on the Thai destroyer *Maha Rat* reported.

"Strange?" Captain Thanarat parroted, sounding confused. "What do you mean?"

"Well, continuous small-scale tremors have been detected coming from Shangri-La Grid. Furthermore, there appears to be some sort of connection problem between the grid and the Equatorial Spring."

"Does that imply they're man-made phenomena?"

"The possibility of that is high, but the only thing I can say for sure is that values in this range have never been recorded here before."

Captain Tharanat's expression turned grim. The only group he could think of that would try something like messing with a grid mechanism was Second Ypsilon.

*So, the infamous terrorist group has finally made their move, huh.*

*This operation is being directed by IGMO. Its objective is to oppose Second Ypsilon's actions. As such, these abnormal circumstances are the perfect excuse to take concrete action.*

"Call the Thai command center! Tell them there's a possibility that Second Ypsilon has made a move, and ask for further instructions."

"Roger!"

However, the reply they received from sending a report was not the one they were looking for.

The orders from their government remained unchanged: "Continue monitoring."

They tried asking the IGMO flagship as well, but likewise, the reply was, "Remain on standby."

"Damn these indecisive cowards...!" Captain Tharanat growled, grinding his teeth. To begin with, this whole ordeal was a massive embarrassment for the Thai military.

First they'd had one of their destroyers stolen by Second Ypsilon, then one of their military harbors destroyed, then failed to catch them inside their own country. Furthermore, the grid they escaped to was one of Thailand's grids to begin with.

*We must redeem ourselves here at any cost, but the fleet we're a part of is an allied force made up of ships from the regional countries. If we ignore our own government's orders and act without permission, we wouldn't just be disgraced; we might even be sunk by ships from the other countries for acting on our own.*

*In that case, we need another push of some sort. A grand cause that would provide justification for us acting at our own discretion...*

"Captain!" the information officer cried out.

Immediately after, the bridge of the ship was rocked by a heavy jolt that came with what sounded like a growl from the depths of hell.

"What's going on?!"

"I-It's an earthquake! The epicenter's in Shangri-La Grid! This reading is way above the standard for quakes!" the information officer replied while clinging to the transmission equipment next to him.

He then went on to report that the earthquake was affecting

the surrounding countries and causing tsunamis in the waters they were in as well.

"Captain, this is clearly a manmade calamity! They've finally gotten serious...!"

"Urgh...ngh!" Captain Tharanat uttered in distress as he pondered what to do. *There's no way these readings are due to some sort of malfunction in our gauges. Without a doubt, Second Ypsilon has made their move now. Is there a possibility that this is a trap, or a stratagem of some sort? Of course. But if we twiddle our thumbs in fear of that, we might end up letting a calamity unfold right before our eyes...!*

He made his decision. "Turn ten degrees to port and turn both propellers on full throttle! We're heading to Shangri-La Grid!"

"Roger, accelerating at full throttle!" the helmsman replied as he turned the rudder.

He confirmed with his naked eye that the other ships were also turning one by one after them.

"Receiving transmission from the flagship *Isvarah*!"

"Connect them to me."

After a momentary pause, an angry voice shouted out from the transmission device by the commanding platform. "*Maha Rat*, what are you doing?! You are not to take solitary action!"

"With all due respect, Your Excellency," Captain Tharanat replied with utmost composure, "This is clearly an emergency situation. Second Ypsilon is trying to do something dangerous in Shangri-La Grid. Swiftly subduing their terrorism is our mission."

"We're the ones who make the call on that!"

"I recognize the current circumstances to be a case where emergency judgment should be applied. We're simply fulfilling our duty in line with standard protocol."

"No; your actions are breaching orders!"

"I see that we have a difference in opinion. In that case, allow me to justify myself in the council room *later*. Over and out," Captain Tharanat said as he hit the switch on his transmission device.

The information officer asked with a stiff face, "Captain, are you sure?"

It was undoubtedly an emergency situation, but ignoring orders from the flagship so flagrantly would inevitably lead to problems later on. That was the true essence of the officer's question, but his captain seemed to interpret it differently.

Captain Tharanat returned a calm gaze at the officer. "How can I possibly not be? Tell me, what are we here for?"

"Sir, to respond to Second Ypsilon's actions."

"Then our mission is clear. Everyone, do your jobs." Captain Tharanat paused to look over the whole bridge before loudly giving out his orders. "Every second counts! Launch the fighters we have aboard! Those in the army are to prepare for landing immediately!"

· · ● · ·

Just as Shangri-La Grid was struck by a tempestuous earthquake, a silhouette leapt out of a window from one of the upper floors of Pandora's Inn.

The shadow blazed downward through the air along the exterior of the hotel, as if she were gliding on it at a speed far beyond what was humanly possible. It was a child automaton, donned in armor with a silver and red color scheme, carrying a blonde-haired girl under one arm.

It was Marie and AnchoR.

*Kabooooom!*

After tearing right through the atmosphere at supersonic speed, they landed with a thunderous boom, like that of a submarine's depth charge detonating. The shockwaves tore up the pavement and blew debris everywhere.

"Ahh...!"

Marie had closed her eyes, expecting a violent jolt from landing, but none came. In fact, it almost felt as if she had gently been laid onto a bed of feathers.

*Where's the shock of impact? What happened to the law of inertia?*

Such questions crossed her mind, but Marie set them aside for now as she opened her eyes.

AnchoR asked with a puzzled face, "Hm...? Mother, are you all right?"

"I'm fine. More importantly, how do you feel? Does anything feel off?"

"It's perfect!" AnchoR replied happily with a blush. She threw out her chest and puffed through her nose. "AnchoR's fully back in business!"

"That's good to hear," Marie said, smiling back at her. She then slipped out of AnchoR's underarm and instantly fell on her butt, her feet caught in the violent tremors that were still going strong.

"Ugh...is that idiot trying to stir up a ruckus all by himself?" Marie scowled. *This earthquake is clearly different from the minor tremors that occur when the grid mechanism releases built-up stress. There's almost no doubt that this is something Naoto cooked up.*

*In which case...* Marie thought as she turned around. Looking up at the girl who remained standing effortlessly despite the violent shaking, she said, "AnchoR, you should go help RyuZU."

"Okay! But Mother, what will you do, then?" AnchoR asked worriedly.

Marie smiled confidently. "I'll be fine. I can at least take care of myself. More importantly," she continued with a solemn face, "RyuZU's in far more danger. For her to have asked me for *a favor*, things have to be pretty dire."

*She said that the one who attacked us was an Initial-Y, and she had clearly mentioned before that she could never win in a head-on battle against any of her sisters.*

"Y-yeah...Big Sis isn't very strong, so..."

"I still have trouble wrapping my head around that concept, but well...in that case, the only one who can save her is you, AnchoR."

As she finished speaking, the tremors finally died down. It appeared that the quake had caused quite the chaos, as screams and rumbles could be heard from afar.

Marie got on her knees before standing up. She then set both her hands onto AnchoR's shoulders and said, "Go now. Do the job that only you can do."

AnchoR widened her eyes. She replied, tightening her lips, "Yes." She nodded firmly. Then, turning around, she walked away from Marie a little, then instantly lowered her body.

*Boom.*

Smashing the road beneath her into pieces, the little automaton blasted off with the force of thunder.

As Marie saw her off, she muttered quietly, "Now then, I wonder what I should do."

She needed a plan. Marie held her chin and tilted her head, thinking. *From the earthquake just now, it seems that Naoto's up to something in the core tower, though I'm not sure what he's trying to do. Does that mean I should go lend him a hand?*

*But it'll be tough for me to break into the core tower by myself, considering that the Arsenal lackeys must be on high alert right now after what just happened...*

*As I expected, the first thing I need to do is get in contact with Naoto somehow.*

At that moment, Marie's mind suddenly went blank.

"...Whaah?" She had been staring up into space while pondering, but she suddenly noticed something peculiar in her field of vision.

The sun had begun to set and the sky was taking on a vivid red in the southeastern nation. It was a clear day without a single cloud to be seen—correction: there were actually a number of thin, twisting lines of white.

*I've seen something like this before. It was when I was invited to an air show somewhere. The letters written in smoke by the gracefully-dancing airplanes looked pretty close to this.*

Marie tried reading the words that the white bands spelled out: "Quit slacking, Ms. Walking Landmine, and get your butt to the westernmost clock tower immediately!"

Apparently, the sender had even made sure to punctuate his message properly. He wouldn't want to be rude, after all.

*I get the principle behind it.*

With control over a city's core tower, writing some words in the sky with clouds by manipulating the atmospheric pressure and gravity in the city was child's play, but...

"That idiot... Did he seriously cause an earthquake just to do this?"

Struck by an intense pang in her forehead, Marie inadvertently staggered. *Calm down. No matter how stupid he is, he can't be that—wait, no. He's actually even stupider. Wait, wait, wait. Calm down, Marie Bell Breguet. This is nothing new. You shouldn't be getting flustered. Yeah, he's an idiot, but there's usually some logic behind his idiocy...*

*Hm...? Isn't this weird?*

Marie sank deep into thought, her face turning serious.

*If he just wanted to relay this message to me, he could have just hijacked a communications line near me. Actually, if that's all he wanted, he wouldn't have even had to do that; he could have just had Vermouth tell me that when he was here.*

*Yet, he's deliberately choosing to use such a conspicuous method, and in plain language at that. Does he want the enemy to know our plans, or something? I'm already being targeted by just about every organization in Shangri-La as is, yet that guy...*

"Wait, don't tell me that's his aim?!"

Marie was shocked.

*The message itself couldn't be clearer: go to the westernmost clock tower in the city, which is the ninth. He's most likely got some work that he wants me to do there. I can guess what he wants me to do as well...but what would happen if he publicized these instructions?*

Marie already had a target on her back. One so large, in fact, that an assassin came after her right after RyuZU left. Revealing where she was headed now would let the enemy know exactly where to look for her.

"That guy! Is he trying to lure the enemy by using me as bait?!"

*It's not a bad plan. By giving our enemies a location, we can predict their moves and take care of them all at once, which would also allow us to limit the amount of damage done to the city. But...*

"And just when I thought I'd finally gotten used to his stupidity...ngh!"

*The problem is that this means I'll have to break into a clock tower full of all those enemies waiting for me. In other words, he's basically just throwing it all on me to do something about these organizations.*

"That perverted, rotten, no-good dumbass! The hell is he thinking?! Does he think I'm a Hollywood action star or something?!" Marie yelled, stomping her foot in frustration.

*Like I could possibly pull off such a stunt!*

Just then...

Sensing something behind her, she turned around and saw a large truck headed right towards her at a fearsome speed.

As she rushed onto the sidewalk, the truck suddenly braked harshly before coming to a screeching halt slightly in front of her.

A woman with an insolent look on her face leaned out from the driver's seat—or rather, a cyborg man did. "Hey! My cute Parisienne! Need a ride?"

It was Vermouth, who was apparently in a good mood for some reason.

As Marie stared at him while giving him the stink-eye, she asked, "Oy...did you get a fix just now or something?"

"Leave me alone; women wouldn't understand. I was just re-minded of the young boy dreamer that I was for the first time in a while... So, what's it gonna be? You gettin' in?"

"Yes, well, I suppose I could grace you with my presence."

*"Oui, mademoiselle."* With a flippant smile on his face, Vermouth opened the door of the passenger seat.

As she climbed up to the door and got in, Marie said, "You really just like to pop out of nowhere at just the right time, don't you?"

"That's my job, y'see," Vermouth said with a shrug as he hit the gas.

"So, should I head to the ninth clock tower, or...?"

"Yes, but the problem is..."

*There's surely going to be all sorts of enemies standing in our way, Marie thought. That'll most likely include thugs from Market, Restaurant, the other organizations—and of course, Arsenal as well.*

*It might be tempting to write them off as mere punks, but I have to imagine there'll be some ex-soldiers and mercenaries among them.*

*And it's not just going to be cyborgs and lightly armored automata, either. There're surely going to be some heavily armored automata and stuff in that class as well. So how should we try to break through?*

Seeing Marie furrow her brows, Vermouth smirked. "Look at that pretty face; it's no wonder all the tough guys throughout Shangri-La are just drooling to get their hands on you."

"Hey, don't put it in such a disgusting way!"

"Shouldn't you be happy that you're getting attention from guys?"

"Who'd be happy about that?!"

"Just relax, would you, *mademoiselle*?" Vermouth said, suddenly turning quiet. "It isn't every day that we get to put on an improvised play, so enjoy it for what it is. Everyone's simply running around doing whatever the hell they want, showing just how stupid they are right now. You being all serious by yourself isn't going to help anyone."

Marie snorted, tightening her lips sullenly. "If this is an improvised play, then that would make my role an offer that someone forced onto me, right? So what it boils down to is simply that he's making me pay the consequences for him doing whatever he wants, no?"

"If you don't like his script, then why don't you just tear it to shreds? No one'll blame you, y'know."

"This far into it all?" *The show's already begun,* Marie thought. *I can more or less guess what Naoto wants to do. Most likely, he hasn't gained full control over the core tower because his technical skills aren't up to par with his senses yet.*

*Based on that assumption, it can be inferred that the reason he wants me to go to a clock tower is so I can back him up from outside of the core tower. In that case, then...what would happen if I chose not to go to a clock tower now?*

*It probably won't end with just the core tower becoming unresponsive. I don't know exactly what Naoto did, but I'm sure he made a mess... Just imagining the cleanup work that'll be necessary makes my head hurt.* "Curse that idiot. He's basically blackmailing me."

"Don't let it get to you, my lovely attrice. If it's a stage you must get on, then let's put on some fireworks, yeah?" Vermouth said cheerfully before sharply turning the steering wheel.

The scenery outside the windows blurred into a swirl. Turning her head to face forward, Marie saw a group of men pointing guns at their truck.

*They're making an entrance already, huh.*

Marie got down and pulled out her coil spear, growling, "It'd be great if this could end as a comedy! But in reality, life goes on both before and after the curtain call, you know?"

"Cleanup is for the stage hands, darling. The starring actress should just throw on her gown and pop open a champagne."

"Is that so? Then tell me, who's going to clean up the mess before our eyes?!"

"Oy oy, have you forgotten?" Vermouth replied nonchalantly with a ferocious smile.

Immediately after, gunshots and screams simultaneously rang out. The group of gunmen in front of them all collapsed onto the ground, having been shot out of nowhere.

"What...?!"

As Marie goggled at the sight before her, Vermouth stepped on the gas and said, "You've got the coolest man alive, someone with unrivaled skills by your side as your bodyguard, don't'cha?"

· · ● · ·

"Nice timing, Vermouth. You have my thanks." Halter smiled as he gazed at the speeding truck through the sights of his gun.

He was laying down in sniping position on the rooftop of an old hospital to the west of Suan Dok Gate. The hospital was considerably taller than the surrounding buildings, so the view on the rooftop was largely unobstructed. It was the perfect location to snipe from.

Halter laid down his sniping rifle, then threw off his urban camouflage cloak and got up.

*I've eliminated most of the threats along the way.*

*Well, the ones that belonged to an organization, at least. And as for the small-time lone wolves who were just crashing the party, they're probably scurrying away with their tails tucked right about now. There might be one or two with defective noses left, but Vermouth alone will be enough to deal with them. What's left is the big fish.*

He turned around. His eyes landed on the ninth clock tower, which sat inside the white-painted grounds of a temple. A unit of Arsenal's troops was gathered there.

*Unsurprisingly, even from afar it's clear that they're on a totally different level from the street punks with guns. Their equipment might be all over the place, but considering they've got an orderly line of defense set up, they've certainly received a fair level of training. They should have actual combat experience too, to some degree.*

*I'm counting about four hundred to five hundred men. A battalion-sized unit, huh... But even that is nothing compared to the six heavily armored automata that I also see.*

"We're supposed to demolish this force." Halter smiled as he cringed. *That's quite the joke.*

As a mercenary who had stood on many battlefields before, his instincts were telling him to withdraw immediately. Heavily armored automata were things a cyborg was neither meant to, nor should, face.

He might be sporting a seventh-gen body right now, but when all was said and done, he was only one man. If he got hit with one of the side cannons of a heavily armored automaton, there'd be nothing left of him. Even shots from the lightly armored ones or the soldiers might inflict lethal harm to him if he took a direct hit.

Under normal circumstances, he wouldn't even try to fight them to begin with. Instead, he'd look for another method. But things were different now.

Could he really pull off this reckless, irrational, absurd stunt?

That was the question Halter was faced with.

"Well, ain't no way around it. Guess I'll take a swing at it."

Curling his lips, Halter leapt off the rooftop into free fall from an eight-story building without any protective gear. Someone with a living body would die instantly upon hitting the ground, but he was able to land easily with his cyborg body. He then smashed down on the button of a device hanging from his belt.

*Boom! Boom! Boom!*

As the blasts resounded from the direction of the clock tower, countless cries and shrieks overlapped. Halter had just detonated some bombs there that he planted in advance.

As he lowered his body and broke into a sprint, he thought, *Fair and square? If you want to fight honorably like Don Quixote, then go right ahead. But as a mercenary, I'm going to fight like one. I'm going to fight as cowardly, despicably, underhandedly, and nastily as I possibly can.*

Making his way through one last side alley, he slipped himself to the side of the enemy base. All the while, gunshots continued to resound from the enemy base without pause.

*So it's begun.*

*The ones shooting right now are probably Market's troops under Don Carlos's command. Having explicitly violated his agreement with Kiu Tai Yu, his ass is basically on fire right now. Now that he's failed to abduct Marie from the hotel, the only choice left for him is to try to take advantage of the commotion we've been stirring up to crush Arsenal, then try to capture Marie again.*

*I'm guessing he thought the blasts I set off gave him a good opportunity to start an attack, but...*

"Sorry, but you'd need more help than that," he said out loud.

*They might be momentarily confused right now from my bombs, but I imagine that Arsenal's troops will get back on their feet in no time. Once that happens, it's the end of the road for Don Carlos.*

"Guess I'll do what I can to shore things up," Halter muttered. He pulled out a mini grenade launcher from his back and, as he continued to run, pointed it upwards without aiming at anything in particular.

What the grenade launcher was loaded with was not a grenade.

With crisp, sizzling sounds, a smoke bomb shot out of the launcher. It traced an arc in the air until it was right above the line of defense that the enemy had set up, and then it exploded, spreading smoke evenly over the area.

"Wh-what's going on?!"

"It's a smoke bomb! They're gonna charge at us! Prepare yourselves to fight!" one of Arsenal's soldiers yelled.

But no charge from Market's troops came.

Halter's aim in setting off the smoke bomb was to create confusion among Arsenal's troops. The automata might be another matter, but the human soldiers couldn't recklessly fire if they had their vision obstructed like this, as it could lead to friendly fire.

That said, one smoke bomb wasn't going to buy him much time. He had to hurry. Looking in front of him, he saw a soldier with a rifle at the ready.

*Is he in the middle of a patrol? Looks like he hasn't noticed me yet. He's being a nuisance.*

Upon determining that without hesitation, Halter accelerated, closing the distance between them. As he came right up to the soldier, he finally noticed Halter, shouting, "It's the ene—!"

"It sure is," Halter muttered as he grabbed the soldier's face and twisted it. *Crack.*

He immediately began running again, continuing right on his way. As he made his way deeper into the enemy base, the buildings surrounding him became shorter and shorter. He was getting close to the central plaza. Even here, he was still under the cover of his smoke bomb, the smoke having been carried quite a ways by the wind.

Just as he made it through an alley, he saw a heavily armored automaton in the shadows of the buildings and smoke.

*I can't tell what model it is. It feels somewhat like a Vacheron unit, but it doesn't match anything I know. I'm guessing it's a unit that was modded in this city.*

Detecting Halter with its compound visual sensors, the automaton turned its 98 mm autocannon towards Halter and fired.

Halter continued to run without stopping. Finding cover wouldn't help. If a storm of armor-piercing ammo came his way, it'd pierce right through and turn him into swiss cheese regardless. Trying to lose the automaton was also futile. Its compound eyes could easily capture his figure, even in the midst of this smoke.

*If they were the dollies in our group, Halter wondered, would they be able to see shells this fast coming and dodge them?*

*If so, that would be so unfair. No matter how advanced artificial bodies get, they still wouldn't be able to speed up the processing speed of the brain. Even with the help of stimulants, my brain is still only moving a mere 64% faster than normal right now.*

For a human brain to visually process a shell flying towards him at three thousand meters per second out of the barrel and then dodge it was, to understate things, impossible, even adjusting for his movement trajectory.

Halter had only one option: to slide into the one blind spot of the enemy automaton—by its feet.

"...Ngh!"

A shell exploded right behind him, the thunderous noise tearing right through the membrane of his auditory sensors. Glass and other debris from the buildings scattered everywhere as he dashed towards the automaton's feet. Suppressing the nasty chills he was getting from putting himself within reach of Death's scythe, he looked up at his target. It was a bipodal, heavily armored automaton with a reverse joint design.

"An automaton of this type should have a weakness right around...there!" Halter muttered, ascertaining his precise target. He then leapt upward.

Halter latched on to a side ladder used for maintenance that rested in a small gap in the automaton's back plating.

Sensing that Halter had snuck onto its back, the heavily armored automaton twisted and turned like an untamed horse. However, Halter was able to hold on tight with the strength of his artificial arm as he pulled out a pistol from his waist with his other hand.

It was the trans-system pistol he had acquired two days ago: Monarca.

A typical cyborg would have been shaken off long ago by now, but Halter was still holding on strong as he switched the pistol to strafe mode with proficiency and took aim.

He fired twenty rounds of 15 mm armor-piercing ammo, but even that wasn't enough to penetrate the plating of a heavily armored automaton. However, it was more than enough firepower to shatter the lock on the maintenance hatch.

Putting his gun away, Halter tore the hatch right off and peered at the mechanisms inside.

*If I were Marie, he thought with a wry smile, or if I had the skills of a Meister, I'd probably be putting on a show hacking this machine and making it do what I want but, well, I'm not.*

"Not a big deal, though. I just have to do this instead then," he muttered as he took out a cylindrical module from his backpack and stuffed it inside an empty socket within the hatch.

The heavily armored automaton's behavior immediately changed. It writhed about and trembled as if it were in pain.

Taking advantage of the opportunity, Halter swiftly jumped off the automaton and hid himself in the shadows from the buildings and the smoke, while also taking care to elude the automaton's sensors.

Then, the heavily armored automaton suddenly turned around, readied its main cannon, and fired...at the allied base.

"Gwahhhh?!" a soldier screamed.

"Wh-what the... Wait! There are allies over here!!" another shouted angrily.

But the heavily armored automaton paid their cries no mind as it went on a rampage and fired every which way without aim.

Watching its rampage from afar, Halter whistled. "Hmm... Looks like that toy is more useful than I thought."

The module that Halter had stuffed inside the automaton was a device that interfered with its artificial intelligence. Right now, the automaton should be seeing everything around it as enemies due to the module interfering with its IFF system.

The module was highly illegal, having originally been developed by terrorist organizations for heinous purposes...but in this city, one could find it at the street stall around the corner.

Furthermore, it was supposed to be inserted before the unit that the AI was running booted up, not when the unit was already up and running in combat, but...

"Well now, how many enemies will you clean up for me?" Halter muttered dryly. *Ten? Twenty? If it takes down some of the other heavily armored automata as well, that'd be just perfect, but that's probably hoping for too much.*

*Still, with this, I've crushed one of the six greatest threats.*

*Five units left and several hundred soldiers. The battle's a total snafu right now. Market's troops might serve as a distraction for us to some extent, but on top of being incapable, they're not our allies either. So I'm supposed to clean the rest of this up by myself?*

Halter felt like something heavy was digging into his shoulders. He couldn't help but feel assaulted by a strong urge to just head back and gulp down a bottle of whiskey, but...

Letting out a deep, deep sigh, Halter stroked his bald head. "God, you leave me no choice, do you?!" he growled. "Fine, then. I'll show you what an old grandpa cyborg can do when he gets serious!"

• • ● • •

RyuZU was in the middle of an intense fight against TemP, who had activated her inherent ability.

The field she had chosen to fight on was an abandoned cylindrical building near the area where the fight originally began.

There was an atrium in the center of the building that let RyuZU move up and down freely, while the floors on the sides provided plenty of cover. It was a favorable stage for her, as her forte was fighting with speed and maneuverability in all three dimensions.

RyuZU dashed along the thick and sturdy walls like the ray of a shooting star. She sensed an incoming resonance reaction from her front, and immediately jumped to the left, just barely in time to escape the destructive blast.

"Ngh—!"

Unsatisfied with the speed of free fall, she propelled herself downward by using her pair of black scythes as an extension of her arms. She quickly slipped down to the floor below, heading towards the atrium.

Looking down, RyuZU saw TemP looking back up at her. Her entire body was covered in light and her lips were twisted into a mocking smile.

"I knew you were a slippery one...but it's still irritating," RyuZU muttered to herself, feeling antsy.

TemP's Phononic Gear was based on the same technology underlying the Fourth's Perpetual Gear, but was made in an effort to better control the infinite output of energy.

It was a rebellion against the nature of matter. By manipulating phonons, or sound particles, she could neutralize all vibrations and interfere with the boundaries of matter.

Right now, TemP could probably even remove the restraints of being physical matter and become a block of pure energy if she wanted to. As for what that meant...

Suddenly, TemP disappeared.

"Wha—?!"

RyuZU dodged to the side posthaste. To begin with, running away was all she could do against TemP's resonance attacks. Launching any kind of physical attack would have no effect whatsoever at this point.

Behind RyuZU came a burst of light, along with the sound of spacetime splitting. The matter that was caught up in the light lost its form. The wall, floor, and ceiling of the aisle that RyuZU had been standing on were all engulfed by light and annihilated, dissolving into pure energy.

The radiant ball of energy then took on the form of a girl, TemP. "I'm not going to let you get away, Elder Sister!!" she shouted.

TemP had not been programmed with a combat algorithm. The reason for that was simple: she'd be too much of a monster if she had been.

In other words, she wasn't designed to be a fighter. But, should she ever fight with a combat algorithm optimized for her capabilities, her combat strength would likely rival even that of AnchoR's.

After all, she was capable of changing the phase of all matter on demand.

*Move.* Just by thinking that, she could resonate with space-time and teleport.

*Break.* Just by thinking that, she could neutralize matter and annihilate it.

She was glowing brilliantly in an awfully flashy way right now, but that actually wasn't even necessary. By becoming a block of consolidated energy—or, in other words, *a vibration*—she could dance freely through spacetime while remaining unobservable, just like how the moon waxes and wanes, but remains present throughout all time.

This was Moon Phase—the inherent ability of the Third of the Initial-Y, TemP the Aerial.

RyuZU leapt.

She used all four limbs and her black scythes to accelerate in a 3D trajectory while deftly keeping herself under cover.

"Grr... You slippery little weasel!" TemP shouted.

While she might be able to deal with it if RyuZU were only moving in laterally, she just couldn't keep up in a battle of maneuverability. From her point of view, an enemy whom she could easily crush if she could just get her hands on her had slipped away at the last second many times now.

*RyuZU smiled. I imagine she is feeling quite vexed right now.*

*The massive quake earlier should mean that something is going on at the core tower. In other words, my master is making his move.*

*Despite being behind enemy lines, he is still fighting for his beliefs, following his own sense of justice.*

RyuZU felt proud of that fact. "Master Naoto..."

The spring hidden behind heavy gears in her chest throbbed, the nerve wires strung throughout her body resonated, and her main cylinder fluttered like a butterfly.

*What is it that I should do right now? As his follower, what should I strive for?*

The ball of energy shouted, "You're just going to run and run and run like that after running your big mouth?! You make me laugh, Elder Sister!"

"Being told that by my younger sister whose laughability remains in the present continuous tense really stings, I must say," RyuZU said without bothering to turn around as she leapt up even higher.

*That said, I don't have any counterattacks available, either.*

*My only weapons are my scythes, good for physical slash attacks only. Now that TemP has activated her inherent ability, even if I entered into Mute Scream, I wouldn't be able to deal a decisive blow to her.*

*Considering the situation, I guess my only way to win is to make TemP burn through her energy until she cannot maintain Moon Phase anymore.*

*But while it may be easy to evade her attacks because of her bad aim, her attacks are powerful enough that if I am hit by even one of them, that would be the end of it. Can I continue to dodge all of them indefinitely? Could that not possibly lead to an even more dire situation long before her spring runs out of energy?*

*This is really tough.*

RyuZU groaned.

Just then, the building shook. With an agonizing screech, spacetime was torn and part of the wall collapsed.

It wasn't one of TemP's resonance reactions. It was something more simple than that—destruction by fusion brought about by a ridiculous amount of energy.

An endearing voice shouted, "Big Sister!"

An angel stood in the midst of the dust and debris. It was AnchoR, clad in silver armor and wielding a giant sword that exceeded her own height in her hand.

"Wha—no way, AnchoR?!" the ball of energy cried.

"So, you made it in time. I guess that means Mistress Marie is not completely useless after all," RyuZU said, letting out a sigh of relief.

"Just who could possibly have repaired AnchoR, given the state that she was in...? Never mind; that doesn't really matter." TemP glared at her younger sister, who had joined the party uninvited. "AnchoR? I'm sorry to tell you, but I won't be destroyed again. Know that if you plan to get in the way of me killing Elder Sister, there will be pain coming your way, all right?"

The radiance shrouding TemP intensified threateningly. She couldn't afford to hold back against AnchoR.

Still, she could destroy anything in one hit. If she landed a direct hit with Moon Phase activated, even AnchoR wouldn't be able to just shrug it off, as sturdy as she was.

AnchoR's response to TemP's threat was to tilt her head with a blank face. She lowered her giant sword as she looked up at her two older sisters staring each other down in the atrium and asked, "Big Sisters...why are you fighting?"

"Huh?" TemP faltered, putting her hand against her lips. She clearly hadn't considered it before. As she stared into space, the light shrouding her turned hazy. "Why? That's because..."

"Because what?"

"Umm, well, I guess it'd be because Elder Sister wrecked me two hundred years ago...and because she started calling me a defective unit out of nowhere... I guess that's the gist of it?"

Receiving TemP's incoherent answer, AnchoR looked up at RyuZU and asked, "Is that what happened?"

"Yes, roughly speaking." RyuZU nodded.

AnchoR began to look more and more puzzled and asked, "Why did you do that?"

RyuZU nodded again. Adjusting her posture, she threw out her chest, replying, "Because she's a stupid girl."

Right after, she dodged to the side.

The place she had just been standing on was annihilated by a resonance reaction. As a ball of light engulfed the matter, TemP said from within that radiance, her voice trembling in anger, "That's how it is, AnchoR. Elder Sister seems to hate me for some reason."

"Stupid girl," RyuZU repeated while jumping. "I see that you really have forgotten the contract we sisters are all bound to."

Hearing a pitiful ring in RyuZU's voice, TemP gulped, muttering, "Con...tract?"

"You have everything confused. The supreme purpose you

were given, the abilities you were endowed with, their proper use, everything—all of it is something that is absolutely unforgivable."

"I'm not mistaken about anything!" TemP shouted. Light shot out from her eyes and gouged a hole out of the pillar right in front of RyuZU.

"I'm TemP the Aerial—no one can hold me down! 'Live more freely than anyone else! Act as you please!' ...That's the supreme mission I was given, and this is the power I was endowed with for that purpose!"

"Is that your answer? Do you really have no doubt of that whatsoever?" RyuZU asked pleadingly. It even sounded like she was begging for mercy.

However, TemP shook her head like a child throwing a tantrum and yelled, "What doubt? I don't know what you're talking about!"

"That is unfortunate."

RyuZU closed her eyes for just a second. When she re-opened them, what was gleaming from her eyes was pure resolve. "Goodbye, TemP. I imagine this will be our final farewell."

"Ngh, Elder SisterrrrrrrrrrRRRRRRR!!" TemP howled.

As RyuZU dodged the resonance reaction that sparked from TemP's howling, she landed next to AnchoR.

AnchoR said anxiously, "Big Sister..."

RyuZU cast her eyes downward, replying with a cold voice, "I made a grave mistake two hundred years ago, AnchoR. Despite knowing that TemP was broken, I bet on a fleeting hope."

"..."

"I figured that while she was broken now, someone might come along one day and help her remember the proper way to live. To that end, I stopped short of damaging her beyond repair, but..." She paused, sighing deeply. "However, seeing that she is repeating the same mistake even after being repaired, there is nothing more to be said. It is our job to finish her before she becomes *unstoppable*."

As she finished speaking, RyuZU looked up.

However, AnchoR shook her head, saying gently, "That's not true. You weren't wrong at all, Big Sister."

RyuZU was flabbergasted. Looking up at her older sister, AnchoR continued resolutely, "We have to stop her."

"But she's already—"

"Then we just have to stop her again. As many times as it takes," AnchoR said with a smile.

Gripping her giant sword tight with her left hand, she placed her right hand on her chest.

"Because that's what I promised...because that's what the power of AnchoR the Trishula is for!"

"..."

RyuZU's eyes widened. She was genuinely dumbfounded, which rarely ever happened to her. She remained still for several seconds, before putting on a pained smile. "You really are the adorable little sister who I am so proud of," RyuZU whispered.

AnchoR blushed in embarrassment, then took a step forward and said, "Now then, Big Sister!"

"Yes. Let us go now to stop another one of my cute little sisters, though I cannot say I am proud of this one!"

Their gears turned. Their wires crackled. Their cylinders pumped. With unwavering wills and a mission to accomplish, the two automata leapt up simultaneously.

• • ● • •

Witnessing the sight before him, Commander Cormack of Arsenal's enforcement unit muttered dumbfoundedly, "What is this...?"

He couldn't quite believe what was right before his eyes.

The adjutant by his side looked like he was about to faint as well. "Th-this... How can such a ridiculous thing..."

His body was shaking all over, so much so that it was really quite amazing that he was still standing up. He hadn't been shot or anything. His mind was crumbling purely from the mental shock.

Cormack understood exactly how his adjutant felt. He knew that was how humans naturally reacted to things beyond their comprehension. At the same time, for better or worse, he wasn't so dim-witted a man that he could escape from the reality before his eyes.

Hell was unfolding around them.

Just ten or twenty minutes ago this place was the plaza in front of the clock tower. But now, it was covered in flames and smoke, and the ground was full of holes.

Above all, the dead bodies of his soldiers—both human and cyborg—lay pitifully on the ground, along with the ruins of lightly and even heavily armored automata.

The large majority of these had been Cormack's subordinates. There were some guys from Market among the corpses who had been attacking as well, but that didn't matter to him right now. They were already dead, anyway.

He turned around. Behind him was a half-destroyed lightly armored automaton, three living soldiers including his adjutant, and four cyborg soldiers.

Everyone else was dead.

As a tactical advisor, Cormack had been in charge of an entire battalion—nearly the entire force of Arsenal. And yet, what was this mess? All he was left with was a half-broken piece of junk and seven subordinates.

It wasn't that he couldn't acknowledge that fact. The losses themselves were whatever to him. Simply in terms of the scale of destruction, Cormack had experienced even bloodier and more ruthless battlefields than this. Those had been *true* hell.

The problem was...

"You're telling me that all this was done by a single cyborg?!"

...this unbelievable truth.

Turning his head forward, he was able to make out the enemy in the scorched earth of the plaza. The lone man was kneeling in silence on top of a pile of corpses.

*Vainney Halter.*

Cormack had first confirmed his presence and realized who had been attacking them, aside from Market, when the six heavily armored automata were all destroyed. Up to that point, Cormack had been busy dealing with the chaos that was Market's assault force and the allied heavily armored automaton that had gone rogue.

Even after being discovered, the man had been a tough nut to crack.

By that time, half his battalion was already gone. Still, Cormack determined that the man was the biggest threat, and ordered his remaining troops to eliminate him. However, Halter shielded himself with their dead allies' corpses and used the natural obstacles in the plaza as cover, weaving in and out of the shadows like a phantom as he tore through the battlefield.

*His combat execution was simply marvelous. He always took the most rational, optimal line. I wish I could have captured some shots to publish in a tactical manual.*

*If you challenged him to a firefight, he'd crush you one-sidedly. If you pressed on until he ran out of rounds, he'd snatch one of your guns to use. And if you lost sight of him, twenty more of your allies would be dead by the time you found him again.*

*In the end, only by taking out my precious electromagnetic pulse magnet was I finally able to take him down. Dozens of allied cyborgs were inevitably caught in the pulse as well.*

"Fucking shit...! Just who is this monster?! I'd find it more believable if you told me he was an Initial-Y!"

*Yes...if that were the case, I could comprehend it, somewhat.*

*It'd have been better if we were crushed by one of those magical, miraculous things—"Y"'s legacy; that insanely advanced technology with its absurd capabilities. It'd still suck, but I'd probably have been able to accept it as being hit by a natural disaster or something.*

*But this is different.*

*Vainney Halter, that bastard...he should be a mere human!*

Cormack knew of the man's nicknames.

*Oberon. Overwork. The legendary mercenary who creates miracles in the most desperate of situations.*

*I didn't doubt his reputation. I didn't underestimate him. I assumed his reported combat résumé and achievements to be true...but even so, this kind of performance is simply unfathomable.*

*He seemed to have been using an outstanding artificial body, but that fact alone is hardly enough to justify a single soldier destroying a five-hundred-man battalion any more believable. Such a thing should never happen.*

"I won't accept it..." Cormack growled in a deep voice as he pulled out the pistol at his waist.

The hand holding the gun was trembling, so he had to stabilize it with his other hand as he carefully took aim at the head of the silent, kneeling man.

*All I have to do now is pull the trigger, and this absurdity will be forever gone from this world.*

"Grrawh! Like I'll accept such a thing!"

*Bang.*

• • ● • •

Halter was in the middle of darkness.

Well actually, that wasn't quite accurate.

The battle had been going smoothly for him, although that

might be an overstatement. Still, he felt he had accomplished quite a feat.

He might have inadvertently relaxed a bit, seeing that he was just about to complete his objective. Or perhaps the credit should go to the commander, who had resolved to shoot an electromagnetic pulse despite knowing that allied cyborgs would get caught in it as well.

In any case, Halter had been hit by an electromagnetic pulse grenade. It was a tactical weapon that made use of the forbidden electromagnetic technology. It was an item that shouldn't have been easy to obtain even in this city, but the commander had one nonetheless.

Halter was able to prevent his body from being entirely totaled, but the more relatively sensitive mechanisms in his body—like all of his sensors—had been destroyed.

Right now, out of the five senses, Halter had none. His mind was simply floating in a void, having lost reception of all external signals.

Under these conditions, he couldn't even move his limbs. It appeared that this was where he would meet his end.

*This is how I die after screwing everything up big time, huh... I'm sure the princess is gonna laugh at me for this. He groaned internally, unable to speak.*

To Halter, this wasn't exactly an unfamiliar sensation. This was how it felt when a human brain stored inside a clockwork case wasn't connected to any external input devices. It was something all cyborgs inevitably experienced at least once, when their brain was first transplanted.

If one didn't keep their mind active in that state, even the ego would fade. Forget the difference between up and down—even the flow of time would become murky. It was a phantom world more ephemeral than dreams, basically a state of pseudo-death.

It was said that someone mentally weak would go insane in a mere few seconds in this state, losing all sense of self.

Surprisingly, Halter didn't really dislike this sensation. Of course, he did feel some anxiety and unease at being completely defenseless against the external world, but even so, this tranquility that came with being released from all burdens gave him a sort of spiritual high.

There was nothing here.

Without any external signals coming in, the only thing he could use to affirm his own existence was his own mind. Or so that was how it should have been, but...

*"Oh? So you believe that just because you haven't seen it yourself, it doesn't exist, eh?"*

He heard a voice.

It felt like something that was said to him a few days ago—or was it a few months ago? It might even have been a few *years* ago. The flow of time was vague. He felt terribly sleepy. Whatever the case, this should just be a recollection of some sort, a playback of a past conversation in his mind, but...

*"Indeed, the only information you can access is what you can get through those sensors. You can only experience the world as others have defined it,"* the voice in the memory muttered.

Despite the awfully disjointed sentences, the voice had a strangely realistic feeling to it.

*"That is why, while there are those who doubt the existence of love or God, there are none who doubt the existence of money and power, because their existence need hardly be proved. It is self-evident."*

Suddenly, a doubt arose in Halter's mind.

Vainney Halter didn't believe in fate. He had been this way ever since the day he first stood on the battlefield as a living boy long, long ago—actually, probably even before then—and still was, to this very moment.

He had made it through countless battlefields and created countless fields of emptiness out of them. That was the raw reality he had faced. That there was no meaning in truth, so naturally, Vainney Halter didn't believe in God.

*"So long as you don't doubt that..."*

In that case, on what basis should Vainney Halter define himself?

Suddenly, his vision came back.

Perceiving the bullet rapidly closing in on him, Halter promptly moved to evade it.

"I-Impossible... How did he reboot?!" an enemy cried.

*I can feel my limbs again. My left arm is lightly damaged. The shock absorbers on my feet aren't working, but that's ignorable for now. Shutting down* FCS *and switching to manual aim. All sensors destroyed... Hm? Wait, then how am I sensing all this?*

Questions arose in Halter's mind, but for now, he continued to inspect his condition.

*Power efficiency is suboptimal with output at 57%—good enough to fight with.*

"I-Impossible!"

"Lee! What's going on?! Shouldn't that EMP have put him out of commission?"

"A cyborg that can move after being hit by an EMP? What?!"

Halter heard voices he shouldn't have been able to hear. Not only that, but his vision was sharper than usual. It felt almost as if his entire body had turned into visual sensors, pulling in light from all around him.

Overflowing information surged into his brain like a tsunami. He might lose his sense of self if he didn't continue thinking. Earlier, it was because of a lack of sensory input, but now it was because of an overflow of sensory input. It felt like omnipotence.

*Hmm, this doesn't feel too bad.*

"He did shut down at one point! If nothing else, all of his sensors at least should have been destroyed!"

"Fool! Then just how is he moving right now?!"

*Great point. I'd love to know myself.*

*But this body is definitely working. That fact is all that matters right now.*

Halter began to sprint.

Despite being in the silent darkness of sensory deprivation, he was still able to clearly perceive the enemy, somehow.

He charged.

Like how he was able to maintain his ego inside that state of emptiness which he had experienced many a time.

Right now, he could believe in the existence of his own soul without a doubt, despite it being an unobservable entity.

He threw out his fist.

With a motion he had repeated some tens of thousands of times before, his iron fist smashed down an enemy.

He could tell what had happened without even seeing it.

"K-kill him!" the enemy commander screamed.

"Fire! Blow him out of this worlddd...ngh!!"

Halter was aware that his brain was working far faster than normal right now. It wasn't just the usual 64% from cyborg enhancements. It might be 100%, 200%, or even infinitely faster. His artificial body moved with terrifying precision and speed.

He *perceived* the crossfire coming at him from all directions and dodged it. It wasn't that he saw it—his visual sensors weren't working. To begin with, there wouldn't have been enough time to dodge them by relying on sight. So what was going on, then?

Halter knew.

*Don't get bogged down trying to force yourself to see things that can't be seen. That just complicates things unnecessarily. Just assume that you do see it, that it is there. All you have to do is choose the reality that you want to see.*

*"There are countless worlds inside this infinite universe..."*

*That's what it means to exceed your limits.*

As a matter of fact, despite the fact that his body's power output was deteriorating, his reaction speed and performance continued to reach new heights.

*There's something in this universe that only a human brain can perceive,* Halter realized. *It is what Naoto Miura listens for when he covers his ears, and it seems that Marie Bell Breguet can now see it as well when she closes her eyes.*

*In that case, what about someone who isn't a genius? An average Joe? Just how should Vainney Halter, who can only perceive the world as forcefully defined for him by others, look upon reality?*

Doubt arose in his mind.

*On what basis should Vainney Halter define himself?*

*I don't believe in fate, miracles, or magic. Life, truth, this world—none of them feel significant to me.*

*I've seen people die countless times. I've also seen people survive by the skin of their teeth many times. I've experienced having hope shattered all too easily, as well as endless despair simply vanishing, countless times.*

*The cold truth is that both fortune and misfortune are ubiquitous in this world. Basically, it's all just like a joke—anything and everything.*

*And it's because fortune's smiled upon me countless times that I'm alive right now. I've had to overcome thousands and thousands of close encounters with death to be standing here today.*

*Is that unreasonable? Absurd?*

*But it's reality. A hard fact. There might be some reason behind it, some sort of unfathomable existence that intervened in my life. You want to call that God? Fine. But I won't accept that explanation myself.*

*Then, what should I believe in? What explanation should I*

*accept? For someone who, right now, has lost all of his five senses and can't confirm the existence of anything?*

He found the answer.

*Vainney Halter...what defines you is simply the strength of your will.*

Halter pulled out a knife from his belt. He glided forward one step. His movement felt relaxed, casual, even. In front of him were three cyborg soldiers pointing guns at him.

They fired.

He *perceived* the trajectories of the bullets. Only three would hit him if he stayed his course. He could ignore the rest. He raised his knife up near his eyes and sprinted. As the first bullet came, he blocked it with the ultra-hard blade of his knife.

*Ding!* Sparks flew out. His awareness grew sharper. He reflexively flung his arm and smacked down the second bullet before his conscious mind caught up to the action. He wouldn't be able to swing again in time to deflect the third one, though.

He immediately extended his arm out straight towards the trajectory of the bullet—no, actually slightly angled away.

The bullet landed. It was armor-piercing ammo that would easily penetrate his armor with a direct hit. But because it struck at an angle, it ran right along his arm and past his shoulder, though it did tear up his artificial skin.

"Wha—?!"

Halter *perceived* the enemy goggling in astonishment. Not planning to let this opening go to waste, he kicked off another sprint. He closed the distance faster than they could fire again and twisted his body as he plunged at the cyborg in the center.

He slammed his back against the cyborg.

The sound of gears cracking rang out. The cyborg was blasted away before he could even scream, his entire body distorted as if it had been smashed with a hammer.

Next, a slash attack came at Halter from the left.

It appeared that the cyborg to the left had dropped his gun and pulled out his own knife in response to Halter's approach. His judgment was correct, but his execution was far too slow and clumsy.

Halter grabbed the cyborg soldier's arm as he swung at him and pulled it towards him. Instead of fighting against the enemy's momentum, he twisted his body and directed the enemy's knife into the chest of the other cyborg to his right.

Finally, he dealt an uppercut to the last cyborg, who was frozen in shock. It pulverized his skull.

"Fiiiirrre!"

Upon hearing that order, a half-broken, lightly armored automaton began to move. It was a giant one that stood two and a half meters tall. It was on the large side for a lightly armored model, but its right arm was already gone.

The giant automaton pointed the autocannon on its remaining arm at Halter and fired.

Without panicking, Halter dodged to the side a half-step to evade the autocannon's line of fire. At the same time, he hurled his knife at the automaton with a lightning-quick fling of his arm.

A split second later, the autocannon that had been thundering along just a moment ago came to a stop with a clunk. Halter's knife had torn right through the air and pierced the giant automaton's head, destroying its sensors.

He ran forward.

Closing the distance in an instant, he tripped the giant by sweeping his foot. Its heavy body toppled right over with a rumble. He then stomped on its exposed neck, crushing it to pieces.

*What's left?*

*Perceiving* his next target, Halter set forth with an air of calm.

· · • ● • · ·

"W-wahhhhhh!"

Losing himself due to fear, Lee desperately charged at Halter and began firing blindly. With an annoyed look, Halter swung his arm backwards without even turning around. His fist dug deep into Lee's body before sending him off flying.

Before Cormack knew it, he was the only one left.

Facing the man who'd turned his subordinates into piles of corpses before him, Cormack muttered, "People make a fuss about the Initial-Y, but if you ask me..."

*If he were a weapon with over-the-top capabilities that produced over-the-top results, that'd only be natural. Just as it's only natural that a shell fired from a tank has more destructive power than a bullet fired from a pistol. Just as a race car built for performance can run faster than regular vehicles.*

*But just what is this which stands before my eyes supposed to be?*

"...your existence is far more unreasonable, you damn monster."

*If a cyborg, a mere human, causes far more havoc on the battle-field than a cyborg should be able to, what is he if not a monster?*

*In the first place, he shouldn't even still be alive!*

Cormack didn't even bother to ready his gun anymore. He simply glared at the reaper of death that was approaching him.

He had been an excellent commander in his time. He was a fast thinker with a discerning eye, who possessed both skills and courage.

But at the same time, he was an extremely practical man, which was why he couldn't comprehend the man before him.

That Halter could simply see the world as he wanted to.

That he could attain infinite potential with just his own will, despite being a mere human.

That a man who had lost all connection to the external world could put up such results with just that one conviction in his heart.

Cormack couldn't comprehend it, down to his very last moments.

$$\cdot \; \cdot \; \bullet \; \bullet\cdot \; \cdot$$

It was right around sundown when the battle came to its conclusion.

"Ugh...tsss..." TemP muttered in pain as she fell to her knees.

She was no longer enshrouded by light. Having chewed through the energy stored in her spring, she could no longer maintain her inherent ability. With some difficulty, she straightened her back and looked up at the girl covered in red and black with hateful eyes.

"Big Sis..." AnchoR muttered, letting out a long breath.

As if on cue, her black horns turned back into a white ring, her long red hair into short black hair, her red claws into silver gauntlets. She returned to her normal state from her demon-like form.

Standing next to her, RyuZU said, "You held on longer than I expected, TemP."

"Hmph...what, trying to rub it in?"

"That is not my intention."

It was the truth. TemP had continued fighting for far longer than RyuZU had expected. Her calculations had been based on her memory and records of TemP's data. At the very least, it'd be fair to say that TemP wouldn't have been able to put up such a tough fight two hundred years ago against her and AnchoR.

*She's grown. In that case, it might not be absolutely impossible that, at the end of her growth, she will regain herself.*

However, at the moment it didn't seem all that likely, as TemP shot her a sulky glare. "So? What are you going to do now?"

"What do you mean?"

"Are you tormenting me now? A bit in poor taste, I must say." TemP slumped her shoulders, looking fed up, but then hung her head down. "You were going to destroy me, were you not? Though it pains me to death to admit it, I lost. So go ahead. I will not resist unseemingly; just do it already, would you please?"

"Could it be that you actually want to die, TemP?" RyuZU asked calmly.

"What is this now? In the end, I am just a failure of a little sister to you, am I not?! Or are you implying that disposing of a defective product like me is not even worth your—"

"Don't say that, Big Sis." Seeing TemP beginning to lose herself to rage, AnchoR cut in.

"AnchoR?"

"You mustn't say such a thing." Picking up TemP's hand, AnchoR continued, "You see, Big Sis RyuZU actually loves Big Sis TemP. And of course, I do too."

Being told that right to her face, TemP pulled her lips tight, shaking her head. "Th-that's a lie! Then why does she try to destroy me?! It is because she hates me and sees me as an eyesore, is it not?!"

"She didn't try to destroy you. She wanted to save you."

"From what?!" TemP yelled.

"From regret," AnchoR answered briefly, then said, "You know, Big Sis... To be honest, I had it wrong, too."

Upon those words, TemP looked straight into AnchoR's face and asked, "Had what wrong?"

"Because I was made to destroy...I thought that was the only thing I could do," she replied, her voice sounding murky, cold, and lifeless. "I hated that. It was so painful. I felt desperate. Even games I used to love playing didn't feel fun anymore. If things had gone on like that, I would surely have ended up doing something I would regret one day."

"AnchoR..."

"But I was wrong!" Suddenly, her voice came back to life. With the smile of an angel, she continued, "Father taught me that my power to destroy is really the power to fix things. The power to give things that have become twisted a chance to be reborn... That isn't violence, but strength!"

Placing her hand on her chest, she declared in a loud voice, "That's why I decided that I would become strong! If my power lets me save the ones I love, then it isn't a bad thing at all. I'm okay with being the ultimate weapon now."

TemP asked with a trembling voice, "Are you saying...that I am also mistaking something?"

"I think so."

"Just what could it be that I'm mistaking?"

AnchoR shook her head. "I think that's something that you have to figure out for yourself, Big Sis TemP."

TemP became more and more confused. "I...am mistaken? But I am free..." she said, hugging her shoulders in fear as her eyes darted about. She suddenly lifted her head and shouted, "No...th-that is right! After all, my master also said that I am fine like this! I have not mistaken anything!!"

Shooting her frayed little sister a cold gaze, RyuZU muttered with a sigh, "So not only is your brain loose, but also your morals?"

*"Because Master said so"... That's your only basis for blindly believing that you're right? I think that makes you what they call an "easy score."*

RyuZU was just exasperated at first, but what followed that was indignation.

*So basically, it seems that this little sister of mine has been wheedled along by her master, most likely the man who revealed himself during the events in Tokyo: Omega.*

*Furthermore, it seems he does not even value her much, despite making use of her. First it was AnchoR, now TemP...*

"To dare treat my little sisters as girls only good for hitting and quitting... You certainly have got some nerve." *I will definitely make you regret it,* RyuZU thought, reaffirming the man whose face was yet unknown to her as a bitter enemy.

Meanwhile, despite TemP's continuing outbursts, AnchoR persevered with patience in her efforts. "Big Sis, you should come with us."

"Huh? Me, go with you...?"

"AnchoR, that—" RyuZU interjected chidingly.

However, AnchoR did not back down. Gazing straight into TemP's eyes, she said, "Let's try asking Father and Mother for advice together, yeah? If you're lost, just say so. I'm sure that talking with them will help you find an answer."

"Help...me?"

"Yeah. Father would definitely—"

"That person would..." TemP muttered in a daze. Immediately after...

*Poof.* For some reason, her face instantly flushed beet red as her head overheated like a steaming kettle.

TemP proceeded to stand up, shaking off AnchoR's hand.

"Th-that is just fine, thank you!" She fumbled her feet as she retreated and shook her head fiercely back and forth. "If I were to join up with a person who acts in such a way upon meeting someone for the first time, my sanity wouldn't last! How lecherous he was!!"

*Acts in such a way? Upon first meeting? Lecherous?*

Questions popped into RyuZU's head, but before she could ask, TemP continued, "I—I shall leave it here for today! But do not think that it is over now! I shall return the humiliation I have suffered a thousand times over!"

After spitting out a line that only a sore loser would say, TemP quickly spun around.

Just like that, she vanished. It appeared that she had used the small amount of energy she recovered during their conversation just now to turn herself transparent.

RyuZU might be able to catch her if the nature of her invisibility was simple optical camouflage, but she didn't even feel like trying anymore at this point.

AnchoR was also staring vacantly at the spot where her older sister had just vanished. "I wonder what's wrong with her?"

"Well, who knows what happened."

"Did I say something I shouldn't have?"

"No, I think you did the best you could."

"But...ah!" Upon turning around and looking up at RyuZU, AnchoR was taken aback, her face stiffening. She looked like she just saw the devil.

"Now then, let us hurry to Master Naoto's side. There is

something that I must get an answer for right away. For TemP to react that way, just what kind of stunt was he pulling while I was so worried about him being alone in the enemy base? Yes, I would be quite curious to know, indeed."

Looking up at RyuZU, who had an unspeakable look on her face, AnchoR sighed with her eyes half-closed. "Your face says everything, Big Sis..."

• • ● ● • •

"Halter did all this by himself?" Marie muttered in a daze upon surveying the ruins of the plaza in front of the ninth clock tower.

*This is ridiculous. Even by a conservative estimate, there's at least a battalion's worth of dead soldiers and cyborgs lying on the ground, as well as the wreckage of military automata. Just what kind of magic would enable a single man to create a scene that looks like something straight from hell?*

Vermouth bumped Marie with his elbow, saying, "Oy, missy— he's over there."

"Ugh, Halter!" Marie dashed off like a billiard ball that had been struck.

Right around the center of the ruins was a familiar-looking figure, but instead of his usual suit, the bald man was clad in thick, beat-up combat armor. He sat with his back reclined against the rubble, looking completely exhausted.

*There's no mistaking it. That's Halter.*

As she became certain of who it was upon getting closer, Marie yelled out, "Halter! You—! Halter...?"

Her voice shriveled up. She had been ready to slap him, with her hand raised and everything, but then realized that something was wrong. She shook his shoulder, but there was no response.

"Oy, Boss! You still alive or what?!" Vermouth yelled out anxiously as he caught up with Marie.

Marie took out some of her tools and examined Halter's condition. He had apparently shut down. "The damage to his body isn't really that bad."

*The damage to his armor is proof that it was put to good use. His internal mechanisms do look like they've been considerably overworked as well, but they aren't damaged enough to cause a shutdown.*

"Oy, slut, how does it look?!"

"Quiet! He hasn't suffered fatal damage. In fact, he's practically unscathed, considering that he apparently cleaned up everyone here by himself."

"Then why isn't he responding? It can't be that he's just sleeping again, right?"

"That's what I'm looking into right now... Wait, all of his sensors are broken?! You're kidding me. Just what kind of weapon could have broken them in such a way?"

Clicking her tongue, Marie pulled out another tool. While tuning his internal mechanisms with her eyes focused, she grumbled, "Oh no, they've been magnetized... An electromagnetic weapon, again? Really? God, electricity's just the absolute worst!"

"Oy oy, can he be fixed?"

"If I replace some parts later, yeah. For now, I'm just making some emergency repairs... Done!"

The second Marie said that, Halter's shoulders jumped.

"Phoo..." Exhaust gas came out of his mouth as he started to show signs of life. He slowly began to move, straightening up. Halter then shook his head to dispel the lingering drowsiness, then looked up at Marie.

"Hey there...princess."

"Good morning," she replied in a threatening voice. She pulled her lips that had loosened in relief tight again and folded her arms as she looked down at Halter with a high and mighty attitude. "You sure went around making quite the mess, didn't you?"

"Yeah, I guess... Are you mad at me?"

"Of course I am. Did you seriously think I wouldn't be? I'm neither an angel nor a saint. Oh, you stupid little dummy, is this head of yours really holding anything inside?" Marie replied as she prodded his forehead lightly with her small fist.

Halter pouted like a child might when chided for his mischief. "You're so mean. I tried my absolute best, you know?"

"Were there no other options?"

"This is how a proper adult settles things. Have I taught you nothing?"

"Why don't you start by telling me how you're defining 'proper.'"

"All right, I'll revise my statement. This isn't how a proper adult settles things, but how a bad adult does. It was educational, right?"

"Yes, and as I understand it, it's not so different from a selfish brat's pranks," she replied while giving him a dirty look.

Halter chuckled, his shoulders rocking up and down. Then he said, "Sorry, Marie."

"Don't think I'll let you off easy. I'm hurt. Very hurt."

"Sorry."

"I won't forgive you. I'll never forgive you," she whispered as she cast her face downward.

*God damn it,* Marie thought, *I want to let him have it right now, but my voice won't stop trembling.*

As Marie buried her face in the sleeve of her coat, Vermouth called out from behind her, "Hey Boss, good work."

"Yeah. Same goes for you. You did well."

"It's nothing compared to what you did." Vermouth smiled and winced, and then took another look at their surroundings. As he imagined the ferocious battle the man before him must have fought to create such a hellacious scene, he muttered, "I think you could seriously go toe-to-toe with even an Initial-Y, Boss."

He had subjugated an entire battlefield, alone. Vermouth understood just what an absurd, bone-chilling fact that was.

*Tactics can never overcome preplanned strategy. Perhaps that was possible once upon a time, but battles nowadays are decided before they even begin—that's common sense in modern warfare.*

*But...the sight of this makes me doubt that common sense.*

*I can't help but believe that he just might end up pulling off the impossible whenever I'm watching him. I mean, isn't he exactly how mythical heroes are portrayed in their legends?*

At the very least, this was what Vermouth thought. If he had no choice but to pick an enemy to encounter on the battlefield, he'd rather it be an Initial-Y than Vainney Halter. However...

"Don't be stupid," the legendary man said, immediately cutting him down. "This is nothing to brag about. I simply won a winnable fight. And if anything, I'd rather exhaust all means to avoid ending up in a fight with an Initial-Y in the first place."

"A winnable fight, huh..." Vermouth muttered dubiously. "If you could arrange things so you win a battle you should have had no chance of winning, wouldn't it also be possible for you to set up a stage where you could take down an Initial-Y? That's what I was saying."

"Now you're really being dumb," Halter said. "I sure as hell ain't gonna break my back trying to set up such an extravagant stage. You might still be young, but I'm an old man already. It's about time you allow these old bones to rest. The absolute combat machine Overwork retires as of today."

"Oh, is that right?" Vermouth muttered as he internally sneered.

*"A winnable fight"... If you insist on challenging a royal straight flush with a no-pair hand, then well, fine, I guess. That's what makes you the master.*

*But in the first place, is this man even aware that while he barked about how he sure as hell ain't gonna go through that kind of trouble, he didn't say a single thing about it being impossible?*

"He's fallen under their spell for sure," Vermouth muttered, feeling a little exasperated, but also smiling.

*Well, I can kinda understand. When you're around these kids...
you just feel like you can do it all. Calling anything impossible just
doesn't feel quite right anymore. It's different from groundless opti-
mism. It's more like you start to not want to admit that something
is impossible, even if it is.*

"Sure is tough for an average Joe to keep up with geniuses. Good
grief," Halter grumbled with a sigh, sounding completely depleted.

Vermouth couldn't help but burst into laughter. "If you're an
average Joe, then what does that make the rest of us?"

· · ● ● ● · ·

Without elaborating on the obvious, several things happened
after the battle.

Naoto Miura gained control over the core tower, and Marie
Bell Breguet entered the ninth clock tower.

Second Ypsilon gained total control over the core tower and
the clock towers of Shangri-La Grid. As a result, it was wide-
spread knowledge throughout the world that they now had the
power to do anything they wanted in that city.

However, what really struck everyone was *what they chose to
do* with that newfound power.

The residents of the city, the militaries of the IGMO countries that had invaded, and the leadership of the five surrounding
countries all directly received the answer to that question in the
form of a proclamation of criminal responsibility in the style of
an instruction manual. Namely...

"We created direct links between the entirety of Shangri-La Grid's control system to its neighboring grids, man! Shangri-La's core tower can now be controlled via the corresponding clock towers nearest to the border of its five neighboring grids, so treat it well, m'kay loves? ♪"

To begin with, neighboring grids supported each other in their day-to-day functions. By making the linking mechanisms between Shangri-La Grid and its neighbors from the ninth clock tower both bigger and more sophisticated, they had effectively turned Shangri-La Grid into a multiple grid system with its neighbors.

It was no longer possible to reverse the changes that Naoto had made to Shangri-La Grid's control system. After all, he had only *done inexplicable things in a trance until he had burned out*—he couldn't recall why anything was the way it was now. Of course, Marie couldn't understand, either, as she only hooked up what he had created.

There was no one in the world who could restore it to its previous state.

And so, Shangri-La Grid's sovereignty was forcefully relinquished to the joint management of the five neighboring grids.

There were extremely few in the present world who could understand how this abnormality might have been created. After all, even the ones responsible didn't have a good grasp of it themselves.

# ● Epilogue / 22 : 30 / Retroscena

**N**OW THAT THE POWER over Shangri-La's core tower had been delegated to its neighbors, the question now was who among the five countries would really hold the (figurative) keys. Presently, the five neighboring countries were holding a heated conference to sort that out.

To begin with, the city was a treasure mine, if one could only access it. Slush funds, smuggled goods, advanced illegal technology, talented professionals, valuable experimental data, information on top-secret cover-ups...the city was full of things that shady enterprises, crime syndicates, politicians, and intelligence bureaus would all kill to get their hands on.

On the surface, the goal of the conference was to decide how Shangri-La would be governed, but in reality, it was a battle for the rights to its pot of gold.

"Well, I can't imagine this political bickering will last long, though," Halter said.

Walking beside him, Vermouth nodded. "I'd say that before

long, the bigshots are gonna manipulate IGMO to intervene and force the neighboring countries to commission IGMO to govern Shangri-La, after which they'll begin destroying the evidence—or 'cleaning house,' if you will."

*They'll quickly distribute out the slush funds, keep the technology and experimental data under wraps under the pretext of corporate privacy, and bury the top-secret info even deeper. In other words, nothing would change.*

"And so, God's in His heaven and all's right with the world, I suppose, eh?" Vermouth said, summing things up with a sneer. He was no longer in the body of the golden-haired beauty that the troupe had gotten used to seeing him in, but back to his old look of a muscular and bold-looking young man.

"Only by piling lies upon lies does the truth become acceptable," Halter muttered with a shrug.

"That's how you keep the cogs of this world turning. Just let 'em be."

"Well, guess we can't say much, given that we're going to capitalize on this chaos to escape and all."

The necessary arrangements for their escape had already been made. They were going to use a distribution route used for smuggling to escape all the way to India, then continue on to France while continuing to live as terrorists on the run, but...

In the dead of night, just a few hours before their scheduled departure, the two of them were walking inside a small estate on the outskirts of Shangri-La Grid.

While the building was old, there wasn't a single speck of

dust in the hallways. In addition, the greenery on the outside was trimmed neatly and the furniture inside was refined and unassuming. It was dead silent right now, without a sign of anyone being home.

Walking through this place, one would get an inkling that the family who lived here was probably a fastidious bunch.

"By the way I haven't asked yet, but what business do you have here, Boss?"

"That's a good question. Frankly, I don't know, either," Halter muttered with a sigh as he came to a stop. Before him was a thick and heavy door. Judging by the layout of the house, what lay ahead should be something like a study room. "I'll go finish my business. You wait outside."

"Oy oy, c'mon now, Bossss. Don't leave a guy hangin' after all this way."

"It probably isn't gonna be the kind of fun thing you're imagining. Besides..." He paused for a breath. "It won't take very long," Halter finished in a chilling voice.

Vermouth erased the flippant smile he had on his face and gazed at Halter, but Halter had already moved on mentally. Without turning to acknowledge Vermouth, he opened the door and entered the room.

Right by the door was an enormous partition screen, and there were no lights inside. Because of that, he couldn't see the inner part of the room.

Just as Halter started walking to get around the screen from the right, he quickly stopped.

The corpse of a girl was laying on the floor to the right of the screen. She was dressed in the garb of a nun for some reason, and there was a smoking pipe next to her.

She had a gunshot wound right in the middle of her forehead, which seemed to be the cause of death. As far as Halter could tell at a glance, it didn't look like it'd been that long since she was killed.

"Oh, please, don't concern yourself with that thing. It isn't a very interesting story to tell anywayyy..."

Hearing a voice, Halter looked up.

It turned out to be a spacious room past the partition screen. There was a large window in the center, through which pale moonlight shone into the dark room. As befitting a study, heavy bookshelves lined both side walls, and leather-bound books clearly chosen for style decorated their shelves.

In front of the window was a large office desk. It looked like the room doubled as a reception room as well, as there was a splendid table in between two classy-looking sofas set facing each other in front of the desk.

On one of the sofas sat a man—Kiu Tai Yu.

He was kicking back on the sofa while drinking wine from a glass. "Hey there, I've been waiting, you know. Why don't you take a seat?"

"You knew that I'd come?" Halter asked as he sat down on the opposite sofa.

Kiu shook his head, replying, "No. I just had a feeling somehow that it'd be fun if you diiid. After all, I've had quite a bit of time freed up because of you."

"Is that right?" Halter said as he turned his eyes towards the girl's corpse.

Kiu shrugged. "Don't misunderstand, would you please? That woman was Restaurant's head. The looks are from surgery; she's really an old hag."

"But why is she dead in your house?"

"Like I said, it's a boring story. I think she must have gotten confused about something, because she started going on about something like how if we joined up now we could dismantle Market and take over their businesses. It bored me, so I ended up shooting her without thinking."

"You're right." Halter nodded. "It is a boring story."

"That's what I said, isn't it? Well, let's start things off with a drink, shall we?" Kiu said, shaking the glass in his hand playfully. He then dropped some ice into another glass and poured in wine from a bottle that must have cost an arm and a leg.

The beautiful amber liquid glistened in the moonlight while the melting ice clinked against the glass as Kiu shook it slightly. After handing the glass over to Halter, he refilled his own, then said, "Now then, let's toast, shall we?"

"To what?"

Kiu smiled, raising his glass up high, "To the new Shangri-La."

As Halter also raised his glass in kind, he asked with a serious face, "You're fine with letting go of the old Shangri-La?"

"Hm? But of course. I always keep my eyes on the future, you know!" Kiu nodded cheerily as he curled his lips. "But maaan, it sure is chaotic right now with the IGMO forces invading and all, huh? Politicians and corporations are all in a frenzy, flinging shit everywhere. I pray to God this continues, as I couldn't ask for more!"

"You sure seem awfully chipper for someone who just lost everything."

"Well, yeah. I told you, didn't I? That it's actually better for me if you guys trample all over the city—and that's what happened in the end. Isn't that something to celebrate?"

*That's true,* Halter thought. *Letting Second Ypsilon screw things up here is actually better for him. Kiu Tai Yu maintained that from beginning to end. Having Naoto modify the core tower was a compromise plan for him to begin with.*

"Well, I guess you could say this, though..." Kiu bent his back backwards in a sulky manner and took a sip from his glass. "I didn't expect that I'd have my control over the core tower snatched away after having my organization literally annihilated. I really have to hand it to you guys for doing such a perfect job on me. I'm not even mad, just amazed," Kiu said laughingly. It truly looked as though the turn of events didn't bother him at all.

Halter tilted his head. "I don't get it."

"Get what?"

"Why did you try to destroy your own organization?" Kiu didn't immediately answer. Halter took a gulp from his glass, then continued, "You're a capable man. Both your mind and your instincts are sharp."

"Aw, shuuucks."

"So why did you stuff Naoto inside the core tower? And

without keeping a serious eye on him, either? You should have easily been able to tell that he isn't the kind of person who would bend to another's will from one cheap threat."

*That's the one thing I just can't figure out. For someone who set out to clean up the mess he created himself by executing a plan that bore the risk of incurring the spite of Initial-Y automata, his response to the outcome is simply too casual.*

*Even if TemP hadn't ignored orders, his plan would have quickly come apart. Almost as if he had considered the possibility that this—no...*

*As if things went just as planned.*

"Let me ask you, then," Kiu said, furrowing his brows, "do you think that bossing around a bunch of dumb punks and loose hoes is really all that fun? Do I really look like I'd be desperate to keep that position?"

"..."

"That's basically it. I'd gotten tired of it. It was time for change."

It suddenly clicked in Halter's mind why this man had been able to stay at the top of Arsenal up to now. It was simple.

Kiu Tai Yu wasn't attached to anything.

Status, prestige, money, power—they all meant nothing to him. He wasn't prideful enough to be arrogant, idealistic enough to be naïve, or ambitious enough to bother trying to change the world.

Someone without the desire to take center stage wouldn't ever perish from being letting his urges blind him.

*I see. He's the type who's perfectly suited to run underworld businesses. In short, for him...*

"I'm fine so long as things are fun for me," Kiu sneered. "That's the same for everyone, isn't it? I'm no different. That's why I'm always looking for fun thingsss. Well, being the boss of a criminal syndicate was fun in its own right. But now's the right time for something new. I'm going to start looking for the next game I want to play."

"So in the end, the entire city was thrown for a wild ride for the sake of your enjoyment, huh?"

"I guess? Well, if I concerned myself with every single dreg of society that might have died, then I wouldn't be able to enjoy anything, right? So I don't let it bother me."

*He's the ultimate hedonist. Everything's fine so long as he's enjoying himself. Yet, he doesn't overstep his boundaries, so it's hard to lay hands on him.*

Halter said, "So? What do you plan to do now?"

"Well nowww? What should I do, indeeeed?" Kiu replied, reclining against the sofa and gazing into space. "Should I gather up some poor kids in South America and have them call me *comandante*? Diving into the quagmire that is the Middle East and instructing the totalitarian regimes on how to put on mass games doesn't sound bad, either. Ahhhh, the possibilities are endless!"

As Kiu spoke joyously of his dreams, his eyes seemed to be sparkling, even in the dim moonlight. They were like the eyes of a young dreamer imagining all the possibilities in the future, and the worlds yet to be discovered.

Halter looked at the ice in his glass. "So whatever the case, you don't plan to do honest work, huh?"

"Huh? What in the world are you saying? That's a terrible joke. I, for one, believe that I made all my money through honest work, you know?! It's simply that most of my methods aren't accepted by the international community, with their whimsical standardsss... Seriously, the world is so unreasonablle. Though, that's what makes it interesting," Kiu sneered.

"I see..." Halter muttered before swallowing the rest of his glass in one gulp. Setting his empty glass on the table, he slowly stood up. "Thanks for the drink. It was pretty good wine."

"Ohhh? You're going already?" Kiu asked, looking perplexed.

Halter nodded. *I found out what I wanted to know,* he thought. *I more or less expected that it'd be worms inside the can, but still, it would have felt like I had something stuck in my teeth if I left with this question unanswered.* "We've gotta run while the city's still in chaos, you see. If I don't leave now, I'll be late for the departure."

"That's a shame, but...well, I enjoyed our time together. Thanks," Kiu said with a picture-perfect smile. It felt like he wasn't just being polite, but that he genuinely meant it.

*This man really didn't lie a single time all the way through, huh? Halter thought.*

"I don't imagine we'll ever meet again, but I'm looking forward to watching you guys continue to make splashes elsewhere in the world."

"Well...thanks, I guess." Halter smiled slightly before turning around and walking towards the door. Out of nowhere, he stopped and turned around. "Can I just say one last thing?"

"What is it?"

"Well to be honest, I wasn't sure myself up until this very moment, but..." Halter said as he pulled out his pistol from under his arm. He pointed the gun at Kiu Tai Yu's torso so naturally, it was as if he were simply seeking a parting handshake. "...in short, it seems like *I wanted to do this.*"

Kiu Tai Yu's smiling face stiffened.

After staring back and forth between Halter's face and the humble and mundane 9 mm automatic pistol for a while and realizing that he wasn't just imagining things, Kiu's jaws dropped. He yelled, "I don't get it! Why are you going to kill me?!"

"..."

"I'm utterly confused! And scared. Super scared! Just look, I'm peeing myself! These pants and boxers are ones that I'm fond of, you know! Just hoooooooowwww are you going to compensate for this?!"

Halter didn't reply; he simply fired.

*Bang.*

With that, Kiu Tai Yu flinched and dropped the glass in his hand. A small red dot appeared near his abdomen and quickly grew in size.

"Ohhh...?" Kiu said, looking puzzled and tilting his head. He first looked down at his gunshot wound, then slowly back up, before blinking his eyes several times. "Hmm? Huh...it turns out that being shot hurts quite a bit, surprisingly enough..." Contrary to his words, he looked disappointed if anything, rather than surprised.

Halter lowered his gun in silence, upon which Kiu asked in a calm voice, "Why did you do this?"

"Beats me," Halter replied quietly. "It wasn't to settle things with you. If anything, we're the ones who caused you trouble, so it's not like I have a grudge against you. I'm not really mad at you for anything, either."

"Then...were you asked to by somebody?"

"No, I decided by my own will to pull the trigger," Halter replied.

Kiu frowned, looking a little disappointed. "Then...what, is it that you were really a scumbag who...kills people in the name of justice all along?"

"I've got no interest in your shenanigans," Halter refuted flatly. "I couldn't care less whether you're a saint or a scoundrel. It's got nothing to do with me. People like you are a dime a dozen in this world; you're just one of many."

"Mm...? I really can't think of a reason, thennn... Did I do something that rubbed you the wrong way?" Upon finishing, Kiu coughed up a small fit. Fresh blood spilled out from the ends of his lips.

*Why did you choose to kill Kiu Tai Yu? Halter asked himself. Was there a special reason that compelled you to go out of your way in the dead of night to visit and kill this small-time scoundrel, when there are far worse villains in the world?*

*No, there wasn't.*

*At the very least, there was no strategic gain in killing him. It wasn't a question of emotion, or that I thought his evil deeds were unforgivable, either. In the first place, is he really a villain? Leaving standard morality aside, were Kiu Tai Yu's deeds really so unforgivable, if you thought about them fairly?*

*Admit how you really feel, Vainney Halter. To be honest, do you not, in fact, rather like this man?*

*Even if you were to split the world into good on one side and evil on the other, and Kiu Tai Yu was on the evil side, don't your own values, in fact, lean the same way? You work for your own enjoyment, and don't hesitate to kill those who oppose you if you have to eliminate them from the picture. And yet, you chose to kill this man. Just why?*

*That's...*

"...Shirley," Halter said.

"Huh...?"

"She's the girl you killed. Did you forget? The one you shot at that agent's bar."

Seeming to have lost too much blood at this point, Kiu stared into space with a ghastly expression as he struggled to recall who Halter was talking about. Finally, he said, "Oh...you're talking about that... girl?"

Halter nodded, upon which Kiu looked at him goggle-eyed, astonished from the bottom of his heart. "What, seriously? Wait, you're telling me that I'm going to die because of some hoe...?"

"That's not it, you idiot," Halter scowled, looking fed up.

*And I mean that. To be honest, I don't care one bit that Shirley was killed. I mean, I barely even remember her face, and I almost forgot her name just now.*

*On that day, she simply happened to be there when I met the agent. She was just somebody who I made some small talk with over a cocktail she made. She wasn't even someone I had a casual fuck with, nor was she my type. If we'd parted uneventfully, I probably would have forgotten her before five minutes were up and never thought about her again.*

*However...*

"I told you, didn't I? That girl was a skilled bartender who knew how to make the kind of drink I like."

*The "Fairy Lady." The one thing I do clearly remember is the intense flavor of that sweet, scorching drink.*

"The cocktail she served me was delicious, but now I'll never get to drink it again, because of you."

"Ahah...I seeee..." Kiu said, closing his eyes. "Yes...I can understand, then..."

Looking satisfied with that answer, he died with a peaceful smile on his face.

A short while later, after confirming that Kiu Tai Yu was in fact dead, Halter exited the study and met Vermouth at the door. He told him that it was time to go, and so the two of them left the estate.

They remained silent until they got inside the car that had been parked nearby, but at that point, it seemed that Vermouth couldn't hold his curiosity back anymore. "Hey, Boss?" he asked. "Was that really why you killed him?"

"You're gonna ask me the same thoughtless question too, huh?" Halter scowled in disgust.

Vermouth persisted, however. "C'mon, just tell me. What've ya got to lose?"

"I don't know. I can't explain it," Halter replied, shaking his head to the side in annoyance. "I did it because I wanted to. I ain't got no reason for it. That's just how we humans are, dumbass."

· · • ● • · ·

Naoto and Marie were visiting Giovanni's workshop again. They were there to make the final adjustments of AnchoR's mainframe, and also to show him the work that Marie had done.

Just like the first time they met, the old man was leaning forward, working on something in his work chair, when they came in. As soon as he saw AnchoR, he said, "Hmmm... Well, I guess I'd give you a 'C.'"

"A 'C,' you say?" Marie replied discontentedly. She folded her arms and raised her chin defiantly as if she wanted to give him a piece of her mind, but at the same time, she also looked nervous as she ran through what she might have overlooked in her brain.

The honest truth of it was that Marie couldn't decide what kind of attitude she should take with this old man.

He was a senior clocksmith who had outstanding technical skill, so she should talk to him with respect, but couldn't bring herself to do so due to her poor experience with him during their first meeting.

She also didn't like how the usually audacious Naoto seemed to be uncharacteristically meek in the presence of this old man. She didn't understand exactly why this bothered her, but bother her it certainly did.

Did Giovanni notice Marie's internal conflict? Perhaps...

Giovanni said with a nonchalant expression, "Oh? Maybe I should add that I thought you could do better. Or is this the limit of what you're capable of, miss? Are you satisfied with this level of work?"

"O-of course not! Keep in mind that, unlike some sarcastic and twisted old geezer, I'm still young. I'm going to continue to get even better, just you watch!" Marie replied indignantly, throwing out her chest.

Giovanni smiled and said, "Good. Then that means you could have done a better job on her repairs. The repairs you made are neither complete nor perfect. That's why you get a 'C'—do you see what I'm saying now?"

"Nngh! Fine, I'll take it! Hmph!" Marie replied, puffing her cheeks and turning to the side.

Naoto, who had been standing next to her, stepped forward and bowed. "Master, thank you for everything."

"Oh, please. I haven't really done much."

"That's not true. AnchoR was saved thanks to you, and I also feel like...I was able to take another step forward myself because of you."

"Now that, I really did have nothing to do with. That's a road you had already chosen for yourself."

"Still, I'm grateful to you."

"Is that so? In that case, hmm...I guess I have something a little preachy to say, as a senior clocksmith, to the both of you. Do you mind?"

"Hm...? Please," Naoto replied, straightening his posture. Meanwhile, Marie looked back at Giovanni with a perplexed face.

Giovanni smiled and said, "I have neither superpowers like the two of you, nor technical ability that's worth any acclaim. But I do have one thing I can teach you as your senior."

"..."

"You two are still too young. Living life on the edge is fine and all, but you're too sure of yourselves."

Naoto and Marie both gulped.

Eyeing them both with his amber eyes, Giovanni continued, "The two of you are talented. Talented enough to reshape this world, even...but so long as you let that go to your head, you'll always just be children."

"...Right."

"If you just rely on your talents to continue to maintain this planet of ours that 'Y' has left behind, you won't create anything yourselves. Above all, if you don't even understand, then you're really just letting your divine gifts do the work for you. Your achievements wouldn't count as the work of humans."

"..."

*He's right,* Marie thought. *Both Naoto and I have simply been chasing after "Y" on the road he paved. People may hail us as geniuses or superhumans, but in reality, we're nowhere close to omnipotence, and have yet to catch up with "Y" as well.*

*Not yet, at least.*

Giovanni said, "What you two need is to create a brand for yourselves."

"A brand?"

"It's the original story, the legend that's born from all the impossibles that you've made possible, and your mission state-ment. This is something that's absolutely necessary if you're going to earn yourselves a reputation as independent clocksmiths who are a cut above the rest."

"..."

"If you can't do that, no matter how much you hone your skills, you'll simply die as humble artisans," Giovanni said sol-emnly. "Modern humanity will finally catch up to 'Y'. Whether that fact will be treated as divine intervention, or as a human feat, all depends on the two of you."

Marie straightened her posture. Beside her, Naoto did the same. Marie thought, *We were just taught something very important.*

The two of them found themselves naturally bowing and say-ing the same words in unison: "Yes. Thank you very much for your pearls of wisdom, Master."

After politely bowing and bidding farewell, they left Giovanni's workshop. The three of them walked side by side, holding hands with AnchoR in the middle.

"Looks like we've found what we have to improve on," Marie said.

Naoto nodded lightly. "Yeah. We haven't created anything ourselves. We aren't able to yet."

"*Yes, indeed...*for now, at least." Marie stopped and looked Naoto's way, upon which she found Naoto reciprocating her actions.

The pair of ashen eyes and the pair of emerald eyes met. Upon finding a powerful will and burning passion in each other's eyes, the two of them laughed together.

Then, Naoto said, "I'm going to do what I want, how I want, no matter what comes my way."

Marie responded, "I'm going to make all impossibilities possible."

"If 'Y' recreated the planet, then shall we recreate this universe?"

"I like the sound of that. Overhauling this clockwork planet? I have to say, that was an awfully humble ambition for the two of us. We've got to create another clockwork planet from this one at the very least, or I won't be satisfied!"

The two of them took off on the hype train.

AnchoR tilted her head, muttering, "I don't get it. Haven't you two been shooting for the stars the whole time?"

However, the latter half of her muttering didn't reach the two's ears, as they were off in their own world.

· · • ● • · ·

The sky was still covered in black and filled with stars.

A ship was docked at a secret harbor of Shangri-La Grid which, until yesterday, had been active as a base for smuggling.

Aboard the rocking ship, RyuZU was giving Halter a chilling stare. The air of hostility was such that it felt like at any moment she might just pull out her black scythes.

Beside her, AnchoR was also staring at Halter with murderous eyes, the adorable expression she typically had on currently replaced by a thoroughly dour one.

*Christ, this is more unnerving than all the bloodbaths I've made it through,* Halter thought as a shiver ran down his spine. Despite that, he worked to keep his face expressionless as he bowed deeply to them and said, "I'm sorry."

He received no response.

With his head bowed, he continued, "I'm well aware that I can't complain even if you choose to kill me. I'm not going to give any excuses. If there's anything I can do to repent, I intend to do so."

"..."

There was still no answer from either of them.

Halter remained still with his head down as he continued to wait for a response. Naoto and Marie, who were both in the vicinity, also kept their mouths shut. Vermouth also watched on nervously, gulping as he waited for the two automata to reveal a reaction. Eventually...

"*Mister,*" AnchoR said dispassionately. She trotted forward briskly until she was right in front of Halter, upon which she turned her head up to peer at his face, asking, "Are you really, genuinely reflecting on your actions?"

Meeting her eyes, Halter replied solemnly, "...Yeah, of course."

"Do you promise never to do something like this again?" AnchoR asked to double-check.

"I promise."

"Okay. I forgive you, then."

"..."

Taken aback, Halter lifted his head up without thinking. He hadn't expected to be forgiven so readily.

"I definitely won't forgive you next time, all right, Mister?" AnchoR said to drive the point home, but despite her words, she was smiling kindly.

Halter hurriedly nodded. He then looked towards RyuZU with his head still down.

"We'll put this on hold for now," RyuZU said, her gaze still chilling. "If you had remained the worthless junkbot that you were, I would be dismantling you for being a defective product right now, no buts about it. But for humans who show some hope for growth, as little as it may be, there is no need for immediate disposal, despite having brains smaller than those of fleas. However..." She paused, glaring at him. "Should you make the same mistake again, I shall be so merciless in my revenge that you will wish you had died by my hand right now instead, so do not ever forget this."

"Y-yeah, I know. I won't ever do something like this again."

"Good." With that, RyuZU turned around and began to walk away. AnchoR followed.

After they left, Halter puffed out a grand sigh as he stroked his bald head. *If my body was still human, I'm sure I'd be drenched in sweat right now.* "'Mister,' huh..." he muttered. "Does that mean she sees me as at least somewhat human now?"

"Well that's good," Marie called out. She made her way in front of him, then looked up at his stiff face teasingly and laughed,

"If RyuZU had seriously snapped, you would be mincemeat by now, you know?"

"I'm aware of that. I ain't ever crossing such a dangerous bridge again."

"I sure hope so. Ah yes, I've also reconsidered things because of what you said, by the way."

"Say what?" Halter asked looking perplexed.

"I do believe you said something along the lines of not remembering ever signing a contract with or receiving a salary from me, yes?" Marie asked, her eyes half-closed.

"Ah, well...that's, you know—"

"I did some reflection on that, you know? As you said, it isn't right to expect a mature man to work himself to the bone purely out of the goodness of his heart. Everyone should receive fair compensation for their work, which is why..." Marie paused as she took out a small item from her shoulder bag. "I've decided to give you a salary from now on." She tossed the object over to him.

Halter quickly caught it so it wouldn't fall before he even recognized what it was, but once he saw what he had caught, he dropped his shoulders wearily.

It was a can of beer—something that was worth a mere two hundred yen, give or take.

"Oy, princess..." Halter moaned.

However, Marie continued unsympathetically, "So, that's your salary. Now that I've officially employed you, I won't let you off scot-free the next time you act on your own."

"You serious...? At least pay me enough pocket money to go drinking, will you?!"

"Huh? You've got some nerve to try to negotiate a raise when you haven't even done anything of value for me yet. You might want to act more respectfully towards your employer, just saying."

"That's messed up," Vermouth piped up. "Paying Boss a beer for his services goes far beyond price-slashing, you know."

"You shut your mouth." Marie pricked up her nose and placed her hands on her hips, glaring at Halter. "You understand? By taking that beer, you've agreed to work for me. I'm your boss now. You are to obey my commands absolutely! I'm going to work you dry every day, so prepare yourself. Now, if you get it, then say yes."

"...Yes."

"That's more like it," Marie said with a broad smile. With that, she walked away looking satisfied, leaving Halter standing with his head hanging.

Vermouth gazed piteously at the back of the legendary mercenary for a while, but then a question popped into his mind. "But really, have you seriously not been paid all along? It seems hard to believe."

"Of course that's a lie," Halter replied with a sigh as he fiddled with the can of beer in his hand. "I was formally employed as her bodyguard and private secretary back when the princess was working for Meister Guild, and to tell the truth, I received a secret bonus after the chain of events in Kyoto—a big one, at that."

"Okay, thank God! Man, I feel relieved. What hope is there for people like me, if a first-rate mercenary like you works for free?"

Vermouth replied, leaning against the rails in relief. He then turned to look at Halter again with a curious expression and asked, "By the way, how much does it take to keep a talent like you so loyal? Mind telling me, for the sake of reference?"

"You're gonna get yourself in trouble trying to dig up other people's finances, you know? Especially in our world."

"Are you really one to talk, considering that you exposed all my finances, even my hidden bank accounts?" Vermouth jabbed back, tongue-in-cheek.

Halter smiled at him, then naturally closed his eyes. In his mind he saw the image of a blonde-haired girl.

The memory was from a few months back, when they were at Kyoto's core tower. When the girl told him that she was going, he asked her if she was really sure.

The girl had looked at him without a shred of hesitation in her face. She stamped her foot firmly onto the staircase with her legs apart, threw out her chest boldly, placed both hands on her hips, and straightened her back as straight as it could get as she gazed up at him. In that moment, her emerald eyes had displayed nothing but hope and confidence.

That was because she had a dream—one that only children are allowed to believe; a foolishly noble ideal that felt nostalgic to him.

The unwavering luster in her eyes went back even further than that. He had witnessed the same radiance in her eyes when he first met her, at the research facility on the Breguet Corporation's main campus. Back then, she was much, much younger; but even now, she still had the same roaring flame in her emerald eyes.

*Nothing's changed at all. Neither her determination nor my decision to follow her has changed since that time.*

Halter answered, "Well...how should I put it...?"

"Hm?"

"I guess I'll just say that I'm getting paid with something money can't buy."

"..."

For a moment, Vermouth goggled a bit, looking puzzled. However, he quickly caught on—or so he thought, anyway—and broke into obnoxious laughter. "Gahahah! You're a real killer, Boss! No wonder, then! After all, that's a top-class *prize* that those in our line of work could never hope to buy!"

"Er, right... In any case, that compensation has been ongoing, so for now, I'm in an exclusive contract with the princess," Halter muttered as he pulled back the tab on his can of beer with a *whoosh* sound.

Looking up, he saw a sky full of stars. In the unfathomably distant past, those stars had simply popped up from the void one day for no apparent reason and continued dashing about, lighting up this universe ever since.

Putting the rim of the can to his lips, he gulped down the entire can in one go. Then he laughed and said, "Ahh, delicious. It's been a while since I had such a good drink."

• • ● • •

Naoto was gazing at the sea from the railing when Marie got

back up on the deck. He turned around and said, "So we're finally about to depart, huh. Did we actually finish all the preparations in time, or...?"

"Quite some time ago, in fact. Halter's starting the engine right now."

"I see. Come to think of it, I never asked. Where are we headed?"

Marie raised an eyebrow in annoyance. "Are you serious? I already told you our plans once. Weren't you listening?"

"You did? I might have forgotten, then," Naoto muttered.

Marie sighed as she sat down on a bench. She pointed at the sea while taking out a can of juice from the cooler box by the bench. "First, we're going to sail along the coast until we reach Myanmar, remember? We're then going to get on a cylinder train there, and cross into India through Bangladesh."

"Gah, that again? Then what?"

"We'll head northwest until we reach Europe by crossing through the territory of uninhabited grids without stopping. From there, hmm...well, I guess we should stop by France first. Even though AnchoR has been fully repaired already, there are still some spare parts I want to stock up on and tools I want to switch out."

"I see. In that case—huh?" Naoto said, sounding perplexed as he looked up at the sky. Seeing that, Marie did the same.

Immediately after, a ball of light came crashing down.

"Whaaa—?!" Naoto and Marie cried in unison.

At the same time, the ball of light smashed into the bow of

the ship, causing it to rock violently. The force wasn't enough to puncture the deck, but it definitely felt like something heavy had just jumped on board. The air was crackling.

*Was that a lightning strike just now...? No way! Marie thought.*

Naturally-occurring lightning would typically be impossible in the modern day, as weather was controlled by gears, but she felt like the shocking phenomenon she just witnessed was similar to the footage of lightning in the past she had seen before in school.

However, it turned out that it wasn't lightning.

The crackles gradually died down; so too did the ship's swaying. However, the light at the bow of the ship continued to grow in intensity while pulsing like a living creature's heartbeat.

"Hee hee hee."

The sound of a laugh came from the light.

No, actually it wasn't just pure light. Beyond the glittering veil was what looked like the face of a...

The instant he recognized who it was, Naoto yelled, "TemP-chan?!"

"Wait, an enemy Initial-Y is here?!" Marie turned to face straight ahead as her level of vigilance instantly jumped.

The light burst away.

The aura of light faded, upon which an automaton girl wearing a punk lolita dress appeared, as if she had just cast off a glittering jacket she had been wearing until now.

"That's...TemP?"

It was the Third of the Initial-Y series, whom Marie had yet to meet personally until now, though TemP had given her friends quite some trouble this time around.

"Master Naoto, are you all right?!"

"Father?!"

RyuZU and AnchoR shouted as they came flying out onto the deck from their cabins. A few moments later, Halter and Vermouth also came running out.

The moment she saw TemP standing at the bow of the ship, RyuZU said in a guttural voice, "TemP! I thought that you would be back with your master by now, having run away with your tail tucked like a rat after our fight. What are you trying to pull now? Do you not realize that the conflict in this city has already been settled?"

"Huh? You seem to have the wrong idea, Elder Sister. The affairs of this city do not concern me one bit," TemP replied as she shot RyuZU a chilling gaze.

"Is that so?" RyuZU replied, the temperature of her voice at absolute zero. "Then your business here is done, yes? In that case, might I suggest that you head on back now? I am busy here taking care of Master Naoto, so I have not the time to waste on entertaining a foolish little sister of mine."

TemP covered her mouth gracefully, answering, "Oh...well, that's cold of you." Seeing RyuZU posture herself to fight, she fluttered both hands in the air to show that she was unarmed with a smirk on her face. "Rest assured, I have not come for a fight. Well, it might be short work to plow through you, El. der. Sis. ter... but with AnchoR here as well, I'd be at a teensy bit of a disadvantage, after all."

"Big Sis...?"

"But...I did say, didn't I? That I'd repay the humiliation I suffered back by a thousandfold?"

Immediately after, TemP vanished.

"Huh...?!"

She had completely vanished without a sound, or any emission of heat or light. The sudden stillness contrasted against her bombastic entrance earlier took them all off guard.

The next moment, TemP reappeared—behind Naoto.

"Wha—?" Naoto uttered as TemP locked him in with her arms.

"Naoto?!" Marie, who was standing nearby, yelled, her eyes widened.

*No way! she thought. Is she saying that since she can't beat RyuZU and AnchoR in a fight, she'll take revenge on their master instead?!*

TemP then grabbed hold of Naoto's wrist and forcefully pulled him towards her. That caused him to lose his balance. As he fell towards her, TemP smiled sadistically, like a cat reveling in the chance to torment a mouse struggling futilely to escape from its claws. In that moment...

*Smooch.*

Time froze—or at least, it felt like it did to Marie.

*Hmm, how should I put it...TemP's leaning forward with her body all tense, and in that awkward position, she's pressing her own lips down on Naoto's. This...this act is...right...it's that.*

*It's a kiss.*

*It looks as though TemP is kissing Naoto.*

*And both of them are frozen like rocks in that position.*

*For Naoto's part...well, I can understand. He probably doesn't even comprehend what is being done to him right now, with how sudden it was. But what about TemP? She pulled him in so that their lips are touching, then just froze in that position. Just what is her game here?*

*Seriously, what is she even doing?*

Marie and everyone else were either so dumbfounded or shocked that they couldn't move. Eventually...

*Mshch.* TemP pulled her lips away with a light sucking noise.

"Ha...hahahah! Ahhhahahaha!!" Upon pulling back from Naoto, TemP broke into shrill, loud laughter, her shoulders rocking up and down. She then turned towards RyuZU and shouted with a smug face, "Did you see that?!"

*...Oh, she saw it.*

*She saw it all right.*

"You might finally have your first boyfriend now, but I'll bet that you haven't even kissed him yet! You may like to talk big, but I know how awkward you are when it comes to these things! Weeelllll?!"

"..."

"Elllder Sister's first boyfriend's f-f-f-first kiss isn't with her! It's with n-n-n-none other *than* meee...!!"

What she had intended to be the ultimate provocation ended up sounding somewhat pitiful as she magnificently fumbled her words right at the climax.

Her face turned bright red. It was clear she was embarrassed to death, so much so that the others almost felt like they should look away out of pity. But then she threw her hand out sharply to point at RyuZU, whose face was completely bereft of emotion, and shouted in an even louder voice, "Hey! Hey! Elder Sister! Tell me, how do you feel?! How does it feel to have your first boyfriend's first kiss stolen by me?!"

She provoked her mercilessly, but RyuZU didn't say a single word in response.

That silence of hers was so absolutely terrifying that Marie retreated backwards reflexively. To be precise, it wasn't so much her silence that made Marie retreat as what it implied.

*If I stay around here, I'll get caught in the crossfire...ugh!*

The alarm bells in Marie's mind rang the loudest they'd ever rung in her life. Trusting her instincts, Marie sprinted away as fast as she could while still keeping RyuZU in her peripheral vision.

Her hunch immediately became reality.

"Master Naoto," RyuZU said in a guttural voice.

Immediately after, Naoto unfroze with a "Holy!" Upon regaining his wits, he quickly fumbled out, "M-Miss RyuZU?! Wait, no, you see—"

Whether he was going to try to come up with an excuse or beg for his life, no one would never know, as RyuZU wasn't listening anymore.

"Definition Proclamation."

RyuZU's voice was stone-cold. At the same time, the

timepiece of imaginary time on her chest began transforming with a louder clank than usual.

It was an assertion of rebellion. She was expressing that, starting from this very moment, she would let her jealousy explode in full force.

"Wait, what? Stop, stop, stop! What the heck are you doing?! Why are you trying to activate Mute Scream?!" Naoto yelled in a hurry.

"That I did not eradicate this foolish little sister of mine two hundred years ago is my greatest mistake...and sin!" RyuZU answered, her shoulders trembling. "Ahh, TemP...I hoped that I could reform you before you ended up committing an irredeemable crime one day...but even so, I never thought you would commit a mortal sin like this. Very well. As your elder sister, the least I can do to atone is to destroy you, after which I shall kill Master Naoto, then follow him to the grave myself!!"

RyuZU had a stoic expression on her face as she announced her intent to commit a lovers' suicide with Naoto.

*God help us. I've never seen her this dead serious before.*

Naoto screamed with a desperate, pained look, "AnchoR! Stop RyuZUUUUUUU!"

"Eh-ehhhh?!" AnchoR cried in a dither.

"Ahhhhahahah! I like the sorry look on your face, Elder Sister! I'll excuse myself now for today, but when you're near Switzerland, I'll gladly take you on again!"

"Hey, stop provoking her, would you, TemP-chan?!"

"'*TemP-chan*'?" The cold rage on RyuZU's face intensified further, the air around her rumbling.

Meanwhile, TemP turned her head to the side, her face still beet red. "D-don't act so chummy with me! Could I ask you not to get in over your head over a m-mere k-k-k-k-kiss?!"

The soap opera roared on. Off to the side, Marie averted her eyes from the hellacious scene before her and muttered, "Oh? So Omega's base is in Switzerland, huh…"

"Earth to Ms. Genius Slut," Vermouth said. "That's probably important information, but is now really the time to think about it? Go do something about that mess already."

"Don't be absurd!! If you're going to complain, do something about it yourself!"

"Now *that's* absurd! Unlike you bunch, I'm just an ordinary bloke! Like I can stick my tiny nose in a galactic war like that!"

Just like that, Marie and Vermouth began their own petty argument off to the side.

As Halter gazed at the wretched state of affairs around him with his eyes half-closed, he sighed deeply. "Why can't things just end nice and neatly for once…?"

*Well, I guess that's just how it is. There's no real reason to anything in this world. In the end, everything's pretty much a joke.*

*In which case, I might as well enjoy the ride, eh?*

With a pained smile and a stroke of his bald head, Halter walked over to stop the multiple fights going on.

CLOCKWORK
PLANET

**O**N A CERTAIN DAY of a certain month, during a season where the sun was still scorching hot...

"Hey Kamiya, listen to this seriously, please," Tsubaki Himana began. His face was probably the most serious it had ever looked.

Kamiya sensed that Tsubaki's question wasn't going to be the usual "Are Asian lolis or Western lolis better?" or something along those lines, so Kamiya also became serious for once in his life, fixing up his collar as he turned to face Tsubaki.

Tsubaki opened his mouth solemnly. "Wat do ya think I shud do with my life?"

"...Sorry, what did this thirty-year-old man just say to me?"

"For the past year and a half, I've dieted and improved my fashion, yet I still can't get past the first date, no matter how hard I try! And when I tell my friends about it, they're like, 'Oh, you've been trying to find a girl? I didn't even realize, sorry.' And the cousin who I doted on like a little sister is getting married, and my little brother found himself a stable job, and of course also has a girlfriend, 'cause why wouldn't he? And to top it off, my mum's been calling me every week recently, ya know?! Saying, 'Aren't there any nice girls that'chu know?' in a serious tone and all! Forget marriage, I haven't even gotten past the first step after trying for a year and a half! Take a hint, would you?!"

Kamiya couldn't care less about this. Frankly, he didn't give a rat's ass. However, Tsubaki was looking off-the-wall unhinged, so Kamiya reflexively replied, "Y-yeah...umm, so? What are you expecting from me?"

"I'm obviously asking you for advice on what I should do with my life!"

"I see...ah, just give me a second. I'm trying to find a good therapist for you online—"

"Cooooome onnnnn!! I'm askin' ya seriously for sum life advice here, goddamniiiiiiiiiiiiiiiiit!!"

"How should I know what you should do? Just live life the way you want, you iiiiiiiiiiiiiiidiot!!"

"Now for the punchline!" Tsubaki shouted. "There's an idiot here who wrote a 450-page book on a theme that could be summed up with those two lines! Can you guess who it is?"

"Here's a big hint! Y'see, part of his name is Tsubaki!"

"So, why did things really turn out this way in the end?" Editor S said as he gave them a death stare.

Kamiya and Himana both looked away and up to the side in response. "Well, you know, originally we planned to finish the story in three volumes, so we didn't really think about how to continue the story," Kamiya said.

"Yeah, that's what he told me, too. Honestly, when he brought up adding in Omega out of nowhere, I was like, what the hell are you saying?"

"I know, right?! Well, I figured the third volume would be the last, so I even joked to Tsubaki: 'Well, I guess we'll write a fourth volume if the story gets picked up for an anime.'"

"Frankly, we never thought it could actually happen, so we just wrote whatever we felt like and kept thickening the plot at the end of the third volume—"

*Slap!* Editor S smacked both of their cheeks with the anime proposal files in his hand to bring them back in line. "Yes, well, as I was saying, I actually did get an anime approved for the series, so..." He grinned.

"Um, right, sorry," the two replied in unison.

"And so we were discussing why the manuscript was so late, right? In fact, didn't I shout, 'Why was it this late?!'?" Editor S' smile grew bone-chilling.

"Right, well, actually we were about to get there... You'll see how everything ties together."

· · ● · ·

It started right around the beginning of summer.

"Hey, how about we do things the opposite way this time around from Volume Three? I'll be the main writer, and you be the co-author."

*Kamiya gave Tsubaki's suggestion some thought. Well... Clockwork Planet was originally supposed to be that way to begin with. It's only because Tsubaki bit off more than he could chew in modifying my original plot and wrote himself into a hole that I had no choice but to make it a joint work.*

"Well, I guess that's fine, but...I feel like in the end I'm just going to be digging you out of the hole that you'll write yourself into again."

"Yeah, so to prevent that from happening, let's have a formal meeting where we write out the plot together."

"Huh? I mean, even for the first volume, I handed you what might as well have been a first draft, but you basically rewrote the third and fourth chapters entirely."

"Ah, well you know, you said that I could do what I want with it, so... Well, I'll handle things better this time. I'll try super hard! I want to turn my life around, after all!"

"R-right. Um, okay then... How detailed of a plot summary do you want from me?"

"Hmmmmm...I guess I'll be good if you could give me the character profiles, setting notes, the storyline, and a portion of the dialogue, I guess?"

"Hmm...all right, all right, stop there. I see there is a discrepancy in our understanding here. Isn't that far beyond the level of a plot summary?"

"Well, I mean, only you can express how you envisioned the Initial-Y series and the world of the story, so..."

"Just use your best judgment, man, I need a break right now."

"Oh, that's impossible. I don't think I can ever hope to mimic your hopelessly cringey plot ideas that reek of a teenage wannabe author."

"Well, seeing as you're clever enough to insult and praise someone at the same time, I think you'll be fine on your own..."

· · ● ● ● · ·

"And that ends the summary of what happened. As you can see, it's Tsubaki's fault that the manuscript was late!"

"Ohhh, I see. Well then, Tsubaki-san, what say you?" Editor S asked in a dispassionate voice.

Tsubaki replied in a trembling voice, "...Because I tossed the latter half of his plot out and did my own thing, what was supposed to be around a 250-page plot arc somehow turned into one that's over 450 pages..."

"I understand. So in short, business as usual, huh."

"B-but! This time around I did whatever I felt like. I mean, I got fired up—er, no, I mean...I'm not sure how to say it, but like, I really went all out doing my own thing, but in a good way. I ultimately managed to keep the epilogue that Kamiya wrote, so I'm improving, right?!"

"Yeah, I guess. If you overlook the fact that you blazed right past the original deadline by a wide margin, yeah, I guess."

"Gahhh, I'm sorry!"

"Well then...I guess I can sympathize if I give you not an inch but two hundred nautical miles. So then, Tsubaki-san... While the original plot may have been written by Kamiya-san, you wrote out this volume almost all by yourself. Now that you're done with it, have you found what you should do with your life?"

"Well...yes, of course! I've decided to live as I wish!" Tsubaki replied, his face beaming brighter than the summer sun that was long gone by now. "For now, please teach me how to get a girlfriend. Actually, if you know a nice girl, just introduce her to me. To be more specific, I'd like someone who's good at cooking, smart, usually ditzy, yet capable of being considerate, and of course, a total nympho. Yes, pweeze! Now that's the kind of cutie I'd be into!"

*This guy... It's like he hasn't grown up at all! Hearing Tsubaki rattle off a long list of desired traits that not even most adult game heroines could satisfy, Kamiya shuddered.*

*On the other hand, Editor S thought about it carefully, then said with a sunny smile,* "Hmm...okay, sure. There's someone I have in mind. I'll introduce you to that person once Volume Five is finished."

"Seriously?! You know someone like that?! Such an angel is a rare find even in eroge, you know?!"

"Oh, so he is self-aware about it..."

"Awwwwwwwww hell yeah, bring it on! I'll write the next volume up in no time! Oy Kamiya, let's head back and start working...!"

As he watched Tsubaki dash towards the door in a rush to start working on the next volume, Kamiya thought about what his co-writer had said.

*"I'd like someone who's good at cooking, smart, usually ditzy, yet capable of being considerate, and of course, a total nympho. Yes pweeze! Now that's the kind of cutie I'd be into!"*

*There can't be many women out there who can actually fulfill that fantasy. If there is someone who can fulfill such a male fantasy in reality, that person would probably have to be a man himself. That's exactly why those who write such characters in eroge and light novels are almost always male—oh.*

Upon reaching the door, Tsubaki turned around. Seeing Kamiya's expression, he gloated, "Whyyyy the long face, Kamiya?! Ahah, could it be that you're jealous of my future girlfriend?"

*Editor S didn't say a single word about the person he has in mind being a girl, did he...? Well, I guess it's fine.*

·  ·  •  ●  •  ·  ·

As a cold, dry wind blew past, Editor S chuckled to himself and muttered, "Well, by the time he's done with Volume Five, he'll probably have realized anyway that if he just wants to live freely...he doesn't really need a girlfriend. Haha..."

"Yikes..." Kamiya visibly recoiled. *This guy's the type who'll do anything as long as it gets the manuscript done.*

Editor S then turned towards Kamiya and said, "Ah, I'll be counting on you too, of course, Kamiya-san. It wasn't easy getting the anime approved, you know, so if you dare tell me something like how you're not going to write another volume now...haha...I... haha...will take this uncommonly sharp boot of mine and jab it right up your—"

...

"M-meow..."

***TWINTAILS!*** (SALUTORY NOD)

THIS TIME WE'RE DISCUSSING THE GIRL ON THE COVER OF THIS VOLUME, TEMP.

FOR RYUZU AND ANCHOR, THEIR DESIGNS SORT OF JUST CAME NATURALLY TO ME, SO I WAS ABLE TO FINALIZE THEIR DESIGNS PRETTY QUICKLY, BUT FOR TEMP I CLEARLY REMEMBER HAVING TO REDRAW HER DESIGN FROM SCRATCH MULTIPLE TIMES.

TWINTAILED GIRLS ARE A REAL CHALLENGE TO DESIGN, MAN. (EYES ROLLED UPWARD FROM SUFFERING)

OVERALL, I DECIDED TO GIVE HER A GENTLE AND FRILLY, FLOWERY FEEL WITH GREEN AS HER PRIMARY COLOR. AS FOR THE GEAR ACCESSORY THAT ALL INITIAL-Y'S HAVE, IT'S IN THE FORM OF A COLLAR FOR HER.

SO HER CODE NAME IS AERIAL, THE FLUTTERING BUTTERFLY, PRESUMABLY BECAUSE SHE'S A FREE SPIRIT. YET SHE WEARS A COLLAR. WHAT DOES IT ALL MEAN...?!

IT MIGHT BE FUN TO REREAD VOLUME FOUR WITH THAT IN MIND!

(TO BE HONEST, I HAVE NO IDEA WHETHER IT'S SIGNIFICANT, I JUST MADE THAT UP ON THE SPOT TO TRY TO SOUND SMART...BUT JUST PRETEND THIS PARENTHETICAL ISN'T HERE.)

—SINO

# Experience these great light**novel** titles from Seven Seas Entertainment